Born in London, Jonathan Lunn started writing at the age of fifteen. He studied history at the University of Leicester, where he became involved in politics. He worked for six years as a spin doctor for the modern-day equivalent of the Whigs. He now lives in Bristol.

Praise for Jonathan Lunn's Killigrew series:

'A hero to rival any Horatio Hornblower. Swashbuckling? You bet'   *Belfast Telegraph*

'A cracking adventure crafted by a writer who has clearly inherited the talent to tell a jolly good yarn'
Newton & Golborne Guardian

'If you revel in the Hornblower and the Sharpe books, grab a copy of Jonathan Lunn's action-packed saga'
Bolton Evening News

'A rollicking tale with plenty of punches'
Lancashire Evening Post

'Full-blooded, action-packed with a wealth of historical background and naval and warfare detail, a spread of characters and a racy narrative make this a rollicking good read'   *Huddersfield Daily Examiner*

Killigrew's Run

Jonathan Lunn

headline

First published in Great Britain in 2004
by HEADLINE BOOK PUBLISHING

First published in paperback in Great Britain in 2004
by HEADLINE BOOK PUBLISHING

A HEADLINE paperback

10 9 8 7 6 5 4 3 2 1

ISBN 0 7553 2068 9

Typeset in Times by
Letterpart Limited, Reigate, Surrey

Printed and bound in Great Britain by
Mackays of Chatham plc, Chatham, Kent

Headline's policy is to use papers that are natural, renewable
and recyclable products and made from wood grown in
sustainable forests. The logging and manufacturing processes
are expected to conform to the environmental regulations of
the country of origin.

HEADLINE BOOK PUBLISHING
A division of Hodder Headline PLC
338 Euston Road
LONDON NW1 3BH

www.headline.co.uk
www.hodderheadline.com

In memoriam
James Hale
1946-2003
Agent, mentor and friend

ACKNOWLEDGEMENTS

Last year saw the tragic death of James Hale who had been my literary agent ever since I wrote my first novel. Over the past thirteen years he edited every novel I have written to date; negotiated publishing contracts for all that were fit for publication; provided the best possible advice on matters both professional and personal; was enthusiastic in his encouragement whenever I had a good idea for a book, and firm but gentle whenever I had a bad one; a convivial and witty host. Without him, this book would never have been written.

Thanks also to Sarah Keen for editorial duties; and to Yvonne Holland and Alastair Wilson, whose sharp eyes and keen and capacious minds can always be relied on to keep me from making a fool of myself on an international scale (at least as far as the books go). Any inaccuracies remain the responsibility of the author.

Thanks are also due to the following for inspiration: William Alwyn, G.I. Brown, Stephanie Cole, Graham Crowden, John Debney, Stewart Granger, Basil Greenhill and Ann Giffard, Bernard Hill, Trevor Howard, Erich Wolfgang Korngold, James Mason, Bill Nighy, Sergei Prokofiev, Julia Sawalha, and Victor Young.

Glossary

chert!	–	Russian equivalent of 'damn'; lit. 'devil!'
drachevo	–	bastard
Ekenäs	–	Swedish name for Tammisaari
Hangö Head	–	Swedish name for Hanko Head
Helsingfors	–	name by which Helsinki was known prior to Finnish independence
inzhener	–	engineer
matros (pl. *matrosy*)	–	sailor
michmani	–	midshipman
mouzhiki!	–	'lads!'; literally, 'peasants!'
nagaika	–	cossack whip
negr	–	Negro
papakha	–	Cossack's woolly hat
sazhen	–	unit of measurement equivalent to seven feet
starshina	–	colonel of Cossacks
telezhka (pl. *telezhki*)	–	crude Russian four-wheeled cart without springs, little more than a box on wheels
utka	–	a waterfowl of the *Anatidae* family
verst (pl. *vehrsty*)	–	unit of measurement equivalent to slightly less than two-thirds of a mile

Commander Christopher I. Killigrew

1824–Born. 1837–Entered the Navy. 1840–Aide-de-Camp to Commodore Charles Napier in Syria. Distinguished himself at St Jean d'Acre. 1842–Served 1842–Served at the capture of Woosung and Shanghae, and in the operations on the Yang-tse-Kiang. Distinguished himself at the storming of Ching-Kiang-Foo, and obtained in consequence his first commission. 1843–Took part in an attack on a large piratical settlement on the Island of Borneo. 1845-7–Active in the oppression of slavery. 1847–Made a Lieutenant. Employed at the destruction of the Owodunni Barracoon. 1849–Actively engaged against the pirates in the South China Sea. 1852-53–Took part in Sir Edward Belcher's Arctic Searching Expedition. Promoted to Commander in consequence. 1854–Appointed to the Ramillies. Commander Killigrew's person bears the marks of no less than eight wounds.

The Killigrew Novels

Killigrew R.N.
The Guinea Coast, 1847

Killigrew and the Golden Dragon
South China Sea, 1849

Killigrew and the Incorrigibles
The South Seas, 1850

Killigrew and the North-West Passage
The Arctic, 1852-3

Killigrew's Run
The Baltic, 1854

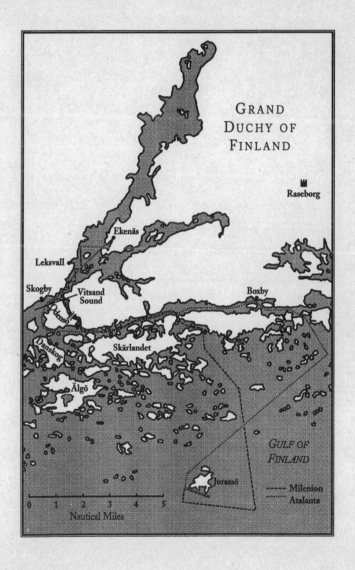

GRAND
DUCHY OF
FINLAND

Raseborg

Ekenäs

Leksvall

Skogby

Vitsand
Sound

Odensö

Boxby

Danskog

Skärlandet

Älgö

GULF OF
FINLAND

Jurassö

Milenion

Atalanta

0   1   2   3   4   5
Nautical Miles

Prologue

_____

Friday 4 August 1854

The channel was wide and deep enough to accommodate any vessel up to a third-rate ship of the line, or so Captain Sulivan of Her Majesty's surveying ship *Lightning* claimed. If Commander Killigrew had heard it from anyone else's lips he would not have believed it, but Sulivan was a wizard at surveying, and he had already sounded the channel, marking it using empty bottles painted white as buoys, and arrows and other markers whitewashed on the rocks on either side.

Killigrew gazed the length of HMS *Ramillies'* upper deck to where Petty Officer Molineaux sat astride the bowsprit, following the line of buoys by the light of the deck lamps. Standing next to Killigrew and Captain Crichton on the quarterdeck, the quartermaster watched Molineaux's signals and relayed them to the two able seamen at the helm.

'Come one point to starboard!'

'One point to starboard it is!' The helmsmen spun the wheel, and the big ship brought her bows round to port, nosing her ponderous way through the treacherous channel. In one of the smaller vessels Killigrew was more accustomed to serving on board, they would have gone up the channel like a rat up a drainpipe. HMS *Ramillies*, however, was no steam-sloop, but a former third-rate ship of the line converted into a blockship: 170 feet from stem to stern, with a burthen of 1,747 tons, 60 guns and an official complement of 660 men; although they had had difficulty getting experienced seamen to sign on board before sailing, and at present the total number in her crew was closer to 500. Of those, one-third were well past their prime, while another third had never sailed on a naval vessel before.

'Right the helm!' ordered the quartermaster, his eyes fixed firmly on Molineaux.

The helmsmen spun the wheel back. 'Helm amidships!'

These occasional exchanges highlighted how unnaturally silent the *Ramillies* was, even for three bells in the first watch. The men of the larboard watch were below decks, in their hammocks, but they each had a good notion of how perilous the passage was, and Killigrew doubted that any of them would be sleeping. The men of the starboard watch were at their stations on deck, standing by, awaiting instructions – which were few and far between while the sails were furled and the *Ramillies* advanced under steam only – and speaking little, and then in hushed tones. Leading Seaman Endicott said something to Able Seaman Iles, prompting him to laugh uproariously; hysterically, even. He quickly cut the laugh short, but too late: the boatswain rounded on him furiously.

'Keep silence, there!' If any Russians in the vicinity had not heard Iles' laugh, they had most certainly heard the boatswain's bellow.

In the silence that followed, Killigrew was all too conscious of the creaking of the ship's rigging and timbers, the slapping of the water against the hull, and the chuntering of the engine. Under steam, the *Ramillies* had two speeds: ahead full, and ahead half. She had been built in 1813, which made her older than most of the men that served on her, but eight years ago she had been converted into a steamer by the installation of a Seaward and Capel

4-cylinder engine in her hold, driving a screw that enabled her to potter along under bare poles at just under six knots. At the moment she crawled along at half speed, but it was still far too fast for Killigrew's liking. It was an hour after sunset and dusk had settled over the Åland Islands. A gibbous moon cast its silvery light over the scene, but visibility was still poor and if Molineaux missed one of the markers in the darkness he would barely have time to spot a half-submerged obstacle before they ran into it.

Killigrew took out a cheroot case of polished tin and extracted one, plugging it in the corner of his mouth while patting his pockets down for his matches. There was only one left in the box, so he took care to cup his hands around it as he lit the cheroot; if it had blown out, he would have had to go without smoking until the *Ramillies* passed through the channel and emerged into Lumpar Bay at the far end of it. Only then would they be safe, and only then would Killigrew feel he could quit the quarterdeck to fetch another box of matches from his cabin. Crichton did not approve of his officers smoking on watch, but strictly speaking Killigrew was not on watch, and besides, he felt there were special circumstances given the tension of the moment. Crichton must have agreed, for he said nothing.

Killigrew shook the match out and crossed to the side to toss it overboard; which, perhaps, had been his real reason for lighting the cheroot, for once there he swung himself up on to the bulwark. Holding on to the ratlines with one hand, he leaned out over the side, gazing down the length of the ship to where the buoys were barely visible in the water up ahead.

He gazed across at the shore to port. At the mouth of the Gulf of Bothnia, midway between Sweden and Finland – an autonomous constitutional grand duchy within the Russian Empire – the Åland Islands were low-lying and thickly forested with pine trees. As the *Ramillies* rounded the next headland, a gap opened in the trees to reveal a Russian fort standing in a clearing, perhaps two hundred yards from the shore. It was not unlike a Martello tower, but broader and taller – nearly fifty feet high – built of brick faced with pink granite. Two tiers of embrasures looked out from the masonry like so many gaps in the toothy grin of a bleached skull. The fort perfectly dominated this stretch of the channel, but fortunately the Russians had abandoned it, withdrawing to rejoin the garrison at Bomarsund, otherwise the other Allied ships that had already passed this way would never have made it.

In his mid-sixties, Captain Graham 'Nose-Biter' Crichton was a tall man of imposing build, with wild white hair and watery eyes that bulged from his fish-like face. The young gentlemen of the gunroom had dismissed him as a genial but mildly dotty old man, until Killigrew had explained that he had earned his nickname on the deck of a frigate in the Great War with France by biting the nose off a French officer in hand-to-hand combat.

'I hope your man Molineaux knows what he's doing, Killigrew,' Crichton remarked, the mildness of his voice belying the strength of the feeling behind it.

'Your man Molineaux': never mind that responsibility for the crew ultimately lay with Crichton as captain of the ship; the black petty officer was one of the five men whom Killigrew had particularly recommended to Crichton, fellow survivors of HMS *Venturer*'s disastrous voyage of the Arctic in search of Sir John Franklin's expedition, and as such he would always be 'your man Molineaux' whenever the captain discussed him with Killigrew.

'I wouldn't be so bold as to say that I've never known Molineaux make a mistake,' he told Crichton. 'But I cannot think of any particular instance off the top of my head.'

'The problem with speaking off the top of one's head is that one is bound thereby to talk through one's hat,' Crichton retorted genially.

Killigrew smiled. 'There are worse parts of one's anatomy to speak out of.'

'How long d'ye say you've known him?'

'Seven years, on and off. More on than off, come to thi—'

Seeing Molineaux gesturing frantically, Killigrew broke off and turned to the quartermaster.

The quartermaster had already seen the gestures for himself. 'Hard a-port!' he snapped at the helmsmen. 'Look lively!'

The helmsmen spun the wheel furiously, and the *Ramillies'* head began to come round, but too slowly. A moment later Killigrew felt the copper sheathing on the keel scrape over the shingle bottom, and then the ship juddered to a halt. The men on deck staggered under the sudden impact.

'Stop engines!' Crichton barked, even before he had righted his stagger across the quarterdeck.

The midshipman stationed by the binnacle unclipped the speaking tube for communicating with the engine room and blew into it to sound the whistle at the other end. 'Stop engines!' The engine stopped so soon after that the chief engineer must have realised they had run aground long before he received Crichton's order.

Killigrew glanced forward anxiously to make sure Molineaux was all right, and saw the petty officer dangling by his arms from the bowsprit. Even as Killigrew watched, Molineaux pulled himself up and swung to safety. Killigrew cursed himself for wasting time worrying about the petty officer when he should have known from experience that Molineaux was perfectly capable of looking after himself.

'Damage report, Mr McGurk!' commanded Crichton.

'Aye, aye, sir.' Although barely fourteen, Midshipman McGurk knew what to do: he hurried down the main hatch to where the carpenter and his team were at their stations on the orlop deck, ready to look for leaks and plug holes in the event of the ship being breached below the waterline.

'Anyone hurt?' called Killigrew. Apparently, no one was, or at least not sufficiently to justify bothering the ship's surgeon. He took stock of the situation: it felt as though the ship was firmly grounded, heeled over at ten degrees with her keel on the bottom. He did not think the hull had been breached by the sound of it: the *Ramillies* might be old, but she was tough.

Molineaux was back on the upper deck, making his way aft. He was not a tall man, but shoulders broadened by years at sea gave an impression of strength and solidity that was by no means misleading. The bonnet on his shaven skull – like a tam-o'shanter, with a red pom-pom – was tipped forward so that it almost touched his eyebrows, and a gold ring through one earlobe gave him a piratical look.

Crichton rounded on him furiously. 'Damn your eyes, man! You were supposed to be following the buoys!'

'I was, sir,' the petty officer replied, politely but firmly. In spite of his African physiognomy, he spoke English with the accent of the back streets of London where he had grown up. 'Begging your pardon, sir, but I reckon that's where I went adrift.'

'Where you went adrift? What the blazes are you blethering about?'

'Reckon some bugger must've moved the buoys, sir. Didn't see the shoal water until it was too late.' If Molineaux was telling the truth, then it was a miracle he had noticed the shoal water at all, and that he had done so too late was hardly his fault.

'Moved the buoys? Who on earth would do such a thing?'

Killigrew glanced towards the fort ashore, and the realisation was like a kick in the stomach from a mule.

Crichton must have realised it too, for he forgot all about berating Molineaux to order: 'Beat to quarters!'

Even as the ship's musician beat his drum and the larboard watch tumbled out of their hammocks to emerge on deck, four of the cannon in the fort boomed – the only four that could be brought to bear on the ship from their embrasures – and spewed forth fists of flame. Was it Killigrew's imagination, or did he actually glimpse one of the cannon-balls skipping across the greensward between the fort and the channel, glowing a dark shade of red in the gloom? The only one that came near to the *Ramillies* crashed over the rocks on the shore to land in the water between shore and ship with a plop.

The Russian gunners in the fort – Killigrew knew at once they were enemies intent on destroying the *Ramillies* rather than allies who had mistaken her in the darkness, because if they had been British or French they would have destroyed her at that range with the first salvo – had used an insufficient charge, and their aim was wildly off. But the *Ramillies* was a sitting duck while she was lodged in the shoals, and sooner or later the gunners would get the range and the direction right. They were not using shell, thank God, but from the way the water bubbled over the round shot that had fallen short of the *Ramillies* they were using red-hot shot, which would do the job just as effectively if it became lodged in the ship's timbers and set them alight.

The Russians must have reoccupied the fort after it had been checked by the landing party from the *Lightning*, and some damned fool had not thought to empty the place of powder and shot. Their gunnery might have left a lot to be desired – from the Russian point of view, at any rate – but whoever had planned this ambush had been no fool: where and how the *Ramillies* was aground, she could bring none of her guns to bear on the fort, only the bow chaser on the forecastle, a ten-inch long gun, and already the ship's gunner was having it loaded and brought to bear through one of the four gunports in the *Ramillies'* prow.

Crichton did not waste time relaying his order through the midshipman standing at the binnacle, but snatched up the speaking tube himself. 'Set on, full astern!' he ordered, and a moment later the deck throbbed beneath their feet once more as the chief engineer threw the engine into reverse to try to draw off the shoal. But the *Ramillies* was caught fast.

The bow chaser boomed, shooting back on its brass racers, and the shell shrieked through the night to where the fort stood, still wreathed in the smoke of its first salvo. The roar of the shell did not last long – fort and ship were exchanging shots at almost point-blank range – before it was cut off by the thunderclap of its explosion, and a great burst of flame filled the night, obscuring the fort from Killigrew's sight with a cloud of dust and smoke. The men at the bow chaser were already reloading while Crichton and Killigrew waited for the cloud to disseminate so they could see what damage had been done.

And then the dust sheeted down and the smoke drifted off to reveal the fort fully intact . . . in appearance, at any rate, and in function as well, as the gunners proved by firing a fifth shot that slammed into the rocks on the far side of the channel, perhaps two dozen yards ahead of the *Ramillies*. A sixth shot followed, then a seventh and an eighth in rapid succession, all three missing but coming closer than before. The Russian gunners were firing independently now, as fast as they could load, aim and shoot.

'This is a fine to-do, eh?' Crichton might have been remarking on a piece of luggage gone astray somewhere between Paddington and Temple Meads. 'We'll have to try to kedge her off, before those damned Russkis make a bonfire of us! Summon the gig's crew, bosun!'

'Sir, if instead of making a cable fast astern we anchor it to those rocks off the port quarter, we might be able to kedge off and bridge our broadside to bear on the fort at the same time.'

'Good thinking, Mr Killigrew. You heard the man, Mr Masterson. See to it.'

'Aye, aye, sir.'

The bow chaser roared again, and this time one of the guns in the Russian fort belched flame before the smoke and dust had had a chance to clear. Now they had got the direction right, if not the range, and the shot screeched through the air overhead to part one of the backstays supporting the mainmast.

Crichton took the telescope from the binnacle to study the

fort as the smoke cleared once more. 'Hardly a scratch on it, rot it! We might as well throw stones for all the damage we're doing.'

'It'll be a different story when we start pounding that fort with round shot.' Killigrew tried to sound breezy.

'Yes, but that will take time; and time is one commodity we do not possess in abundance.' Crichton handed him the telescope and Killigrew studied the fort for himself.

'There may be another way, sir.'

'Oh?'

'A shore party. I'll take the pinnace with a dozen blue-jackets and twenty jollies and see if we can't take that fort by storm.'

'Muskets against granite, Killigrew?'

'Muskets and grenades, sir. We have some on board. If we could get close enough we could toss a couple through two of those embrasures, then go in through the back door.'

'The back door will be locked.'

'If love laughs at locksmiths, sir, that's nothing compared to the howls of derision they provoke in Molineaux.'

'Very well. But keep an eye on the *Ramillies*: don't get caught in front of the fort when I'm ready to fire a broadside.'

'I'll take a couple of blue lights. When one goes up, you'll know the fort is ours and you can belay the broadside.'

'Smart thinking. Carry on, Mr Killigrew.'

The commander turned to Molineaux. 'Summon the pinnace's crew.'

'Aye, aye, sir.' Petty Officer Wes Molineaux was one of the *Ramillies*' boatswain's mates, and as such he wore a boatswain's call around his neck. Now he used it to pipe the pinnace's crew to the davits while Killigrew ordered the ship's armourer to issue them with muskets and cutlasses, and Crichton ordered Marine Lieutenant Neville to summon a squad of nineteen men.

Satisfied that everything had been set in motion, Killigrew descended the after hatch and made his way to his cabin

9

where he buckled his gun belt around his hips. A tall man with the athletic build and graceful movements of a dancer, he wore a pea jacket over his waistcoat and shirt – the arrival of summer had finally brought temperate weather to the Baltic – and his peaked cap sat on his thick, dark hair at a jaunty, insouciant angle. The ordeal he had suffered in the Arctic had left its cruel mark on his saturnine features, and he looked older than his nine-and-twenty years.

If their Arctic ordeal had left him weak in body, in spirit he felt stronger than ever. Having faced death in that cold, lifeless land, he had determined that henceforth he would squeeze every last drop of enjoyment out of the remainder of his life. In his hurry to get HMS *Ramillies* ready to go to sea, Crichton had taken on more than his fair share of Queen's hard bargains, yet when they showed a lack of seamanship that would have tested the patience of a saint, Killigrew could laugh it off and upbraid them with a joke, refusing to blight a single moment with bitterness or anger. Now he viewed the insanity of the world – and of the Royal Navy in particular – with a smile; not the twisted sneer of a man who only laughed at any mortal thing so that he might not cry, but the hearty chuckle of one who could always see the funny side. It should have been intensely infuriating, but it was a smile that was infectious.

So far the campaign had been a dull one: the Baltic fleet had sailed from Portsmouth five months earlier, before Britain and France had even declared war on Russia in support of the Turks, who had been fighting the Russian aggressors for nearly a year now. News of the declaration of war had reached the fleet when it had been anchored in Køge Bay off Copenhagen. Since then the *Ramillies* had been largely confined to blockade work, discouraging the ships of the Russian navy from emerging from behind their maritime fortresses, while smaller vessels – paddle-sloops and frigates – had garnered all the glory of raiding defenceless Finnish ports and burning merchant barques and fishing boats.

He returned on deck to find Neville's marines assembled in the ship's waist, pipeclayed crossbelts showing pale against their red coatees, Brunswick rifled muskets slung from their shoulders, black shakoes making them look taller than they were – and even bare-headed none of them could walk beneath an average door without ducking. Killigrew had ordered the armourer to break open a box of grenades, and two of the marines were given haversacks stuffed with the gunpowder-packed orbs to carry.

In their pusser's slops, the pinnace's crew were a marked contrast to the parade-ground-smart marines: all wore the traditional blue jackets and bell-bottomed trousers that passed for a uniform on board HMS *Ramillies*, but there all attempts at standardisation ended: some wore bonnets, others had tied their neckerchiefs over their heads as bandannas, giving them a distinctly piratical look that was emphasised by the wide variety of weapons they carried: muskets, cutlasses, tomahawks and boarding pikes. They were short, squat men, for the most part, as if generations of natural selection had produced a breed of seaman well suited to living in the cramped 'tween-decks of a man o' war, shoulders broaded by pulling on oars and pushing on capstan bars, knuckles hardened by brawls in every tavern from Portsmouth to Dunedin.

The pinnace was lowered from the davits and Killigrew and the crew shinned down the lifelines. The commander sat down in the stern sheets while the crew took up their oars and moved the boat to the foot of the accommodation ladder, where Lieutenant Neville and his men descended, taking their places on the thwarts between the oarsmen, with a minimum of swearing about clod-hopping jollies from the seamen – the marines returning the compliments with their own jibes about tars.

Another Russian gun boomed, and this time the round shot smashed through the bulwark, throwing large splinters of wood in all directions. From the pinnace, Killigrew could not see if anyone on deck was hurt, but it was a reminder – as if

11

one were needed – that time was not on their side.

'Shove off!' he ordered. 'Out oars and give way with a will!'

The bow man pushed the pinnace's prow out from the *Ramillies*' side and the oarsmen put their backs into it, taking their stroke from the starboard after-oar. Killigrew had already picked out a rocky cove on the shore, sheltered by an escarpment from the view of the fort, and he ordered the coxswain at the tiller to make for it.

As the pinnace moved across the water, at least one of the Russian guns tried to drop a round shot on it, which suited Killigrew just fine: the shot did not even come close enough to drench the boat with spray, and every shot fired at the pinnace was one less fired at the *Ramillies* herself; and the gun crew would waste time realigning the gun on the ship once the pinnace had reached the safety of the shore.

It was less than fifty yards from the ship to the cove, and with a dozen strong backs heaving at the oars they covered it in next to no time. As soon as Killigrew felt the pinnace's keel scrape over the shingle bottom, he vaulted over the side and waded up through the chill water on to the rocky shore. The seamen and the marines went after him, leaving the coxswain and the bow oarsman behind to make sure the pinnace was secure before following.

Crouching low, Killigrew scrunched across the pebbly shore, picking his way between boulders until he came to the escarpment. Turning to face the men coming up behind him, he motioned for them to stay back and stay low, before scrambling up the slope to peer over the crest towards the fort. The four guns that could be brought to bear were still firing intermittently at the *Ramillies*, sending round shot flying over the heads of the men on the shore with a sound like canvas ripping.

He glanced back towards the ship. Lieutenant Masterson had succeeded in anchoring a hawser to a huge boulder further down the shore, and although the high bulwark hid the deck from Killigrew's sight, he could imagine the hands heaving at the capstan bars, trying to drag the ship's stern round to bring her broadside to bear on the fort. Not fast enough, though: even as he watched, a shot slammed into the ship's side, punching a hole through the timbers. He thought of the splinters of wood flying across the lower deck, doing far more damage to life and limb than the shot itself; and if the shot was red-hot, and it lodged in the timbers . . . but the fire-control parties would be on stand-by, ready to rush pails of water to any blaze as soon as it was discovered. A lucky shot through the magazine, however . . . best not to think about it. Killigrew consoled himself with the thought that the Russians did not seem to be enjoying many 'lucky' shots: three out of every four shots from the fort still missed the hull altogether, and at that range too . . . shocking-bad gunnery. The *Ramillies'* ten-inch bow chaser, by comparison, was firing fast and accurately, but in vain: the shells continued to burst harmlessly against the fort's granite face.

Killigrew lifted his head above the level of the escarpment, and something stung him on the cheek in the same instant that a musket shot sounded between the cacophony of booming cannon and bursting shells. His first fleeting thought – that he had been shot – was dismissed when he realised that a bullet had struck one of the rocks close to his head. In any case, he quickly withdrew below the crest of the escarpment. Perhaps the shot had been lucky, but if so it was the kind of luck that came from having a sharp eye and a rifled musket.

'There's claret on your dial, sir,' said Molineaux, in the low voice he might have used to advise the commander that his flies were undone. Killigrew raised a gloved hand to where the splinter of stone had stung his cheek, and it came away with a few drops of blood smeared over the fingertips, black against the white kid leather. He cursed: it was hardly life threatening, but getting blood off leather was the devil's own job and the marine who kept his rig looking respectable would not thank him for it in the morning.

'What do we do, sir?' asked Lieutenant Neville, young enough to have a head full of dreams of glory and empty of common sense. 'Charge 'em?'

'Do that, and we'll carpet the ground between here and the fort with our dead,' Killigrew warned him. 'They've got sharpshooters on the roof. You and your men keep your heads down on this side; I'll lead the bluejackets round the back and see if we can't find a way inside there. Aikman, pass that bag of tricks to Molineaux.'

'Very good, sir.' The marine handed the haversack to the petty officer, and looked very relieved to be rid of its weight.

'Bluejackets to me!' ordered Killigrew. 'Keep your heads down, your mouths shut, your eyes and ears open, and follow me!'

As the marines crept to the crest of the escarpment and began a desultory fire on the fort, Killigrew led the bluejackets round to the right, following the shore to begin with. He had seen the lie of the land from the upper deck of the *Ramillies*, including a shadow that ran perpendicular to the channel, to the north: not a gully as such, but ground sufficiently dead to give them cover to within fifty yards of the fort.

'This is it,' he told Molineaux and the other seamen with him when they reached the beginning of the ditch. 'From here on in we crawl. Make sure everyone's musket is at half-cock, Cox'n, and bring up the rear to make sure no one gets left behind.'

They scrabbled along as fast as they could, Killigrew conscious that the *Ramillies* was taking a pounding as the majority of shots began to hull her. When they had gone a couple of hundred yards they were level with the tower, but Killigrew crawled on: he was banking that all eyes in the fort would be turned towards the *Ramillies* and the marines on the beach, so he wanted to come at it from behind. When he judged he had crawled another hundred yards, the sulphurous stench of gunsmoke drifted from where the Russian guns boomed and the ten-incher's shells exploded. He stopped, removed his scabbarded cutlass from his hilt, balanced his cap on the end of it, and slowly raised it above the level of the dead ground. When no one took a pot shot at it, he lifted his head and saw the fort all but hidden by the drifting smoke.

He turned to look down the line of seamen crawling up behind him. Molineaux was right behind him, not one iota impeded by the heavy haversack he carried, and behind him was Able Seaman Gilchrist.

'I want you to wait here and make sure everyone gets as far as the smoke before they leave this ditch,' Killigrew told him, drawing his revolvers from their holsters one after the other and making sure they were loaded and primed. There was no need to whisper: the guns were making so much noise, he could have bawled the 'Hallelujah Chorus' at the top of his voice, had he known the words, and no one in the fort would have heard him. 'Give Molineaux time to reach the back of the fort, then start sending them over one at a time.'

Gilchrist nodded.

Killigrew tucked one of the revolvers back in its holster, holding the other in his right fist. 'Same goes for you, Molineaux: give me time to reach the fort, then follow. Gilchrist, if you see Molineaux fall, tell the next man to pick up the haversack on his way.'

'Oh, never mind me, if I get shot!' grumbled the petty officer. 'It's the grenades that matter.'

'That's pretty much the long and the short of it,' Killigrew agreed cheerfully. He was used to Molineaux's occasional flashes of insubordination, and had learned to turn a blind eye to them: the petty officer was too good a man to alienate by harsh treatment. 'But try not to get killed: we need you to unlock the door.'

'And what if *you* get killed, sir?'

'Then you're in charge,' Killigrew told him, picking himself up and running through the smoke towards the fort. The smoke got thicker the closer he got, tearing at his lungs and bringing tears to his eyes. Then he broke out into fresh air and the fort loomed over him, less than thirty yards off. One of the embrasures was directly ahead of him, and he could see the dull light of an oil lamp illuminating the figures who served the gun in one of the loopholes on the far side. There was no telling if they were looking in his direction, but he reasoned he would know about it sooner rather than later if they were.

His feet pounded the sod as he powered himself the last few yards, one hand before him to soften his impact against the masonry, before dropping down at the foot of the wall, breathing hard. Once – not so long ago – a short dash like that would not have left him panting, but that had been before his ill-fated voyage to the Arctic. Even the year that had passed since his return had not restored all the muscle to Killigrew's ravaged limbs, not that he had ever been a muscular man to begin with. In the four months since HMS *Ramillies* had sailed from Portsmouth with the rest of the Baltic Fleet, he had been exercising on a daily basis, trying to build his strength up, but he still had a long way to go before he regained the peak of fitness he had known before.

When his breathing became normal and his heart rate had slowed, he made his way round to the right until he came to the door at the back of the fort, crouching below the level of the embrasures. His palm was moist inside his glove where he gripped the revolver and his heart pounded, but he felt joyously alive, his senses sharpened by the thrill of the moment.

Molineaux burst out of the smoke a few moments later, the haversack over one shoulder. He dropped down beside Killigrew, lowering the haversack to the ground and crawling across to examine the lock on the door.

'Can you pick it?'

'Two, maybe three minutes,' Molineaux told him, taking a little wallet of lock-picks from the pocket of his jacket. More than sixteen years had passed since he had turned his back on the life of crime he had learned on the back streets of London as a child, but he had not forgotten the skills and nor had he thrown away his set of 'betties', a fact for which Killigrew had had cause to be grateful more than once in the past.

As Molineaux went to work on the lock, another seaman emerged from the smoke, ducking down to crouch by Killigrew against the side of the fort, and five more had arrived by the time the petty officer moved back from the door, nodding curtly to the commander to signify that the door was unlocked. Killigrew returned his revolver to its holster, unstrapped the top of the haversack and passed out grenades to the others while they waited for the remaining five to join them. When the coxswain brought up the rear, Killigrew took a grenade out for himself. He reached for his box of matches, and realised he had used his last one.

'Give me a light, Molineaux.'

The petty officer stared at him. 'Don't look at me, sir. You're the one who smokes.'

'Cox'n!'

'Sir?'

'Matches.'

'Haven't got them on me, sir.'

'Come on! Someone must have some matches!'

Eleven faces stared back at him blankly.

'Someone's going to have to go back for lucifers,' said the coxswain.

'There's no time.' God alone knew what kind of state the *Ramillies* was in by now. Killigrew drew a revolver and held the grenade's fuse to the muzzle: he would have to hope that the sound of the guns would mask the shot, or that if it did not then everything would happen too quickly for anyone inside the fort to have time to react.

He squeezed the trigger. The burst of flame ignited the fuse, which sputtered into life. He held it for Able Seaman Patchett to light the fuse of his own grenade from it. As soon as Molineaux saw the fuse on Patchett's grenade was burning, he hauled on the door handle.

The door refused to budge.

Killigrew had about three seconds left to get rid of the grenade. He was about to hurl it away from him when Molineaux gave the door another tug and this time it opened. Killigrew lobbed the grenade through, and Molineaux slammed the door shut again.

Patchett had already allowed the next seaman to light another grenade from his, and now he threw it through the embrasure above his head. Four more grenades followed in quick succession, trailing smoke from their hissing fuses, and then the first exploded.

Molineaux had moved to one side of the door, which was just as well because it was blown clean off its hinges to land about twenty feet away. The other explosions followed rapidly in a crescendo of sound, and then there was a deafening boom that seemed to tear the whole world apart, followed by an even louder one that made the ground shudder, and brick dust sheeted down the side of the wall. It was swept up in the burst of rapidly expanding gases that leaped through the embrasures all around the tower with an ear-splitting roar.

Killigrew was so dazed by the size of the blast, he hesitated before charging through the door, stunned. One of the grenades must have set off the powder in the fort's magazine. Gilchrist was shouting something: Killigrew saw his lips move but, deafened by the blast, heard no sound. No time to worry about that, or the danger that more explosions might follow: it was too much to hope the explosion had killed everyone in the fort, and the longer he hesitated the more time they would have to recover. Drawing his second revolver from its holster, he charged through the doorway, roaring incoherently.

The place was as hot as hell, and dust and smoke filled the air, choking him. A man loomed at him out of the darkness, naked, his clothes blown from his blackened body. Killigrew shot him twice in the chest at point-blank range before he realised that the man presented no threat to anyone. He looked around for the stairs leading to the first floor, and saw another man in a long, drab grey greatcoat stagger towards him. He pointed the revolver in his left hand and squeezed the trigger. Killigrew was not much of a shot even with his right hand, and the revolver was not the world's most accurate weapon, but at that range even he could not miss and the man went down. Killigrew was aware of Molineaux and the others charging in behind him, blazing away with their muskets at anything that moved before drawing their cutlasses.

He saw another Russian emerge from a doorway and shot him, stepping over his body to find a curving flight of steps leading up to the first floor. He pounded up the steps four at a time, saw a figure silhouetted in the doorway above and put two more rounds in him. Stumbling over the man's corpse, Killigrew emerged on to the first floor, still roaring, firing both revolvers alternately at anything in a grey greatcoat. There was no shortage of targets, and a moment later the hammers of both revolvers fell on empty chambers.

A Russian lunged at him with a bayoneted musket. Dropping one of the revolvers, Killigrew caught the musket by the barrel and forced the bayonet aside, using his other revolver to club the man, whose flat forage cap provided little protection from the blow. As the man fell, Killigrew slipped the revolver into its holster but was still trying to draw his cutlass when an officer charged at him with a sabre. The blade of Molineaux's cutlass came arcing down, slicing through flesh and bone, and the officer fell before he got within three feet of the commander. Another Russian thrust his bayonet at Killigrew's stomach, but the commander had his cutlass in his hand now and he parried instinctively, kicking the man in the crotch and hacking at his neck as he doubled up. Killigrew looked around – the air was a little clearer up here – and saw a hole in the floor immediately above where the magazine must have exploded. Three of his men were running up another flight of stairs, which must lead to the roof; he heard

19

more shots, and then silence from above, and suddenly there was no one left to kill.

Gasping for breath and feeling shaky, Killigrew turned to Molineaux, who was wiping the blade of his cutlass clean with a rag. 'Much obliged, Molineaux.'

'My pleasure, sir.'

'Where's Gilchrist? Find him and tell him to send up a blue light, before the *Ramillies* opens up with a broadside.'

Molineaux nodded and hurried back downstairs. The three men who had gone on to the roof to deal with the sharpshooters up there returned, two of them supporting the third, who nursed a bullet hole in his upper arm.

'Is it bad, Rawlins?'

'I've had worse, sir,' the seaman replied cheerfully. 'Right glad of it, I am too. Didn't want to go back to England without a souvenir. I'd never've been able to show me face in the Ramage Arms without summat to prove I weren't shirking.'

'That's the spirit, Rawlins. Take him out into the fresh air, Stoddard. Patch him up as best you can and take him back to the pinnace.'

'Aye, aye, sir.'

As Killigrew made his way back downstairs, he heard a whooshing sound outside, and had reached for the hilt of his cutlass before he realised it was only the noise of Gilchrist's signal rocket. Forcing himself to relax, he emerged into the ground floor where the coxswain greeted him with a salute.

'I'm afraid Wilcox is dead, sir. One of the Ivans managed to squeeze a shot off before Patchett could pay him off. And Kearney's in a bad way.' He indicated an able seaman who lay on the floor amongst the corpses of Russians with two of his shipmates crouching over him, offering him what comfort they could. His stomach had been slashed wide open by a bayonet and his entrails were spilling out.

'Take him outside into the fresh air and rig up a litter so we

20

can take him back to the *Ramillies*.' Killigrew would have preferred to summon Mr Dyson ashore, but from the way the Russian shots had been slamming into the hull before they had attacked the fort, he suspected the surgeon and his two assistants would have their hands full in the sick berth. 'Same goes for any other wounded. Including the prisoners.'

'The rest of our wounded are still standing, sir,' reported the coxswain. 'Which is more than I can say for the Russian wounded: about six of 'em.'

Killigrew stooped to retrieve the revolver he had dropped earlier. 'Any other prisoners?'

The coxswain grinned. 'Begging your pardon, sir, but you didn't say anything about taking prisoners.'

'Did we win, sir?' asked Kearney, his eyes shining brightly, in spite of the pain he was in: pain that was evident from the sheen of sweat on his ashen face. Despite Mr Dyson's skill, Killigrew doubted the young seaman would last the night.

'Yes.' Killigrew's voice was raw. 'We won.'

Kearney managed a wan smile as he was carried out. Following him out, Killigrew felt sick. He supposed he himself would get a mention in dispatches for the brief action, perhaps even a mention in *The Times*' 'Naval Intelligence' column. Wilcox and Kearney would get mentions too, perhaps, but only in the casualty list. It was a poor reward for men who had given their lives for their country . . . not even their country, Killigrew corrected himself bitterly, but for Turkey and the Eastern Question, a question they did not even understand. He was not sure he understood it himself. He remembered joking about it in the wardroom on the voyage from Portsmouth: anyone who knows the answer to the Eastern Question doesn't understand the question. It did not seem so amusing now.

Molineaux must have seen the grim look on his face. 'Pretty light butcher's bill, sir, considering.'

'One man dead,' Killigrew snapped back. 'And Kearney

like to follow him. That's two men too many.'

'And how many if we'd done it Neville's way?' Molineaux shouldered his musket. 'This is war, sir. Coves get scragged. There ain't a man in the *Ramillies* who ain't a volunteer. Wilcox and Kearney knew the risks. Better that British soldiers and seamen die fighting for their country than innocent women and children get slaughtered by the Russians in Bulgaria.'

'It was the Turks who perpetrated the Bulgarian massacres, Molineaux, not the Russians.'

'Same difference.'

'It doesn't trouble you that we're fighting to defend the Ottoman Empire?'

Molineaux laughed harshly. 'Don't kid yourself, sir. It's British trade we're fighting to defend, never mind the poor bloody Bulgars. You think the government'd give a dam what the Turks or the Russians did to the Bulgars, if the Tsar didn't have his beady eye on India?'

Killigrew nodded. As usual, Molineaux was able to see beyond the self-righteous stuff and nonsense in the newspapers to cut to the heart of the matter.

'Russia, Turkey . . . not much to choose between them, s'far as I can tell,' the petty officer continued. 'You can worry about the rights and wrongs of it if you like. Me, I'm going to concentrate on staying alive.'

The breeze had cleared the smoke by now, and Killigrew was able to see that while the Russian guns had punched a few holes in her sides above the waterline, there was no sign that the red-hot shot had set the *Ramillies*' timbers alight. That was something to be grateful for, at least.

He saw Neville approaching at the head of his squad of marines. 'Damned good show, sir!'

'One dead and seven wounded, one seriously,' Killigrew told him. 'How are your men?'

'Not a scratch on 'em, sir.' Neville at least had the decency to sound apologetic. 'Just like you, to keep my lads standing in the wings while your bluejackets steal all the glory.'

'Well, I'm sure my bluejackets will damn me to hell for it tonight.' Killigrew took out a cheroot, plugged it in the corner of his mouth, and reached for his matches before catching himself with a grimace. He turned back to Neville. 'You wouldn't happen to have a light on you, by any chance?'

I

War Tourists

Thursday 10 August

It was the usual damned shambles, Killigrew thought sourly.

The French took their soldiering seriously: that much had been obvious from the speed with which they had set up their camp within hours of landing, and the methodical manner in which they had established their mortar batteries within range of the Russian forts.

But with the English – and at times like this he preferred to think of himself as Cornish, which was something else entirely – it was altogether another matter. Here, as in all things, the culture of the gifted amateur pervaded, although in what way these particular amateurs were gifted remained a mystery, unless not being overburdened with brains might be considered a gift.

The Åland Islands had no shortage of beasts of burden, and the French had commandeered plenty. It simply had not occurred to the officer commanding the landing party from the British fleet – Captain Hewlett of HMS *Edinburgh*, Rear Admiral Chad's flagship – to commandeer any horses of their own, a happenstance that gave rise to a good deal of muttering amongst the British seamen who hauled at the drag ropes.

What they were hauling was one of three thirty-two-pounder long guns that had been brought ashore at Tranvik Point from HMS *Belleisle*. Now the guns – along with a good supply of shot, shell and cartridge – had to be dragged the four and a half miles to where the Royal Engineers were setting up a breaching battery. Weighing two tons, each gun rested on a stout wooden sledge, and needed 150 men to drag it on rollers over the dusty, uneven ground to where the sappers were building a rampart of sandbags and earth-filled wicker gabions. A band from one of the ships in the bay behind them led the way, playing martial airs like 'Heart of Oak' and 'The Girl I Left Behind Me' to encourage their efforts.

Dragging the guns was backbreaking work. Leaving the other officers present to rush about bawling unnecessary orders, Killigrew had stripped off his pea jacket to haul at the ropes alongside his men, while half a dozen petty officers – including Molineaux – were appointed to each sledge to steady it with handspikes as it rolled, pitched and slewed about the dusty track. Others picked up the rollers as they emerged behind the sledge, replacing them at the front. Beyond the forest of pine trees that lined the rocky shore, the rollers sank into the soft earth of ploughed fields, and the sweating, puffing seamen turned the air as blue as their jackets with their salty language.

'Bloody hot work, eh?' said 'Red' Hughes, a Welshman whose sallow face was pitted by smallpox.

'Aye,' agreed Seth Endicott, a tall, lanky man with greasy fair hair and thick Scouse accent. 'Eh, it's just as well we didn't have to drag sledges as heavy as this'n in the Arctic.'

'I can keep going for ever,' said Hughes, and added: 'On Trubshaw's Cordial!' As always, it provoked a burst of hilarity from the men pulling on the drag ropes; all except Molineaux, who scowled. Some kind of in-joke at Molineaux's expense, as far as Killigrew could tell.

'All right, my buckoes,' he gasped. 'That's enough gabbing – a little less yack and a little more back, if you catch my drift.'

The men strained at the ropes, faces red with exertion, bare feet slipping and sliding in the dust. The fleet had been issued with boots for the men to wear ashore, but the Naval Commissariat Department – staffed by more 'gifted' amateurs, Killigrew did not doubt – had seen fit to supply boots that were all two sizes smaller than the average seaman's foot.

Glancing at the seamen's feet now, Killigrew could not help noticing that Molineaux wore a particularly fine pair of boots. 'Those didn't come from the commissariat,' he observed. 'You bought those yourself?'

'Yur, well, you know how uncomfortable the navy-issue ones are. Even when they're the right size.'

'Where did you get them?'

'Some cove called Tricker.'

'Tricker . . .' Killigrew almost lost his grip on the drag rope. 'Not . . . Tricker's of St James's?'

'That's the place.'

'But . . . that's where I get mine!' And a pretty penny they cost him too. He wondered how Molineaux could afford them on a petty officer's pay; given the Londoner's curriculum vitae, Killigrew could be forgiven for wondering if he had acquired them by entirely honest means. But now was not the time to ask him, not with his shipmates listening.

The last half a mile was the worst. The guns had to be hauled up a boulder-strewn slope to the eminence where the sappers had located their battery. Now the guns were in view of one of the Russian forts the enemy gunners began to send the occasional cannon-ball skipping towards them.

Seeing the tars struggling to haul the guns inch by inch up the slope, some French soldiers camped nearby left off what they were doing to take their places at the drag ropes alongside the British allies. This prompted huzzahs and heartfelt cries of '*Vive la belle France!*' from those seamen

26

who had breath left in their aching lungs.

By now the Russian gunners were dropping shells close enough to shower the men with dust and soil, but their guardian angels earned their wings that day: there were no fatalities, and thanks to the assistance of the French soldiers the three guns were all in position by one o'clock in the afternoon.

A young officer of the Royal Engineers saluted Killigrew. 'Lieutenant Lennox,' he introduced himself. 'Aide-de-camp to General Jones.'

'Commander Killigrew, HMS *Ramillies*. Anywhere my men can get a bite to eat?'

Lennox smiled. 'It's all been arranged: our cooks are preparing something for them now. What about you? You're welcome to be a guest in our mess.'

'That's very kind of you.'

Lennox stepped up on to the rampart, took the telescope from under his arm and levelled it towards the Russian positions, studying them for a moment.

'What do you think?' Killigrew asked him.

'Well, it would have been a formidable position if the Russians had finished the defences. But given that they began work on these forts about forty-five years ago and they're still not finished, I'd say a reasonable date for the projected completion would be some time in the early twentieth century.'

'Looks like we got here just in time, then.'

Lennox lowered the telescope. 'I should say we'll have this nut cracked in about a week.'

'A week!'

'Too long, you think?'

'Surprisingly short. But siege warfare never was my forte.'

Lennox proffered the telescope so Killigrew could see for himself. The main fortress of Bomarsund stood on the coast, facing across the narrow channel that separated Prästö Island from Bomar. Semi-circular in shape, it presented a casemented battery five hundred yards long towards Lumpar Bay. It had embrasures for 120 guns in two tiers, although Killigrew had only counted five dozen muzzles. The fortress was built of brick faced with hexagonally cut blocks of the local pink granite, the embrasures and the arches of doorways framed with whiter stone. The iron roof was covered with several feet of sand as protection against mortar shells.

Four round forts – identical to the one Killigrew and his men had taken six days earlier – were arranged around the flanks of this fortress to provide covering fire in the event of an attack from the sea. Each stood about half a mile from the main fortress. The British had designated them the north, west, south and east forts according to where they lay in relation to it, although strictly speaking the south fort lay to the south-west. Earthworks ran from this fort to the main fortress, and it was clear that if the war had not intervened then more fortifications would have been built linking the south, west and north forts; the east one stood on Prästö Island, across the channel from the main fort. Incomplete as the fortifications were, they nonetheless presented a formid- able appearance to Killigrew's eyes as he surveyed them now from the landward side.

Lennox indicated the west and south forts. Both stood on knolls that dominated the whole vicinity. 'We'll have to take both those forts before we can launch an assault against the main fortress.'

'I found lobbing a few grenades through the embrasures works wonders,' said Killigrew.

Lennox smiled thinly. 'Ah, yes, heard about your little adventure at the Ango Fort the other day. That's doing it the hard way. It's a miracle your casualties were so light.'

A lesser man might have taken umbrage at the implied slight, but Killigrew only smiled and raised an eyebrow. 'Oh? And how would you have done it?'

'Artillery barrage, of course. Pound away with shells, and

keep pounding away until it collapses. No need to risk the lives of your men in hand-to-hand combat.'

'It was the lives of the men on board the *Ramillies* that concerned me.'

'Yes, well, the *Ramillies* should never have found herself in that position. Not that it was your fault,' Lennox added hurriedly. 'But troops should have landed to occupy that fort, prevent the Russians from sneaking back inside when our backs were turned.'

'I couldn't agree more!'

'But it only goes to prove what I've been saying for years. No disrespect, but the age of battleships is over. Look at what happened to the Turks at Sinope: one shell in the magazine, and the whole ship goes up. Swinging on board enemy ships to capture them will soon be all in the past. That thing has had its day.' Lennox indicated the sword at Killigrew's hip.

'You mean, who needs a cutlass, when you can blow your foe apart at a thousand yards?'

'Precisely! Modern armaments are much more efficient.'

'Efficient! I'd never looked at it in quite that way. I'd always thought that one sought to gain a military advantage by gaining a tactical or strategic advantage: getting the weather gage of the enemy; or dominating the high ground, as you landlubbers would say. You make it sound as if it was our job to kill as many of the enemy as possible.'

'That's the way the world is going.'

'Rather a dangerous approach, wouldn't you say? Given that we're at war with one of the most populous countries in the world; and one that's ruled by men who don't care how many of their soldiers they send to their deaths.' Killigrew shook his head. 'Not sure I approve of all this long-distance pounding. Call me an old-fashioned romantic if you will, but I can't help feeling that if gentlemen must kill each other without the courtesy of being formally introduced first, they should at least have the courage and decency to do it face to face: to look into the eyes of their opponent even as they snuff their lives out with the thrust of a bayonet or the stroke of a cutlass. Trying to kill men who are little more than stick figures in the distance, or barely glimpsed shadows behind far-off embrasures . . . one doesn't feel one's trying to kill another human being at all.'

'Much easier that way, wouldn't you agree?'

'Oh, it's easier, all right: too easy. Too easy to forget that those distant figures are men of flesh and bone, like you and me, with mothers, wives, sweethearts, ambitions and dreams. How many dreams are shattered with each burst of a shell? Slaughter without guilt.' Killigrew shook his head. 'If this is to be the way of the wars of the future, then no good will come of it.'

He turned his attention to the south-east, where Lumpar Bay shimmered beneath the sun. He could see two screw frigates, a sailing frigate, a steam corvette and a first-class paddle-sloop positioned to support the French landing at Tranvik Point, where two paddle-steamers towed barges packed with soldiers across from the four troopships. In addition, more ships were arrayed in two lines across the bay, out of range of the Russian batteries: four screw ships of the line, including the *Ramillies* and Admiral Pénaud's flagship, the *Inflexible*; five French sailing ships of the line; ten more paddle-steamers; two hospital ships; the Imperial yacht *la Reine Hortense*, which had brought General Baraguay d'Hilliers and his entourage out from France; and a cutter. Not to mention the Åland Islanders' own bum-boats; several British merchant schooners owned by enterprising captains selling alcohol and other forbidden pleasures to the fleet; and four pleasure yachts.

'Is that an iron steam yacht?' Killigrew asked Lennox incredulously.

The lieutenant nodded, scowling. 'The *Vesta*, Lord Newborough's yacht. And beside it the *Gondola*, Lord Lichfield's.' He scowled. 'Damned war tourists, come to see us risk our lives for Queen and country as if this were a blasted entertainment at Astley's, rather than an actual war.'

'Now I know how the gladiators of old must have felt when they stepped out into the dust of the Circus Maximus for the amusement of the citizens of Rome.'

'Ghoulish bastards,' Lennox grated, staring towards the yachts.

'Oh, don't criticise them,' Killigrew said cheerfully, but a hard edge entered his voice as he continued. 'Let them see what war is really like. I wish every damned voter in Britain could be here today to see it stripped of the veil of newsprint, revealed in all its bloody, horrid reality. Perhaps then, the next time our government gets into a squabble with another country over some obscure problem of international diplomacy, they'll remember soldiers and seamen maimed or dying in terrible agony, and the widows and orphans they leave behind them, and think twice. Perhaps then they'll start considering war a last resort, rather than the first.'

'The Russkis have got her range now,' Rodney Maltravers, thirteenth Viscount Bullivant, remarked with the air of an expert as another round shot slammed into the hull of the paddle-frigate HMS *Penelope*. 'See that? They must be usin' red-hot shell. Couldn't reach her at that range, otherwise.'

'I thought red-hot shot was used to set the ship's timbers on fire?' asked Lord Dallaway.

'That too,' acknowledged Lord Bullivant. 'But it's the range, that's the thing, d'ye see?' He turned to where Dallaway – the young man he hoped would one day be his son-in-law – stood beside him at the yacht's taffrail. 'Well, don't just stand there, young feller – get your camera thingy up on deck and take some photographical pictures, damn your eyes! You won't get a show like this every day of your life.'

'It wouldn't work,' Lord Dallaway, a pioneer of the photographic art, remarked with the air of a man who very much wished it were otherwise. 'Even with my fastest-acting photographic paper, it takes at least thirty seconds for an image to form – the splinters flying from the hull wouldn't even register. Besides, the rocking of the deck would make everything blurred.'

The Russian gunners slammed shot after shot into the frigate's hull. Two of the Allied ships were firing their ten-inch guns at the main fortress on the coast, trying to discourage them. Another cloud of smoke belched from one of the embrasures of the main fortress. While the general din of the engagement made it impossible for Bullivant and Dallaway to distinguish the shriek of the shot, they clearly saw timbers burst from the far side of the *Penelope*'s hull. In the same instant a small boat below was smashed to smithereens, killing one man instantly and throwing the rest into the waves.

'Oof!' exclaimed Bullivant. 'Did you see that? Went straight through her, it did! In one side and out the other!'

'Why the deuce doesn't her captain move her?' demanded Dallaway. 'The Russkis will pound her to matchwood if he stays there much longer.'

'I don't know,' admitted Bullivant. 'Looks like the damned fool's run himself aground on a hidden shoal . . . look, here comes another steamer to pull her off.'

In the saloon of the yacht, the Honourable Araminta Maltravers sat in the corner and tried to blot out the voices of her father and Lord Dallaway as they watched the battle from the deck with their opera glasses. Instead she concentrated on Thackeray's *The History of Henry Esmond, Esquire*, which lay open in her lap. She was in her late twenties, a tall woman with light brown hair and a strong-jawed face, long lashes framing her cool grey eyes and a hint of freckles dusted across the sides of her nose.

'I say, Araminta!' Lord Dallaway's voice sounded immediately above her. She looked up, startled, to see him peering at her through the skylight in the deck head.

'I do not recall giving you permission to address me by my first name, my lord,' she told him frostily.

The young aristocrat looked hurt. 'Why ever not? I mean, we're practically engaged as it is.'

'No. You proposed to me – I turned you down. That does not make us "practically engaged" by any stretch of the imagination.'

'Oh, I'm sure you'll come round to my way of thinking sooner or later.'

'Nicholls!'

The door to the saloon opened almost at once, and Araminta's maid entered. 'Yes, miss?' she asked with a curtsy.

'Would you do something for me, Nicholls?'

'Yes, miss?'

'If I ever come around to Lord Dallaway's way of thinking, would you put a pistol to my temple and pull the trigger?'

Nicholls considered the request. 'Wouldn't it make more sense to put the pistol to Lord Dallaway's temple before that happens, miss?'

'Good thinking, Nicholls. Whatever would I do without you?'

The maid was too fond of having steady employment to answer that one as truthfully as she would have liked, so she said nothing.

'Don't be like that, Araminta!' protested Dallaway. 'You know how much I love you.'

'How can I forget, when you keep reminding me every ten minutes? I wish your faculty of recollection were as well developed: you might remember the countless times I've told you that your feelings are not reciprocated.'

'Well . . . at least come on deck and watch the battle with your papa and me.'

'Watching a load of men in silly uniforms trying to kill one another may be your notion of entertainment, my lord. It isn't mine, I can assure you. Now be so good as to go away and leave me in peace.' She bowed her head over her book.

'Araminta!' her suitor exclaimed.

'Nicholls?'

'Yes, miss?'

'The blinds.'

'Yes, miss.' Nicholls crossed to the centre of the room and reached up to draw the blind beneath the skylight, blotting out Dallaway's face. 'Will that be all, miss?'

'Yes, thank you, Nicholls.'

No sooner had the maid withdrawn, however, than Lady Bullivant entered. 'Araminta?'

'Yes, Mama?'

'What are you doing down here, reading? Why don't you come up on deck?'

'So I can watch a load of foolish men trying to kill one another? No, thank you.'

'You don't have to watch the battle. It's a lovely day. Why not come up and get some fresh air?'

'I'd rather not, if it's all the same with you.'

'You'll hurt your father's feelings. He arranged this trip for you, you know. We thought it might do you some good. You know you haven't been yourself lately.'

'Mama, that's utter nonsense, and you know it. For one thing, Papa doesn't have any feelings. For another, if you wanted to take me on a voyage to cheer me up, why not ask me where I would like to go? If you'd suggested the Mediterranean, I might have said yes. I've always wanted to go to Italy.'

Lady Bullivant grimaced. 'All right, I'll admit the choice of destination was your father's rather than mine. But all the same, it really is lovely outside: the sun's shining, the sky is blue, there's not a cloud in the sky—'

'Unless you count the smoke coming from the steamers and the cannons.'

'—and the trees look delightful—'

'What a shame they're obscured by all those hulking great ugly ships.'

Lady Bullivant closed the door behind her and lowered her voice. 'You're thinking about *him*, aren't you?'

Araminta bowed her head over her book once more. ' "Him"? Who's "him"?'

'You know very well whom I mean. You cannot fool me – I am your mother, after all.'

'I haven't given *him* a second's thought in years. And anyhow, even if I were thinking of *him*, I would hardly think that bringing me to see the navy fighting a battle would help to take my mind off him.'

'Look, even if he is out there – and we don't know that he is – I'm sure he'll be all right.'

Araminta looked up at her mother. 'You know something? I hope *he* is out there. And I hope he gets his stupid, ugly, thick skull blown off by the Russians, and rots in Hades where he belongs!' She slammed down her book, stood up and flounced out of the saloon. The effect was marred only marginally by her having to reopen the door to free her skirts.

Exhausted but triumphant after hauling the three guns to the battery, the bluejackets collected their dinner from the cooks of the Royal Engineers and collapsed by the tents of the camp to eat. The distant sound of shell and shot drifted up from the direction of Lumpar Bay, where the ships of the fleet exchanged salvoes with the batteries of the main fort, but the seamen had enough problems of their own and were glad that someone else was being subjected to the attentions of the Russian gunners.

'Red' Hughes massaged his blistered and bloody feet. His nickname referred not to his hair – which was a mass of tight, black curls – but to his habit of spouting communist dogma at the least provocation.

'How far do you reckon we dragged those guns today?' he asked Molineaux.

'Tom Tidley reckoned it at four and a half miles when we surveyed the route yesterday.'

'Four and a half miles!' groaned the Welshman. 'Felt more like four and a half *hundred* miles to me.'

'I heard Cap'n Hewlett say we'd achieved a feat unprecedented in the annals of naval history,' said Endicott.

'Oh, yur?' Molineaux asked sceptically. 'What was that? Getting Red to pull his weight for once?'

Hughes scowled. 'Kiss my bum, Wes!'

Endicott lay back on the ground and clasped his hands behind his head. 'I'll be glad when they pipe "down hammocks",' he sighed. 'I think I'm going to sleep for a month after today.'

'Chance would be a fine thing,' said Molineaux. 'Don't get too comfortable, will you, lads? There's another three guns to bring up tomorrow.'

Endicott groaned.

'Another three guns?' said Hughes. 'You've got to be joking! You know what this is, don't you? Exploitation of the working classes.'

'Stow it, Red!' warned Molineaux. 'It's bad enough breaking our backs dragging guns up for the sodgers, without having to listen to your commie claptrap at the end of it. It ain't as if the officers didn't bear a hand.'

It was sixteen years since he had joined the navy. A 'snakesman' in his youth, he had signed on board HMS *Powerful* to evade the peelers, intending to desert at the first opportunity. Funny how things rarely turned out the way one expected. In those days, of course, you joined a ship for a voyage, a commission of three years if it was a navy ship, but you did not 'belong' to the navy. You could pick and choose which captain you served under, and if you liked the life you could join a new ship after the old one paid off, following a suitable break to blow all your earnings on booze, gambling and whores.

But it was all changing now. Anticipating the difficulty it would have finding experienced seamen for the fleets in time of war, the Admiralty had finally become convinced of the need for continuous service: nowadays you joined the navy for ten years minimum. They were in the middle of the changeover period, with both old and new systems in place. Many of Molineaux's shipmates had signed on as ten-year men, but the petty officer was reluctant to commit himself. The pay was better if you signed on as a ten-year man, and you could still choose the ship you served on for your first commission. But after that you went to whichever ship the navy sent you to. Molineaux preferred to size up a captain before he decided whether or not he wanted to serve under his command. Hell, for all he knew, they might send him back to the Arctic! Besides, ten years . . . it seemed such a long time. He liked the navy; he just was not sure he liked it *that* much. He would be in his forties by the time he got out.

On the other hand, his one ambition in life was to be made a boatswain, and there was no getting away from it: the ten-year men would always be preferred to short-service volunteers when the Queen's warrants were handed out. Still, he had three years' grace in which to make up his mind.

He glanced across to where the French soldiers were setting up another camp nearby, pitching their tents wherever they could find space. Chasseurs in sky-blue coats and red *képis* bustled to and fro, heading out on patrol or to relieve picquets, while more and more seemed to march up from the landing point with every passing moment. Foraging parties marched into the camp driving herds of cattle, which were promptly butchered at a large tent set up as a slaughterhouse to provide meat for the troops.

Endicott saw a *vivandière* in a blue jacket and red pantaloons, a cask of brandy in the small of her back and a brace of pistols at her hips. He blinked, and rubbed his eyes as if in disbelief. When he opened them again, the apparition was still there, no matter how much he blinked. She was selling tobacco to a couple of infantrymen, while a burly soldier stood on guard by her stall to make sure none of the rough and licentious soldiery took advantage. Molineaux wondered who made sure the guard did not take advantage.

'Hey, Wes!' called Endicott.

'What?'

'That feller's a judy.'

'Yur – she's a *vivandière*.'

'Come again?'

'A *vivandière*. They sell fancy goods and stuff to the Frog sodgers.'

'And their army allows it?'

'They're employed by the army. The Frogs are into all this equality for blowers stuff. Why, yer *vivandière*'s practically a woman sodger. 'Cept she don't do any fighting, of course.'

'She's wearin' kecks.'

'They're called "bloomers", shipmate.'

'Bloody disgustin', I call it. Eh, she's not bad-lookin', though but. Have you ever noticed how lasses from Cat'lic countries always make more of themselves than lasses from countries where they're all psalm-singing Methodies? Don't get me wrong – I'm not saying that your Paddy, Frog, Wop or Dago judy is actually better looking than an English, Scowegian or sauerkraut-eating haybag; just that they take more pride in their appearance.'

'Do you mind? My lass happens to be a sauerkraut-eater!'

Endicott did not seem to hear him. 'I reckon their religion must have summat to do with it. Y'see, yer Cat'lic lass, she believes she can sin as much as she likes, but as long as she goes to confession and says as many "Hail Maries" as the priest tells her, all her sins will be forgiven and she can still get into heaven. But yer protestant lass, there's nowt she can do to extrapolate her sin, so she's got to behave herself. Only Cat'lic judies are up for it all the time . . . what's wrong, Wes? Why are you looking at us like that?'

Molineaux shook his head, torn between wonderment and disgust. 'Do you have to think hard to come up with so much gammon, or does it just come naturally?'

Endicott shrugged. 'I'm just sayin', like.' He nodded to the *vivandière*. 'Eh, what do yer reckon me chances are wi' that one?'

38

'About ten thousand to one – and that's before I take into account the fact you don't speak a word of French.'

'I can speak French. Well, a bit. Anyhow, who needs to speak the lingo? The language of love is understood all around the world.'

'Now, don't go making trouble, Seth. The Frogs won't like it if a British seaman starts trying to get spoony with one of their lasses.'

'Hey, if she's up for it, she's fair game. Watch and learn, Wes: you're about to see a master at work.' Producing a comb from his pocket, Endicott walked over to the *vivandière*'s stall, trying in vain to tame his tangled locks.

''Afternoon, Molineaux.'

The petty officer turned and saw Killigrew walking towards him. ''Afternoon, sir.'

The commander glanced across to where Endicott was leaning across the *vivandière*'s counter to whisper in her ear. 'Is Endicott getting something from that *vivandière*?' he asked.

'Yur, right!' snorted Molineaux. 'In his dreams, maybe.'

'I didn't know he spoke French . . .'

The *vivandière* straightened with a shocked expression on her face, and gave Endicott a stinging slap across the cheek.

Molineaux chuckled. 'Oh, I think he made himself understood.'

As Endicott reeled from the stall, the soldier set to stand guard over her grabbed him by the neckerchief and delivered a powerful punch to his nose. The seaman staggered back almost as far as where Molineaux and Killigrew stood. Despite the blood that poured from his nostrils, Endicott was back on his feet in an instant. He would have flung himself at the soldier to avenge the assault if Molineaux had not grabbed him and dragged him away in the interests of maintaining the Anglo-French alliance.

'*Pardonnez-vous mon ami, mam'selle, m'sieur,*' he called over his shoulder at the *vivandière* and her guard. '*Il est un crétin.*'

Killigrew handed Endicott a linen handkerchief to stanch the flow of blood. 'What did you say to her?'

'I don't understand it, sir.' The Liverpudlian looked genuinely bewildered. 'I only asked her if she'd let us kiss her.'

'Oh, Lor'!'

'All right, maybe I were being a bit 'ard-faced, but not enough to justify a smack in the gob!'

'Do you want to tell him, Molineaux, or shall I?'

'Seth, when a Frenchman says he wants to kiss a woman, he doesn't mean he wants to kiss her.'

'These Frenchmen are crazy!' Endicott tapped his forehead emphatically. 'What *do* they mean, then?'

Molineaux glanced at Killigrew, and whispered in Endicott's ear.

The Liverpudlian's face cleared. 'Oh, is that all? For a moment there, I thought you were going to say it meant summat *really* dirty. So what *does* a Frenchman say when he wants to kiss a lass?'

Molineaux scratched his head. 'Dunno. What about you, sir? What do you say to a French lass when you want to kiss her?'

Killigrew smiled bashfully. 'Well, not that I've had much experience with French ladies . . .'

The two ratings looked at him sceptically.

'. . . but I would imagine one simply waits for the right moment, and then kisses without asking. Best to go about it handsomely, though – make your intentions clear, give the other party a chance to indicate that your attentions are unwelcome, if necessary.'

Molineaux saw a man in the uniform of a mate come running up from the direction of Tranvik Point, and pointed him out to Killigrew and Endicott. 'Here comes Mr Latham, sir.'

A young man with a mop of straw-coloured hair and deeply sunken eyes in a thin face, Francis Latham skidded to a halt in front of Killigrew and snapped to attention, saluting

40

awkwardly. 'Captain Crichton presents his compliments, sir, and requests the presence of the shore party back on board at your earliest convenience,' he gasped breathlessly, his normally pale face now red from running.

'Something amiss, Mr Latham?'

'It's the *Penelope*, sir – she's run aground on Presto Island, within range of the enemy guns. The Russians are throwing everything they've got at her.'

'Sounds like a case of all hands to quarters.' Killigrew strode briskly to where the rest of the men lounged about, resting from their labours. 'Listen up, lads! I know you're all tired and it's a lot to ask, but the *Penelope*'s got on shore under the Russians' guns, and—'

Hughes and the others leaped to their feet. 'Where do you want us, sir?'

'The captain's sending boats to pick us up at the cove west of Grinkarudden,' said Latham.

'Come on, lads!' said Molineaux. 'Look lively, while there's still enough of the *Penelope* left to rescue!'

With a great cheer, the seamen charged in a mob towards the French battery facing the west fort half a mile away. Almost at once the Russian gunners opened up, sending cannon-balls skipping across the open heath land. But the west fort could only bring a few guns to bear, and their rate of fire was as slow as their aim was poor. Nevertheless, it was a hair-raising sprint, with Latham leading the way and Killigrew bringing up the rear with Molineaux and a few other trusted hands, to make sure that no one was wounded and left behind. At last they had skirted the back of the French battery and entered the trees beyond. The Russian guns started lobbing shells at the pines, but they were firing blind now, and succeeded in doing no more damage than stripping a few branches and slaughtering some wildlife.

When the seamen reached the cove, they found the boats already waiting for them. The petty officers took a head-count of the men in their divisions. Having established that their guardian angels were still working flat out, they climbed into the boats and pulled hard to where the *Ramillies* was anchored on the other side of the bay. As the men scrambled up the lifelines to the bulwarks, Killigrew ascended the accommodation ladder and pulled himself through the entry port, not forgetting to doff his cap in obeisance to the quarterdeck, where he presented himself to Captain Crichton.

'Reporting for duty as ordered, sir.'

'By God, Killigrew, you don't lag behind when there's work to be done, do you? Too late this time, though: *Hecla, Gladiator* and *Pygmy* have already towed the *Penelope* clear. Not before time, either: she was taking a fearful pounding. The Russkis must've hulled her in a dozen places. The chief had to order them to throw her guns over the side to lighten her. How did it go ashore? Did you get the guns up to General Jones?'

'Only half of them, sir: it was heavy going. Captain Hewlett respectfully requests that the men who went ashore this morning be allowed to rest, and asks that you send a hundred and eighty fresh men ashore tomorrow to help drag the remaining three guns to the battery.'

Crichton nodded and turned to the yeoman of the signals. 'Signal *Edinburgh*, Flags: Captain Hewlett shall have as many men as he requires.'

'Aye, aye, sir.'

'Permission to go ashore with them tomorrow, sir?' asked Killigrew.

'Not granted.' Crichton smiled. 'You're not the only officer in the *Ramillies*, you know. Time to let someone else get a whiff of grapeshot, eh? Masterson can go ashore tomorrow; you've earned a rest.'

'Aye, aye, sir. There is one other thing: the lads who were ashore this morning were called away before they had a chance to eat . . .'

'Say no nore. Mr Saunders! Tell Sawyer to prepare a hot

meal for the men who were ashore this morning.'

'Aye, aye, sir.' Midshipman Saunders saluted and headed for the fore hatch.

'I'd recommend them for an extra tot of rum at "up spirits", sir,' added Killigrew. 'They've earned it.'

Crichton nodded. 'Make it so, Mr Killigrew. I shall want a full report of your activities ashore by the end of the first dog watch.'

'Aye, aye, sir.'

'Carry on.'

II

What Did You Do In The Russian War, Daddy?

Thursday 10–Friday 11 August

Molineaux had a pounding headache by the time he crawled into his hammock that night after piping 'ship's company's fire and lights out'. He closed his eyes and lay very still, hoping that he would fall asleep, and the headache would be gone by the time he awoke, but sleep was elusive. Finally he gave up, creeping below the bodies of the other men snoring in their hammocks, and made his way forward to the sick-berth. The place was quiet at that time of night, with only Mr Charlton there, reading one of his books on homeopathic medicine.

A snub-nosed lad with dark curly hair, Humphrey Charlton was only recently qualified as an apothecary and this was the first time he had served on board one of Her Majesty's ships. As soon as Charlton had come on board, the news that Crichton had employed a homeopathic practitioner as one of the *Ramillies'* two assistant surgeons had spread through the lower deck like the plague, and about as welcome.

'What's homeopathic medicine when it's at home?' Endicott had asked.

'Something to do with curing like with like,' explained Molineaux.

'Oh, aye? Does that mean that if you get one of your legs blown off by a round shot, Mr Charlton's going to amputate the other?'

Now Molineaux stood on the threshold of the sick-berth and eyed Charlton dubiously. 'Er . . . is Mr Dyson around, sir?'

'Tucked up in his bunk, at this time, I should imagine,' said Charlton.

'What about Mr Yates?'

'Ditto. Anything I can help you with?'

'I was just after some Dr James's powders, sir.'

'Headache?'

'Thumping.'

'You don't want Dr James's powders,' said Charlton. 'I've got just the thing for you.' He crossed to the dispensary and took out a bottle of an oily, yellow-tinged liquid. Removing the stopper, he dipped a medicine dropper inside. 'Open wide!'

'Ahh!'

'Now, don't swallow this – let it rest on your tongue until it's absorbed.' Charlton let the tiniest trace of the liquid drop on Molineaux's tongue. It had a sharp yet sweet taste, not entirely unpleasant.

'Wha' i' i'?' asked Molineaux, taking care not to let his tongue touch the roof of his mouth.

'A new chemical: a compound of glycerine, oil of vitriol and spirits of nitre. Taken in small doses, it induces violent headaches.'

'Well, thank you very much, sir!' Molineaux forgot all about not touching the roof of his mouth with his tongue. 'When I said I wanted something for a headache, I meant I wanted to get rid of one, not get a new one!'

'It's a homeopathic cure,' Charlton explained patiently. 'If you haven't got a headache, it will give you one. If you've already got one, it *should* cure it.'

'Yur, right!' snorted Molineaux. He snatched up the bottle and glanced at the label: pyroglycerin. 'Sorry, sir, but with all due respect, you can keep your blooming homeopathic cures!' He tossed the bottle to Charlton, who blanched and caught it with an expression of profound relief.

'*Don't do that!*' screeched the assistant surgeon.

'Don't do what?' asked Molineaux, alarmed by the unwarranted panic in Charlton's voice.

'Throw this bottle around like that. This stuff is highly explosive!'

'What do you mean, sir, highly explosive?'

'I mean what's in this bottle is enough to blow this sick-berth apart and reduce the two of us to our constituent atoms.'

'Go tell it to the marines!' scoffed the petty officer. 'You're spinning a yarn, ain'tcher?'

'No, Molineaux, I am not.'

'Lumme! Does the cap'n know you're storing explosives in the dispensary?'

'Why? Do you think he'd mind?'

'I reckon there's a distinct chance he might have some objection, sir, yes . . . lumme!'

'What's wrong?'

'You maniac! . . . sir. You just put some of that stuff in me gob!' Deciding it was time to make his excuses and leave – before Charlton offered him a gunpowder suppository – Molineaux turned on his heel and returned to his hammock very gingerly.

The first lieutenant, Masterson, had already gone ashore with two hundred of the *Ramillies*' crew first thing the following morning. Killigrew was attending to some paperwork after breakfast when someone knocked at the door to his cabin.

'Come in!'

The door opened and Molineaux stood there. 'You sent for me, sir?'

'Yes, Molineaux. I've been meaning to ask you about your boots.'

'My boots, sir?'

Killigrew nodded. 'Don't take this the wrong way, but . . . I cannot help but wonder how you can afford a pair of Tricker's on a petty officer's wages.'

'I didn't steal them, if that's what you mean.'

'I dare say. Nevertheless, I'm intrigued to know how you came by the money.'

Molineaux looked uncomfortable. 'With all due respect, sir, I ain't sure that's any of your business.'

'All I'm asking is that you'll give me your word of honour that you earned the money honestly.'

'Well, I wouldn't say I *earned* the money, exactly . . . but I didn't break any laws, if that's what you mean.'

'A legacy?'

'Not exactly, sir. More a sort of . . . windfall.'

On the upper deck, the ship's bell tolled twice, and in exactly the same instant a chiming sound came from Molineaux's pocket. 'Oops!' The petty officer pulled out a gold watch and fiddled with the winder. 'Sorry, sir . . . forgot to switch off the chimes of me repeater . . . sir?'

Killigrew was staring at the watch, open-mouthed. 'That must have been some windfall, Molineaux,' he stammered at last.

The petty officer grinned. 'I ain't complaining. Not enough for me to retire on, you understand. More sort of . . . pocket money, if you will. Thought I'd treat myself to a few luxuries.'

'So I see. Molineaux, are you quite sure you didn't—'

Mr Charlton appeared in the corridor behind Molineaux. 'Sorry to interrupt, sir. Wondered if I might have a word?'

'Hmph . . .? Oh, yes, of course. We'll continue this conversation some other time, Molineaux. Carry on.'

'Aye, aye, sir.' The petty officer touched the front of his bonnet and was about to leave when Charlton addressed him. 'How's the headache this morning, Molineaux?'

'Fine; no thanks to you, sir. Pyro-bloody-glycerin indeed!' Molineaux turned smartly on his heel and made his way forward to the mess deck.

'What was all that about?' asked Killigrew.

'It seems Molineaux doesn't seem to have much faith in my homeopathic cures, sir,' explained Charlton, taking the petty officer's place on the threshold.

'He's not the only one,' grunted Killigrew. 'Did you want something?'

'Sick list, sir.' The assistant surgeon held the said paper down at his side.

The two of them stared at one another.

'Well, are you going to give it to me?' Killigrew asked Charlton at last.

'You're not going to like it, sir.'

'If it was a rattling good yarn I was after, Mr Charlton, you may rest assured that I would not opt for the daily sick list.' Then a horrid thought occurred to him. 'Christ! Don't tell me the cholera's back!'

'You'd best see for yourself, sir.' Charlton finally handed him the report.

Killigrew cast an eye over it. The names of Willoughby and Gidley – second and third lieutenants respectively – leaped out at him. 'Oh, Lor'!' he groaned when he saw what ailment they were suffering from. He looked up at Charlton. 'We'll have to tell the Old Man.'

'Won't that be rather embarrassing for Willoughby and Gidley?'

'I should say it will be *extremely* embarrassing for Willoughby and Gidley. Pass the word for them to join us in the captain's day-room. You'd better have Mr Dyson join us too.'

'Yes, sir.'

While Charlton went off to search for the two lieutenants, Killigrew made his way to the captain's quarters. 'Sick list, sir,' he announced once he had negotiated his way past the marine sentry on duty that morning.

Like Killigrew, Crichton was up to his ears in paperwork as usual. He took the sick list from his commander and initialled it without even glancing at it.

Killigrew coughed into his fist. 'You might like to take a closer look at this one, sir.'

Crichton looked again. 'Oh, hell!' he exclaimed. 'Pass the word for Willoughby and Gidley.'

'I already took the liberty of asking them to join us, sir.'

'Thank you. Take a seat, Killigrew.' Crichton tidied up his papers and presently they were joined by Charlton, Dyson, Willoughby and Gidley. The captain invited the surgeon and his assistant to be seated, leaving the two lieutenants to stand there on the carpet like a couple of naughty schoolboys who had been caught tippling the chaplain's brandy.

'Do you know about this, Dyson?' asked Crichton.

The surgeon looked bewildered. 'About what, sir?'

'Tell him, Killigrew.'

The commander took a deep breath. 'It would seem our second and third lieutenants have contracted a social disease, Mr Dyson.'

Willoughby and Gidley both blushed and squirmed, as well they might.

'Don't beat around the bush, Killigrew,' snapped Crichton. 'They've both copped a burner.'

Dyson peered at his assistant. 'Are you certain, Charlton?'

'All the symptoms are there, sir,' said the assistant surgeon. 'Extreme pain in the male member when passing water, purulent mucus discharge—'

'Thank you, Mr Charlton, we all know what the symptoms of gonorrhoea are,' Crichton interrupted hurriedly. 'What's your prognosis?'

'Fortunately we've discovered the infection in the early

stages, sir. With the swift application of a course of mercury treatment, I think we can soon have them back on their feet again.'

'But I suppose they'll need to be off duty until then,' snorted Crichton. 'Can't have 'em running off to the necessary every five minutes when they're officers of the watch, hey? Until then, we'll move Adare up to second, Lloyd to third, and so on.' He glowered at the two lieutenants. 'Damme, I'd've expected such carelessness from a couple of the hands, but from you two? I'm very disappointed in you. Have you got anything to say for yourselves?'

'Sorry, sir,' mumbled Willoughby and Gidley.

Crichton sighed. 'I ought to punish you, but between your symptoms and the cure, I think that's punishment enough ... though you can be assured I'll be deducting your pay for every day you're unfit for duty.' He turned to Charlton. 'Does anyone else on board know about this?'

'Only Barr, sir,' said the assistant surgeon. Barr was the sick-berth attendant.

'Then it will be all over the ship within the hour,' sighed Crichton. 'No point in cooking up a covering story to hide your shame; not that you deserve it anyhow. Go on, get out of my sight, the pair of you—'

'One moment, sir,' said Killigrew. 'May I ask them a question?'

'By all means.'

Killigrew turned to the two miscreants. 'Any notion where you might have picked it up?'

Willoughby and Gidley exchanged glances.

'Answer the question, damn it!' snarled Crichton. 'This is no time to be coy.'

'There's a schooner moored in Ångholmsfjörd, sir,' volunteered Willoughby. 'Can't remember it's name – something beginning with M, *Mil*-something. They have ... ah ... ladies ... on board. It's very high class,' he added hurriedly. 'All the officers of the fleet have been using it—'

'Oh, *very* high class!' snorted Crichton. 'A schooner chock-a-block with poxed cyprians! Mr Dyson, would you make arrangements to have these two idiots transferred to the *Belleisle*?'

'Yes, sir.'

Willoughby, Gidley, Dyson and Charlton withdrew from the day-room. Only Killigrew lingered.

Crichton rubbed his face wearily. 'Damn it! This is all we needed.'

'We'll manage somehow, sir,' Killigrew said confidently.

Crichton looked up at him, as if surprised to discover the commander was still there. 'Was there anything else, Mr Killigrew?'

'Just a thought, sir. I don't doubt Willoughby was exaggerating when he said that all the officers of the fleet have visited this schooner – I haven't, for one, and I know that isn't your cup of char, but . . . even if only a few dozen have been on board, well . . . it could be a major problem for the fleet.'

'You're right, of course. I suppose I'll have to write a letter to all the captains of the fleet, warning them and their crews off this damned floating bordello. Perhaps you'd pass the word for Mr Latimer on your way out?'

'Certainly, sir. But by the time your letter gets around the fleet, it could be too late for some poor, innocent fools.'

'Yes, of course. Can we impound this vessel, put them under arrest?'

'I don't think that's legal, sir.'

'Oh, damn and blast! Still, we could send a boarding party over to her to clear off any naval people, and see if we can drive her away from the fleet. Check their papers, search them for contraband, generally make life difficult for the crew, that sort of thing. Make it clear they're not welcome, perhaps find enough evidence to arrest them on some trumped-up charge. Take the first cutter and a score of men.'

'Me, sir?'

'Who else? You're good at that sort of thing; and don't

stand there pretending you don't know what the inside of an accommodation house looks like.'

Killigrew was tempted to ask what Crichton meant when he said he was 'good at that sort of thing' – as if he had made a career out of boarding floating brothels – but he could not in all conscience argue with the captain's second accusation. 'I'd've thought it would be a job for one of the lieutenants, sir.'

'Masterson's ashore with the guns; can't send Willoughby or Gidley, obviously; wouldn't trust Lloyd to tie his own bootlaces; and Adare probably thinks gonorrhoea is one of King Lear's daughters. No, Killigrew: I appreciate it may seem a little *infra dig.*, but it's got to be you.'

The commander sighed. 'Aye, aye, sir.'

A thick fog was rolling down Ångholmsfjörd by the time the cutter approached the sound where half a dozen merchant ships and bum-boats rode at anchor. Killigrew ordered the crew to lie on their oars, and took his miniature telescope from his pocket to survey the scene. The sun had set, but there was still a pale glow in the sky to illuminate the masts that rose above the level of the fog, and he could easily make out the ships' lights shining through the gathering dusk.

It was a good place for the floating grog shops to do business: naval officers were passing up and down the channel constantly, moving between the squadron engaged in Lumpar Bay and the rest of the fleet waiting at Ledsund. If some of those officers' boats took a little longer to make the journey than necessary because they had stopped here to replenish their personal stocks of alcohol, or to enjoy the embraces of a young lady of easy virtue, their superior officers would be none the wiser.

Killigrew snapped the miniature telescope shut and returned it to the pocket of his pea jacket. 'All right, lads, now listen carefully. One of those vessels is the one we're after.'

'Is it a Russian spy ship, sir?' asked the coxswain.

Killigrew shook his head. 'It's a floating cunny warren . . .'

The men cheered.

'Don't get your hopes up. We're here for business rather than pleasure. And in case any of you were thinking of boarding the whores, I should warn you that at least two of 'em are fireships, and I'm informed that certain officers from the fleet have already burned their pokers . . .'

'Willoughby and Gidley,' murmured someone, and the others nodded.

Killigrew grimaced. 'Yes, well, we don't want it happening to anyone else, so our job is to make life very uncomfortable for the crew of the ship we're looking for. We'll board her as if she was a slaver: be rough, but not too rough. Corporal, make sure your men's muskets are unloaded. Bruises by all means, but not cuts, hoist in?'

'Aye, aye, sir.'

'We'll go on board hard and fast. Search the ship from stem to stern, get everyone up on deck: crew, bluejackets, tarts, everyone.'

'What if one of 'em's an officer, sir?' asked Molineaux.

'I'm sure I don't have to remind you of the penalty for striking an officer, Molineaux; but if they're lieutenants or below, don't let them pull rank on you. If they don't like it, just refer them to me. If they're captains or above, you'd best use your discretion.'

'And if we find a commander?'

Killigrew smiled. 'Find out if he's got seniority on me before you do anything else.'

The men laughed.

'All right, lads, give way together.'

The crew dipped their oars once more and the cutter moved across towards the fleet of bum-boats and floating grog shops.

'Bloody hell!' muttered Powell. 'I joined the navy to get a crack at the Russkis; didn't think I'd end up boarding a floating brothel.'

'Dunno what you're complaining about, Hal,' Joyner retorted. 'At least you ain't married. 'Ow am I going to explain this one to my missus?'

'This'll be a story to tell our grandchildren,' said Molineaux. 'How we boarded a cunny warren in the great war with Russia.'

Hughes began to sing: 'Farewell and adieu to you fair trading ladies; farewell and adieu to you ladies of trade. For we've received orders for to—'

'All right, keep silence in the boat there!' Killigrew did not mind a little banter amongst the hands when things were not too serious, but they were drawing close to the ships now, and the hull of the first loomed out of the fog at them. 'I know we'd all rather be boarding a Russian warship, but don't go thinking this isn't a very serious matter.'

They rowed in and out between the ships riding at anchor while Killigrew tried to match one of them to the description Willoughby had given him: a fore-and-aft rigger schooner of about 170 tons, a hundred feet from stem to stern and twenty-three feet broad. It was difficult to gauge the dimensions of any of these ships in the fog, and he hoped in vain that a whore leaning at the rail of one might invite him on board for a good time, thus giving the game away.

He was starting to think he was on a wild-goose chase when the cutter rounded the stern of one of the grog shops and he saw a handsome yacht beyond. The curtains behind the gallery windows were drawn, but he could see a slit of light shining between them, and hear laughter and the chink of cutlery on china. The name carved on the scrollwork below the window was illegible in the gloom until he shone the light of a bull's-eye on it: *Milenion*.

'That's the one,' he murmured to his men. 'Make for the accommodation ladder, Cox'n.'

'Aye, aye, sir.' The coxswain put the tiller over, bringing the cutter in towards the yacht's side. Standing at the bulwark smoking a pipe, a crewman watched them approach with idle curiosity. Killigrew ignored him, jumping for the accommodation ladder as soon as it was within reach and climbing up to the entry port.

The crewman tried to block his path. ''Ere, you can't just barge on board like this! This here's a private yacht.'

'I'll do as I please, my bucko!' Killigrew drew his revolver from its holster and waved the muzzle in the crewman's face: it was unloaded, but with any luck the man would not notice in the half-light.

Apart from the coxswain, who remained in the cutter and made her fast to the accommodation ladder, the rest of the men swarmed up on the schooner's deck, fanning out to cover the other crewmen with their muskets. Glancing about, Killigrew saw that the schooner was well kept, the deck holystoned as white as that of a man o' war.

'What the devil's going on?' A smartly dressed man in a peaked cap came up through the after hatch. He was in his mid-fifties, a hard-faced man with a neatly trimmed beard emphasising the point of his jaw. 'Who are you?'

'Commander Killigrew, HMS *Ramillies*. Are you the owner of this vessel?'

'I'm Captain Thornton, the master. The owner is—'

'Where can I find him?'

Thornton regarded him stonily.

Killigrew thumbed back the hammer of his revolver.

Thornton sighed. 'You'll find him dining in the saloon, aft.'

'Thank you. Corporal Harding, you and your men remain on deck and keep these fellows covered. Molineaux, make your way down the fore hatch and work your way aft, flushing out everyone below decks. I don't care if they have to tumble up with their trousers round their ankles.'

Molineaux grinned. 'Aye, aye, sir.'

'Powell, Joyner . . . you two come with me.'

Accompanied by the two able seamen, Killigrew descended the after hatch. Below decks was illuminated by oil lamps set in gimbals on the bulkheads. Willoughby had not been exaggerating when he had described this as a high-class establishment: teak panelling, brass handrails brightly polished, even a thick carpet underfoot. The owner of the vessel must have been raking it in, to make a voyage in a ship of this quality pay its way. Even the crewmen on deck had been wearing a uniform of sorts.

They passed a number of cabin doors. 'Shouldn't we search 'em, sir?' asked Powell.

Killigrew shook his head. 'Leave them to Molineaux and the others; I'm after the pimp who runs this barge.' Besides, he could hear no sounds emanating from any of the cabins, none of the giggles, moans of passion, creaking bed springs or whip cracks he might have expected from a vessel like this. Presumably it was a quiet night. It was just as well: he was terrified of kicking in one of the doors and catching a rear admiral *in flagrante delicto* on the other side.

He could hear a murmur of voices coming from the door at the far end of the passage, presumably leading into the saloon. He glanced over his shoulder to make sure Powell and Joyner were still with him. 'Ready?' he murmured. They both nodded.

Killigrew kicked open the door and strode through into the saloon. The compartment was luxuriously appointed, even compared to the *Ramillies'* wardroom: plush velvet drapes, mahogany furniture, and what looked suspiciously like a Persian rug on the floor. The younger of two women screamed, and the white-coated steward who had been serving supper to the two couples at the table dropped a serving dish in fright.

Killigrew levelled his revolver at the man sitting at the head of the table. 'All right, which one of you whoremongers is the owner of this floating bordello?'

The man's jaw dropped. He was sixty or thereabouts, dressed in black cassimere pantaloons and an alpaca swallow-tail coat, a gold watch chain hanging across the front of his white satin waistcoat beneath a muslin cravat. His ruddy face was dominated by a Roman nose and a splendid set of white whiskers.

Killigrew's jaw dropped too.

'You!' exclaimed the thirteenth Viscount Bullivant.

'My lord!' stammered Killigrew.

He did not recognise the younger but equally well-dressed man seated at Bullivant's right – thirtyish, pink-faced, with ginger hair and extravagant side-whiskers – but the older of the two women was familiar enough: in her late forties or early fifties, elegantly dressed but well past her prime, with a lantern jaw and iron-grey hair pinned up in a bun: Lady Bullivant.

The younger woman, sitting with her back to him, twisted in her chair. Seeing him, she blanched. 'Kit!'

'Killigrew!' spat Lord Bullivant, rising to his feet and throwing his napkin down on the table as if in challenge. 'What the devil's the meaning of this intrusion, sir?'

The commander hurriedly returned his revolver to its holster. 'I can explain everything, my lord. You see, I thought this ship was a floating brothel . . .'

Bullivant turned puce.

The younger woman rose to her feet and turned to face him with slow deliberation.

Killigrew grinned sheepishly. 'Hullo, Minty. Long time, no see.'

The Honourable Araminta Maltravers dashed the contents of her wine glass in his face.

He licked his lips. 'Mm! The 'forty-six. An excellent year—' He broke off and ducked hurriedly as she threw the glass at his head. It shattered against the bulkhead behind him. 'Perhaps I'd better take my leave?'

'I'll say you had!' snarled Bullivant. 'By God! If you ever come near me or any members of my family ever again, I'll have you horsewhipped to within an inch of your life! Damn your eyes, Sir James Graham will hear of this!'

Sir James Graham was the First Lord of the Admiralty: a

Whig, but a Whig in the Tory Lord Aberdeen's coalition government, and Killigrew knew for a fact that Bullivant and Aberdeen were on the best of terms. If it had been his intention to end his career prematurely, he could not have done it more spectacularly if he had mooned the Queen.

'My most sincere apologies. Naturally, I'll pay for any damages,' Killigrew added lamely.

'Oh, you'll pay, right enough!' Bullivant roared apoplectically. 'You haven't heard the last of this, Killigrew! By God, I'll see to it you're kicked out of the navy for this! Now get out!'

'My lord.' Killigrew bowed out of the saloon, closing the door behind him, while Powell and Joyner snickered.

In the passage, he heard a woman squeal in protest, and saw Molineaux emerge from one of the cabins with a petite, dark-haired, elfin-faced young woman firmly gripped in a half-nelson. 'Let go of me, you black-faced heathen brute!' she protested.

'Look at this one, sir!' the petty officer grinned. 'Dressed as a dollymop. Kinky, eh?'

'Let her go, Molineaux.'

'Sir?'

'She really *is* a maid. This yacht belongs to Lord Bullivant.'

'You mean, his lordship's running this floating brothel?'

'No, Molineaux. We've got the wrong ship.'

The petty officer hurriedly released the maid. 'Sorry, miss . . .'

She whirled and drew back a hand to slap him. He raised his arms to protect his face, so she punched him in the groin. He doubled up with a gasp, and she turned and disappeared back inside the cabin, slamming the door behind her and sliding the bolt.

As Molineaux followed Killigrew up the companion ladder clutching himself, he was pursued up on deck by the well-dressed young man who had been dining with the Bullivants.

'Killigrew? You are a bounder, sir!'

The commander ignored him. 'Back in the cutter, every-one. Take a head count, Cox'n.'

'Killigrew!' persisted the young man. 'I am talking to you, sir!'

The commander turned to face him. 'But I am not listening to you, sir.'

'You, sir, are a bounder.'

Killigrew shrugged. 'It's been said before.'

'You are not only a bounder, sir. You are a dastard and a coward.'

'Sticks and stones.' Killigrew made for the entry port to follow his men back down to the cutter.

'One moment, sir!' The young man tugged off one of his kid gloves. Grabbing Killigrew by the shoulder, he spun him round and slapped him in the face with it. 'Sir, I challenge you to a duel!'

'Duelling is illegal,' Killigrew reminded him.

'Back in England, perhaps . . .'

'If, as I suspect, this vessel is registered in England, I think you'll find that English law applies here on board every bit as much as it does on Piccadilly.'

'Then we'll go ashore, by God!'

'You may go ashore, sir. I have my duties on board the *Ramillies* to attend to.'

'Am I to understand that you are refusing to give me satisfaction?'

Killigrew rolled his eyes. 'My word, he's finally got it!' he remarked to no one in particular.

'You, sir, have no honour!'

'None at all. Look, you want a duel? Very well. As the injured party, I have choice of weapons.'

'Injured party, sir? And just how is it you consider yourself the injured party?'

'I have offered you no insult; I do not even know your name . . .'

'It is Dallaway, sir! Lord Dallaway! And I demand satisfaction!'

'Yes, I think we've got past that point. You were the one who struck me, so I am the injured party.'

Dallaway waved dismissively. 'As you will. It makes no difference to me, sir – I am equally adept with swords or pistols.'

'And I also have choice of time and place.'

'As you will.'

'Then for the time and place, I choose here and now.'

Dallaway smiled wolfishly. 'Nothing would give me greater satisfaction.'

'That remains to be seen.'

'Your weapon of choice?'

'Hmph? Oh . . . fists.' Killigrew punched him on the nose. Dallaway went down with blood streaming from his nostrils.

'There,' said Killigrew. 'Honour is satisfied. Good evening to you, sir.'

He climbed through the entry port and descended to the cutter, taking his place in the stern sheets. 'Shove off, Molineaux! Up together, lads. Give way with a will!'

'Good God, man!' Crichton was appalled when Killigrew reported to his day-room later that night. 'I send you to do a simple little job like drive off a floating brothel, and you manage to insult one peer of the realm – a close personal friend of the prime minister, no less – and assault another.'

'Yes, sir. It was entirely my mistake. I'll bear full responsibility and take the consequences.'

'And deprive me of the best second-in-command I ever had? You'll do no such thing. I'm sure if I have a word with the chief we'll be able to sort this mess out somehow.'

'Thank you, sir. What about the real floating brothel? She must still be out there somewhere . . .'

Crichton grimaced. 'Forget about the floating brothel, man.

60

I've sent word to the other ships in the fleet. That will have to do. We've got more important fish to fry. Carry on.'

'Aye, aye, sir.' Killigrew saluted and withdrew, wishing he shared Crichton's belief that things could be cleared up so easily. Sir Charles Napier might be commander-in-chief, but to judge from the tone of some of the editorials in the newspapers brought out to the fleet from England, public opinion was turning against the rear admiral for his failure to attack Kronstadt. The attack on Bomarsund might deflect some of the criticism, if all went well, but Bullivant had Lord Aberdeen's ear, and if the prime minister put pressure on the navy to have Killigrew dismissed, Napier's patronage would not be enough to save him. Besides, Napier himself had always been fickle, and had grown increasingly testy with his subordinates as the campaign had progressed; given his own troubles, he might not hesitate to sacrifice the commander to protect his own back: he was in no position to defy Lord Aberdeen.

Emerging from Crichton's day-room, Killigrew encountered Willoughby, supervising his marine servant who was packing his things for his transfer to the *Belleisle*.

'By the way, sir, I remembered the name of that schooner – it was the *Millicent*.'

It took the combined efforts of Lieutenants Lloyd and Adare and the marine to remove Killigrew's hands from Willoughby's throat.

III

The Guns of Bomarsund

Saturday 12–Wednesday 16 August

The crew of the *Duke of Wellington* were paraded on the upper deck for divisions when the lookout at the maintop spotted the schooner approaching. 'Sail ho!' he bellowed down to the deck.

Captain Gordon cupped his hands around his mouth. 'Where away?'

'Fine off the starboard bow!'

One of the lieutenants took the telescope from the binnacle and raised it to one eye. 'Can you make her out?' asked Gordon.

'She's flying the White Ensign . . . but I don't think she's one of ours.'

'What makes you say that?'

'She's a schooner, sir.' The lieutenant handed Gordon the telescope so he could see for himself.

'Royal Yacht Squadron,' said Gordon. 'Or one of the other clubs permitted to fly the White Ensign.' He handed the telescope back to the lieutenant. 'The *Milenion*?'

'I do believe you're right, sir.'

Rear Admiral Michael Seymour – a tall man with a patrician face and greying hair swept back from his temples, iron-grey side-whiskers creeping across his prominent cheek-bones like cant hooks – crossed the quarterdeck to join them at the bulwark. 'The *Milenion*?'

'Lord Bullivant's yacht, sir,' explained Gordon. 'He's one of the war tourists who've accompanied the fleet out here.'

And a personal friend of Lord Aberdeen, thought Seymour. 'Captain Gordon, you will order your men to dress the yards.'

'Sir?'

'You heard me, man! I want the yards dressed, as a mark of respect to a peer of the realm.'

'Aye, aye, sir. Bosun, pipe the men aloft.'

The men swarmed up the ratlines and out on to the yards until there was not an inch of horizontal timber in the ship's tops that did not have a seaman standing on it. The wind was light, and even with all sails drawing, the *Milenion* made slow progress as she sailed across the Ledsund to where the *Duke* was anchored.

The *Milenion* dropped anchor a short distance from the *Duke* and lowered her gig from its davits.

'Looks as though his lordship intends to honour us with a visit, sir,' said the lieutenant.

'Full compliments, Captain Gordon,' said Seymour. 'Marine guard, drummers, side party.'

'Aye, aye, sir.' Gordon turned to the senior officer of marines on the quarterdeck. 'Guard at the entry port – a ruffle of drums when his lordships sets foot on the deck.'

'Very good, sir.'

The *Milenion*'s gig rowed across to where the *Duke* was anchored. 'What boat is that?' called the marine sentry at the entry port.

'Lord Bullivant, yacht *Milenion*, Royal Yacht Squadron!' responded the gig's coxswain. The gig bumped against the *Duke*'s side beside the accommodation ladder, and Lord

Bullivant gazed unhappily up at the entry port, some thirty feet above him.

At 270 feet from stem to stern, with a burthen of 3,700 tons and a complement of 1,100 men, HMS *Duke of Wellington* was indisputably the mightiest man-o'-war in the world. With 130 thirty-two pounders arrayed on three decks and a sixty-eight pounder mounted on traversing rails on the forecastle, she carried sufficient firepower to discharge a ton and a half of iron at every broadside. She rode at anchor under bare poles with the other mighty line-of-battle ships at Ledsund that were too large to navigate the shallow Ångösund to Lumpar Bay where the rest of the fleet supported the attack on Bomarsund. A slim funnel rose abaft her foremast to betray the presence of the 780 horsepower engine in the depths of the ship, driving a screw propeller to manoeuvre her in defiance of wind and tide.

Lord Bullivant said something to one of the gig's crew, and the man ascended the entry port to approach one of the boatswain's mates.

'His lordship requests a bosun's chair, sir,' reported the boatswain's mate.

'Well, don't just stand there, man! Rig one up!'

'Aye, aye, sir.'

A boatswain's chair was rigged up and lowered from one of the yards to the gig below, and presently Lord Bullivant was swinging above the upper deck. 'Well, lower me down! Can't afford to hang about here all day!'

'If you'd just stretch your legs, my lord, you'll find that your feet are only a couple of inches off the deck,' Captain Gordon told him as tactfully as possible.

'Stretch me legs? What do you think I am, made of India rubber?'

Disgusted, the two seamen holding Bullivant up exchanged firm nods, and a moment later the boatswain's chair came crashing down to deposit Bullivant sprawling on his back amidst a tangle of rope. The boatswain descended on the two hands with a face like thunder, but both knew that whatever punishment he had in store for them, it was going to be worth it.

Ashen-faced, Rear Admiral Seymour hurried forward to help Bullivant to his feet. 'My lord! My most sincere apologies, my lord. Rest assured, the men responsible will be punished most severely for their carelessness.'

'I should damned well think so too,' snarled Bullivant, dusting himself down. 'Now then, where's Napier?'

'Napier, my lord?'

'Yes, Vice Admiral Sir Charles Napier. This is the flagship, ain't it?'

'Sir Charles has transferred his flag to HMS *Bulldog* for the duration of the attack on Bomarsund, my lord. Perhaps I may be of service?'

'And who the blazes are you?'

'Seymour, my lord. Rear Admiral Michael Seymour. I,' he added self-importantly, 'am the captain of the fleet.'

'I thought Napier was in charge?'

'He is commander-in-chief, my lord. I am his second in command.'

Bullivant wafted him away dismissively. 'I want to speak to the organ grinder, not his monkey.'

'Ah ha ha ha ha ha!' said Seymour.

Bullivant looked around the deck, as if doubting the veracity of the rear admiral's claim that Napier was not on board. Finding no trace of the commander-in-chief, he turned back to Seymour. 'Well, if Napier ain't here, I suppose you'll have to do,' he said wearily. 'Now see here, Seymour: I want to make a complaint.'

'A complaint, my lord?'

'Yes, a complaint! Damme, do I have to say everything twice? A complaint against one of your officers. Commander Christopher Killigrew, to be precise.'

'The Arctic explorer?' asked Seymour. It was news to him that Killigrew was in the fleet, although on reflection he was not all that surprised.

65

'That's the feller. Damned scoundrel came on board the *Milenion* last night, roughed up my crew, broke one of the doors, accused me of running a brothel, and then had the gall to strike the son of a good friend of mine: Lord Dallaway!'

'An officer of the Royal Navy?' Seymour exclaimed incredulously.

Bullivant rounded on him. 'You calling me a liar?'

'No, my lord, not at all. Far from it. You may rest assured, that I shall have the matter looked into at once.'

'Never mind looking into it, Seymour. I want the damned feller punished. Keelhauled, flogged, strung up from the yard-arm, whatever it is you do to damned scoundrels like that in the navy.'

'We don't inflict capital or corporal punishment on officers of the Royal Navy any more, my lord, except for the gravest of crimes—'

'You don't? No wonder the damned navy's gone to pot. No damned discipline, these young bucks nowadays. I've a good mind to complain to Lord Aberdeen!'

'However, if Commander Killigrew is guilty of the things you say he is, you may rest assured he'll be dismissed the service in disgrace.'

'Well, I suppose that will have to do. I want him finished, Seymour, do you understand? Finished!'

'He will be, my lord, I assure you!'

'Hmph!' Bullivant snorted, as if he would believe it when he saw it. 'You'd better not be flannelling me, Seymour, or I'll see that you stay on half-pay for the rest of your life. That's all. Good day to you, sir!' The viscount turned on his heel and stalked across to where the boatswain's chair had been hoisted once more, but on second thoughts descended to his gig via the accommodation ladder instead.

Seymour watched him being rowed back to the *Milenion*, then ordered his flag lieutenant to follow him and descended the after hatch.

'Close the door behind you,' he ordered, when they entered

the great cabin, and then rounded on the flag lieutenant. 'Know anything about this fellow Killigrew, Tremaine?'

'Yes, sir. As a matter of fact, I had the misfortune to sail with him on board the *Tisiphone* when she was posted to the Guinea Coast a few years ago. Not an association I'm proud of, I hasten to add.'

'Really? I thought he was a national hero, after that Arctic business.'

'From what I heard, the voyage of the *Venturer* was a total shambles, sir. Killigrew should have been court-martialled instead of promoted.'

'You think there might be some truth to Lord Bullivant's accusation?'

'I don't doubt it, sir. Killigrew's a scoundrel, sir, an absolute scoundrel. He swears, he smokes, he consorts with the wrong sort of women . . . damn it, sir – pardon my French – but he even reads the *Manchester Guardian*!'

'Good God! What is he, some sort of anarchist? What's a fellow like that doing in the Royal Navy?'

'Making a nuisance of himself, by the sound of things.'

'Think I'd better meet this fellow for myself. I don't suppose you know which ship he's in, do you?'

'*Blenheim*, I think.'

'Very well. Take a cutter up to Lumpar Bay to arrest him. The charge is conduct unbecoming an officer of the Royal Navy. We'll court-martial him as soon as Bomarsund is reduced.'

Tremaine smiled triumphantly. 'With pleasure, sir.'

'Holloa, sir!' exclaimed Killigrew, delighted to see his former captain. 'What are you doing here? I thought the *Jenny Dacre* was back at Ledsund.'

'Came up in my gig,' explained the Honourable Henry Keppel, a younger son of the Earl of Albemarle. The captain of HMS *St Jean d'Acre*, Keppel was less than five feet tall, his face framed by flaming red hair and long side-whiskers, his blue eyes twinkling. 'Thought I ought to come and see for myself how big a mess Old Charlie makes of the attack on Bomarsund.'

'You mean, the Chief doesn't know you're here?' exclaimed Killigrew.

Keppel grinned. 'What he doesn't know can't harm him.'

There was no love lost between Keppel and Vice-Admiral Sir Charles Napier. It dated back nearly a quarter of a century, when Napier had been captain of HMS *Galatea* and Keppel had been one of his lieutenants. Killigrew had heard the story while serving as a midshipman under Keppel's command on board HMS *Dido* during the Opium War. On a cruise to the West Indies, Keppel had had his heart set on attending a ball held at Government House in Kingstown by Sir John Hill, the governor of St Vincent and a friend of Keppel's father. On the day of the ball, Napier had ordered Keppel confined to his cabin – on a trumped-up charge, to hear Keppel tell it – just to spite him. Keppel had none the less contrived to go ashore disguised as an officer's servant, and had been enjoying himself dancing with the young ladies of the island when Napier himself had turned up in the ballroom. Keppel had only escaped court-martial thanks to Sir John's intervention.

The past few weeks had not improved relations between the two men. There had been reservations about appointing Napier commander-in-chief of the British fleet that was being sent to the Baltic: he had a reputation for being a loose cannon with a habit of exceeding his orders, and there were fears that he would send the ships of the fleet to their destruction by ordering them to attack the granite batteries of Sveaborg or Kronstadt. In the event, he had gone to the other extreme, and Keppel made no secret of his disappointment that for once in his life Napier was sticking to his orders: in this case, to prevent the Russian fleet from escaping into the North Sea, and to 'look into the possibility of doing some-thing in the Åland Islands'. In the months since the fleet had arrived in the Baltic, both Sveaborg and Kronstadt had been reconnoitred, but – without going in person within a mile of either – Napier had declared both unassailable without gun-boats or mortar vessels, much to the swashbuckling Keppel's disgust.

'You won't tell him you caught me playing hookey, will you?' Keppel asked Killigrew.

The commander grimaced. It was awkward to find himself caught between two men who had both acted as his mentors at different stages of his career. He liked both. Sometimes he suspected that the reason they did not get on was that they had too much in common: both reckless rebels who refused to play by the rules.

Instead he excused himself to buy himself time. 'If you'll pardon me a moment, sir?'

Keppel waved magnanimously.

Killigrew turned to the *Ramillies*' gunner. 'When you're ready, Mr Gatiss.'

'Aye, aye, sir.' Gatiss turned to the gun crew and screamed: '*Fire!*'

Keeping his eye steadfastly fixed along the sights of the long gun, Endicott pulled the lanyard downward with a jerk, bringing his left hand smartly on his right. The hammer snapped against the quill tube and a puff of smoke escaped the vent; the gun boomed deafeningly in the same instant, belching forth a great cloud of flame and smoke and shooting back on its truck until the preventer tackle brought it up short.

'Stop the vent,' ordered Gatiss.

Endicott forced in a vent-plug with his left hand, keeping his thumb on it, and half-cocked the lock with his right.

Killigrew levelled his telescope and saw the shell explode about thirty feet short of the target, and a little to the left, throwing smoke, dust and clods of earth high into the air. The next gun in the battery fired, and then the one after that. The two French batteries continued their bombard-ment, while down in the bay below, the *Edinburgh* and the

69

fourth-rate screw ship *Ajax* were keeping up a diversionary fire. All three batteries ashore hurled shot and shell at the Russian fortifications as fast as their sweating gun crews could fire and reload, filling the air with noise and smoke, and every now and then a Congreve rocket would shoot from its frame, trailing smoke along its erratic course before exploding against any target but the one it was aimed at.

The flag lieutenant's error in naming the *Blenheim* as Killigrew's ship had given him a reprieve, at least. Another of the blockships in Lumpar Bay, the *Blenheim* was anchored less than a cable's length from the *Ramillies*, but a cable's length made all the difference. Having put Tremaine straight about where the commander might be found, Captain Pelham had hoisted a signal to the *Ramillies* advising Crichton that the cutter now rowing towards his ship had come to arrest his second-in-command, and he would be advised to place the miscreant under arrest. The fact that the signal had been sent at all carried a broad wink advising him to do exactly the opposite, and while Tremaine had been ascending the accommodation ladder on one side of the *Ramillies*, Killigrew had been shinning down the lifelines to Crichton's gig on the other.

'Make yourself useful ashore,' Crichton had called down to him from the bulwarks. 'God knows, you're no help to anyone out here in the bay, and you'll be even less use kicking your heels in the *Duke*'s lazaretto. And for heaven's sake, try to stay out of the Chief's way until I can have a word with him.'

With which dubious benediction Killigrew had returned ashore once more, and had spent the last two days helping to put the finishing touches to General Jones's battery.

'Reload,' he told the gun crew, and checked his fob watch. 'I'm timing you.'

'Aye, aye, sir,' said Gatiss. 'Run in!'

Each man in the fourteen-man gun crew knew his place

and his duties. Endicott helped Joyner and Powell overhaul the side tackles while the rest of the gun crew manned the train tackle, hauling the gun back until the muzzle was clear of the embrasure and ready for reloading.

'Well!' said Endicott. He had been appointed captain of the gun, and Killigrew was curious to see how well the leading seaman would conduct himself. Normally the ship's joker – although there was room for plenty of jokers on a ship as large as HMS *Ramillies* – today Endicott was being seaman-like and professional.

Killigrew turned back to Keppel. 'Sorry about that, sir. You were saying?'

'Just that I remember when I hurt my back in a fall from the accommodation ladder during the China War. A certain midshipman under my command took the opportunity to go adrift and take part in the assault on Chinkiang-fu. When I learned of his gallantry in that desperate assault, I promoted him to mate. What I really ought to have done was have the young rogue court-martialled.'

Killigrew sighed. 'You were never here, sir.'

Keppel beamed. 'That's the spirit, my boy.'

'Sponge!' ordered Gatiss.

Joyner and Powell stepped inside the breeching together. Another man handed the sponge to Powell, who forced it hard home to the bottom of the bore and gave it two round turns to extinguish any fire left in the gun. He withdrew it hand over hand and gave it two smart taps against the underside of the muzzle to knock off any burning or foul fragments.

'You've already met Molineaux, I think?' Killigrew asked Keppel, gesturing to where the petty officer stood at the adjoining embrasure, holding a musket.

Keppel glanced at the petty officer and nodded. 'China, wasn't it? But you were only an AB back then,' he added, indicating the badge of distinction on the sleeve of Molineaux's blue jacket.

Turning back from the embrasure to face Keppel, Molineaux touched a finger to his bonnet in a casual salute. 'Virtue rewarded, sir,' he replied with a broad grin.

Keppel returned his grin. 'I dare say you have many fine qualities, Molineaux – but somehow I doubt virtue is one of them!'

'Load!' ordered Gatiss.

The powder-man passed a fresh, flannel-wrapped cartridge to Joyner, who put it seam-sideways and bottom-first into the muzzle to prevent the seam of the cartridge getting under the vent, which would cause a misfire. He thrust it down the bore to the full extent of his arm. The assistant loader passed shell and wad to Joyner, who put them into the muzzle. He was about to uncover the fuse when the rising shriek of an incoming shell warned the men to throw themselves flat on the earth. Endicott ducked down by the side of the breech, and the enemy shell exploded immediately outside the fort, showering them all with clods of earth.

Only Keppel and Killigrew had not ducked. 'So, you're Nose-Biter's second in command, eh?' Keppel remarked to Killigrew, flicking a clod of earth from one of his epaulettes. 'How is the old rogue?'

'Full of beans, as always.' Killigrew removed his cap to brush dust from it with a kid-gloved hand. 'Frustrated with the tedium of blockade duties, but then aren't we all?'

'I know how he feels. Why the Chief doesn't attack Kronstadt I don't know. He's turning into an old woman in his dotage.'

Joyner kept his hand over the head of the fuse until Powell had taken the rammer from the assistant sponger and thrust it into the muzzle. Assisted by Joyner, he forced cartridge, wad and shot home to the bottom of the bore. Endicott thrust the priming wire into the vent to prick cartridge. He nodded to Powell, who withdrew the rammer.

'With all due respect, sir, attacking Kronstadt isn't going to be like attacking this place,' Killigrew told Keppel. 'The Russians haven't even finished the fortifications here. And we'll need gunboats and mortar vessels to attack Kronstadt, if we're not to run aground in the shoals. The Chief's asked the Admiralty to commission some, but they keep fobbing him off.'

'Your loyalty to the Chief does you more credit than your choice of patron.' Keppel shook his head sorrowfully. 'He's lost his nerve. You know it, and I know it. We should have attacked the Russian fleet when we had the chance, while it was trapped outside Sveaborg by the ice.'

'Run out!' ordered Gatiss.

The gun crew manned the tackles and ran the muzzle out through the embrasure.

'That report was never confirmed, sir,' Killigrew reminded Keppel.

'But he should have ordered the fleet up to see for himself,' the captain pointed out.

Killigrew could not argue with that.

'Prime!' ordered Gatiss. Endicott inserted a quill tube in the vent.

'Nevertheless, an attack on Kronstadt without gunboats and mortar vessels would have been foolhardy,' said Killigrew.

'We don't need gunboats and mortar vessels to attack Kronstadt,' Keppel opined. 'We should have built rafts to carry our guns over the shoals to get in range of the Russian batteries.'

Because of his linguistic skills – Killigrew spoke fluent Swedish and had a smattering of Russian besides – he had spent enough time on board the flagship to be aware of the various plans submitted to Napier when the fleet had reconnoitred Kronstadt six weeks earlier; and he knew the arguments against them. 'Deuced difficult things to control, rafts. We might simply have provided targets for the Russian gunners. Increase range to twelve hundred and fifty yards,' he added to Gatiss. 'Same target as before.'

'Aye, aye, sir. Point!'

The handspike-men picked up their handspikes while the rest of the crew attended to the side-tackle tails.

'Russian gunners couldn't hit a barn door at point-blank range with a blunderbuss,' snorted Keppel. 'Anyhow, you don't win wars by being cautious. I'd've thought you of all people would appreciate that.'

'Me, sir? Why me?'

'Right a bit,' said Endicott, gazing along the barrel. 'Bit more . . . no, that's too much . . . well!' he concluded, when the gun was lined up to his satisfaction. He placed the tube lanyard over the neck-ring and retreated as far from the gun as the length of the lanyard would permit, while the rest of the gun crew replaced the side tackles and resumed their former positions. Endicott stood with his feet spread, his weight distributed evenly.

'I remember a time when you used to be a real fire-eater, just like your father.'

Killigrew grinned ruefully. 'Well, perhaps I'm an older and wiser man now.'

'Elevate!'

'Heaven forbid! I can understand Old Charlie turning into an old woman at his age, but a young feller like you has no excuse. Or did you lose your nerve in the Arctic?'

Keppel said it genially enough – from anyone else, it would have sounded like an accusation of cowardice – but it gave Killigrew pause for thought. 'I don't think so, sir,' he said dubiously.

The handspike-men placed their handspikes on the steps of the gun carriage, under the breeching, and raised the gun off the quoin. Hughes withdrew the quoin. The handspike-men lowered the gun slowly and steadily until Endicott said: 'Well!'

Keppel clapped Killigrew on the shoulder. 'Don't be like that, dear boy! I was only joking. Surely you can't tell me you prefer blockade duties to a chance to cross swords with the foe?'

Hughes forced in the quoin. 'Down!'

Killigrew smiled wanly. 'I wouldn't argue with that, sir. By the way, I heard you had a little excitement the other day.'

'Hmph? Oh, nothing much: just a run-in with a Russian two-decker off Hangö Head. The *Ivan Strashnyi*. She was in New York, of all places, the last I heard; must've been trying to get back to rejoin the fleet at Kronstadt. Managed to hull her in a few places, but she ran into a fog bank and gave us the slip. By the time the fog had lifted, she'd vanished completely.'

'Sunk?'

'I don't think so. Couldn't find a trace of flotsam.'

'Ready!' bawled Gatiss.

Killigrew frowned. 'She couldn't have made it into Helsingfors or St Petersburg; our blockades would have caught her.'

Hughes cocked the firing lock and withdrew. The right rearman attended the train tackle.

'Galling, isn't it?' Keppel remarked. 'Here we all are, itching for a fight, and the only Russian ship not protected by one of their fortresses has done a disappearing act!'

'Fire!'

Killigrew glanced at his watch before raising the telescope once more. He saw the shell explode against the side of the north fort.

'Capital shooting, Mr Gatiss: bang on target. But too slow, my buckoes, much too slow. Imagine this was a gunnery exercise instead of the real thing: what would Captain Crichton say? Run in! Look lively, there! Come on, my buckoes, put your backs into it! Those Russkis are laughing at how slow your rate of fire is!'

The bombardment continued through the morning. At eleven o'clock the *Amphion* and *Bulldog* joined the *Edinburgh* and *Ajax* in shelling the main fort to provide cover for the boat crews of the *Blenheim*, who landed the ten-inch pivot gun from the blockship's bow at the earthwork fort at Grinkarudden. Captain Pelham accompanied the gun in person, and soon had it hurling shells past Rear Admiral Pénaud's battery to pound the main fort.

The west fort – captured by the Chasseurs de Vincennes in the early hours of the preceding day, but abandoned when the Russians themselves began to shell it to drive them out – exploded a short while afterwards. When the smoke cleared, only a charred and blackened ruin was left standing on the knoll.

The paddle frigates *Valorous* and *Hecla* joined the fray shortly after that to support Pelham's gun, and fifteen minutes later – on the dot of noon to be precise – the ships anchored in the bay below fired broadsides in salute as a mark of respect to their French allies to commemorate the Emperor Louis Napoleon's birthday; the ships engaged with the main fort fired with shotted guns. As the afternoon wore on, five more ships – three of them French – joined in the bombardment, and before long the engagement had become general.

While the ships engaged the main fort, General Jones's battery hammered away at the north fort, until one side was breached and the Russians within had no choice but to hang out a flag of truce. Without waiting for terms to be agreed, the marines and bluejackets coolly marched forward to take them prisoner.

The prisoners – over a hundred of them – spent the night under guard in the British camp, and the next morning they were fed breakfast before being escorted to the north landing place with a strong escort of marines. Jones's battery, meanwhile, had now turned its guns on the main fort and the bombardment was resumed with increased intensity. With two of the forts put out of action, and a third isolated to the east on Prästö Island, it was all over bar the shouting. Captain Pelham's gun was doing the most damage and the Russians knew it: they concentrated their fire on his position, whereupon Napier promptly responded by ordering the ships in the bay to increase their fire to one round shot and one shell every five minutes. Combined with the effects of the mortars in the French breaching battery, this forced the Russians in the main fort to surrender at noon, and the men in the eastern fort capitulated shortly after that.

The Allied losses at the end of the nine-day siege were astonishingly light: two bluejackets killed on the *Penelope* when she had run aground beneath the guns of the main fort, a colonel of the Royal Engineers and a marine in Jones's camp, and a dozen or so wounded, including one of General Jones's aides-de-camp, who had accidentally shot himself in the thigh while chasing a Russian spy who had infiltrated the camp disguised as a woman. The French losses were rather higher – a couple of dozen – which was not surprising seeing that they had done most of the hand-to-hand fighting; but not nearly so high as the Russian losses, not to mention the two thousand or so Russian soldiers who had been captured, along with the fortress of Bomarsund itself.

As the prisoners were marched out, Killigrew went down to the fort to offer his services as an interpreter. He found that most of the Russians seemed to be drunk, either with defeat or vodka, perhaps a little of both, to judge from the bottles scattered about the place. Laughing, dancing and singing, they tore off their uniforms and spat and stamped on them, as if capture by the Allies was the best thing that could have happened to them. Suddenly, Killigrew was amazed: not that the fortress had fallen so quickly, but that it had taken so long. Apparently, the Russian soldiers feared their own officers and NCOs more than they did the enemy. He spent most of that night interrogating Russian rankers – the officers spoke French, and could be interrogated by others – but learned little from them that the Allies did not already know.

Early the next morning, he found himself staring down at the corpses of some Russian soldiers awaiting burial. They had been arrayed on the ground in neat rows and covered with linen shrouds. Most of the men he had spoken to the previous evening had been ridiculously young or ridiculously old. He did not doubt that the faces beneath those shrouds were much the same; unless they had been torn open by bullets, or shredded by the percussive effects of an exploding shell. He felt a pang of guilt – not the guilt of a man who survives a battle and wonders why when so many of his comrades had fallen about him, which he had felt after the storming of Chinkiang-fu – but the guilt of a man who has taken life without knowing why. He knew all about the causes of the war: Christ knew, they had been debated long enough in the newspapers in the lead up to the war. So many reasons for fighting the Russians, so few of them good ones. He could not see how butchering old men and boys on an island in the middle of the Baltic prolonged the life of the Ottoman Empire; as if it needed prolonging, which he very much doubted. He had killed enough times in the course of his naval career, without so much as a qualm, but usually the men were pirates or slavers: scum without whom the world was a better place, not unwilling conscripts like these poor devils.

'Reckon we did them a favour,' said a familiar voice. Killigrew looked up to see 'Plummy' Vowles, the cutter's coxswain, standing a short distance off, leaning on his musket.

'How so?' the commander asked sharply.

'It ain't much of a life, being a Russian serf, from what I hear, sir. Maybe they're better off dead.'

'And would you have been grateful to a man who took that decision on your behalf when you were living on the back streets of Portsmouth?'

The petty officer thought about it, and grimaced. 'I reckon not.' His voice seemed to come from a long, long way away.

Killigrew tried to reply, but then a wave of nausea swamped him and his legs turned to water. The fort spun around him, and the last thing he remembered was the ground rising up to meet him as his legs crumpled.

IV

Passage to Ekenäs

Wednesday 16–Thursday 17 August

Killigrew could not have been unconscious for more than a couple of minutes, but by the time he awoke the ever-efficient Vowles had him on board a boat carrying him back to the *Ramillies*.

'I'm quite all right now,' insisted Killigrew. 'You can take me back ashore.'

'With all due respect, sir, you didn't look all right when you passed out just now,' said Vowles. 'Besides, the cap'n wants to see you. And it couldn't hurt to let the sawbones look you over.'

As soon as he was on board the *Ramillies*, Killigrew made an oral report of his activities ashore – one that omitted any mention of his fainting – that Crichton accepted, pending a fuller written report. After dispatching the ship's steward to fetch him a mug of coffee, Killigrew sat down in his cabin and began to work on his report. The first paragraph was always the toughest – once he got steam up, he could dash off reports in his sleep, almost – and he was still wrestling with it when he heard the marine sentry posted outside the door to

Crichton's quarters pass the word for Mr Killigrew.

He presented himself in the captain's day-room for the second time in half an hour. This time Dyson sat at the captain's elbow.

'I understand you fainted ashore shortly before you came back on board, Mr Killigrew,' Crichton said sternly.

Killigrew flushed. *Thank you, Vowles.* 'I wouldn't say "fainted", sir. More of a dizzy spell. It soon passed.'

'You lost consciousness for the best part of two minutes,' grated Crichton. 'What do you call that, if not fainting?'

'I'm perfectly fine, sir, I assure you.'

'Are you?' said Crichton. 'I wonder. Mr Dyson?'

'How do you feel now, Killigrew?' asked the surgeon.

'Never felt better.'

'No nausea, vomiting?'

'No.'

'How are your bowels?'

'Answer the question,' Crichton put in, when Killigrew hesitated and looked tempted to protest.

'As well as can be expected, sir.'

'Regular motions?' asked Dyson. 'Good, firm stools?'

'Not that it's any of your business, but—'

'The health of the people on this ship is precisely Mr Dyson's business, Mr Killigrew,' Crichton said coldly. 'It had occurred to us that you might have contracted cholera.'

'Mr Dyson is more than welcome to examine a sample the next time I have cause to use my chamber pot, sir.'

'I'm sure that won't be necessary,' the surgeon said hurriedly, and turned to Crichton. 'I think we can rule out cholera, sir. How would you describe your health overall?' he asked Killigrew.

'As I said before, I never felt better.'

'Except that's not entirely true,' said Crichton. 'Don't think I haven't noticed how out of breath you are when you reach the top of the accommodation ladder; and Dyson tells me that you fell asleep at the dinner table last Thursday.'

Killigrew smiled. 'It was a long day. You'll recall we were rather busy helping to land the guns that day.'

'I hadn't forgotten. But while falling asleep at the dinner table is something to be expected in a man of my age, you'll own it is unusual in a man not yet thirty.'

'What's this all about, sir?'

'Everyone knows you had a hard time in the Arctic,' said Dyson. 'Frozen, half-starved, badly mauled by a polar bear, suffering from scurvy . . .'

'It's a year since I returned from the Arctic, sir,' protested Killigrew. 'I'm fully recovered from my ordeal, I can assure you.'

'To be brutally frank, I have to disagree,' said Dyson. 'You don't recover from an ordeal like that overnight; or even in months. It can take years. Some people never recover. It's become increasingly apparent that your ordeal took a greater toll on your health than you're prepared to admit. My diagnosis? Physical and mental exhaustion. The efforts of the past few days have simply proved too much for you.'

'That's nonsense, sir—'

'Be quiet, Killigrew! What's your recommendation, Mr Dyson?'

'He needs rest, and lots of it. He should never have returned to full active duty so soon. If I were you, I'd have him shipped home on the next boat. The seat of war is no place for a man in his condition. Sorry, Killigrew, but it's for your own good.'

'All right, thank you, Mr Dyson,' said Crichton. 'Carry on.'

'Yes, sir.' The surgeon rose from his chair and left the day-room.

'Sit down, Killigrew,' said Crichton.

'I'm quite comfortable as I am, sir.'

'It wasn't an invitation.'

The commander pulled out a chair and sat down.

'What am I to do with you, Killigrew? I don't want you to

think that I'm ungrateful. If it hadn't been for your unceasing labours and your knack of organisation, we'd never had got the *Ramillies* ready in time to put to sea with the rest of the fleet, and no one knows better than I how much work you've been putting in over the past few days. It's no wonder you've over-taxed yourself. But I need officers I can rely on. If we have to go into battle, I'll have enough on my plate, without having to worry about whether or not my second in command is going to faint on me.'

'It won't happen again, sir.'

'Know that for a fact, do you?'

'Sir, the navy's my life. If you send me home now, it'll be the end of my career: even if I do make a full recovery, I'll always be remembered as the man who was sent home from the Baltic. The man who was broken by the Arctic. I'll never find another captain who'll take me on.'

'Don't think I want to do this, Killigrew. Damn it, I can scarcely afford to lose an officer of your calibre, especially with Willoughby and Gidley down with the pox. But with this business with Lord Bullivant hanging over your head, perhaps it's for the best. If I ask one of the other captains to lend me a senior lieutenant until a replacement for you can be sent out from England—'

Outside the day-room, the marine crashed his musket against the deck. 'Mr Saunders to see you, sah!'

'Send him in,' sighed Crichton.

The door opened and Midshipman Saunders was ushered inside. 'Sorry for the intrusion, sir, but we've just received a signal from the *Bulldog*: you and Mr Killigrew are to go on board at once.'

Crichton and Killigrew exchanged glances. 'Well, Mr Killigrew! It seems the decision is about to be taken out of my hands.'

Once on board HMS *Bulldog*, Crichton and Killigrew were ushered down to the captain's day-room, where they were surprised to find Napier in ebullient mood.

'Ah, come in, gentlemen, come in. A fine week's work, aye? Bomarsund taken; and with hardly a loss on our side! That should silence ma critics in Westminster. And now we've shown that granite batteries are no' invulnerable to bombardment, we can think about launching attacks on Sveaborg and Kronstadt. No' this year, o' course – too late in the season for it, now – but next year . . . if I get ma gunboats and mortar-vessels.' The older Napier got, the stronger his Scots accent seemed to become. 'Can I offer you both a drink?'

Killigrew and Crichton exchanged glances. 'Thank you, sir.'

The *Bulldog*'s steward poured them each a tumbler of scotch, and they drank to the downfall of the Russians.

Vice Admiral Sir Charles Napier, KCB, GCTS, KMT, KSG, KRE, was known as 'Black Charlie' to his friends and family on account of his unusually swarthy complexion and his once-black hair; affectionately as 'Old Charlie' to the seamen who served under his command; as 'Mad Charlie' by his political enemies in London, who viewed him as a dangerous maverick; and as 'Dirty Charlie' by some of his subordinates, because of his slovenly approach to his dress. Earlier in the campaign Killigrew had seen the commander-in-chief wearing a bright red suit with large yellow buttons and facings, which he had won in a bet, and presumably worn for another. Today he wore a rumpled admiral's tailcoat over his portly stomach, with a rainbow-coloured handkerchief spilling from a pocket and a dusting of snuff on the lapels.

'Am I to take it, then, sir, that I am not under arrest?' asked Killigrew.

Napier blinked at him. 'Arrest? Bless ma soul, nay! Whatever gave you such a peculiar notion?'

'But last week, when Lieutenant Tremaine came on board the *Ramillies*, he told me he'd been ordered to put Killigrew under arrest,' said Crichton. 'That he was going to be court-martialled for conduct unbecoming an officer and a gentleman.'

Napier grimaced. 'Seymour being a little too efficient as usual.'

Killigrew smiled. 'Efficient? Or officious?'

'Now, now, Killigrew. That'll do.' But Napier said it with a smile. 'Unlike Seymour, I dinna take ma orders from passing war tourists, even if they are close personal friends of the prime minister. I've spoken to Seymour about it, and he's agreed to withdraw the charge.'

'But what about Lord Bullivant, sir? Won't he write a letter of complaint to Lord Aberdeen?'

Napier chuckled. 'I dinna think Lord Bullivant will be writing any letters of complaint to the prime minister in the near future, gentlemen. It seems his lordship has gone and got himself captured by the Russians.'

'Captured!' exclaimed Crichton.

Napier nodded, grinning. 'Seems the damned ass took his yacht too close to the Finnish coast a few days ago and was overhauled by a stray Russian paddle-sloop. I only learned all this a couple of hours ago from a dispatch from Plumridge: one o' his steamers stopped a Finnish fishing boat out of Eckness and the master told him all about it.'

Like most officers in the British fleet, Napier had immense trouble pronouncing local place names correctly: Ekenäs became 'Eckness', Älvsnabben became 'Elgsnabben', Nott-vik became 'Nottich' and Bränklint became 'Tzee' (Killigrew was still trying to work out that last mispronunciation).

'But . . . surely they can't hold him?' protested Crichton. 'I mean, he's a civilian, damn it.'

'They can and they will,' Napier said grimly. 'A British citizen captured in Russian territorial waters in time of war . . . oh, they'll hold on to him, right enough. I've always said this was nae place for war tourists, and Bullivant's proved it!'

'You don't think they'll execute him for spying, do you, sir?' said Killigrew.

'Och, I doubt it. I mean, he's a peer of the realm . . . they canna seriously believe he was engaged in espionage. However, they'll no' let him go without getting something in return. We'll have to negotiate for his release. Or rather, *you'll* have to negotiate, Mr Killigrew.'

'Me, sir?'

Napier nodded. 'You'll take a boat into Eckness under a flag of truce and parley with the local authorities there. Offer them a fair exchange: Lord Bullivant for Major-General Bodisco. I dare say Sir James Graham will give me merry hell for surrendering the commanding officer of Bomarsund so soon after we captured him, and in exchange for a useless civilian at that. But better that than having the PM give me merry hell for allowing one of his cronies to languish in durance vile a moment longer than is necessary.'

'With all due respect, sir, Commander Killigrew is in no condition to undertake a job as important as this,' said Crichton. 'I was just about to dismiss him from the *Ramillies* on grounds of ill health when we got your signal.'

'Ill-health?' Frowning, Napier peered at Killigrew. 'He looks well enough to me.'

'He's still not fully recovered from his Arctic ordeal, sir. He fainted ashore only this morning.'

'Is it true, Killigrew?'

'Just a dizzy spell, sir. I've never felt in better trim.'

'Capital! Well, ill or no', it canna be helped.'

'Are you sure you want *Killigrew* to do this, sir?' asked Crichton. 'I mean, I don't imagine he's Lord Bullivant's favourite naval officer at the moment—'

'Which is precisely why I chose him. Oh, I'm no' naïve enough to imagine Lord Bullivant will forgive him for that little altercation on board the *Milenion* the other evening simply because he effects his release from the Russians.

But it will make it damned hard for him to press for Killigrew's dismissal if he owes him a debt of gratitude.'

Killigrew replaced his scotch on the sideboard, untasted. 'I'd rather not, if it's all the same with you, sir.'

Napier stared at him. 'Whut d'ye mean, you'd rather not? Do ye no' see I'm trying to do you a favour?'

'Yes, sir, and believe me, I appreciate it. But there's more to what happened on board the *Milenion* than meets the eye. You see, the Bullivants and I . . . well, we've met before. If it had simply been a matter of a misunderstanding and a broken door to be repaired, I'm sure his lordship would have settled for damages and an apology. The only reason he's pursuing this matter so vindictively is that I've crossed his bows in the past.'

Napier rolled his eyes. 'Is there anyone whose bows you've no' crossed yet, Mr Killigrew? But surely that's all the more reason for you to at least try to get back into his good graces?'

'I'm not sure I was ever in his good graces to begin with, sir. Believe me, I think it would simply be too awkward – for the Bullivants as well as myself – if I were the one sent to arrange their release.'

'Is there something you're no' telling me, Killigrew?'

The commander grimaced. 'Miss Araminta Maltravers and I were once engaged to be married.'

Crichton's jaw dropped. '*You* were engaged to Lord Bullivant's daughter?'

'Bless ma soul!' exclaimed Napier. 'You kept that fair quiet, didn't you? When was this?'

'Two and a half years ago, back when I was a lieutenant, sir. His lordship didn't want the engagement announced in all the usual places.' Killigrew grinned ruefully. 'Come to think of it, he didn't want the marriage to take place at all.'

'I'm no' surprised!' said Napier. 'Nae disrespect intended, Killigrew, but the thought of Miss Maltravers being married

87

to an impecunious naval lieutenant . . . and one wi' your radical sympathies . . . I wonder his lordship allowed it at all!'

'He did try to buy me off, sir. And when that didn't work, he sent a couple of pugs around to my rooms in Paddington to work me over.'

'And?'

'They weren't exactly first-rate pugs, sir. And well past their prime.' Killigrew could still feel their fists pummelling his stomach. 'I think I can say I gave as good as I got.'

'Good for you. Still, I canna help but think you might've been wiser to take the money.'

'It was an insultingly small offer, sir.'

'I know you, Killigrew. He could have offered you a small fortune, and you'd've told him to go to the devil. So, whut brought Miss Maltravers to her senses?'

'Nothing, sir. It was I who broke off the engagement.'

'*You* broke off the engagement?' Napier spluttered incredulously.

'You're lucky you weren't sued for breach of promise!' remarked Crichton.

'What would have been the point, sir?' Killigrew pointed out. 'Lord Bullivant would have spent more on lawyers' fees than he could have hoped to win in damages from a lieutenant on half-pay.'

'Let me make sure I understand this aright, Mr Killigrew,' said Napier. 'You were engaged to the daughter of one of the wealthiest and most influential peers in Britain . . . and a damned bonny lass to boot. You refused her father's attempt to buy you off, resisted his attempts to frighten you . . . and then broke off the engagement anyhow?'

'I could see there was no future in it. Lord Bullivant would have cut Miss Maltravers off without a penny. She said she was willing to live on my income, but . . . well, I just knew she wouldn't be able to live like that, not after her upbringing.' That was true enough, but it was only part of the story.

Napier sighed. ''Pon ma word, Killigrew! Sometimes I wonder if you're the noblest man I ever met, or simply the biggest fool.'

'Probably the latter, sir. But you must see now . . . it would be hopelessly awkward if I were to be the one sent to negotiate their release.'

'Well, awkward or no', I'm no' asking for volunteers: I'm ordering you to do this . . . for your own good, even if you're too much of a bletherhead to see that for yourself. This is too important to be left to a lieutenant – the Russkis respect a bit of gold braid – and you're the only officer I can spare who speaks Swedish. You have some Russian too, I think?'

Killigrew could see he was not going to get out of this. 'Just a little, sir.'

'Perfect! Any questions?'

'Just one, sir. What if the Russians aren't willing to exchange Bullivant for Bodisco? You'll admit, they can be a little . . . unpredictable.'

'In that event, I expect you to act upon your discretion. Weigh up the situation and act accordingly. But whatever else happens, make sure you get Lord Bullivant and his family back to safety. Do I make maself clear?'

Killigrew saluted. 'As crystal, sir.'

They took their leave of Napier and were rowed back to the *Ramillies* in Crichton's gig. By the time they returned on board, Killigrew had resigned himself to the task the commander-in-chief had set him, and thought about what lay ahead. 'If I'm to go to Ekenäs, sir, I'll need to consult someone who's already been that way lately. The passage is intricate, from what I hear.'

'Good thinking, Killigrew. You have someone in mind?'

'I was thinking of the *Hecla*'s master.' Three months earlier, the *Hecla* had accompanied the screw frigates *Arrogant* and *Dauntless* when they had steamed up the Ekenäs inlet to cut a merchant barque out of the harbour as a prize of war.

'All right, take my gig and ask Captain Hall if you can have a word with his master. Take Mr Dahlstedt: he can go with you when you sail up the inlet.'

In his late twenties, Dahlstedt was the *Ramillies'* pilot, a half-pay lieutenant in the Swedish navy currently attached – in a strictly unofficial capacity – to the Royal Navy. Sweden had ceded the Grand Duchy of Finland to Russia some seventeen years before he had been born there, but he nonetheless felt more loyalty to Sweden than he did to Russia, and had emigrated shortly after the death of his parents. His father had been a master in the Finnish merchant marine, and Dahlstedt had learned how to sail almost as soon as he could walk, so he had been welcomed into the Swedish navy.

'It will save time if I take the *Ramillies* back through the Ångösund while you're on board the *Hecla*,' Crichton continued. 'We'll wait for you back at Ledsund. If we sail tonight, we can be off Eckness by dawn.'

When Killigrew told Dahlstedt what they had to do, the lieutenant seemed delighted to be able to offer his services, and cheerfully accompanied Killigrew to the *Hecla*, where Captain Hall was more than happy for them to pick his master's brains. The master having told them all he knew about the perils – navigational and military – of sailing up the Ekenäs inlet, Killigrew and Dahlstedt cadged a ride on a dispatch boat that took them back down the Ångösund to where the *Ramillies* rode at anchor not too far from the *Duke of Wellington* and the other capital ships of the British fleet. As dusk approached, the blockship weighed anchor and steamed out of the Åland Islands for Ekenäs.

HMS *Ramillies* flew a large white flag from her mainmast when she dropped anchor off the south coast of Finland the following morning, so there could be no mistaking her peaceful intent. Although she was really too large for the task in hand, Napier felt he could spare her from his fleet for the three or four days it would take to make the exchange. Besides, since General Bodisco was a guest on board, and soon to be replaced by Lord Bullivant and his family, it seemed only fitting that they should travel in style on board a ship of the line.

The *Ramillies* anchored a couple of miles out from the coast, which was screened by a labyrinthine mass of islands and skerries. Even with Dahlstedt on board to guide them, the water was too shallow to risk the ship any closer in. Since Ekenäs lay about five miles up a narrow inlet from the coast, the cutter's crew was in for a long pull. But as usual finding volunteers had not been difficult, even after it had been pointed out that they would not be taking firearms, despite the fact they could not be sure what kind of a reception the Russians would give them, white flag or no.

As soon as the *Ramillies* anchored off the Ekenäs archipelago, Killigrew assembled on deck the men he had chosen to go ashore with him. In addition to Dahlstedt and the cutter's crew of eleven, Killigrew took Mr Charlton, and Mate Latham as an aide. Theoretically the twenty-five-foot cutter would carry forty people in calm weather, so if all went well there would be enough room in the boat to carry not only Lord Bullivant and his family but also the crew of the *Milenion*: no more than fifteen, Killigrew calculated. It would be cramped and doubtless his lordship would complain, but that could not be helped. As for Lord Bullivant's yacht, that would be staying behind in Ekenäs with the Russians: whatever the outcome of the negotiations, no one could deny the schooner was a legitimate prize of war.

'I'll keep General Bodisco on board until we've reached an agreement with the Russians,' Crichton told Killigrew as the cutter was lowered from its davits. 'I expect you'll have to make at least two trips, so I'll have a relief crew standing by when you get back.'

'Thank you, sir.' Killigrew wore his full-dress uniform: double-breasted navy-blue epauletted tailcoat, trousers, white kid gloves and cocked hat. He wore his dress sword at his side, for show rather than as a weapon – although he kept the blade honed to a razor's edge – but left his brace of revolvers in his cabin. Latham wore his dirk – more of a short sword than a knife – again for show, but otherwise they would all be unarmed, although Killigrew did not doubt that Molineaux had his Bowie knife hidden in its sheath in the small of his back. And the other seamen would have their fi'penny clasp knives; much good those would do them if there was any shooting.

'Given it's a long haul to Eckness, I'll wait here until six this evening. Are you quite certain you're up to this?'

'I'm fine, sir. Please stop worrying: it'll be a stroll in the park.'

'Just try to be careful.'

The cutter's crew shinned down the lifelines to the boat, followed by Killigrew and Latham, who took their places in the stern sheets as the cutter was manoeuvred to a point below the accommodation ladder, so that Charlton and Dahlstedt could climb down and join them. Endicott and Hughes fixed the cutter's mast in the mast step and ran a white flag up a halyard so that it fluttered above their heads in the sou'westerly breeze.

'Shove off!' ordered Killigrew. Molineaux cast off the heaving line and pushed the cutter's bows away from the *Ramillies*' side with the boat-hook. 'Out oars. Give way together.'

Taking their stroke from Able Seaman Powell at the starboard after-oar, the rowers pulled at their oars, powering the cutter away from the *Ramillies*. Once they were no longer shielded from the wind by the blockship's hull, Killigrew ordered the sails set, and the oarsmen were able to rest as the canvas bellied in the breeze off the port quarter. It was not an unpleasant way to spend a morning: the sun was shining, the Baltic surprisingly temperate in August. He watched the *Ramillies* grow smaller and smaller behind them. Ahead, the mass of islands presented one long, unbroken façade of rocky shores and pine forests, but he knew from the chart that there were plenty of channels leading through to the Ekenäs Inlet.

Dahlstedt directed the coxswain to steer to port of the first cluster of islands. Once level with the western-most they turned to starboard, and presently the *Ramillies* was hidden from view behind the islands they had just passed off the starboard quarter. There were more low-lying islands up ahead, ranging in size from the tiny, smoothed rocks of the skerries that barely projected above the water to some isles a mile or two in length. The Finnish coast was visible to port, but some five miles south-west of where they wanted to be. They passed between two of the larger islands – the one on the right shielding them from the coastal town of Lappvik, according to the chart – and emerged on the other side of the strait to see more islands beyond. In some places there were fishermen's huts sheltered amongst the pines lining the shores, but there were few real landmarks and the larger, tree-covered islands had a uniformity that would have had Killigrew hopelessly lost without a compass and chart. Fortunately, Dahlstedt seemed to know where they were going.

'Steer to port of this next island,' the pilot told the coxswain.

'Is it much further to Ekenäs?' Killigrew asked him in Russian. Dahlstedt had been giving him lessons, and Killigrew insisted that the two of them always conversed in Russian, so that he could practise his tenuous grasp of the language.

'Vitsand Sound lies just beyond this next island, between Odensö and the mainland. The channel narrows to a cable's length, and then broadens out into the Ekenäs Inlet. From there it's another three miles to the town itself.'

Killigrew nodded. It was already half-past ten; he reckoned they would be in Ekenäs by noon.

'Shh!' Latham held up a hand for silence. 'Hear that?'

Killigrew listened. All he could hear was the gentle flapping of the canvas and the slop of the waves against the cutter's strakes. He shook his head and regarded the mate quizzically.

'Red-flanked bluetail,' Latham explained.

'Red-flanked what, sir?' asked Powell.

'Bluetail,' Latham told him. 'It's a kind of bird.'

'Good eating, sir?' Endicott asked disingenuously, winking at Molineaux.

'No!' snorted Latham, who had yet to learn to tell when the hands were ribbing him, and thus became the butt of many of their jokes. 'Bluetails are no bigger than robin redbreasts. You'd have to catch and cook a lot of them to have a meal!'

They rounded the next island and entered the Vitsand Sound. The entrance to the Ekenäs Inlet was about a mile off: the forested shores of Odensö and the mainland formed a funnel into it. Within half an hour they were close enough to see that a chain had been stretched across the narrow strait to prevent the passage of ships. When *Arrogant, Hecla* and *Dauntless* had been here three months ago, there had been a cable here, which the seamen had been forced to hack through to gain access to the inlet; evidently the Russians had decided to replace it with something stronger in the aftermath of the British raid. Supported by rafts every hundred yards or so, the heavy chain nevertheless sagged so much it hung beneath the waves: an effective barrier for a deep-draughted ship, perhaps, but no obstacle at all for a cutter with a draught of two feet.

A battery of four light field guns stood on the left shore, protected by a rampart of earth-filled wicker gabions. Killigrew could see Russian artillerymen in drab grey greatcoats and flat, peaked caps working the guns.

'Battery coming up to starboard, sir,' Latham reported about two minutes after Killigrew had seen it for himself.

'They can see our white flag clearly enough,' Killigrew replied mildly, nevertheless removing his cocked hat and waving it at the artillerymen, to reassure them that their intention was peaceful.

The cutter was in mid-channel when the first gun boomed, at a range of a little over a hundred yards. The report sounded dull and flat, yet the plume of smoke bursting over the gabions was unmistakable.

'Salute?' Dahlstedt asked dubiously.

The shriek of a cannon-ball hurtling through the air with a sound like canvas rending quashed his hope. It landed in the water only thirty yards from where the cutter glided over the waves, throwing up a great plume of white spray.

'Warning shot?' Dahlstedt was an incurable optimist.

'Let's heed their warning,' said Killigrew, determined not to take any unnecessary chances. 'Furl the sails and out oars.'

The second shot landed close enough to drench the men in the cutter. 'Jesus Christ!' blasphemed Able Seaman Sheppard. 'The bastards are trying to kill us!'

'Can't they see our white flag?' moaned Latham.

'Make for the shore to starboard!' Killigrew told Vowles, pointing.

As the rowers strained at the oars, the coxswain put the tiller over to port. 'Come on, you buggers! Put yer backs into it!'

Another shot landed even closer, drenching them a second time. Latham rose to his feet and cupped his hands around his mouth. 'Flag of truce!' he yelled. 'Stop firing, for Christ's sake! We've come to parley!' He moved between the rows of double-banked oarsmen to indicate the white flag flying above their heads.

'For God's sake, Latham, sit down!' snapped Killigrew. 'Are you trying to—'

His words were drowned out by the boom of the fourth cannon, and his body was twisted around violently as the boat spun clockwise; or rather, the stern spun clockwise, for a cannon-ball had hit them squarely amidships, smashing the cutter in half. Everything went red as one of the oarsmen disintegrated in a crimson mist and the air was full of dust and splinters.

V

Prisoners of the Russian Bear

_____

9.00 a.m.–11.00 a.m., Thursday 17 August

The world seemed to spin around them – Killigrew glimpsed a body flying through the air, cut clean in two at the waist, entrails spilling out – and then the stern tipped over and Killigrew was thrown backwards over the transom.

The water was icy-cold, even in summer. Killigrew went under, the world beneath the waves oddly quiet and peaceful after the cacophony of the artillery barrage. He opened his eyes to see the water full of seamen, twisting and turning beneath the waves. A vermilion cloud stained the water, and the two halves of the wrecked cutter floated above them.

He had not had time to gulp down a lungful of air before he went under, and when his head broke the surface he whooped the breath back into his body. Even through the water in his ears he could hear the cheers of the Russians in the battery. There were a dozen men in the water: they did not need to be told to strike for the south shore. Killigrew looked around, saw someone thrashing about wildly nearby, and swam across to help him. It was Latham, screaming as he flailed about, the water around him full of blood. Killigrew hooked a hand under his jaw and pulled the mate after him as he backstroked for the shore. It was only a hundred yards or so, and he was a strong swimmer: he had been born with a caul on his head, and so could not be drowned, if you believed in old wives' tales.

The old wives said nothing about bullets, however, and, as the rattle of musketry sounded on the north shore, musket-balls kicked up little spurts in the water all around him. The Russians had to be using sharpshooters armed with rifled muskets, to judge from the accuracy of their shooting. Killi-grew saw Able Seaman Brooks shudder in the water as a bullet slammed between his shoulder blades, and he floated face down.

The others reached the shore well ahead of Killigrew, but Molineaux came back and waded out into the shallows to help him with Latham. The two of them each took an arm and dragged the mate out on to the rocky shore. Latham was quiet now. He had passed out, and it was easy to see why: he had lost both his legs below the knees, and blood jetted from the stumps to stain the pale rocks crimson. But they were still close enough to the north shore for the sharpshooters to send bullets soughing about their ears, so they took an arm each and dragged the mate into the cover of the trees beyond.

Most of the others were already crouched there amongst the bracken. Killigrew was relieved to see the assistant surgeon amongst them.

'Mr Latham is wounded, Mr Charlton. See what you can do for him.'

Charlton took one look at Latham's blood-pumping stumps, and blanched. In his brief time in the navy, the only cases he had been called upon to attend were constipation, hernias, venereal disease, cholera, and smallpox. None of those prepared a man for the sight of a fellow human being with a limb or two ripped off, his lifeblood flooding out through severed arteries.

'I lost my medicine chest!' he stammered.

'Do what you can!' Killigrew snapped back.

The assistant surgeon swallowed hard and crouched over Latham. Killigrew turned to the rest of them to take a quick head count: Dahlstedt was there, and Molineaux, Endicott – who had lost his bonnet in the water and was tying his neckerchief over his head in its place as a bandanna – Coxswain Vowles, Able Seaman Hughes, and Ordinary Seaman (Second Class) Ben Iles. That left five men missing. 'Where are Phipps, Ridley, Powell, Joyner and Sheppard?'

'Phipps and Sheppard were sitting amidships,' Molineaux reminded him. 'That last shot cut right through them.' His matter-of-fact tone belied that he had lived with these men below decks for the past five months. 'Poor bastards never stood a chance. And I think someone got hit by a splinter – might've been Powell. Whoever it was, he was wounded so bad, I doubt he made it ashore.'

'What about Phil?' asked Endicott.

'Brooks is dead,' Killigrew told him. 'Caught a ball in the water. Ridley and Joyner?'

'Bill never could swim a stroke,' said Vowles. 'Daft bugger.'

'Us seen Sam reach the shore ahead of us,' said Iles, a big, one-eyed seaman with the broken nose and scarred knuckles of a pugilist. The eye patch made him look even more piratical than Molineaux, and anyone who saw him would never imagine he had not lost the eye swashbuckling on the high seas, but in a bonfire night accident in Bristol. ''E made it a' the trees . . .'

Killigrew cupped his hands around his mouth. 'Ridley! Sam Ridley! Where are you?'

They listened. The only reply was the chirruping of the birds in the boughs above them.

'Shall we search for him, sir?' suggested Molineaux.

Killigrew shook his head. 'We stick together. If that

lubber hasn't sense enough to stay with his shipmates, he can take his own chances.'

'What do we do now, sir?' asked Vowles. 'Press on overland for Eckness?'

Killigrew shook his head. 'It's got to be three miles to Ekenäs from here—'

'Nearer thirteen, overland,' Dahlstedt corrected him. 'Getting on to the mainland will be easy enough – there's a bridge over the channel – but once on the mainland we've got to get around the eastern arm of the Ekenäs Inlet.'

'How far to the south coast of this island?'

'No more than a mile, sir.'

'What are our chances of finding a boat when we get there?'

'Odds on, I'd say. Plenty of fishermen's huts hereabouts.'

'Then that's the way we'll lead. Lord Bullivant and his family will have to take their chances for now.' Killigrew very much doubted the Russians would harm them. 'We have to get Mr Latham back on board the *Ramillies*, where Mr Dyson can attend his injuries. And we've got to report what happened here. Old Charlie will have to find some other way to exchange Bodisco for Bullivant.'

Charlton had finished binding Latham's stumps with a couple of handkerchiefs, which were already soaked with blood. He stood up, wiping his bloody hands on the front of his tailcoat. 'What if we can't find a fishing boat when we get to the south coast? Latham isn't going to last long without proper medical attention.'

'You have a better suggestion, Mr Charlton?'

'We surrender – some of us, at least – and hand him over to the Russians. They can look after him better than I can without medicines or surgical implements. I'm volunteering to stay with him. The rest of you can go on without me.'

'No, we take Latham with us.'

'Damn it, sir! He'll die without proper medical attention!'

'And you think the Russians will give it to him, after they

100

fired on a boat sailing under a white flag?' Killigrew shook his head. 'No, we'll try to take him back to the *Ramillies*. Tie his hands together so I can carry him on my back.'

Molineaux removed his neckerchief so they could bind Latham's hands, and they managed to get him on Killigrew's back. 'Molineaux, you lead the way,' ordered the commander. 'Iles, bring up the rear. Make sure no one straggles. Come on, let's look lively! The Russians know we're here, and it can't be long before they send Cossacks to ride us down.'

Molineaux had no compass, but enough of a sense of direction to find the way, and Dahlstedt was at his elbow at every step. Weighed down by the unconscious Latham, Killigrew was the only straggler, falling behind the others as they hurried through the trees. His legs soon ached, his head swam and he gasped for breath. A couple of years ago he could have carried the slight mate for a mile without even breaking into a sweat, yet now his clothes, which had quickly dried out in the warm summer forenoon, were soon soaking with sweat instead. He hated this feebleness that had plagued him since his return from the Arctic and wondered if he would ever again be the healthy, strong young man who had sailed in search of Franklin.

'Wan' us a' take 'ee, sir?' offered Iles.

'It's all right, Iles. I can manage.'

'Wi' all due respec', sir, you'm look ready to drop. An' then us'll 'ave two to carry, 'stead o' jus' one. Let us carry 'ee.'

'All right,' Killigrew conceded reluctantly.

Between them they managed to get Latham on to Iles' back. The mate was ashen-faced, the blood dripping from the makeshift bandages Charlton had tied over his stumps. But Iles carried him easily and, relieved of the burden, Killigrew found the going much easier.

Iles was a rum feller, Killigrew reflected. Unlike most big men who – with one or two notable exceptions – tended to be gentle giants, Iles was an aggressive swine, always looking for a fight, especially when he had 'drink taken'. In the five months since he had joined the crew of the *Ramillies*, hardly a week had gone by without his getting into a brawl with one of his shipmates on the lower deck. Yet he always obeyed orders without question, and catch him in the right mood and he could be as gentle as a lamb.

Having fallen behind to make the transfer, they hurried to catch up with the others, and found them gathered in a glade a few hundred yards further on. Molineaux had drawn his Bowie knife and held it in one hand, the other raised for silence, his face a picture of concentration.

'What is it?' asked Killigrew.

'Horses, sir,' said Molineaux. 'Lots of 'em.' He pointed off through the trees. 'That way.'

'Let's keep moving,' decided Killigrew. 'We'll go this way.'

Before they had gone another hundred yards, however, they saw a figure riding through the trees on a stout, shaggy pony. Dressed in a long, dark blue tunic and a woolly *papakha* on his head, he was unmistakably a Cossack. He shouted something over his shoulder in Russian, and galloped forward to intercept them, unslinging his carbine and levelling it at the British seamen.

'*Stoi!*'

Molineaux flung his Bowie knife. It turned end over end before burying itself in the Cossack's throat, right up to the hilt. As the Cossack tumbled from his saddle, his finger tightened on the trigger of his carbine, blasting a plume of smoke up at the boughs above.

The petty officer shooed the horse away so he could get at the Cossack's body. He retrieved his Bowie knife, wiping the blade clean on the Cossack's tunic. He pulled an ancient flintlock pistol from the dead man's sash and tossed it to Killigrew, who caught it. Molineaux took the carbine, and a cartridge from one of the pouches stitched across the breast of the Cossack's tunic. He was still reloading the carbine when a dozen more riders materialised through the trees from all directions, surrounding them with carbines levelled.

Killigrew threw down the pistol at once and raised his hands. 'Drop the carbine, Molineaux,' he ordered. 'It's useless to resist.'

'Your officer speaks wisely,' the leader of the Cossacks said in tolerable, if thickly accented, English. He was a tall, broad-shouldered ruffian with a shaven head and a bushy walrus moustache.

Scowling, Molineaux lowered the carbine to the ground by its strap.

The leader of the Cossacks swung himself down from the saddle and walked around Molineaux, looking him up and down as if he had never seen a Negro before. He said something in Russian to his men that made them laugh. Then he hunched his shoulders, bent his legs, and curled his arms under his armpits, making a noise like a chimpanzee. The Cossacks found this hilarious, although their carbines did not waver for an instant.

Killigrew saw Molineaux clench his fists at his sides. Normally one of the most cool-headed men the commander had ever known, the petty officer had a fiery temper when people made jokes about the colour of his skin, and the leader of the Cossacks was going to get a broken jaw if Killigrew did not intervene quickly.

'You are the senior officer of these men?' he asked.

'Starshina Vyacheslav Petrovich Chernyovsky,' the Cossack leader replied, turning from Molineaux to Killigrew.

'Commander Christopher Killigrew of HMS *Ramillies*,' Killigrew returned. He wanted to protest about the way his boat had been fired upon while sailing under a white flag, but there were more pressing matters to attend to. 'One of my men urgently requires medical attention.'

Iles had taken Latham from his back and laid him gently on the ground. Now Chernyovsky looked down at the wounded mate. He drew a sabre from his belt and thrust the tip into Latham's heart.

'You murdering swine!' gasped Charlton.

Molineaux was just as enraged, but unlike Charlton he felt that actions spoke louder than words. As Chernyovsky turned to face the assistant surgeon, he caught sight of the petty officer charging at him. He raised his sabre to defend himself, but Molineaux caught him by the wrist and drove a fist into his face. Chernyovsky staggered away, blood gushing from his nostrils. Before Molineaux could follow up his attack, however, another Cossack urged his pony forward. He struck the petty officer on the back of the neck with the stock of his carbine. Two more dismounted and seized Molineaux between them. Although conscious, he was too dazed to resist as they searched him and found his Bowie knife. Chernyovsky rallied, wiping his nose on his sleeve and scowling at the blood. He still had the sabre in his hand, and it looked as though he was going to slash Molineaux across the face with it.

'Starshina Chernyovsky!' snapped Killigrew. 'My men and I were under a flag of truce when we were fired upon.'

'This *negr* pig dared to strike me!'

Molineaux must have misheard the word '*negr*' – Russian for 'black' – for he struggled furiously in the grip of the two men who held him.

'You murdered a British officer in cold blood!' protested Charlton.

Chernyovsky lost interest in the petty officer and turned to face the assistant surgeon with an amused smile. He laid the blade of his sabre across Charlton's neck. 'I will kill another, if you are not silent.'

Charlton blanched and swallowed.

'We are prisoners of war,' said Killigrew. 'I demand that we are treated as such.'

Chernyovsky rounded on him. 'You are in no position to demand anything, Commander.'

104

'We were on our way to see the military governor in Ekenäs. I have an important message for him from Vice Admiral Sir Charles Napier. I suggest you take us to him at once.'

Wiping more blood from his upper lip with his sleeve, Chernyovsky regarded Killigrew appraisingly for a few seconds. 'Bring them,' he ordered his men at last.

Marching under the guns of the Cossacks, Killigrew and his men reached the north-east side of Odensö Island, where a narrow channel was all that kept the island from being a peninsula. Where the channel was narrowest – no more than fifty feet wide – a low, rickety wooden bridge spanned the deep water below. The bridge was in urgent need of repair, and Chernyovsky sent half his men over first – one at a time, each man leading his horse – before ordering Killigrew and his men to follow.

From the bridge they marched another mile and a half through the forests until they emerged to find themselves at a cove overlooking the Ekenäs Inlet. Killigrew had studied a chart of the place before he had left the *Ramillies*, and it was easy to match the landscape to the calotype-like memory of the map in his mind's eye. The inlet split into three arms, the longest running north-east by north all the way up to the village of Pojo. The middle arm ran east-north-east, and the shorter ran due east for less than a mile before it split into three more, much smaller arms. The town of Ekenäs stood near the end of the promontory between the longer two arms – from the shore of the inlet, Killigrew could see the whitewashed tower of the church rising up above the shingled roofs of its pretty wooden houses less than a mile away – and to reach it overland would have required a march of eleven miles, around the shorter two arms of the inlet.

A wooden landing-stage ran out into the cove, and a thick cable reached across to the south side of the island just below the promontory, where a flat ferry stood at a second landing-stage about five hundred yards away. One of Chernyovsky's men dismounted to ring the bell, and the five men who worked the ferry hauled it across to the south landing stage.

Chernyovsky exchanged a few words in Russian with the man in charge of the ferry, a squat, neckless fellow with crew-cut hair. He cast his piggy eyes over the prisoners, then hawked and spat over the rail. 'Angliskis! I defecate on Angliskis!' he told them in broken English.

The ferry was large enough to carry Chernyovsky's troop, horses and all, along with the prisoners. The ferrymen hauled on the rope, pulling them across to the island, while the fellow with the crew cut sang a sonorous shanty to help them keep time.

'What *is* that tune?' asked Charlton.

'I think it's "The Song of the Vulgar Boatman",' Molineaux said with a grin.

Once on the island, they were marched across to where a long wooden bridge spanned the channel that separated them from the promontory. From there it was a short walk to Ekenäs itself, a small town of wooden, two-storey buildings painted red and white. As the prisoners were marched through the narrow, cobbled streets, the townsfolk stared at them curiously: coarsely dressed fishermen, or respectable-looking burghers in broad-brimmed black hats, sober black frock coats and colourful waistcoats, their wives and daughters in embroidered bodices and pretty shawls.

A couple of merchant barques vied for space with fishing yawls in the harbour, but the scene was dominated by the two ships tied up at the wharf: a Russian paddle-sloop, 160 feet from stem to stern, and the *Milenion*. Two *matrosy* – Russian seamen – stood on guard at the foot of the yacht's gangplank in tight-fitting, bottle-green jackets, like a dragoon's, their feet encased in Wellington boots, forage caps worn on one side of their crew-cut heads. Excepting that it had no paddle-box boats, the sloop was little different from the ship

Killigrew had served on three years ago, the *Tisiphone*; except that while the Royal Navy now considered the paddle-steamer *Tisiphone* obsolete, this sloop, merely by virtue of having a steam-engine, represented the cutting edge of technology as far as the Russian Imperial Navy was concerned.

While Molineaux was marched off with Vowles, Endicott, Hughes and Iles, Chernyovsky and two of his men dismounted to escort Killigrew, Charlton and Dahlstedt to a handsome town hall on one of the streets running parallel with the harbour.

Inside, they were shown into an outer office where a clerk did some paperwork at a desk while three civilian petitioners sat on a bench against one wall. The clerk, a petty jack-in-office like any of his breed anywhere in the world, ignored Chernyovsky and his prisoners until the *starshina* whacked his Cossack whip down against his desk, startling him. Chernyovsky barked at him in Russian – Killigrew caught the words 'three English prisoners', but that was about it – and the clerk rose to his feet and disappeared through an inner door.

Conscious of the scrutiny of the three civilian petitioners, Killigrew, Dahlstedt and Charlton stood stiffly to attention in their brine-stained uniforms. All three of them had lost their hats, and cut bedraggled figures. 'Perhaps if we point out that you're Swedish, you'll be more fairly treated,' Killigrew murmured to Dahlstedt out of the corner of his mouth, for Chernyovsky's benefit as much as for the pilot's.

'Eh? Oh! Yes. Yes, of course.'

The clerk re-emerged through the door and said something to Chernyovsky, and the three Cossacks marched the prisoners through the door, down a corridor to a large office where a man wearing a white uniform with lots of gold braid sat at a desk. He rose to his feet as Killigrew, Charlton and Dahlstedt were brought in. Chernyovsky spoke at length to the officer, who nodded and studied the three prisoners while the *starshina* was speaking.

'*Kto-nibud' govorit po-Russki?*' the officer asked Killigrew when Chernyovsky had finished speaking.

'A little, but my Swedish is better.'

The officer regarded him in surprise. 'So, we will speak Swedish. I am Lieutenant-General Ramsay, military governor of the Ekenäs district.'

'Commander Christopher Killigrew, of Her Majesty's Ship *Ramillies*, at your service,' Killigrew replied, wondering how a Finn came by a Scottish name like Ramsay. 'These gentlemen are Mr Humphrey Charlton, one of our assistant surgeons, and Mr Sten Dahlstedt, a Swede who is kind enough to serve as one of our pilots.'

Ramsay regarded Dahlstedt curiously. 'Sweden is neutral in this war, Herre Dahlstedt.'

The pilot shrugged. 'The British pay well.'

'I hope it is worth it, for your sake. You need not expect any special treatment on account of your nationality, Herre Dahlstedt. You have chosen to serve alongside an enemy of Russia, and you will be treated accordingly.' Ramsay smiled. 'However, as officers and gentlemen, if the three of you are prepared to give your paroles, I'm sure it can be arranged for you to be billeted in comfort.'

'First things first,' said Killigrew. 'I wish to protest in the strongest possible terms.'

'Protest? About what?'

'First, that my cutter was fired upon by one of your batteries as it passed through the Vitsand Sound under a flag of truce. Five of my men were killed.'

Ramsay frowned. 'That is a very serious allegation, Commander Killigrew. I will have it looked into immediately.'

'There is nothing to look into,' Killigrew told him. 'My cutter was sunk. Otherwise we would have sailed into the harbour here, instead of being captured in the woods by Starshina Chernyovsky and his brigands. Second, I also wish to protest at the cold-blooded murder of one of my officers, Mate Francis Latham.' He jerked his head at Chernyovsky.

'The *starshina* here stabbed him with his sabre when he was defenceless.'

Ramsay asked Chernyovsky a question in Russian. The *starshina* replied indifferently, with a shrug. Ramsay's expression was that of a man who did not like what he was hearing, but could not do much about it. Theoretically, as a lieutenant-general he outranked a *starshina* – the Cossack equivalent of a colonel – but Ramsay was a Finn, and Chernyovsky was a Russian. Although Finland might in theory be integrated as part of Russia, Killigrew suspected that things were not so clear-cut between the Russian and Finnish authorities.

'Starshina Chernyovsky tells me that the officer in question was mortally wounded,' Ramsay told Killigrew. 'That his act was one of mercy.'

'Mr Charlton here will tell you that Mr Latham could have survived with prompt medical attention.'

'I am sorry for the death of your comrade, but ... my hands are tied. Such things happen in war, yes?'

Killigrew was not satisfied with that, but it was the closest thing he was going to get to an apology, so he would have to accept it – for now. In the meantime, he had gained the initiative in this interview, and he was determined to hold on to it. 'And now we must turn to the matter that brought us to Ekenäs in the first place: the seizure of the civilian yacht *Milenion.*'

Ramsay chuckled. 'Ah, yes. Our belligerent Lord Bullivant and his family. Civilians of an enemy power captured in Russian territorial waters in time of war. Even you must confess we would be well within our rights to execute them for espionage ... yes, Commander, even the ladies.'

'I should point out that Lord Bullivant is a personal friend of Lord Aberdeen.'

'Yes, so he pointed out to me during our first meeting. Do not concern yourself too much about Lord Bullivant and his family, Commander. They are being well treated.'

'Vice Admiral Sir Charles Napier has instructed me to inform you that he is willing to exchange General Bodisco for Lord Bullivant and his family, and the crew of his yacht.'

'General Bodisco is Vice Admiral Napier's prisoner?' Ramsay asked in surprise.

'Bomarsund surrendered yesterday.'

Ramsay frowned, then shrugged. 'So. I do not have the authority to order the release of a prisoner as important as Lord Bullivant. I have referred the matter to my superiors in Helsingfors.'

'What about us?' demanded Killigrew. 'Since we were captured under a flag of truce, you have no right under the custom of war to hold us as prisoners.'

'As I have said, I will have the matter looked in to. In the meantime, I crave your patience. If you gentlemen will give me your paroles, I will have you billeted locally until this matter can be resolved. Fair enough?'

Killigrew was reluctant to give his parole: if the Russians decided that he and his men were to be held as prisoners of war, all the fiends in Hell would not stop him from trying to escape. He was damned if he would give his word of honour that he would not attempt to do so. 'We'll give you our paroles not to escape until such time as we've had a response from your superiors,' he told Ramsay, wondering how long it would take: the optical telegraph connected Ekenäs with Helsingfors and could relay messages back and forth in a matter of minutes, but Russian bureaucracy was notoriously slow. 'However, I must stipulate two conditions.'

'Oh?'

'I want to see Lord Bullivant and his family and be assured from their own lips that they are being treated well.'

Ramsay smiled. 'Nothing could be simpler. Lord Bullivant and his family are guests at my house. This afternoon you shall join us for dinner. I think that will assure you they are being well treated. Your second condition?'

'I also want to see my men, and the crew of the *Milenion*, to be assured they are also receiving proper treatment.'

'I think this can be arranged. I have your parole?' Ramsay proffered his hand.

Killigrew shook it. 'Conditional on the terms we agreed.'

Molineaux and the others were escorted to a large barn on the outside of the town. A padlocked chain around the handles of the barn door held them fast, while four guards – Russian infantrymen in grey greatcoats and caps – patrolled the outside of the building with muskets and pistols. The doors were unchained, Molineaux and his shipmates ushered inside, and the doors closed behind them.

There were eleven men already in there, arranged about the stalls or in the hayloft in various attitudes of lassitude. They all looked up as the five seamen entered, and some of them rose to their feet. Molineaux recognised them as the crew of the *Milenion* from their poncy uniforms.

'Who are you?' demanded one, the bearded, hard-faced man Killigrew had confronted on the deck of the *Milenion* a week earlier. 'Speakee English?'

'Better than you, mate,' said Molineaux. 'Petty Officer Wes Molineaux of HMS *Ramillies*. These coves are Andy Vowles, Seth Endicott, "Red" Hughes and Ben Iles.'

'I'm Captain Thornton, master of the yacht *Milenion*. This is Mr Mackenzie, my mate; Mr Uren, my bosun; and Jack Burgess, Tommo Fuller, Joe O'Leary, Charlie Ogilby, Dick Searle, Ned Yorath and Nick Attwood.'

'Everyone calls me "Doc" on account of me being the ship's cook,' said Attwood.

'Oh, and this is Mr Todd, the steward,' Thornton added, indicating a fellow in a white coat. 'The *Milenion* is Lord Bullivant's yacht, we were stopped and taken in tow by a Russian paddle-sloop—'

'We know,' the coxswain said coldly. 'If it wasn't for you

111

lot, we wouldn't be here right now.'

'Eh?'

'Old Charlie Napier heard about what happened to you,' explained Molineaux. 'He sent us to get you out.'

'You've come to rescue us?'

'We were originally sent to negotiate your release, but the bastard Ivans fired at our boat. Killed six of our shipmates, they did. I 'spect Mr Killigrew is negotiating our release right now.'

'Mr Killigrew?' echoed Mackenzie, a small Scotsman with a mop of boyish black curls. 'Cap'n, was that no' the name o' the navy officer that boarded the *Milenion* last week?'

'Aye, that it was,' agreed Thornton, staring hard at Molineaux. 'Thought I recognised you from somewhere. You're the nigger petty officer who was with him that night, aren't you?'

Molineaux smiled thinly. 'The first time someone calls me a "nigger", I let it pass. Then I warn them not to do it again. The second time . . . well, just consider yourself warned, Cap'n Thornton; you and all your crew.'

'I'd take him seriously if I were youse lads,' Endicott said cheerfully. 'The last cove who called him a "nigger" got his jaw broke.'

'Last cove but one,' Molineaux corrected him, thinking of Chernyovsky. But sooner or later, he had already promised himself, he was going to settle the score with that Cossack bastard for what he did to Mr Latham. 'Any notion of where they're holding Lord Bullivant, Cap'n Thornton?'

Thornton shook his head. 'We haven't seen hide nor hair of him since we were brought ashore.'

Hughes snorted derisively. 'Typical bloody aristo! I'll bet he's got his feet up in some Russki aristo's mansion, with a good cigar and all the brandy he can guzzle, while the rest of us rot in this stinking barn.'

'Watch it!' growled Mr Uren, the *Milenion*'s boatswain, a tall, lantern-jawed fellow whose jib had the cut of a man who'd done service on one of Her Majesty's ships. 'That's our boss you're talking about.'

'Boss my eye! He's just a capitalist, exploiting the working-class proletarians and then casting them aside like broken machinery when he no longer has any use for you. You lot are no better than Russki serfs, mindlessly kowtowing to your lord and master—'

'Red?'

'Aye, Wes?'

'Stow it.'

'Don't mind him,' Endicott told the Milenions, jerking a thumb at Hughes. 'He read some political pamphlet a couple of years back, and now everything's got to be bourgeoisie exploitation this, capitalist oppression that and working-class struggle for freedom the other.'

'And where's your precious Commander Killigrew right now, d'you think?' demanded Fuller. If somewhere up in Heaven God had a mould from which all sailors were cast, Fuller was closest to the original: about five feet tall, broad-shouldered, with muscular arms so hairy the tattoos that marked them were almost hidden. 'With 'is feet up next to 'is lordship's, I shouldn't wonder, sipping brandy from the same decanter and smoking a cigar lit from the same lucifer.'

'I doubt it,' Molineaux said with a smile. 'I get the feeling there ain't much love lost between Mr Killigrew and your Lord Bullivant after we boarded the *Milenion*. Besides, if I know him, he'll be figuring out a way to rescue us all, including your precious Lord Bullivant.'

'Sounds like a reg'lar Ben Backstay,' sneered Fuller. 'I s'pose 'ee's going to cut 'is way through 'alf the Russki army to do it, if 'ee 'as to?'

'If he has to,' said Molineaux, still smiling.

'Don't you knock Mr Killigrew,' snarled Hughes. 'He got us out of the Arctic; any man who could do that isn't going to let a few thousand Ivans get in his way.'

'Arctic?' echoed Mackenzie. 'You mean . . . he's *that* Killigrew? Then you must be *that* Petty Officer Molineaux!'

'And I'm *that* Leading Seaman Endicott, and he's *that* Able Seaman Hughes,' put in Endicott, jerking his head at his shipmate.

Mackenzie turned to Vowles.

'Don't look at me,' said the coxswain. 'I wasn't there. I ain't *that* anyone,' he added, with a trace of wistfulness in his voice.

'Be this cove Killigrew famous, then, Mr Mackenzie?' asked Yorath, a West Country man from his accent.

'Famous?' echoed Mackenzie. 'Do you no' read the newspapers, Ned? They were taking part in the search for Franklin a couple of years ago. Their ship got trapped in the ice a thousand miles from civilisation. It were Commander Killigrew – although I think he was only a lieutenant then – who led the survivors to safety, fighting polar bears, cold and starvation every step of the way.'

'Aye, well, fighting polar bears is one thing,' said Fuller. 'Fighting the Russian bear is summat else altogether.'

'Have you lads figured a way out of this coop yet?' asked Molineaux, turning his attention from the occupants of the barn to the structure itself.

'What do you mean?' asked Thornton.

'Well, don't tell me you were planning to spend the rest of the war as prisoners! You want to make leg-bail, don't you?'

'We don't need to. All this will be sorted out as soon as the Russians realise who Lord Bullivant is. This is all just a big misunderstanding.'

'Yur: the kind of misunderstanding that can get a cove scragged.' Molineaux tested the planks in one wall of the barn, wondering how much it would take to batter a hole through.

'Forget it,' said Thornton. 'I doubt it would take much to break out of this barn, but if you did there are four guards outside armed with muskets.'

'Yur, I cooled them on the way here. But there's sixteen of us. Muskets or no muskets, we could overpower 'em.'

'Without any of us getting killed? You and your lads can try it if you want, but we're going to sit tight.'

'Sure, tha's 'bout your speed, ain't it?' sneered Iles. 'Thought you'd got yourselves a right cush place, working on Lord Bullivant's yacht, din't you? Bet you got a proper shock when 'ee told you 'ee wanted to sail to the seat o' war in the Baltic; an' an even bigger 'un when you got taken pris'ner.'

Mr Uren rose to his feet. 'And just what do you mean by that?'

'Us'd've thought us made meself plain enough. With England at war, able seamen like 'ee should be servin' on one of 'Er Majesty's ships, not takin' it easy on board a yacht.'

Searle rose to his feet. 'You calling us cowards?'

'Us ain't calling 'ee anything, I'se telling 'ee.'

Searle swung his fist at Iles' head, but the big man was waiting for it. He ducked below the swing and drove his fist into Searle's stomach. As Searle doubled up in agony, Iles kneed him viciously in the face and the sailor went down.

Grinning, Iles turned to his shipmates. 'Useless, gutless bastards,' he crowed. 'Us don't need this lot to win the war any rate.'

'Er . . . Ben?' Endicott jerked his head to where Fuller was charging across the barn towards him.

Iles turned just in time to receive the attack face-on. Fuller got his hands around Iles' throat and the two of them went down, rolling over and over in the mud and straw.

'All right, break it up, you two!' snapped Molineaux. 'Bear a hand, Seth.'

Along with Endicott, he tried to prise Iles away from his opponent, but it was not until Uren and Ogilby had pulled their own shipmate away from the brawl that they were successful. Fuller continued to struggle in their grip, but Uren and the other man had him fast. 'That's enough, Fuller!' snarled the boatswain.

'You 'eard what 'ee said, Mr Uren!' protested Fuller. 'An' 'ee duffed up Dick!'

'I'll bloody duff you up if you don't simmer down!'

'Want some more, do 'ee?' Mirroring Fuller's struggles, Iles continued to wriggle in the grip of Molineaux and Endicott. 'Come 'ere, you big bag o' wind! Us'll settle your 'ash!'

'Pipe down, Ben!' snarled Molineaux. 'Or I'll settle a bloody sight more than just your hash!'

Uren and Ogilby released Fuller, and Molineaux and Endicott released Iles. Fuller made a show of dusting himself down while Iles straightened his rumpled clothes . . . and then, as if at some mutually agreed signal, the two of them lunged at each other once more.

The others prised the two brawlers apart a second time.

'Now listen: whatever paths led us to where we are now, none of us asked to be prisoners of the Ivans,' Molineaux told them all. 'But that's the way it is. Unless we want to stay that way for the rest of the war, we're going to have to work together.'

'Stink-pot!' Fuller spat at Iles.

'Prannock!' the Bristolian spat back.

Fuller lunged at Iles a third time. This time Uren managed to catch him before the two of them collided. Iles strutted and preened himself in a manner not calculated to improve relations between the navy seamen and the civilian sailors. Deciding that diplomacy was all about give and take, Molineaux caught Iles by the lughole and dragged him across to the far corner of the barn.

'Now listen to me, you bloody lubber. I shan't warn you again: I've got enough troubles without having to pull you off some bloody yacht sailor every three minutes. You pull that trick one more time and when we make leg-bail I'll leave you behind so the Ivans can practise on you with their knouts, hoist in? Now you sit down – here – and stow it, unless you want me to choke your luff.'

Iles settled down on a bale of hay to sulk. Molineaux left him to it.

As he was walking back across the barn, Uren came across to meet him. 'Are you really going to try to escape?'

'Just you watch me. The drum Cowcumber Henson can't crack ain't been built. Are you and your lads going to help us?'

'Why risk our necks? It's like Cap'n Thornton says: it's all just been a big misunderstanding.'

'For you and your lads, maybe; but I hear tell the Russians execute prisoners of war, and I don't want to have it confirmed the hard way. And since they've put us in the same gaff as you, it seems to me they don't look at you lot as being any different from us.'

From the look on Uren's face, he took Molineaux's point. 'Have you got a plan?'

'I'm working on it.' Molineaux climbed to the hayloft and crossed to the hatch over the door.

'Nailed shut,' Mackenzie called up to him.

So it was, Molineaux noted, but even so, he thought a couple of good kicks would be enough to smash it open. Peering out through a gap between two boards, he saw the two pairs of sentries pass each other below, circling the barn clockwise and counterclockwise respectively. He waited a minute, and they passed each other at the same place again; and again on the third circuit. The Russians might not be much good as sailors, but they could march with maddening precision. Or was that something he could use to his advantage?

He climbed back down to the ground and kicked one of the planks out of a stall. It splintered free with a crash, and he hid it under the straw, waiting for the guards to unlock the door and come charging in to investigate the noise. But the guards did not materialise. Either they had not heard the crash or, more likely, did not consider it worth investigating. That was the Russkis all over: they only knew how to obey, and if

117

something arose that was not covered by their orders, they would stick to what they had been told to do. Order an Ivan to guard a room in a house, and then set fire to it, and the silly sod would just stand there until the smoke overcame him and he burned to death.

Molineaux took the plank from its hiding place and hefted it in his hands, testing it as a potential weapon.

'And just what do you intend to do with that?' asked Thornton.

'I've been watching the guards,' explained Molineaux. 'They always pass each other at exactly the same spot, right in front of the door . . .'

'And at the back of the barn too,' said Thornton. 'It's been driving me mad for five days now. What of it?'

'All we have to do is wait until they're in front of the door, then kick in the hatch and drop down on them. If we caught them by surprise . . .'

'If you didn't kick the hatch open on the first try, you'd be jumping on to their bayonets,' Thornton pointed out reasonably.

'That's a chance I'm willing to take. If we can overpower them all together, get their muskets . . . it's only half a mile to the harbour, we go through at night when the streets are quiet, bash the Ivans guarding the *Milenion*, and you can sail off.'

'What about you?'

'I ain't going anywhere without Mr Killigrew; and I don't imagine he's going anywhere without your precious Lord and Lady Bullivant.'

'I thought you said he'd be figuring on a way to rescue you?'

'I dare say he is; but it'd be presumptuous of me to wait for him.'

Thornton shook his head. 'Madness. We'd all be killed. I forbid you to try it.'

'Yur, well, no one says I've got to take orders from you.'

'Someone coming!' Vowles hissed from the door.

'All right, lads, this is it!' whispered Molineaux. 'I'll bash the first one that comes through the door, the rest of you rush the others and grab their muskets.' He took up position beside the door, clutching the plank, and the Milenions watched with mild curiosity as the rest of the Ramillies positioned themselves facing the door.

Molineaux heard the chain rattle as someone turned the key in the padlock. The chain was pulled free of the handles, and the shadow of a man fell across the threshold as the door was opened.

'Wes!' yelled Endicott. '*No . . . !*'

It was too late: Molineaux was already swinging the short plank. Something in Endicott's warning tone made him try to pull back the swing, so that it did not land as heavily as it might have done. Even so, he landed a fairly solid thwack on someone's skull. The man sprawled on his back at Molineaux's feet, to reveal half a dozen Russian soldiers standing behind him, their muskets levelled at the petty officer.

Molineaux grinned sheepishly. 'Hullo!' he said brightly.

Then he looked down at the man he had hit, who was rolling about with both hands clamped to his forehead.

'Oh, Lor'!' Molineaux exclaimed in horror when he saw who it was.

VI

The Man from St Petersburg

11.00 a.m.–3.30 p.m., Thursday 17 August

The Russian infantry officer who had escorted Killigrew to the barn was kind enough to soak his handkerchief in a nearby water trough and hand it to the commander to use as a compress. Sitting on a bale of hay in one corner of the barn, Killigrew pressed it to the graze on his temple and wished the throbbing in his skull would die down.

'Sorry, sir,' said Molineaux. 'Thought you was one of them.'

'I'm glad to hear it,' Killigrew gasped, blinking through the waves of nausea that washed over him.

'You sure you're oh-kay, sir?'

'Nothing a glass of Dr James's powders won't cure.'

The petty officer glanced towards the door at the soldiers who stood there, keeping a watchful eye on the prisoners. 'How come they brought you here? They're not going to put an officer like you in with the ratings, are they?' Molineaux was indignant at the very thought.

'No, no. I just came by to make sure they were looking after you.'

'That's very kind of you, sir.' Molineaux looked about the barn. 'Well, it ain't Brown's, but if a stable was good enough for our Lord, I reckon Mother Henson's boy can just about put up with a barn. Not sure I care for the company, though.'

'The company?'

'The Milenions. Bunch of lazy, gutless cowards, if you ask me. They seem to think Lord Bullivant's name will be enough to get them out of here, and don't want to risk their precious hides trying to make leg-bail. But me and the other Ramillies are champing at the bit, sir. Just say the word, and we'll give it a go. There's eight of us, and only eleven of them . . .' Molineaux was one of those seamen who believed that one Englishman was worth two Frenchmen, and ten Russians; when the seaman in question was Wes Molineaux, there might have been some truth in the assertion.

'And they've got guns,' Killigrew pointed out. 'Anyhow, it may not be necessary; possibly the Milenions have the right notion.'

'Sir?'

'I've been speaking to the military governor of these parts. Seems like a reasonable sort of fellow. I don't think he believed me when I told him we were fired upon by one of his batteries, but he's having the matter looked in to. Apparently Lord and Lady Bullivant are staying at his mansion just out of town, so they're being well looked after.'

'Is he willing to trade them for General Bodisco?'

'Not without referring it to his superiors in Helsingfors; but I cannot see any benefit for Russia in keeping them captive, can you?'

'What about us, sir?'

'Well, we arrived under a flag of truce. I'm having dinner with Lord Bullivant at the governor's house this afternoon, so I'll let him know about the circumstances under which we were captured. If the Russians refuse to release us, he can get Lord Aberdeen to raise merry hell about it in the House of Commons. The Russians will give in sooner or later.'

'But it could take months, sir. And I don't intend to be a prisoner of the Russkis for that long.'

Killigrew smiled. 'Me neither, Molineaux. Me neither. But you and the lads sit tight for now and we'll see how things play out.'

'Aye, aye, sir.'

Killigrew rose to his feet and walked over to where the *Milenion*'s master sat with his first mate. 'Captain Thornton? Commander Killigrew, at your service.'

Thornton rose to his feet, but did not accept the hand Killigrew held out to him. 'We've met.'

'So we have. Unfortunate that the circumstances of our second meeting should be even less propitious than the first, but that's by the by. Sir Charles Napier has sent me to get you and your men safely out—'

'Us? Or Lord and Lady Bullivant?'

'All of you, with any luck. How are the Russians treating you?'

'I've no complaints so far.'

Killigrew glanced at the Milenions and saw that one of them had a badly bruised face. 'What happened to him?'

'One of your men assaulted him.'

'Which one?'

Thornton pointed the man out.

'Iles!' barked Killigrew.

'Sir?'

'Come here, Iles.'

'Aye, aye, sir.' The seaman jumped up and crossed to where Killigrew stood.

The commander indicated the battered man. 'Is this your handiwork, Iles?'

'That it be, sir. But 'ee started it.'

'He said we were cowards!' protested the battered man.

Killigrew nodded. 'You and I shall discuss this further once we're back on board the *Ramillies*,' he told Iles firmly, by which the bluejackets present knew at once that the seaman

122

was in for a severe dressing-down, and a dressing-down from Commander Killigrew was not something to be taken lightly. 'In the meantime, Mr Charlton, Mr Dahlstedt and I are working hard to secure the release of us all. It would be nice to know that when we finally succeed, we shall return to this barn to find that you have not all killed one another in the meantime. Hoist in?'

Iles hung his head. 'Aye, aye, sir.'

'Carry on.' Still pressing the damp handkerchief to his grazed temple, Killigrew indicated to the Russian officer that he had seen all he wished to see, and was ready to be taken to his billet. As he was marched back through the streets, in spite of his steaming headache he was careful to note every landmark that might help him find his way back to the barn, as he had done on the way there.

Just in case.

Lieutenant-General Ramsay sent his coach and four to collect Killigrew from the home of Herre Grönkvist, the Finnish burgher on whom he had been billeted, at a quarter past one. After a hot bath and an hour's nap – during which time the burgher's servants had somehow contrived to restore his uniform to something approaching its former glory – Killigrew's headache had subsided, and he was feeling better than he had done for several days.

As the carriage rattled through the cobbled streets of Ekenäs, Killigrew followed the route the coachman took to Ramsay's home. The house itself, if by no means palatial, looked comfortable enough: a wooden, two-storey building with roses climbing up the trellises on either side of the porch, and picture windows with quaintly carved shutters. By the time the coachman reined in the carriage, the butler was already opening the front door. Killigrew alighted and was shown into the drawing room, where he found Lady Bullivant and her daughter seated in plush armchairs with a middle-aged woman – Ramsay's wife, presumably – while Lord

Bullivant stood by the stone hearth with Lord Dallaway, chatting to Ramsay over glasses of champagne. The ladies were as elegantly dressed as they had been that night on the *Milenion*, and both looked cheerful and animated. But then, this was hardly the durance vile Killigrew might have expected to discover them languishing in. If he was here as their rescuer, he certainly did not feel like it.

Ramsay smiled benignly when he saw him. 'Ah, Killigrew. My lords and ladies, may I present Commander Christopher Killigrew?' He spoke French for the benefit of the English gentlefolk present.

When Bullivant recognised the commander, he turned puce. 'We've already met,' he said coldly, and turned to Ramsay. 'This is the damned feller who's come to negotiate our release?'

'So he tells me.'

'I suppose this is Admiral Napier's idea of a joke. Can't say I appreciate his sense of humour. Mind you, what can you expect from a damned Whig?'

'I'm sure Sir Charles' only concern in selecting me for this delicate mission was that I have a smattering of Swedish,' Killigrew said smoothly. If not the whitest of lies, it was certainly a very pale shade of grey.

'I'm not sure I understand . . .?' said Ramsay.

'I once had the gross misfortune to be engaged to Mr Killigrew,' explained Araminta.

'Never did approve of the match,' snorted Bullivant. 'The thought of any daughter of mine being married to a mere naval officer . . .!' He shook his head in disgust.

'Never mind, darling,' Dallaway told Araminta. 'You're better off without him.'

'I realised that a long time ago,' she sniffed.

'Perhaps a glass of champagne, Commander?' Ramsay said, to break the uncomfortable silence that ensued.

'Thank you, sir.'

Ramsay rang a small glass bell and a flunkey entered.

'Champagne for Commander Killigrew, Renholt.' Ramsay turned to Lady Bullivant. 'As one of the conditions of his parole, the commander insisted on being allowed to see you, to be assured that you were being treated well.' The general chuckled. 'I think he had a notion that you were chained in some subterranean dungeon with slime dripping down the walls.'

'Well, I'm delighted to see that nothing could be further from the truth.' Killigrew accepted the champagne flute the flunkey passed him. 'I would ask after the ladies' wellbeing, but I've only to look at them to see they are both the very picture of health . . . and of loveliness, may I be so bold as to add?'

Lady Bullivant sniffed, and Araminta rolled her eyes and looked away with a contemptuous curl of her lips.

Killigrew glanced at Ramsay for help. The general returned his gaze with an expression of sympathy bordering on pity.

The commander cleared his throat. 'To tell the truth, when Sir Charles invited me to undertake this mission, I was delighted to accept it. I felt it would give me a chance to make amends for my boorish behaviour at our previous encounter.'

'Really?' snorted Bullivant.

'I cannot imagine anything you can do that could make amends for your boorish behaviour, Mr Killigrew,' sniffed Araminta.

The commander became uncomfortably conscious of how loud the ticking of the grandfather clock in the hall sounded.

'Any news from Helsingfors?' he asked Ramsay.

'It seems the matter has gone beyond Helsingfors. I received a telegraph from St Petersburg just before noon: the Tsar sent a special emissary to assess the situation as soon as he received word of the Bullivants' capture. He should be here some time today.'

'That should help expedite matters.'

'Yes.'

'Indeed.'

Tick . . .

. . . tock . . .

. . . tick . . .

. . . tock.

'The weather seems to be remarkably fine today,' said Ramsay.

'Yes, but I think it will rain before long,' said Killigrew.

The clop of hoofs and the crunch of wheels on the gravel drive alerted them to the approach of another carriage. 'Ah, that will be our sixth and final guest,' said Ramsay, in the same relieved tone with which the Duke of Wellington had doubtless remarked upon the arrival of Marshal Blücher at the field of Waterloo.

Bullivant knitted his brows. 'Your sixth guest?'

Ramsay smiled. 'The gentleman who brought us all together . . .'

'Not sure that's anything to be grateful for!' Bullivant glowered at Killigrew.

'. . . Captain-Lieutenant Count Mikhail Yurievich Pechorin.'

Killigrew saw Araminta lower her gaze, her cheeks flushed. He frowned. 'Captain-Lieutenant . . .?'

'Count Mikhail Yurievich Pechorin,' Ramsay told him. 'The captain of the *Atalanta*, the paddle-sloop that brought in the *Milenion*.'

' "Brought in"?' Killigrew chuckled. 'That's one way of putting it.'

Araminta glared at him acerbically. 'Count Pechorin is a *true* gentleman,' she said primly. 'But then, good breeding *always* shows.'

'Good breeding,' agreed Killigrew. 'Or in-breeding.'

'I beg your pardon?'

Christ, did I say that out loud? wondered Killigrew. 'I said: "Good breeding, indeed".'

The door opened and those seated rose to their feet at the entrance of a man in the uniform of a captain-lieutenant of the Russian Imperial Navy: not the regulation black-green, but

126

the pure black favoured by the more dashing officers posted away from St Petersburg, and immaculately tailored if Killigrew was any judge. Count Pechorin was thirty or thereabouts, a tall man – Killigrew was five foot eleven in his stockinged feet, but the count towered four inches above him – with the broad shoulders, narrow waist and strong thighs of a ballet dancer. His clean-shaven, square-jawed face was undeniably handsome, crowned with boyish blond curls beneath his jauntily tilted peaked cap. The Cross of St George adorned his broad chest, and a gilt-hilted sabre hung at his left hip.

'My dear Lord Bullivant!' this dashing figure announced in faultless French. 'Delighted to see you again! I trust Ramsay hasn't been boring you with stories of his heroism as a young ensign?'

The general grinned good-naturedly, as if pleased to be the butt of the captain-lieutenant's humour.

'Not at all,' Bullivant assured with a smile.

'You are well, I trust?'

'Capital, thank'ee, Count. And yourself?'

'All the better for seeing your charming wife again. Lady Bullivant . . .' Pechorin glanced from Lady Bullivant to her daughter and back again, frowning with mock bewilderment. 'Are you quite certain you are not sisters, and are only pretending to be mother and daughter to make game of me?'

'Oh, Count Pechorin!' protested Lady Bullivant. 'You are the most incorrigible flatterer!'

'Then be flattered I find you delightful enough to be worth flattering. And Miss Maltravers . . . what can I say? The first time we met, I was astounded by your beauty. Yet what I find even more astonishing is that each time we meet, my astonishment grows rather than decreases. You look lovelier than ever.' He took her hand and planted a kiss on it.

Araminta flushed bright crimson and moved her lips, but no sound would come out.

'Are you all right?' Ramsay asked Killigrew, who raised a hand to clutch at his chest while Pechorin paid his respects to Fru Ramsay.

'Just an attack of bile,' said Killigrew.

'And Lord Dallaway.' Although Pechorin continued to smile, there was a thinness in it now, and Dallaway's response was equally frosty. *Hullo*, thought Killigrew, *some friction there, I think*. But of course: Lord Dallaway could only have been brought on board the *Milenion* as a prospective husband for Araminta, and he had not cared for the warmth with which she had greeted Count Pechorin's arrival. From the look in Pechorin's eyes, the antagonism was mutual. Killigrew could not help thinking that if Pechorin did not like Dallaway, that was a point in the Russian's favour.

Pechorin turned to face Ramsay and Killigrew. 'And who is this? An officer of Her Britannic Majesty's Royal Navy? Have the British invaded Ekenäs yet again? How many barques laden with salt will you take this time, Commander?'

Pechorin's reference to the *Arrogant*'s dubious feat of cutting a merchant ship out of the harbour made Araminta laugh merrily as if the count had just come up with a *bon mot* that would have turned Sheridan or Dr Johnson green with envy.

'Count Pechorin, may I have the pleasure of presenting Commander Christopher Killigrew of HMS *Ramillies*? Commander Killigrew is here to negotiate the release of Lord Bullivant and his family.'

Pechorin tutted. 'Surely you would not be so cruel as to rob Ekenäs society of these charming ladies so soon, Commander?'

'If Lord Bullivant and his family are content to remain here, then no one would be happier than I to leave them to it,' Killigrew replied with a thin smile.

'Killigrew, Killigrew . . .' Pechorin frowned. 'No relation of the Lieutenant Killigrew who so distinguished himself in the Arctic last year?'

'I was there,' Killigrew admitted reluctantly. 'Not sure I can honestly say I "distinguished myself" . . . although I damned near *ex*tinguished myself.' He grinned at the jest, but his gaze met only blank faces.

'Yes, I'd heard that the expedition was something of a disaster; although you seem to have been promoted to commander on the strength of it?' Pechorin smiled. 'How like you English, to celebrate your failures in an attempt to delude yourselves into thinking them victories.'

'We are not all so lacking in fibre as Mr Killigrew,' sneered Dallaway.

Pechorin looked him up and down with a smile of amusement. 'So I see, my lord.'

Renholt returned to announce that dinner was served. As they filed through into the dining room, Dallaway took time off from glaring daggers at Pechorin to catch Killigrew by the arm. 'We still have unfinished business, you and I,' he hissed in the commander's ear.

Killigrew shook his arm free. 'I think not,' he said quietly.

'I beg to differ.'

'Is there a problem, gentlemen?' asked Ramsay, who had already taken his place at the head of the table.

'Only a matter of honour,' said Dallaway, taking his place next to Lady Bullivant and opposite Araminta, who sat beside her father. 'A quality of which Mr Killigrew seems to be singularly bereft.'

Killigrew smiled as he sat down in the only chair left: next to Dallaway and opposite Pechorin. 'Honour being in such short supply, I prefer to ration mine.'

Ramsay knitted his brow. 'I'm not sure I understand . . .?'

'Lord Dallaway challenged Mr Killigrew to a duel,' Bullivant explained while Renholt made his way around the table, filling everyone's wine glass. 'Mr Killigrew refused to accept.'

'To the contrary,' said Killigrew. 'I accepted, and we fought there and then: on my terms.'

'Fisticuffs,' Bullivant explained to Ramsay, rolling his eyes.

Pechorin looked bemused. 'Hardly the preferred way for a gentleman to settle an affair of honour.'

'I was merely mindful of the law, which prohibits duelling,' explained Killigrew.

'Really?' Araminta said disdainfully. 'Are you quite sure you were not mindful of the fact that Lord Dallaway is the finest swordsman in all England?'

Pechorin chuckled.

'Something amuses you, Count?' asked Dallaway.

Pechorin shook his head. 'Nothing of importance, milord.'

Dallaway took umbrage. 'No, do tell me, Count,' he said in the hectoring tone of a schoolmaster berating a boy for sniggering in class. 'What is it you find so amusing?'

It was Pechorin's turn to take umbrage. 'I was merely reflecting that being the finest swordsman in all England is a somewhat dubious accolade. No offence intended, I assure you, my lord,' he added hurriedly as Renholt returned with a tureen of consommé and began to ladle it out. 'But you understand, if you had told me you were the finest swordsman in all France, or all Italy, we might have more cause to be impressed.'

'And you are an expert on fencing, I suppose?' sneered Dallaway.

'I dabble a little,' said Pechorin.

'Count Pechorin is being too modest,' said Ramsay. 'He has won the fencing championships of all the Russias for the past three years in a row.'

'But Russia, like England, has no reputation for good swordsmanship,' Pechorin said quickly. 'I'm sure I am no match for his lordship.'

'We could find out easily enough,' said Dallaway.

'Indeed,' said Bullivant. 'Since we're fortunate enough to have the finest swordsmen of our respective countries here in this room, we should have a match; see who comes out on top, hey? My money's on Dallaway.'

Pechorin shook his head. 'I think not. It would not be seemly: Lord Dallaway is a prisoner of war; what would people say?'

'Pay no need to my status,' said Dallaway. 'I'm game if you are . . . or could it be you're afraid?'

Pechorin smiled at the accusation and shook his head.

'I see no harm in a friendly little bout, provided both parties are in agreement,' said Ramsay. 'But we will need an independent judge . . .'

'Why don't you act as judge?' suggested Bullivant, and Dallaway nodded. 'I know you're a Russian, but I think we can rely on your impartiality as a gentleman of honour.'

'You flatter me, my lord. But then Count Pechorin will have no one to second him.'

'I'll second the count,' said Killigrew. For reasons of his own, he wanted to see this, and was determined not to let the absence of a second for the Russian impede matters. 'If you're willing, Count Pechorin?'

'I should be honoured,' said Pechorin.

'Trust you to side with the Russians, Killigrew!' sneered Bullivant.

'If we can lay aside the fact that our countries are at war for the duration of dinner, I see no reason why we cannot extend the truce for a fencing bout,' Killigrew returned evenly.

After that, conversation was rather stilted at the dinner table until the dessert wine had been served. The ladies withdrew to the drawing room while the men made their way out on to the neatly clipped lawn at the back of the house. Renholt emerged with four swords: two épées *boutonnées*, and a couple of sabres. 'You did not say whether the gentlemen wished to fence *boutonnés* or *sans boutons*, sir.'

'*Boutonnés* or *sans boutons*, it's all one to me,' Dallaway said blithely, stripping off his tailcoat and handing it to Lord Bullivant.

Pechorin removed his tunic. '*Boutonnés*, I think.'

'If you haven't got the nerve . . .' sneered Dallaway.

The count smiled. 'I was merely thinking that we should keep this friendly. You are a . . . ah, shall we say, a guest? . . . in my country. It would not do if a man in Russian custody were to be injured.'

'And I dare say you'd like it even less if a Russian officer were injured by a British civilian,' said Bullivant.

'As our guest, you may have first choice,' Pechorin told Dallaway.

The young aristocrat chose one of the épées, and Pechorin took the other.

'The usual rules,' said Ramsay. 'First to five hits wins.'

Dallaway and Pechorin stood facing one another.

'Salute!' ordered Ramsay.

The two combatants raised their swords to one another.

'*En garde!*'

The ring of steel against steel rang out across the garden as Dallaway lunged and Pechorin parried. Dallaway's first thrust was a feint, of course, and when his blade changed direction Pechorin was too slow to parry it.

'*Touché!*' Pechorin called it himself, backing away from the fight.

Dallaway smiled.

'*En garde!*' commanded Ramsay.

The two men closed again. This time it was Pechorin's turn to make the first lunge, but Dallaway parried it quickly, touching the Russian a second time on the follow-through.

Pechorin grinned ruefully. 'It seems English fencing is better than I gave credit for.'

'*En garde!*'

Dallaway lunged and feinted; this time Pechorin parried successfully and riposted, parrying Dallaway's counter-riposte. The two parted, and Pechorin lunged, his thrust turned aside at once by Dallaway's parry and riposte.

The two of them fenced back and forth across the lawn,

watched intently by Ramsay, Killigrew and Bullivant. Pechorin was good, there was no hiding that, but he seemed totally out-classed by Dallaway, who maintained the initiative and kept the Russian on the defensive. After a couple of minutes of some of the best fencing Killigrew had ever seen, Pechorin received another hit.

'So much for Russian swordsmanship,' Bullivant muttered to Killigrew. 'Fancy a wager?'

'All right,' said Killigrew. 'Ten guineas on Count Pechorin.'

Bullivant stared at him. 'You'd back the Russian? As you will. A fool and his money . . .'

By now Pechorin seemed to be getting into the swing of it, but Dallaway kept him on the defensive, and after a couple more minutes he hit the Russian a fourth time.

'Care to concede now, Count?' jeered Dallaway.

'It's tempting,' Pechorin admitted. 'But I'll see it through to the end, if it's all the same with you. My luck's bound to change sooner or later.'

'Luck ain't got nothing to do with it, Count,' said Dallaway. 'It's all about speed, agility and skill.'

The two men squared off again. '*En garde!*' called Ramsay.

Dallaway and Pechorin crossed swords once more. Like Pechorin, Killigrew dabbled in fencing himself, and he had to admit Dallaway was a fine swordsman; but what happened next came as no surprise to him at all. The aristocrat lunged; Pechorin parried with a careless flick of his wrist, and touched Dallaway in the shoulder.

'*Touché!*' said Ramsay.

'A very palpable *touché*,' agreed Killigrew.

Bullivant scowled. 'Sheer luck!'

'You heard Lord Dallaway, milord: luck ain't got nothing to do with it.'

The épées clashed again. The faces of the two men told the whole story: Dallaway was grimly determined, wearing the expression of a man racked by chagrin at having allowed himself to grow overconfident; Pechorin's was calm – bored, almost – and a moment later he had touched Dallaway again.

When they set to once more, Dallaway was all over the place, his rage and frustration getting the better of him as Pechorin effortlessly held him at bay. Just as Killigrew had suspected, the Russian had been toying with Dallaway all along, letting him get the first four touches as he learned the Englishman's set pieces and got a feel for his fencing style, without ever doubting that, once he set to in earnest, he would have no difficulty defeating Dallaway.

Before long Pechorin had drawn level, and the next touch would be the decider. Dallaway's face was the picture of a man trying to rein in his temper; Pechorin's, an impassive mask. Dallaway rallied, and as the two blades flashed back and forth in the sunlight it looked as though the bout might go either way. The glinting blades moved so fast it was almost impossible for the spectators to keep track. Then Pechorin sprang back with a cry of '*Touché!*'

'Wide!' Dallaway appealed to Ramsay.

'Difficult one to call,' said the general, and turned to Bullivant and Killigrew. 'What do you gentlemen think?'

'I'm afraid it looked to me as though Pechorin touched him,' said Killigrew.

'Nonsense!' said Bullivant. 'I saw nothing of the kind.'

'I'm inclined to agree with M'sieur Killigrew,' said Ramsay. 'I think that was a touch.'

'What?' Dallaway protested incredulously. 'He never touched me!' He turned to Pechorin. 'Once more: the decider.'

'There is nothing left to decide,' Pechorin said quietly. 'I touched you: you felt it as surely as I did, whether or not the general saw it.'

'It was wide, I tell you!'

'Let it pass, milord,' Killigrew said softly. 'You know the rules: the judge's decision is always final. Now be a good sport, and accept your defeat with grace.'

'I'll do no such thing!' protested Dallaway. 'Damn you, Pechorin! Face me and fight me. The bout has yet to be decided.'

Pechorin turned away. 'And I say there is nothing left to decide. Had we been fighting for real, you would be dead.'

Dallaway caught him by the shoulder and spun him back to face him. 'Then we'll do it for real! The sabres, you!' he called to Renholt.

'You'll do no such thing!' snapped Ramsay. 'This was only intended to be a friendly bout. I think things have gone far enough.'

'General Ramsay is quite right,' said Pechorin. 'Let's call it a draw and shake hands, eh?' He proffered his hand.

Dallaway knocked it aside. 'You'd like that, wouldn't you? Better than you losing face when I beat you!'

'Then I concede,' said Pechorin. 'This matter has gone quite far enough.'

'What's the matter, Count?' jeered Dallaway. 'Afraid?'

'Come now, my lord!' protested Killigrew. 'There's no need for that sort of talk. Count Pechorin has been gracious enough to concede. Let the matter lie there, eh?'

'I don't want his damned charity!' spat Dallaway. 'We finish this! Now!'

'There is no point.' Pechorin crossed to where Renholt stood and handed back his épée, hilt first.

Dallaway ran across after him, throwing aside his épée and drawing a sabre from one of the scabbards held by Renholt. He slashed at Pechorin's head, but a cry of warning from Killigrew alerted the count; although in retrospect he would wonder if the count had needed any warning. Pechorin ducked beneath the sword-stroke, drew the other sabre held by Renholt and swung the blade at Dallaway.

Killigrew and Ramsay were already running to intervene, but both were too late. Dallaway staggered back, his hands pressed to his stomach, blood running between his fingers. Even as they watched, the colour drained from his face. He stared at them with an expression of shock, and then his legs seemed to give way. He dropped down on to his hands and knees, the rent in his waistcoat, shirt and stomach parting to allow the coils of his entrails to flop to the grass below.

'Run for the surgeon, quick!' Ramsay shouted at Renholt, who dropped the scabbards he held and dodged around the outside of the house.

Dallaway stared down in incomprehension at the guts spilling from his own stomach. He flopped on to his back and tried to stuff them back through the obscene opening in his abdomen, but it was like trying to push a spring back into a burst mattress. As Killigrew cradled his head, Dallaway clutched at his tailcoat with bloody fingers. He shouted incoherently until the surgeon arrived from the town. Killigrew and Pechorin carried Dallaway into the billiards room and laid him on the table, where a couple of Ramsay's flunkeys assisted the surgeon in his hopeless task of trying to save the aristocrat's life.

Seeing there was nothing more they could do, Ramsay, Pechorin, Killigrew and Bullivant retreated to the general's study, where Ramsay poured them each a generous measure of white rum from the decanter.

'It was self-defence,' Pechorin said numbly. 'You all saw . . . he came at me . . . I had to defend myself.'

'Nonsense!' growled Bullivant. 'It was cold-blooded murder, damn you! By God, I intend to have some pretty strong words to say to Lord Clarendon when I get back to England. You saw it, didn't you, Killigrew? This fiend butchered him!' He levelled a shaking finger at Pechorin.

'It was self-defence,' said Killigrew.

Bullivant gaped at him. 'What? How the deuce can you side with these Russian devils, against one of your own countrymen?'

'Justice knows no nationalities.'

Bullivant's face hardened. 'I might have known you'd side with them! It wouldn't surprise me if you were a Russian spy, the way you've comported yourself these past few days! You're a disgrace to the uniform, man! A disgrace!' He slammed down his glass and headed for the door.

'Where are you going, my lord?' asked Ramsay.

'Someone has to break the news to his intended,' snarled Bullivant, and slammed the door behind him on his way out.

'My fault,' said Ramsay. He seemed even more shaken than Pechorin. 'I should never have agreed to the match. I should have seen what it would lead to.'

Killigrew shook his head. 'You couldn't have predicted that Dallaway would behave the way he did. Pechorin's right: he had no choice. It was self-defence. My report to Admiral Napier will make that quite clear.'

'Thank you. But it will not help Lord Dallaway, I fear.'

There was a knock at the door. 'Come in?' called the general.

The door opened and the surgeon entered, his hands and shirtfront alike drenched with blood. He shook his head sorrowfully.

Ramsay was still in a state of shock an hour later, after Killigrew had returned to his billet in town, Pechorin had gone back on board the *Atalanta*, and the Bullivants had retired upstairs, Araminta bravely refusing a dose of laudanum to help her cope with the shock.

The general wondered what arrangements to make for the deceased. It would be easy enough to bury him here in Ekenäs, but he probably had an ancestral mausoleum at his home in England. His family would want his body shipped back in a sealed coffin, and that in itself would be difficult to arrange; if instructions came from St Petersburg permitting him to let Lord Bullivant and his family go in exchange for General Bodisco, the coffin could be sent with them. And as much as he mourned the young man's death sincerely, he would not have been human if he had not wondered how Dallaway's death would affect his own career. His superiors would be furious, blame him with negligence in allowing a prisoner of war to be killed in so foolish a manner; well, whatever punishment he received, he told himself, it would be no more than he deserved.

He heard the doorbell ring faintly and wondered who could be calling. Probably an ensign from the barracks to report another crisis – they'd run out of champagne in the officers' mess again.

He recognised Renholt's knock on the library door. 'Come in.'

The flunkey entered. 'A Colonel Nekrasoff to see you, sir.'

'Colonel Nekrasoff? I don't believe I know any Colonel Nekrasoff.'

'Of the Third Section of His Imperial Majesty's Chancery.'

Fear gripped Ramsay's innards like an iron claw. 'You'd best show him in,' he stammered.

Two men swept into the room, both dressed in an ornate, sky-blue uniform with gold epaulettes. The senior of the two was in his early forties, a dark-eyed, handsome fellow with wavy black hair, a colonel's aiguillettes hanging across his left breast. His companion was a younger man with a pale, thin face.

'Lieutenant-General Ramsay?' The dark-eyed man extended a kid-gloved hand, which Ramsay shook nervously. 'Colonel Radimir Fokavich Nekrasoff, of the Third Section. This is my aide, Lieutenant Kizheh. Do forgive the intrusion, but as I'm sure you'll appreciate we have an unfortunate situation on our hands which the Tsar is very keen to get cleared up as swiftly and painlessly as possible.'

Ramsay's first thought had been that Dallaway's death had brought the colonel, but even in his distracted state he realised that Nekrasoff could not have been alerted to the English lord's death in time. 'You're the Tsar's envoy?'

Nekrasoff nodded. 'Naturally, I'll require your complete and unquestioning co-operation.'

'Of course.'

'Where are the Bullivants at present?'

'Upstairs. There has been a terrible tragedy—'

'What sort of tragedy?'

'Lord Dallaway ... he had a fencing match with Count Pechorin. Pechorin won, and Dallaway lost his temper and struck at the count with a sabre; Pechorin evaded it and mortally wounded him.'

'Lord Dallaway is dead?' demanded Nekrasoff.

Ramsay nodded. 'The count acted in self-defence; the responsibility is all mine.'

'Good!' said Nekrasoff. 'One less to concern us. What about the crew of the *Milenion*?'

Ramsay was so stunned by Nekrasoff's attitude, it took him a moment to recover himself and answer the colonel's question. 'Under guard in a barn on the outskirts of town, along with Commander Killigrew's men.'

'Commander Killigrew?'

'The British officer who was sent to negotiate Lord Bullivant's release. Unfortunately, it seems that one of our batteries fired upon his cutter as he approached the town. He claims he was sailing under a flag of truce at the time. I'm having the matter looked into.'

'Oh dear. That *is* unfortunate.' Nekrasoff looked mildly pained. 'I was not informed of this.'

'It only happened this morning. I sent a telegraph to St Petersburg as soon as I learned of it.'

'Where is this Commander Killigrew now?'

'Billeted in town, along with the other officers who were captured with him. They've all given their paroles.'

'How many officers?'

'Just three, including Killigrew. The others are Mr Humphrey Charlton, an assistant surgeon; and a Herre Sten Dahlstedt, a Swede acting as the *Ramillies*' pilot.'

'The *Ramillies*?' asked Nekrasoff.

'Commander Killigrew's ship,' said Ramsay.

But Nekrasoff had not been addressing him. 'A third-rate

ship of the line,' Kizheh recited by rote. 'Sixty guns, four-hundred and fifty horsepower, seventeen hundred and forty-seven tons, crew of six hundred and sixty. Captain Graham Crichton.'

'Hm. General Ramsay, I wonder if you'd be so good as to send a patrol to report on the *Ramillies*' current position?'

'That will not be easy. She'll be anchored offshore, beyond the islands of the archipelago.'

'Nevertheless, I require it. And I'll need hourly updates.'

'I'll see what I can do.'

'Thank you.'

'Commander Killigrew informs me that Vice Admiral Napier is prepared to exchange General Bodisco for the Bullivants and their crew.'

'How *very* generous of him,' sneered Nekrasoff. 'No, I think we can manage without the man who lost the Åland Islands.' He turned to Kizheh. 'Find the local telegraph station and signal headquarters. I want all the information we have on Commander Killigrew, and . . . what were the names of the other two, Lieutenant-General?'

'Mr Humphrey Charlton and Herre Sten Dahlstedt.'

Kizheh nodded and wrote their names in a pocketbook with the stub of a pencil before leaving.

Nekrasoff turned back to Ramsay. 'What about the calotypes Lord Dallaway took?'

'Hold on a moment . . .' The general turned back to his desk and took out a wodge of photographs. 'Here they are.'

Nekrasoff looked at the first one, a young woman looking bored standing on the deck of a schooner. 'Who's this?'

'Lord Bullivant's daughter, the honourable Araminta Maltravers.'

'And the ship?'

'We believe it's the *Milenion*.'

Nekrasoff flicked through the rest of the calotypes. There were pictures of Miss Maltravers in the Tivoli Gardens in

Copenhagen, of Miss Maltravers on the battlements of Elsinore Castle, Miss Maltravers on the steps of the Royal Palace in Stockholm, Miss Maltravers in the grounds of the Drottningholms Slott, Miss Maltravers in front of a windmill in the Åland Islands. None of them contained any military secrets, and in each and every one she wore an expression of unutterable boredom.

'What about the calotypes taken on Jurassö?' demanded Nekrasoff.

'They were never developed. The crew of the *Atalanta* seized the *Milenion* before Lord Dallaway had had a chance to get his undeveloped plates back on board. Pechorin's men had never seen a camera before, they didn't know what they were dealing with: half the plates were exposed, the rest simply shattered before they could be brought back to Ekenäs.'

'So, other than what they tell us, we've no way of knowing what they saw on Jurassö?'

'Or what they didn't see,' Ramsay added pointedly. 'You do intend to release the Bullivants, don't you?'

The colonel smiled. 'What happens to the Bullivants is, from now on, no concern of yours, General. Later today they will be moved to a secure location a few *vehrsty* from here, along with the crew of the *Milenion* and Commander Killigrew and his men. Where is Lord Dallaway's body?'

'In the billiards room. Renholt will show you . . .'

'My men will deal with his body. Oh, I'd also be obliged if you'd let me have any records relating to the capture of the *Milenion*, and of Killigrew and his men. Including any journal or diary you may keep. Have you mentioned them in any private correspondence?'

'Of course not.'

'Splendid. All references to the fact that the Bullivants or Commander Killigrew and his men were ever here are to be expunged from the records. Do I make myself plain?'

Ramsay felt sick. 'These are good people, Colonel. A little

foolish, perhaps, but they have been guests under my roof . . .'

Nekrasoff shook his head. 'They were never here, General. Their "goodness" is something I shall leave to God to judge. My loyalty is to the Tsar. I trust your own is just as unwavering?'

'Of course!'

'Good. Count Orloff tells me that His Imperial Majesty was very pleased with the way you handled the attack on this town three months ago, given the limited resources at your disposal. It would be a shame if a man of your undoubted abilities were to be assigned to the salt mines of Siberia.'

VII

The Third Section

3.30 p.m.–5.00 p.m., Thursday 17 August

Killigrew lounged on his bed in Herre Grönkvist's house, smoking a cheroot, and wondered if Dallaway's death would delay the Bullivants' release. Had it occurred in England there would have been a police investigation – or rather, a provost marshal's investigation, since the prisoners had been under military jurisdiction – but in either event there would have been a wealth of paperwork to be dealt with before any of the witnesses could be released. And Russia was supposed to be an even bigger bureaucracy than England, if such a thing were possible.

On the other hand, perhaps the Russians would waive such matters, given how influential the Bullivants were, and whatever the viscount himself might say, the case seemed pretty cut and dried to Killigrew. Perhaps he could use the incident to his advantage: to the Russians it might seem embarrassing, but if he volunteered to stay behind and act as a witness, signing any statements the Russians wanted to the effect that Pechorin had acted in self-defence – provided they were written in English rather than Russian – then in return the

Russians might be prepared to let the others go in exchange for Bodisco.

Hearing a carriage pull up on the cobbles outside, he stood and glanced out of the window. A *telezhka* drawn by six horses had pulled up in the street outside, with two gendarmes dressed in sky-blue uniforms seated on the driving board. The police, come to take his statement, he supposed. He wondered if the senior officer amongst them would have sufficient authority to make a deal.

One of them climbed down from the driving board and disappeared below the window. Killigrew heard the doorbell jangle. He buckled on his sword belt and made his way downstairs to find Herre Grönkvist talking to the gendarme. They both looked up as Killigrew descended the stairs.

'I suppose you want my statement?'

'Commander Killigrew?' asked the gendarme. Killigrew nodded. 'I'm Lieutenant Kizheh: I've been sent to fetch you.'

'To the local police office?'

Kizheh shook his head. 'To meet Colonel Nekrasoff, my superior. He's been sent from St Petersburg to clear up this matter.'

Killigrew's reaction was one of relief. It would be easier to make a deal with a senior officer from St Petersburg, who would be empowered to negotiate. 'It's about time too,' he said, and turned to his host. 'Thank you so much for your kindness, Herre Grönkvist. When I return to England I shall have nothing but good to report of Finnish hospitality.'

Ashen-faced, Grönkvist merely stared at Killigrew as if he was looking at a ghost, and made the sign of the cross.

Frowning, Killigrew followed Kizheh out into the street, where the second gendarme jumped down from the driving board and made his way round to the back of the *telezhka*. He began to unlock the padlock that secured the door.

Kizheh held out his hand to Killigrew. 'Your sword, Commander.'

'But I've given my parole—'

144

The lieutenant drew a percussion pistol from the holster at his hip, pulled back the hammer and levelled it at Killigrew.

Scowling, he drew his sword and handed it to Kizheh, hilt first. 'I shall protest about this in no uncertain terms to General Ramsay.'

'The matter is out of General Ramsay's hands.'

The other gendarme got the door open, and Kizheh gestured with the pistol. Killigrew started to climb inside, and then hesitated. The interior was bare, apart from straw strewn across the boards. Charlton and Dahlstedt were already inside, the latter lying on his back, his face badly battered.

Killigrew started to turn to protest to Kizheh, but the other gendarme gave him a shove in the small of the back so that he fell inside. The door was promptly slammed behind him and padlocked.

'Charlton? What's going on?' Killigrew called in the darkness.

'Your guess is as good as mine, sir. These fellows just told me I was being taken to see some Russian colonel chap, and shoved me in here.'

As Killigrew's eyes adjusted to the darkness, he found enough light filtered up through the gaps between the planks in the floor for him to be able to make out where Charlton crouched over Dahlstedt. 'What happened to him?'

'They picked him up next. He took one look at their uniforms, and tried to make a break for it. He's lucky they didn't shoot him.'

'That was a damned fool thing to do.'

The floor of the *telezhka* jerked beneath them as they rattled off over the cobbles.

'Third Section,' groaned Dahlstedt.

'Eh?'

'The Third Section of His Imperial Majesty's Chancery. In England you would say secret police, yes?'

'Secret police?' echoed Killigrew. 'Hardly secret, if they wear uniforms.'

'They do not all wear uniforms. In Russia, you never know who is an informer for the Third Section. Your next-door neighbour, the butcher's boy, perhaps even your own wife.'

'Why the devil would the secret police be interested in us?'

'In Russia, the secret police are interested in everything, from high treason and espionage to dissidents and public morals.'

'Confound this crazy country!' exclaimed Charlton. 'There's obviously been some kind of misunderstanding.'

'For God's sake, man!' protested Dahlstedt. 'When are you going to learn? You are not in a civilised country now. This is Russia.'

Killigrew took a deep breath. 'All right, Herre Dahlstedt. What can we expect?'

'Interrogation. Torture. Execution, if we're lucky.'

'And if we're unlucky?'

'Exile to the Siberian salt mines.'

'Used to play in an abandoned tin mine when I was a boy. Not sure I'd care to spend the rest of my life working in one. Hellish dirty places.' Killigrew got down on his hands and knees and swept the straw to the sides of the floor, the better to see the gaps that outlined the planks. He found a knot in the grain and pressed his thumb against it until it popped out the other side. Putting one eye to the hole, he could see the ground rushing past beneath the *telezhka*. They were moving along at a fair clip. He took his penknife from his pocket, opened the blade and inserted it into the gap between two planks, shaving slivers of wood from the edge of one.

'We'll be in St Petersburg before you break out that way,' said Charlton.

Killigrew ignored him, patiently working the blade back and forth in the gap, shaving wood first from one plank, then the one next to it, widening a chink about two inches long. After about a quarter of an hour, he judged the gap was wide enough. He unbuckled his sword belt, unthreaded the empty scabbard, and inserted the buckle in the gap.

Now even Dahlstedt was sitting up to watch.

'Charlton, come and give me a hand.'

'What do you want me to do?'

'Stand on this buckle, push it down to one side. Make sure you keep your foot off this central plank.'

Charlton put his foot on the buckle. He pressed nearly all his weight on it, until one plank bent upwards and the other dipped to create a gap a couple of inches wide. Killigrew thrust his scabbard into it, and started to lean on it. 'Charlton, you pull from the other side.'

'The guards will hear the planks snap,' warned Dahlstedt.

'I hope so,' said Killigrew. 'If they do, they'll stop to investigate, and we can jump them.'

'Armed with a penknife? Against muskets?'

'Better a quick death from a bullet than slow, lingering torture. Wherever they're taking us, I don't think we'll have much of a chance to escape when we get there.'

Killigrew pushed on the scabbard, Charlton pulled, and the planks groaned in protest.

'We're going to break the scabbard!' grunted Charlton.

'Never mind the scabbard! Pull, damn you!'

The plank snapped with a crack like a rifle shot. Charlton stumbled against the side of the carriage while Killigrew fell against him.

'Uncommon strong scabbard you've got there,' said Charlton.

'British craftsmanship versus Russian workmanship.' Killigrew grinned. 'Which did you think would give first?'

'We're not stopping,' said Dahlstedt.

'We will in a minute.' Killigrew stamped on the broken plank, pushing it down until it touched the ground below and splintered away entirely with another crack.

The three of them glanced towards the front end of the box. If anything, the *telezhka* was travelling even faster. 'Damned fellows must be deaf,' grunted Charlton.

'They can't hear it above the noise of the wheels on the

road. Damn! I was afraid of that.'

'Now what?'

'We do it again.'

It took Killigrew and Charlton another twenty minutes to remove the adjoining plank, creating a gap in the floor of the *telezhka* some two feet wide. The three of them gazed down at the road rushing past beneath.

'Now what do we do?' asked Charlton. 'Wait until we stop?'

'Can't risk it. We may not stop until we reach our destination.' Killigrew thrust his head through the gap, looking around at the underside of the carriage. He worked one end of his sword belt into the gap between two planks where they had snapped off, so it was anchored by the buckle. Then he positioned himself over the gap, arms and legs supporting him on either side.

'You're not seriously going to try climbing out while we're moving?' gasped Charlton. 'Damn it, man! You'll break your neck!'

'I'll take it under advisement,' said Killigrew, lowering his body through.

'I thought you were supposed to be taking it easy?'

'It seems the Third Section has other plans.' Gazing down between his legs, Killigrew saw a spar of the axle bridge. Withdrawing one leg after him, he braced it against the bridge, and then the other. Slowly, gingerly, he worked his body down until he was as far towards the rear of the *telezhka* as he could get, and lowered his heels to the ground. They juddered against the road; it was at moments like this he realised why he spent so much money on a good pair of boots. He took the other end of the belt in both hands and dropped to the ground.

He shot out between the rear wheels of the *telezhka* and was dragged along on his back at something approaching ten miles an hour. It was agonising: he could feel every pebble, every piece of gravel on the road hitting his body even through his tailcoat, waistcoat and shirt. It was only a matter of seconds before the fabric was worn through and his skin was abraded on the road.

The running board below the back door was just above his head. He grabbed hold of it and rolled on his front, trying to keep his weight on his toecaps rather than on his knees or, worse, his crotch. Pulling himself in to the back of the *telezhka*, he reached up with the other hand and tried to grab the padlocked chain securing the door. He just missed, and fell back down again. The impact on his arm was appalling. His other arm, flailing, hit the road, and only his kid glove prevented the skin being flayed from his hand.

His knees felt as though they were on fire, and he could feel the leather in the toes of his boots wearing down. *This time*, he told himself, *or I'm going to be crippled for life*.

He missed on his next attempt, almost losing his grip on the running board with his other hand. The knees in his trousers were worn out now, and his boots were almost down to his socks.

He lunged again, caught hold of the padlock, then grabbed the chain in the other hand and hauled himself up. It took all his strength in his arms and shoulders to pull himself up until he could brace his feet against the running board. He straightened, clinging to the back of the *telezhka* and sobbing for breath. He had skinned his knees badly and the blood ran down the tattered remnants of his trousers. *Some rest cure!*

As soon as he had caught his breath, he grabbed hold of the top of the box and pulled himself up, using the handle on the door for a foothold. The driving board at the front of the box was so low, he could not see the heads of the two gendarmes. He crawled along the roof and peered down to see Lieutenant Kizheh seated there next to the driver.

All right, so all I have to do is swing down, catch Kizheh unawares and knock him off before he even knows I'm there. Then all I've got to do is deal with the driver.

He took his penknife from his pocket once more, opened it, and gripped the blade between his teeth.

The clop of the horses' hoofs sounded a hollow note as the *telezhka* drove on to a long, narrow wooden bridge. Looking up, Killigrew saw the bridge crossed a deep ditch to where an imposing granite castle stood on a huge rock. At the far end of the bridge there was a gateway where two gendarmes armed with muskets stood on guard.

A very low gateway.

'Oh, Lor'!' he gasped, the knife falling from his mouth. He picked himself up and turned and ran back across the roof of the *telezhka*, launching himself into space just as the carriage passed through the gate.

His body thudded painfully against the planks of the bridge. He rolled over to lessen the impact, then felt the edge beneath him. As he slipped out into space, he grasped wildly for something to hold on to, and managed to grip one of the stanchions of the railing on that side. He caught hold of it with the other hand and pulled himself up until he could crook one elbow around it, his legs hanging in space. Glancing back over his shoulder, he saw a drop of some thirty feet to the bottom of the ditch.

Footsteps sounded on the planks of the bridge. He looked up to see the two sentries strolling across to stand over him. One of them said something in Russian – Killigrew didn't quite catch it – and the other laughed. The first unslung his musket and levelled it at the commander. Killigrew thought he was going to shoot him there and then; but the gendarme only kept him covered while the other man hauled him to safety.

They marched him towards the castle, one of them giving him a shove between the shoulder blades every few yards. The heel had come off his right boot, making him limp. They had almost reached the gate when three more *telezhki* rumbled across the bridge, forcing Killigrew and his two escorts to press back against the railings.

150

They followed the vehicles through the low gate into a gloomy courtyard with a curtain wall on three sides and a stone keep on the fourth. A wooden gallery ran around the inside of the curtain wall with a dozen Third Section gendarmes armed with muskets ranged along it, gazing down in the courtyard below. Other gendarmes jumped down from the driving boards of the *telezhki* while more emerged from a doorway, lining up with their muskets unslung and ready. Killigrew counted about two dozen in total, and to his jaded eye it did not look as though the Third Section recruited its gendarmes on the basis of intelligence or civility.

The door of the first *telezhka* was already open. Charlton jumped down and turned to help Dahlstedt climb down after him. They raised their hands when they saw the muskets levelled at them.

Kizheh looked in the back of the *telezhka* and saw the hole they had made. 'Sanitary arrangements not to your satisfaction, gentlemen?' he asked. Then he turned and saw Killigrew. Taking in his ragged, bruised and bleeding condition, he smiled. 'Nice try.'

The door to another *telezhka* was opened and a guard gestured with his musket. Molineaux appeared in the doorway and hesitated before jumping down while he cast a critical eye over his new surroundings. Endicott, Hughes, Iles and Vowles followed him out, along with two of the Milenions. Captain Thornton and the rest of the Milenions were herded out of the other *telezhka*.

'Molineaux!' called Killigrew. The petty officer looked around. 'Belay my last order!'

The petty officer nodded. One of the guards rammed the stock of his musket into Killigrew's stomach. He doubled up in agony, and sank to his knees, but that was even more painful. He was hauled to his feet, and the prisoners were marched through a doorway in the side of the keep. A narrow flight of stone steps led down to a subterranean chamber lit by a few oil-lamps. The place stank of bat droppings: the floor was slippery with the filth. While the sailors were stopped and searched outside the door to one cell, Killigrew, Charlton and Dahlstedt were marched down a corridor past several other doors to the one at the end. The door was unlocked and they were thrust through into the cell beyond to find Lord Bullivant already within.

He rose to his feet and bore down on Kizheh. 'Now look here, this is intolerable! I demand to speak to whoever's in charge!'

'All in good time, my lord. Well, gentlemen, what do you think of your new home?'

'I think you should give your housekeeper her cards,' said Killigrew.

Kizheh smiled. 'Welcome to Raseborg Castle. It's been abandoned for the past three centuries, so the facilities are a little basic, but it will more than suffice for our needs.' He retreated from the cell and the door was locked from the outside. Killigrew heard his footsteps and those of the guards clacking back up the stairs.

The only light came through the grille in the door. It was stout, and so new Killigrew could smell the sawdust on it: the Third Section must have had it installed specifically for the purpose of holding them prisoner here. The carpenter had done his work well: the lock was only accessible from the other side, and it was so strong there seemed little point in throwing his shoulder against it. He was in enough pain as it was.

He felt a wave of nausea sweep over him, and then his vision flickered and he felt the cell spin around him.

'I suppose this is your notion of securing my release?' snorted Bullivant.

But Killigrew had passed out.

On the other side of the dungeons, Molineaux and the other sailors were ordered to remove their belts, neckerchiefs and bootlaces before they were herded into the first cell.

'What do they want with us belts, neckerchiefs and bootlaces?' asked Endicott.

'Prob'ly worried we're going to hang ourselves,' Vowles said morosely.

'Us wouldn't give 'em the satisfaction,' said Iles.

Molineaux handed over his belt with more than a pang of regret. The man who had initiated him into the fine art of breaking into places – and breaking out of them, if necessary – when he had first started out as a young snakesman had taught him that a good leather belt was one of the most indispensable weapons in the escapologist's arsenal.

'I want a receipt for that lot,' said Hughes, handing over his belt, neckerchief and bootlaces. One of the guards pushed him roughly through a doorway.

The gendarme who searched Molineaux did a thorough job: he even found the set of burglar's lock-picks that he still carried with him for ... well, for situations just like this. Unsure of what to make of them, the gendarme called over an officer and showed him the tools.

'My hussif,' explained Molineaux. It was worth a try.

The officer did not look convinced, however, and Molineaux was thrust through the door without his picks, his unlaced boots flapping on the flagstones.

The cell was fairly large, but then it needed to be. Eventually there were sixteen of them in there: the five Ramillies and the eleven Milenions, including Todd the steward. The door slammed behind them and was padlocked from the outside.

The prisoners surveyed their new quarters with jaded eyes: a granite-walled chamber perhaps twenty feet square, with only the one door, and a window high up in one wall the only source of light. There were no beds: the only furniture in the room was a single bucket.

'Not bad,' said Endicott, taking in their new surroundings. 'I've stayed in worse. Not that a woman's touch wouldn't go amiss, mind you: lace curtains on the window,

153

some nice bolsters for the armchairs, a few knick-knacks on the mantelpiece . . .'

'I like what they've done with the dank,' said Molineaux. 'It wouldn't be yer proper dungeon without the regulation amount of slime dripping down the walls; I'm glad to see they've done us proud here.'

'They bring us to a place like this, and all you can do is crack jokes?' Thornton snapped angrily.

'Got to keep our spirits up,' Molineaux said cheerfully.

'What's the point?' Todd slumped down in one corner. 'We're going to die, aren't we?'

'Nah,' said Vowles, making himself comfortable on the floor. 'They'll swap us for some Russki prisoners.'

'That's just the officers, Andy,' said Hughes. 'Ratings like you and me don't get exchanged. Britain and Russia may be at war, but still our capitalist-imperialist oppressors conspire to subjudicate the working man . . . ow!' he added when one of Molineaux's boots bounced off his head.

'But we ain't even navy sailors!' protested Tommo Fuller, whose face was still bruised from his altercation with Iles. 'We shouldn't be here at all!'

'You're right!' scoffed Iles. 'What were it brung your lord and master to the seat of war, any rate? Looking for adventure, were 'ee? Well, 'e's got it in spadefuls now!'

'What are they going to do with us?'

'Oh, kill us, I reckon,' Molineaux said airily.

'What?' spluttered Thornton.

'That your notion of keeping us spirits up, Wes?' Endicott asked with a crooked grin.

'Keeping our spirits up is one thing, but we've got to face facts.'

'But . . . they can't!' protested Thornton. 'Sir Charles Napier knows we're here; that's why he sent your Commander Killigrew to negotiate our release.'

'Fat lot o' good 'e's done,' Fuller added sourly.

'I reckon Old Charlie picked Mr Killigrew for this mission

because he was afraid something like this might happen,' said Molineaux.

'Don't he like Killigrew, then?'

'It's not that; he knows that Mr Killigrew's got skills other than negotiation.'

'Well, Old Mother O'Leary's boy isn't waiting around for some bastard Ivan to put a bullet in the back of his head,' said one of the Milenions. He threw his shoulder at the door. He was a big, strong lad, but the door was bigger and stronger.

'You're wasting your time,' said Ned Yorath.

Hughes turned to Molineaux. 'You can pick locks, can't you, Wes?'

'Sure. But that jigger's padlocked on the other side, and they took my betties.'

'What about the window?'

Molineaux crossed to the wall below it and got down on all fours. 'Stand on my back and see if you can bend the bars, Ben.'

Iles complied, but after several seconds of grunting and straining he was forced to admit defeat. He stepped down off Molineaux's back. ''Sno good: they'se too firmly cemented in. Now, if I 'ad a file, maybe . . .'

'Brilliant!' said Yorath. 'I'll ask the guard, shall I? See if he'll bring us one.'

'Stow it, Ned,' ordered Uren. 'Squabbling amongst ourselves won't do us a blind bit of good.'

'Come on, Wes!' pleaded Endicott. 'This is your field of expertise. Didn't you once tell us your mate Foxy could break out of any gaff? He taught you everything you knew, didn't he?'

'Yur, but I don't think he was ever a prisoner of the Tsar . . .' Molineaux looked about the cell, searching for inspiration. He stared at the bucket. Then he stood up, crossed to the door and peered through the grille. There was no sign of any sentry, but he knew there would be one not far off. 'Sing, lads.'

'Eh?' said Vowles. 'What do we want to sing for?'

'Keep our spirits up, of course.'

'I think Wes has got an idea,' said Endicott. 'Now, how about a rousing chorus of "The Girl I Left Behind Me"? Hearty as you like.'

Endicott began singing, and Iles, Hughes, and Vowles joined in the refrain while the Milenions watched them in disbelief. Molineaux walked across to the slop pail, kicked it on its side, and stamped on it, reducing it to its constituent staves.

'Brilliant!' said Vowles. 'Now what are we going to crap into?'

'Your kissing trap, if you don't put a sock in it,' Molineaux told him. 'Stretch out your arm.'

Vowles sighed and lifted one arm. Molineaux caught hold of his cuff, and with one yank he jerked the sleeve clean off the jacket. He grinned. 'Pusser's slops, eh? Typical Brummagem rubbish.'

'Oi! What did you want to go an' do that for?'

'You'll see. Anyone need to pump ship?'

The others exchanged glances. 'Not right now, Wes,' said Hughes. 'Besides, you broke the bucket . . .'

'Come on, lads. Surely one of you must have a full bladder? Think of fountains playing musically; water flowing from a pump; cataracts tumbling down rocky hillsides; great cascades of water gushing through narrow gorges, splashing liquidly over rocks with a merry tinkling sound; vast rivers in flood . . .'

Sweat broke out on Vowles' brow. He bit his lip, then stood up and clutched himself, hopping from one foot to the other. 'Oh Christ, Wes! Now you've been and gone and done it! And after you broke the bucket too . . .'

Molineaux tossed the sleeve into one corner of the room. 'Do it on that.'

As peculiar as the request sounded, Vowles was in no state to argue. He fumbled frenetically with the buttons on his flies and relieved himself over the sleeve with a gasp of satisfaction.

'That's it, Andy. Make sure you spread it all over, get it soaked through and through.'

'Has Wes finally gone out of his head?' asked Hughes.

Endicott shrugged. 'I dunno what he's after, but you can be sure he's got a plan. Watch and learn, lads, watch and learn.'

Vowles shook off the drips and tucked John Thomas back in bed.

Molineaux took a deep breath. 'All right, lads: now comes the unpleasant part. If we ever get out of this alive, I hope you all remember the sacrifice I'm about to make. Just promise me you'll never speak of it.'

The others exchanged bewildered glances, but all became clear when Molineaux picked up Vowles' dripping, urine-soaked sleeve.

'Eurgh!' protested Yorath.

'I know, I know,' said Molineaux. 'It's a dirty job, but someone's got to do it. My plan, my hands. Red, make yourself useful and stand against the wall so I can cool out the window.'

Hughes complied, without much show of enthusiasm, and clasped his hands to make a step-up. Molineaux scrambled up to stand on his shoulders. The bottom of the window was level with the ground outside: even as he peered through, a dozen booted feet marched past. Molineaux waited until the tramp of boots had faded, and wrapped the sopping sleeve around two of the bars, tying it tightly in a knot. 'Hand me up one of them bits of wood, Seth. The longest you can find.'

Endicott picked up one of the staves of the broken bucket and passed it up. Molineaux slid it through the loop of the sleeve and began to twist it. Each turn of the stave tightened the sleeve's grip on the bars.

'It'll never work,' snorted Vowles.

'You'm wrong,' said Iles. 'It *be* workin'.'

'Jesus!' said Uren. 'It is too!'

157

'Mad, am I?' Molineaux asked with a grin.

Then the plank snapped in two and he fell off Hughes' shoulders, sprawling on the flagstones.

'You were saying?' asked Vowles.

'Rotten!' Molineaux spat in disgust.

'Of course!' scoffed Vowles. 'It's a slop bucket. What did you expect? You know what's really funny? You got your hands covered in my piddle . . . for nothing!'

'Shurrup, Andy,' snarled Endicott. 'At least Wes is trying. I don't hear you coming up with any clever notions.'

A silence fell over the prisoners as they pondered their fate. Molineaux was beaten, and if there was one thing he could not bear, it was to be beaten. He sat down with his back to the wall, racking his brains for inspiration and massaging his stockinged feet. *You're a Henson*, his mother had always taught him. *You can do anything.*

He frowned, fingering the woollen thread of his socks. Then he ran a finger over the mortar between the granite blocks that formed the walls of the cell.

It could work.

No. It *would* work.

'Lads?'

'What now?' Hughes demanded impatiently.

'We're getting out of here.'

'Aye, right,' snorted Vowles.

Molineaux plucked one of the brass buttons off his jacket and used it to scrape at the mortar.

'We're going to tunnel out?' scoffed Vowles. 'Brilliant! It only took the cove in that book fourteen years, and he had a spoon.'

As Molineaux scraped at the mortar, a small pile of mortar grains formed on the floor at the base of the wall: not much, but it was a start. 'Seth?'

'Aye?'

'Come over here.'

Endicott crawled across to join him.

158

'I want you to scrape at the mortar with this button.'

'I hate to agree with Andy, Wes, but he's right: it'll take for ever . . .'

'We're not tunnelling out. We're going through that window. See this little mound of dust I've made here? That's what I'm after.'

'What do you want with it?'

'You'll see. Trust me.' Molineaux took off his sock. He pulled at it, but his mother was too good at knitting: he had to bite into the fabric to snap the woollen threads.

'We're all hungry, Wes,' said Vowles. 'But surely if we wait long enough, the Ivans are bound to bring us something to eat?'

'Borsch, or Wes's sweaty socks,' said Endicott. 'Talk about being caught between the devil and the deep blue sea!'

The woollen thread finally snapped, and once Molineaux had got started the rest came easily. He unpicked his sock until he had nothing more than a dozen lengths of woollen thread, a few inches long. He took one of the threads and dipped it in the puddle in the corner of the room where Vowles had relieved himself over his sleeve. Then he crossed back to where Endicott was making a tiny pile of mortar grains.

'That's good, Seth. Now make another pile further down.'

Molineaux plucked a couple more buttons from his jacket and tossed them to Hughes and Iles. 'Get to work, lads. I want mortar dust, and lots of it.'

'Totally off his head,' was Vowles' diagnosis.

Molineaux took the urine-soaked thread and dragged it through the tiny mound of mortar dust until it was coated all over. Then he laid the thread to one side, picked up another, and repeated the process. After half an hour of scraping, dipping and dragging, he had two dozen threads of wool, coated in mortar dust.

'It'd be nice to know where all this is leading you,' said Thornton.

159

'Out of here, with any luck.' Molineaux left the threads to dry, and sat down with his back to the wall, tipping his bonnet forward over his eyes. 'Let's have a doss, lads. I've a feeling tonight's going to be a long one.'

Killigrew was awoken by Charlton gently slapping him on the cheek. The commander raised a hand to his head. 'Who hit me?'

'No one. Hate to be the one to break it to you, Killigrew, but I'm afraid you fainted again.'

Killigrew grimaced and glanced around the cell. Dahlstedt was hunched in one corner: there was no sign of Bullivant. 'Where's his lordship?'

'They took him a few minutes ago.'

'Heard any shots since then?'

'No. Why? Surely you're not suggesting they'd . . .? They couldn't!'

'They could and they would!' growled Dahlstedt. 'The Russians don't hold their nobility in the same awe you English do. They think nothing of executing their own aristocrats if they think they're a threat to the Tsar. You think they're going to be any more concerned about an English aristocrat? The Russian secret police make people disappear all the time. We're just the latest victims of the White Terror.'

'But they wouldn't dare!' protested Charlton. 'Dirty Charlie knows we're here . . . and the Russians must know he knows. There'd be an uproar back in Britain if news got out that Lord Bullivant and his family had been executed in cold blood, along with three British officers and a score of seamen.'

'The Russians will just deny it ever happened,' Dahlstedt said wearily.

'No one would believe them.'

'I expect the Russians must be used to no one believing their bare-faced lies by now,' opined Killigrew. 'What can our

160

government do? Declare war on Russia?'

They heard footsteps on the stairs outside, and presently the door was opened and Lord Bullivant pushed through, adjusting his collar and lapels with an aggressive thrust of his jaw.

Lieutenant Kizheh indicated Dahlstedt. 'You next.'

The Finn rose to his feet. 'Well, gentlemen, see you after the war.'

'Don't let the bastards grind you down, Sten,' said Killigrew.

Dahlstedt smiled sadly and marched out. The door was slammed and locked behind him.

Lord Bullivant shot his cuffs. 'Damned impertinence! I'm going to have some pretty sharp things to say about that feller when I get out of here. He's an absolute disgrace!'

'*If* you get out of here,' said Charlton.

'What feller?' asked Killigrew.

'Colonel something or other. Russki chap. Speaks good English, though. Impudent swine tried to get me to sign a confession.'

'Confession to what?'

'Espionage, would you believe? Me, the thirteenth Viscount Bullivant, accused of something as low and grubby as spying! He's got a nerve!'

'You didn't sign it, did you?' asked Killigrew.

'Certainly not! What do you take me for?'

'Thank Christ for that! Did he torture you?'

Bullivant stared at him. 'Of course not! He wouldn't dare.'

'I wouldn't be too sure of that, my lord.'

'You know what he said? He said he was going to give my daughter to his men . . . "to amuse themselves", as he put it . . . if I didn't sign. The man's a disgrace to the uniform!'

'From what Dahlstedt's been saying about the Third Section, I don't think it's possible to be a disgrace to that particular uniform,' said Killigrew.

'Wait a minute,' protested Charlton. 'He said he was going

to give Miss Maltravers to his men, and you still refused to sign? Jesus Christ, my lord! It's only a bit of paper! You'd sacrifice her honour for that?'

'Ah-ha!' Bullivant said triumphantly. 'I knew he was bluffing. He wouldn't dare.'

'You were quite right not to sign, my lord,' said Killigrew. 'Oh, not because he was bluffing – I'm sure he wasn't – but you sign that confession, and we're all dead men and women. And I dare say your daughter would still be used cruelly beforehand.'

'But . . . this is ludicrous! We were merely on a pleasure cruise! You're not suggesting they'd kill us, for that? This is all a ghastly mistake!'

'Exactly,' said Killigrew. 'And the Russian government would rather execute an entire aristocratic family – not to mention three British officers and a score of seamen – than confess to making a mistake. Too embarrassing to admit that they captured a civilian yacht, fired on a cutter sailing under a flag of truce and murdered a British officer in cold blood,' said Killigrew. 'So they've got to dispose of the witnesses.'

'Us, you mean,' Charlton said glumly.

Another ten minutes passed before Lieutenant Kizheh returned with Dahlstedt. The door was opened and Dahlstedt fell through on to the floor. Charlton and Killigrew rolled him on his back, and saw that the pilot's face was a mask of blood.

'Oh, Jesus!' gasped Charlton. 'His hands! Look at his hands!'

Dahlstedt's hands had been smashed to a bloody pulp. The pilot bared his teeth in a grimace of pain, revealing that one had been knocked out. 'He guessed I was Finnish,' he muttered.

'You next,' Kizheh told Killigrew.

VIII

Nekrasoff

5.00 p.m.–8.30 p.m., Thursday 17 August

Kizheh and the two guards led Killigrew to the courtyard, and then back into the keep via a second door nearer the gate. Most of the interior of the keep was taken up with a large and airy chamber, with light entering through crumbling windows on three of the four walls. This must have been the great hall of the castle once, but there was no sign of its former medieval splendour now, just bare granite walls where rich tapestries would have hung in days of yore. A wooden staircase up one side led to a gallery that ran round the walls above them. There was a raised dais at one end, where a dark-eyed man in an ornate sky-blue uniform sat behind a table.

Kizheh and the two guards withdrew, closing the door behind them, revealing another man standing against the wall beside the door, stripped to his shirtsleeves. Although not tall, he was broad-shouldered and bull-necked. Killigrew guessed the man was not present for his sparkling repartee: he had blood on his shirt, doubtless a souvenir from Dahlstedt's interrogation. He jerked his head towards the man on the dais, indicating that Killigrew should approach.

Killigrew's feet clacked unevenly as he walked across the bare wooden floor, still limping with the heel gone from one of his boots. The officer seated behind the table looked up from his papers as he ascended the steps leading to the dais.

'Ah, Commander Killigrew. Permit me to introduce myself: I am Colonel Radimir Fokavich Nekrasoff, of the Third Section of His Imperial Majesty's Chancery.' His English was flawless, spoken in smooth and urbane tones. 'Do forgive the melodramatic surroundings: I'm afraid these were the only premises available for me to set up my temporary headquarters.' He rose to his feet and leaned over the table to proffer a kid-gloved hand.

Killigrew folded his arms.

Nekrasoff looked pained. 'Oh dear,' he drawled sardonically. 'It's not going to be one of those interviews, is it? I was rather hoping we could keep this civilised.'

'As civilised as your interrogation of Herre Dahlstedt was?'

'Herre Dahlstedt is a Finn: a Russian citizen, aiding the enemies of the Tsar, and therefore a traitor.' Nekrasoff indicated the other chair. 'Do take a seat.'

Killigrew hitched up the hems of his ragged trousers before sitting down and crossing one leg over the other.

'You, on the other hand, are a British officer captured in war—'

'Illegally attacked while sailing under a flag of truce.'

'So you say. But the men in the battery that fired upon your cutter all deny that you were displaying any such flag.'

'There's a surprise. What time is it?'

Nekrasoff took out his fob watch and glanced at it. 'Just after five. Why do you ask?'

'I'm supposed to report back on board the *Ramillies* by six this evening. If I don't, Captain Crichton's going to sail up the inlet and bombard Ekenäs.'

'Oh, I doubt it. You see, I know as well as you that even if

164

the *Ramillies* could get past the chain across Vitsand Sound, she's too deep-draughted to sail up the inlet. No, perhaps he'll send a second cutter to investigate. This one will be allowed to reach Ekenäs, where an officer will greet the crew to inform them of the demise of yourself and your men when your boat was blown out of the water by one of our batteries. A tragic waste of life, but that's what happens when you fail to display your flag of truce adequately.'

'And just how do you intend to explain the disappearance of the Bullivants and the crew of the *Milenion*?'

'We'll simply tell them the truth: they've been interned under suspicion of espionage. His lordship's signed confession will provide all the justification we need.'

'Even if he were guilty – and please don't insult my intelligence by pretending you believe that for a moment – Russia would gain more support amongst the neutral powers if Lord Bullivant were subsequently released rather than executed.'

'To tell the world of the atrocities he and his wife and charming daughter were subjected to in order to extract that confession?' Nekrasoff smiled. 'I think not. Fortunately, once his confession is signed, a nasty bout of cholera is going to decimate the inhabitants of this castle.'

'The sort of epidemic that strikes down only Britons, and leaves Russians miraculously unharmed, I suppose?'

'Precisely.'

'And naturally you'll incinerate the bodies to prevent the epidemic from spreading, so no one will be able to prove that it wasn't cholera that killed them.'

'Very good! I can see you have an aptitude for this kind of work.'

'No, but I've met enough psychopathic maniacs to have some understanding of how their twisted minds work.'

'Oh, really, Mr Killigrew! Must you degenerate to childish name-calling? I had hoped to find you above such behaviour.'

'Then how else do you justify the kind of needless slaughter you're planning? What can you possibly gain from such wanton butchery?'

'The embarrassment of the British government in the eyes of the other European powers. We are well aware that Britain and France are wooing the support of neutral countries like Prussia, Austria and Sweden. When it's revealed that a personal friend of Lord Aberdeen has been engaged in something as underhand as espionage, well ... I think even your French allies will be reluctant to be associated with such goings-on. But Lord Bullivant is merely the icing on the cake. No; for me the real prize of this sorry affair is yourself, Commander.'

Killigrew laughed out loud. 'Me! Are you sure you're not confusing me with someone else? Someone important?'

'You do yourself an injustice.' Nekrasoff produced a pair of wire-framed spectacles and put them on to refer to the notes on the table in front of him. 'Commander Christopher Iguatios Killigrew. Born on board HMS *Cambrian* on the fifteenth day of October 1824, grandson of Rear Admiral Richard Killigrew, son of Captain John Killigrew and Medora Bouboulina. Joined the navy in 1837, aged twelve. Served as an aide-de-camp to Commodore Charles Napier in the Syria Campaign, 1840. Seven years later Napier – by then a rear admiral – recruited you as a spy for the Slave Trade Department in Whitehall.'

'So you've got a copy of the *New Navy List* at Third Section headquarters. I find that less impressive than the fact you could find someone there who could read.'

'Last winter you were identified in Helsingfors, posing as an ichthyologist as a cover for your attempts to recruit Finnish pilots like Herre Dahlstedt for Napier's Baltic fleet.'

'May I ask what the relevance of this is?'

'Oh, come now, Commander. There's no need to be so coy. Do you really think we haven't guessed that you're Napier's chief of intelligence?'

'Chief of intelligence?' Killigrew exclaimed in astonishment, and laughed. 'You think I'm Napier's chief of intelligence?'

'You deny it?'

'I very much doubt Sir Charles even has such a thing as a chief of intelligence. If he does, it certainly isn't me.'

'Why else would he take you to his meeting with the King of Sweden in April this year?' Nekrasoff smiled. 'You see, we Russians have our agents too, just like you.'

'The only reason I accompanied Sir Charles to King Oskar's court is because I happen to have a smattering of Swedish, and he wanted an interpreter he could trust.'

Nekrasoff tugged off his kid gloves. 'I dare say we could play this game for hours: me accusing you of being Napier's chief of intelligence, you denying it. But why waste each other's time? I don't want a signed confession from you. With all due respect, I very much doubt that *your* death will cause the same international furore as Lord Bullivant's. However, the Russian Admiralty would very much like to know where and when Napier plans to attack next.'

'So would a lot of officers in the British fleet, myself included. I doubt he's even made up his own mind as yet. Certainly he hadn't when I saw him the day before yesterday; or, if he had, he didn't see fit to confide in me.'

'You honestly expect me to believe your Admiralty hasn't already drawn up a detailed timetable for how Napier should conduct his campaign in the Baltic?'

'Well! At least it's reassuring to know you clearly don't have any spies in the Admiralty, otherwise you'd know we simply aren't that organised.'

'But surely Napier must have said *something* to you?'

'Sir Charles has said many things to me,' said Killigrew. 'Usually along the lines of, "Care for a whisky? Pour me one while you're at it", or, "'Pon ma word, Killigrew, can ye translate? Ah canna unnerstant a damned wurd this feller's sayin'." ' The commander did a fair impersonation of the admiral.

Nekrasoff laughed. 'You know, you're rather an amusing fellow, Killigrew. I shall be sorry to have to torture you.'

'Ah, yes. I was wondering when we would get round to that.'

'Well, I wouldn't presume to insult your honour by suggesting that you reveal any military secrets without being subjected to at least a modicum of pain.'

'I'm grateful for your consideration.' Killigrew jerked a thumb over his shoulder at the bull-necked gentleman standing against the back wall of the chamber. 'I suppose this is where Sweet William back there gets to work me over with his fists until I talk?'

'Nothing so crude, I assure you. Please, come with me.' Nekrasoff rose to his feet and led the way up the steps to the gallery. As Killigrew started to rise, the bull-necked man put a meaty hand on his shoulder, in case he got any foolish notions about trying to escape.

'Oh, Sergeant Ustimovich can be most effective at extracting information from ordinary people,' Nekrasoff continued as the brawny sergeant marched Killigrew up to the gallery. 'But I very much doubt a man who marched eight hundred miles through the Arctic wilderness could be persuaded to betray his country over a few punches, no matter how powerful and well-placed. Indeed, I rather think he would beat his own knuckles raw before you were ready to confess even what you had for dinner last night.'

'Pickled tripe, since you ask. I suppose it would be too much to hope that the dining arrangements in this hostelry are more satisfactory?'

Nekrasoff paused outside another door at the far end of the gallery, and turned to face Killigrew with a smile. 'Well, perhaps I can start by offering you a drink.'

He pushed the door open to reveal a large, circular chamber. The middle of the room was dominated by a chair: the sort of thing the more progressive dentists had started to use, except that this one had straps for wrists and ankles, and a sort of vice-like band for the head. A small Oriental stood there. He had a straggly beard and wore his hair long as if to compensate for the way it had receded from the dome of his scalp. He smiled unctuously, like a barber inviting his next customer to take a seat. There were about two dozen pails of water arranged about the floor on the other side of the chair.

'Please, be seated,' said Nekrasoff.

Killigrew would rather have sat on a fakir's bed of nails, but Ustimovich saw to it he did not have a lot of choice in the matter. He was forced into the chair, and Ustimovich and the Oriental strapped him in place.

'I see from your file that you've spent a lot of time in China over the years,' said Nekrasoff. 'Perhaps you're already familiar with the Chinese water torture?'

'I understand the general principle.'

'Leong here is actually a Siberian, strictly speaking, but he's had many years of working for the Third Section to perfect his art.'

'You realise, of course, this is a complete waste of time?' Killigrew asked Nekrasoff as Leong clamped his head in the vice.

'Every man has his breaking point, Mr Killigrew. Even you.'

'I don't doubt it. But supposing I were to tell you now that Napier's next target is Kronstadt, to save myself undergoing all that suffering? Would you believe me? Of course not. So you torture me, and at length I reveal that the target is Sveaborg. Now you're not sure: was I lying the first time, and telling the truth the second? Or telling the truth the first time, and lying the second in the hope you'd find a lie more convincing than the truth? Or was I lying *both* times? Is Reval the real target?'

'Give me the same answer three times in a row, Mr Killigrew, and then – perhaps – I shall believe you.'

Leong inserted a couple of cork plugs in Killigrew's nostrils, and then forced a brace into his mouth to hold his jaws apart. It made him gag, and he spat it out at once. Ustimovich promptly slammed a fist down on his stomach. Killigrew gasped, the wind driven from his body, and tried to double up, but the restraints held him down.

'Do try to co-operate, Mr Killigrew,' said Nekrasoff. 'You'll find it a good deal less painful in the long run.'

'Kronstadt,' said Killigrew. 'The next target is Kronstadt.'

'Oh, I'm sorry, Mr Killigrew. I should have explained. When I said I wanted the same answer from you three times in a row, answers given before the first application of the treatment don't count.'

Leong forced the brace back into Killigrew's mouth, and laid a large silk handkerchief over his face. He prodded the centre of the handkerchief to create a dip in Killigrew's mouth, and started to pour water on it in a steady stream from one of the buckets.

The pressure of the water forced the handkerchief down past Killigrew's tongue, sliding past his uvula and making him gag. Water seeped through the silk to trickle down his throat, but the worst of it was that sac of water blocking his mouth, sliding obscenely into his oesophagus to cut off his breathing. He wanted to retch and gasp for breath at the same time, but could not. He was suffocating, choking and drowning, all at the same time.

But you can't drown, he told himself. *You were born with a caul on your head.* The ludicrousness of that thought – he was not remotely superstitious – made him want to laugh. He clung on to it, something to focus on to take his mind from the vile sensation of the water-bulging silk in his throat. He struggled to turn his head in the vice, to pull his arms free from the restraints, anything, *anything* to bring it to an end. Had he known which of Russia's maritime fortresses Napier intended to attack next – and had he been in a position to speak – he would gladly have blurted it out there and then. The room spun around him. He felt himself blacking out. Caul or no caul, he knew he was drowning. For all Leong's supposed expertise he was going to kill him before he even had a chance to tell Nekrasoff what he did not know . . .

The water stopped and the handkerchief was withdrawn from his mouth. With tears streaming from his eyes, he gasped the sweet, sweet air into his lungs, and presently Nekrasoff's smug, smiling face swam into his hazy vision, his eyebrows raised quizzically. Killigrew tried to talk, but the brace in his mouth prevented him from articulating.

'Remove the brace,' ordered Nekrasoff.

Leong complied.

'Kronstadt,' sobbed Killigrew. 'The next target is Kronstadt.' God, he hoped he was wrong.

Nekrasoff nodded. 'Do it again, Leong. Longer, this time.'

After supper, Captain Crichton made his way to the upper deck of the *Ramillies*. The sun sank slowly towards the horizon, lengthening the shadows cast by the pine trees crowding the islands to the north. Carrying a logboard, Lieutenant Masterson followed him on to the quarterdeck to replace Lieutenant Adare as officer of the watch.

'Still no sign of Killigrew and the others?' Crichton asked Adare.

'No, sir.'

Crichton glanced at his fob watch, then took the telescope from the binnacle and levelled it in the direction of Ekenäs. He swapped the telescope for the speaking trumpet, and raised it to his mouth. 'Aloft there! See any small boats to port?'

While keeping an eye out all around the ship, the lookout at the maintop had been keeping a particular watch for the cutter, but nevertheless he raised his telescope to one eye to take yet another look before responding. 'No, sir!'

'I don't understand it,' Crichton remarked to Adare. 'It's

not like Killigrew to be late. You don't suppose something can have happened to him, do you?'

The lieutenant shrugged. 'Any number of things might have detained him, sir.'

Crichton shook his head. 'Not Killigrew. He knows how concerned we'll be for him and his men. If there's no sign of him, it must be something deuced serious.'

The last grain of sand in the hourglass by the ship's bell ran out, and the marine on duty at the belfry rang the bell four times to signify the end of the first dog watch. Adare took his leave of Crichton and carried the log board below to write up the ship's log.

'Permission to take the second cutter to Ekenäs to investigate, sir,' offered Masterson.

'Not granted, Masterson. I can't afford to have you disappear with a second cutter and crew!'

'We have to do *something*, sir.'

'I'm well aware of that,' growled Crichton, and sighed. 'We'll give him another hour. I'll be in my day-room. Pass the word immediately if any of the lookouts should spy a small boat.'

'Aye, aye, sir.'

Crichton returned to his day-room, where General Bodisco sat smoking a cigar, the debris of supper littered on the table before him.

'Still no sign of Commander Killigrew?' Bodisco asked in French.

'None at all. I really cannot conceive what can have become of him.'

Bodisco smirked. 'Perhaps he got lost?'

Crichton glowered. 'Mr Killigrew does not get lost.'

'Nevertheless, the delay does not speak well of British efficiency.'

'If there is a delay, General, I'm sure it is on the Russian side,' Crichton told him frostily.

'And if he does not return?'

'Then you, my dear General, will be taken back to captivity in England.'

'Nothing could suit me better,' said Bodisco, well aware that he would be billeted in comfort with a family of quality. 'Since I lost Bomarsund to your Admiral Napier, I suspect a warmer welcome awaits me in England than the one I shall receive on my return to St Petersburg.'

Molineaux picked up one of the woollen threads he had coated with mortar dust: a cursory examination revealed it was dry now, or at least as dry as it was likely to get in the dank cell.

He rose and looked up at the barred window once more. 'Give us a bunk up, Seth.'

Endicott nodded and stood with his back to the wall below the window. Molineaux stood on his shoulders. 'Go to the door and play crow, Red. Sing out if you hear anyone coming.'

Hughes nodded and moved across to peer through the grille, occasionally glancing over his shoulder to see what Molineaux was doing.

The petty officer looped the mortar-coated thread around one of the bars, and began to saw it gently back and forth.

'That'll never work!' scoffed Vowles.

Molineaux took away the thread to feel the surface of the bar with his fingertips: there was definitely an indentation there. 'How much do you want to bet?' he asked, and began sawing again. It made a slight rasping sound, and whenever he heard guards approaching outside he stopped what he was doing and ducked down out of sight below the window, but resumed his task as soon as the coast was clear. After ten minutes the mortar embedded in the thread had all been worn away, but he had expected nothing less: that was why he had made a dozen such makeshift fret saws.

What was important was that he had made a considerable cut into the bar.

Progress slowed as he neared the centre of the bar. There he had a greater thickness of metal to cut through; for a while it seemed as though his third thread-saw was making no progress at all, even though it was relatively fresh. He sawed away, forcing himself to be patient rather than pull too tightly on the threads, snapping them. His wrists and fingers were soon sore and aching. Then he was past the halfway mark, and the going became easier, until there was only a sliver of metal joining the two ends of the bar; then, with a pop, that too was gone.

He jumped down from Endicott's back. 'Take a breather, Seth,' he ordered, and as the Liverpudlian moved away he stood in his place. 'Climb up on my shoulders, Ben. See if you can bend that bar.'

Iles stood on Molineaux's shoulders, and the petty officer grunted with the effort of supporting his weight. 'Sure, us can bend it,' said Iles.

'Plummy! Now bend it back into position, so it don't look as though there's anything amiss.'

Iles grunted again, and jumped down off Molineaux's shoulders. ''Ow's that?'

Molineaux stood up and examined the bar with a critical eye. There was a marked kink in it now; he told himself he should have waited until two bars were cut through before getting Iles to see if he could bend it. But if Iles could not, then sawing through the second bar would have been so much wasted effort. He told himself the kink was only so obvious because he was looking for it.

'All right, Red, your turn: back to the wall. Andy, take his place at the door.'

While Vowles assumed the duties of lookout at the grille, Hughes stood beneath the window so Molineaux could climb on his shoulders and attack the next bar with another thread. He had used up seven to cut through the first bar; he would have to squeeze every grain of abrasion out of the remaining five if he was to cut through a second without needing to make more.

Crichton was working in his day-room when he heard the ship's bell ring twice. He drained the ink from the nib of his pen, wiped the residue on his blotter, and put on his cocked hat to make his way up on deck.

Lieutenant Lloyd stood on the quarterdeck, on duty as officer of the last dog watch. 'Still no sign of Killigrew and the others, sir.'

Crichton took the telescope from the binnacle and surveyed the waters to the north to see for himself, then used the speaking trumpet to address the lookout at the maintop. 'Aloft there! Any sign of the cutter?'

'No, sir!'

Crichton returned the speaking trumpet to the binnacle. 'Pass the word for Mr Masterson.'

'Aye, aye, sir. Pass the word for Mr Masterson!'

Masterson came on deck so swiftly, Crichton suspected he had been awaiting the summons. The first lieutenant saluted briskly. 'Still no sign of Killigrew, sir?'

'No, Mr Masterson. Does your offer to take the second cutter in to investigate still stand?'

The lieutenant's face lit up. 'Most certainly, sir!'

'Make it so, Mr Masterson.'

'Aye, aye, sir.' Masterson turned to the boatswain. 'Call away the second cutter's crew, Mr Pemberton!'

Once the second cutter was lowered from the davits, Masterson and the crew shinned down the lifelines and took up the oars.

Crichton crossed to the entry port to call down to the lieutenant. 'No heroics, Masterson! Just find out what happened to the others, if you can, and come straight back here. No attempts at rescue or negotiation, do you understand? I don't want to have to send another boat to look for you!'

'Aye, aye, sir.'

The bow man pushed the cutter's head out from the *Ramillies*' side, and Crichton watched as the crew rowed in the direction Killigrew had disappeared with the first cutter twelve hours earlier.

'What if *they* don't come back, sir?' asked Lloyd.

Crichton glowered at him for voicing the thought.

Someone dashed a pail of cold water in Killigrew's face, and he woke up to find himself still strapped in the chair.

'Still with us?' asked Nekrasoff. 'Thought we'd lost you, there.'

Killigrew blinked, wanting to shake the water off his face but unable to move his head. 'Did you have to do that? I was having rather a nice dream.'

'You passed out on us.'

'Sorry. Been doing that rather a lot lately. The surgeon on the *Ramillies* puts it down to overwork.' It was a strain to be his usual flippant self during the ordeal, but he was damned if he would let the Russians think he was weakening; even if he was. Every man has his breaking point, and Killigrew was getting close to his. The problem was, even if he reached it, what could he tell them?

'Just tell me the truth about where Napier's next attack will be, and the suffering will come to an end,' said Nekrasoff. 'It isn't that much to ask, is it?'

'Kronstadt.' Killigrew closed his eyes. He felt as though he had been put through the wringer. 'How many times do I have to tell you? It's Kronstadt.'

'That six times now,' said Leong.

Nekrasoff sighed. 'I think the only thing we've established today is that Napier's next attack will *not* be against Kronstadt. Still, that only leaves Sveaborg and Reval. You know something? I'm starting to think he really *doesn't* know.'

Leong removed the clamp from Killigrew's head, and started to unbuckle Killigrew's right leg.

'What are you doing?' demanded Nekrasoff.

'You no want him back in cell?' asked Leong.

176

'Good heavens, no! I no longer have any use for him. Just kill him.'

It seemed to take Molineaux for ever to saw through the second bar, and yet somehow the tenth thread-saw had more life in it than any of the others. He did not even need the twelfth: the second bar was sawn through before he had been using the eleventh for more than a couple of minutes. He pressed his face up against the bars: he could just make out half a dozen guards patrolling the gallery, but they did not seem to be paying too much attention to what was going on in the courtyard below – not that there was much to see, yet – and he doubted they would be able to see much in the gathering gloom as the sun sank towards the horizon, casting the courtyard into deep shadow.

He jumped down from Hughes' back. 'Stay there a moment, Red. Ben, can you bend those bars right up?'

'Consider it done.' Iles climbed on Hughes' shoulders and bent them right back. He jumped down again. 'You go first, Wes. You earned it.'

'All right. The rest of you wait here until I signal. I'll take a look-see, make sure the coast is clear and see if I can get my bearings.'

Molineaux climbed on Iles' shoulders and pulled himself up through the remaining bars. It was a tight squeeze to get his broad shoulders through – he had nasty visions of being stuck there when a patrol came by, and the Russians amusing themselves by kicking his head in – but at last he was through. He crawled quickly across to one of the *telezhki* parked nearby and hid between the wheels before any of the guards above saw him. Glancing back across to the low window, he saw Endicott watching him anxiously. He was about to wave for the Liverpudlian to follow him when he heard a sound from one of the doors leading out of the keep: someone coming. He signalled for Endicott to stay put.

The legs of four more guards emerged from the door and

crossed to stand beside the *telezhka* where Molineaux was hidden. At first he thought he had been spotted and they had come to get him. But they just stood there, talking and laughing amongst themselves in their incomprehensible gibberish.

Endicott was mugging at him from the window: *Now what do we do?*

Molineaux mugged back: *How should I know?*

What they needed was some kind of diversion.

A shot sounded from the round tower above the courtyard. None of the guards moved, as if it was nothing out of the ordinary. Molineaux heard a lucifer being struck, and saw a pool of light on the cobbles around the Russians' legs as they lit a cigarette. Then he saw three more pairs of boots emerge from the keep, one of them the brightly polished boots of an officer. They crossed to the carriage and disappeared. A moment later, the carriage was driven out of the courtyard, the hoofs and wheels rumbling on the wooden bridge beyond.

With a sick, sinking feeling, Molineaux realised that the first of the prisoners had just been executed.

IX

Escape from Raseborg

8.30 p.m.–8.55 p.m., Thursday 17 August

Nekrasoff left the circular chamber and signalled for Usti-movich to accompany him, leaving Leong alone with Killi-grew, the commander still strapped to the chair. The Siberian drew the pistol from his belt and pulled back the hammer.

Feigning semi-consciousness with the upper half of his body, Killigrew struggled to free his right leg from the half-undone buckle. There was some give in it, enough to reassure him that with a bit of effort on his part he could work his leg free, given time. But Leong was already aiming the pistol at his forehead.

Killigrew clamped his mouth shut and expelled air force-fully through his nostrils. One of the cork nose plugs went wide, but the other caught Leong in one eye just as his finger tightened on the trigger. Killigrew felt the blast scorch his cheek as the bullet slammed into the plush leather beside his head. Leong dropped the pistol and clapped a hand to his face with a cry. With a supreme effort, Killigrew dragged his right leg free and slammed the sole of his boot into Leong's face. The Siberian was thrown back against the wall, and sank to the floor amidst the unused pails of water.

Killigrew's hands were strapped to the chair on either side of his head, but by straining his neck he was able to grip one of the leather straps between his teeth and pull it free of the buckle. Once he had got one hand free, he unfastened the other, and was about to release his left leg when Leong came at him again with a dagger.

Killigrew caught him by the wrist and the two of them struggled. The commander was stronger. He forced the blade down towards his restrained leg, using the metal to saw through the leather strap. Leong dropped the knife and chopped Killigrew across the neck with what, from his time in the Orient, he recognised to be a *wu-yi* blow. The commander felt agony lance through his neck and up into his skull. He rolled over and dropped to the floor, but Leong flipped nimbly over the foot of the chair and drove another *wu-yi* blow into his chest. A high kick slammed Killigrew back against the far wall with the distinct impression that at least three of his ribs had been broken. As Leong came at him again, Killigrew tried a little *wu-yi* of his own, hacking at the Siberian's neck with the edge of his right hand. Clutching his throat, Leong spun away from him with a gasp.

'Good Lord!' exclaimed Killigrew, staring at his own right hand in disbelief. 'This *wu-yi* stuff really works!'

But Leong rallied and came at him again. Killigrew sidestepped his next punch, caught him by the arm and slammed him against the wall. He crooked an arm around the Siberian's throat, gripping him in a half nelson, and forced his face down into one of the unused pails. The water bubbled as Leong gasped, struggling furiously to break free of Killigrew's grip. The commander held him there with his face immersed in the pail, pressing his throat against the rim of the bucket. Leong's struggles subsided, but Killigrew kept his face in the water until there was no possibility that the Siberian could have any breath left in his lungs. Grabbing a fistful of Leong's long hair, he pulled his head out of the pail and gazed into his bulging, lifeless eyes.

Sobbing for breath, Killigrew let the dead man's head flop back into the pail, and leaned against the wall. He felt another wave of nausea sweep over him. *Oh God, not now, please not now . . .*

The dizziness passed. He crossed to the door and opened it a crack, peering out. No sign of any guards. Hearing a sound in the courtyard, he crossed to one of the narrow windows and looked down in time to see Nekrasoff and Ustimovich climb into a carriage parked alongside the four *telezhka*. The coachman whipped up the horses and drove into the tunnel leading out of the castle. Four greatcoated gendarmes stood around in the courtyard below, sharing a cigarette beside one of the *telezhka*, while another six stood on sentry duty on the outer gallery, their sky-blue uniforms pale in the gathering gloom. If the sun was only just setting, it must be about half-past eight, given the length of the summer evenings in the Baltic. Had the torture session really only lasted a few hours?

He was about to leave the chamber when he saw two more guards coming down the gallery towards him. He ducked back out of sight before they saw him, and looked around desperately. Leong's pistol lay on the floor, but a cursory search of the Siberian's body did not turn up any ammunition, just a box of matches. He tucked the pistol in his belt anyway, and picked up two of the empty pails.

By the time he emerged from the chamber, the two guards were only a few feet away, but they were not expecting to see a prisoner on the loose. '*Dobryi den*',' Killigrew greeted them cheerfully.

'*Dobryi den*',' they replied instinctively, still taking in his dishevelled appearance.

He brought the two pails up sharply on either side of one guard's head. The man crumpled. As the other struggled to unsling his musket, Killigrew drew the empty pistol from his belt and pressed the muzzle against his jugular. Ashen-faced, the guard raised his hands. Killigrew took the musket from him, handed him the unloaded pistol in exchange, and slammed the musket's stock into his jaw.

He dragged the two unconscious guards back into the chamber one after the other. Picking the one closest to his own build, he stripped off his boots, trousers, tunic, and greatcoat, exchanging them for his own battered half-boots, tattered trousers and sodden tailcoat. At least the gendarmes of the Third Section seemed to have a better standard of personal hygiene than the Russian soldiers he had met at Bomarsund. He put on the gendarme's helmet – something between a shako and a *képi* – slung both their muskets over one shoulder, and pocketed Leong's matches.

He made his way downstairs to the great hall and took an unlit oil-lamp from a wall niche. Removing the stopper from the reservoir, he poured the contents all over the wooden floor, struck a match, and threw it down into the still-spreading puddle of oil. It ignited at once, the bright yellow flames leaping high towards the ceiling.

He staggered out into the courtyard, pretending to cough and retch. '*Pozhar! Pozhar!*' he cried out: Fire, fire!

The guards at once broke away from their positions to investigate. As the four men who had been sharing a cigarette rushed past Killigrew and into the great hall – the flickering flames showed clearly through the crumbling windows – one of them paused and put a solicitous hand on the commander's shoulder. '*Ty v poryadke?*'

'*Da, da!*' Still coughing and retching – with one hand raised to his mouth to help hide his face – Killigrew waved the man away. The Russian hurried into the keep and Killigrew slipped down the stairs to the dungeons. He was making his way along the passage when someone grabbed him from behind, snaking an arm round his neck and half-choking him.

'Savvy English, Ivan?' a familiar voice hissed in his ear.

'Molineaux! For God's sake, let go! It's me, Killigrew.'

'You don't sound anything like Killigrew.'

'Neither would you, with someone half choking you!'

After a moment's hesitation, Molineaux released him, dragging the muskets from his shoulder. He slammed Killigrew against the wall and covered him with one of the muskets.

'Lumme! It *is* you, sir! Sorry about that: didn't granny you with them Russki togs on. What are you doing dressed like that, anyhow?'

Killigrew rubbed his neck ruefully. 'I didn't think it would be a capital notion to wander around Third Section headquarters dressed as a British naval officer—'

'*Stoi!*' a voice called down the corridor behind them. '*Chto sdaesh'sya!*'

The two of them turned to see another guard there, aiming a musket at them. '*Kapat' mushket!*'

'He wants you to drop the muskets,' explained Killigrew.

'Should I?'

'I think it would be safest, for now.'

Molineaux lowered the muskets to the floor.

'*Otstuplenie!*'

'Translation, sir?' asked Molineaux.

'He wants us to step back.'

Killigrew and Molineaux backed off. The guard advanced until he stood over the muskets. '*Chem vy zanimaetes' éto mes?*'

Endicott stepped up behind the guard and prodded him in the back. 'Hands up, Ivan. Handsomely does it!'

'*Chto sdaesh'sya!*' Killigrew translated helpfully. But the guard had got the gist of it, and spread his arms, holding his musket by the barrel in one hand. Endicott snatched it from him. Molineaux hurried forward and snatched up the other two muskets, tossing one to Killigrew and smashing the stock of the other into the Russian's jaw. The guard crumpled, and Endicott ripped a ring of keys from his belt, throwing them to Killigrew. The commander caught them in his left hand and used them to unlock the furthermost door. He threw it open,

183

and Lord Bullivant, Charlton and Dahlstedt looked up at him.

'Killigrew?' exclaimed Bullivant. 'What the devil are you doing, dressed like that?'

'I'm on my way to a fancy-dress ball,' Killigrew snapped back impatiently.

'Well, now you're here, you can take me to see the feller in charge of this establishment. I've got a few choice words to say to him about the abominable way we've been treated, I can tell you!'

'I've got a better idea,' said Killigrew.

'Oh?'

'Let's get the devil out of here! Herre Dahlstedt, are you all right? Can you walk?'

The Finn nodded. 'I think so.'

'Good. Give him a hand, Charlton.'

Killigrew withdrew from the cell and crossed to the next door. Glancing through the grille, he saw Lady Bullivant, Araminta, and a woman in a maid's uniform: the same maid Molineaux had had a run-in with on board the *Milenion*. Killigrew unlocked the door, and they looked up as he threw it open.

Withdrawing the keys, he threw them to Molineaux. 'Get the others out.'

'Aye, aye, sir.'

Killigrew turned back to the ladies. 'Are you all right? Did they hurt you?'

'I'll say they did!' Araminta retorted indignantly. 'One of those Russian brutes gripped me *quite tightly* by the arm! I'm sure I must have the most horrid bruise!'

'A bruise! Good gracious, how absolutely terrible for you! God damn it, I'll give you something worse than a bruise, if you don't get off your backsides and out of that cell at once!'

'Now really, Mr Killigrew!' protested Lady Bullivant. 'There's no need for that sort of language, I'm sure . . .' Her eyes flickered past Killigrew and widened in alarm, and Araminta's hands flew to her mouth to stifle a scream.

He turned to see what had frightened them, expecting to see a dozen Russians coming towards them, but it was only Molineaux, Endicott, Hughes and Iles. Killigrew had to admit, between Molineaux's earring, Endicott's bandanna, Hughes' pock-marked face and Iles' eye patch, they did look less like four ratings of Her Majesty's Navy than four ruffians straight from the pages of Ellms' *The Pirates Own Book*.

'It's all right, they're with me,' he hastened to reassure the ladies. 'This is Petty Officer Molineaux, Leading Seaman Endicott, and Able Seamen Hughes and Iles.'

Araminta recovered quickly from her fright. 'Mr Molineaux and I have already met. Good evening, Mr Molineaux.'

The petty officer grinned and touched his bonnet with a finger. ''Evening, miss.'

Killigrew had forgotten they had met three years earlier, when Lord Hartcliffe and his friends had been taking part in the Squadron Cup at Cowes. One of Hartcliffe's friends had fallen ill at the last moment, and Molineaux had been drafted in as a replacement. Araminta had come on board as a friend of Hartcliffe's; that had been the first time Killigrew had met her.

She glanced at Killigrew. 'I might have known he'd've dragged *you* into this,' she told the petty officer.

'Where would Aeneas be without his faithful Achates?' asked Killigrew.

'Or Don Quixote without his Sancho Panza?' Araminta suggested, smiling sweetly.

Killigrew laughed at that, and was about to turn away when Molineaux called out a warning. Killigrew whirled in time to see the guard the petty officer had knocked out rising to his feet, drawing a large bayonet from his belt. He charged at Killigrew, swinging the blade.

There was no time for the commander to unsling his musket. He jumped back beyond the reach of the blade's arcing tip, and caught the man by the wrist. The Russian slammed him back against the wall and tried to force the blade into his stomach. Killigrew twisted his wrist and turned the bayonet back, pushing the blade home in his opponent's stomach with a massive effort. The Russian staggered back, clutching the protruding haft with blood pouring over his hands.

Araminta raised her knuckles to her mouth and let out a little cry of fright. *Oh, Jesus, don't you dare faint on me*, Killigrew thought sourly. But whatever its faults, the British aristocracy were built of sterner stuff than that.

Lord Bullivant stared down at the dead Russian in astonishment. 'Good God, man! I believe you've killed him!'

'I believe I have,' Killigrew agreed drily.

'You oh-kay, sir?' As the others poured out of their cell to where Endicott was distributing their belts and bootlaces, Molineaux came back down the corridor to investigate Araminta's shocked cry.

'Yes, no thanks to you! Can't you knock someone out for more than a few seconds?'

Seeing the dead Russian, Molineaux grinned. 'Sorry, sir. Forgot how thick these Russkis' skulls are.'

'Look, what the devil's going on here?' demanded Lord Bullivant. 'We can't just go . . . *breaking out* . . . of this place. I'm starting to think we're in a ticklish enough position as it is, without you navy types making it worse by murdering guards!'

'We're pressed for time, my lord,' Killigrew explained, 'so I'm going to keep this short and simple, and not spare the ladies' sensibilities with euphemistic circumlocutions. If we don't get out of here now, the Russians are going to kill us all.'

'Don't be ridiculous, man! They wouldn't dare!'

'They've already tried to kill me once. You were next on their list; once they'd tortured you to extract a confession of espionage. Then they were going to kill the others, and tell our government that we all died in a cholera outbreak.'

'But that's outrageous! Are you quite certain you haven't

misconstrued the situation, somehow?'

'You know something, my lord? That very same thought occurred to me. I tried to ask Colonel Nekrasoff to explain it to me again, just to make sure I hadn't misunderstood him, but it was rather difficult to articulate my concerns on account of how one of his minions was torturing me at the time. Now, you can stay here, and when the rest of us get back to the fleet I'll send a report to Lord Clarendon suggesting that he protest to the Russian government in the strongest terms; or you can shut up, do exactly as I tell you, and maybe – just *maybe* – I can get you, your family and your crew back to safety. So if you'll excuse me, my lord . . .' Killigrew turned and made his way towards the stairs.

'You damnable, jumped-up young whippersnapper!' Bullivant called after him. 'How *dare* you talk to me like that? I'll have you dismissed the service for this!'

'Go and take care of his lordship for me, would you?' Killigrew asked Hughes as he pushed his way through the crowd of sailors gathered at the foot of the stairs. 'If he gives you any trouble, you have my permission to deck him. I've a feeling he's going to be a lot easier to handle unconscious than conscious.'

'Aye, aye, sir.' Hughes grinned; the idea of getting to punch a member of the aristocracy held considerable appeal for the Welsh communist.

'Molineaux, Endicott, you two come with me. The rest of you follow. And keep silence!' Killigrew unslung his musket and climbed up the stairs. He paused at the doorway at the top, motioning for the others to keep back, and peered out across the courtyard. The blazing keep above threw a hellish, flickering glow over the scene. There were no guards in evidence – with any luck they would all be in the keep, fighting the blaze – but they were not going to be able to get horses hitched to enough *telezhki* to get them all back to Ekenäs without someone noticing.

Killigrew glanced back down the stairs. 'Vowles, Iles – to me!'

The two men squeezed past the others to join the commander with Molineaux and Endicott at the top of the stairs. Killigrew handed his musket to the coxswain. 'Molineaux, give your musket to Iles so he and Vowles can keep us covered.'

'What are we going to do, sir?'

'There are two dozen of us, all told. With two men on the driving board of each *telezhka* the rest of us should be able to fit into two of them. There isn't time to harness horses to any more . . .'

'Eh, what's a *telezhka*, sir?' asked Endicott.

'One of those carriages,' Killigrew explained patiently.

'If we leave any of them carriages, sir, the Ivans will only use them to chase us,' Molineaux pointed out.

'Not if we sabotage them first. Captain Thornton!' he called back down the stairs. 'Is there a carpenter in your crew?'

'What do you want a carpenter for?'

'I haven't got time for foolish questions, Thornton. Just answer the question, is there or isn't there?'

Thornton sighed. 'Go see what he wants, Burgess.'

One of the Milenions climbed up the stairs. 'Jack Burgess, sir.'

'See those two tel— those two carriages on the left?'

'Aye, sir.'

'Think you can sabotage them?'

Burgess rubbed his jaw, and grinned. 'Aye, I think I might be able to manage that. I'll need a couple of shipmates to bear a hand, though.'

'Take your pick.'

'Ben! Ned! Show a leg, there!' Burgess turned back to Killigrew. 'What about the Russians? You're not expecting us to—'

'Vowles, Iles and Endicott will take care of the Russians.

188

Vowles, Iles, I want you two to go up on the gallery. There are doors leading out on to it from either end of the keep. Vowles, you take the one on the left, Iles can take the other. Endicott, you take the door at ground level. Try to kill 'em so they fall where you can get their muskets. And don't waste any shots. Use your stocks if you can.'

'Aye, aye, sir.'

'What about me, sir?' asked Molineaux.

'You're going to help me hitch the horses to the carriages.'

'Me, sir?'

'You have a problem with that, Molineaux?'

'You know I don't like animals, sir.'

'They're horses, Molineaux, not polar bears.'

'Even so, sir . . . I don't know the first thing about all them reins and harnesses and such like . . . there must be someone here who'd be more use to you than I would.'

Killigrew sighed. 'All right, all right! Anyone here got any experience of handling horses?'

The sailors exchanged glances. No one volunteered.

'Come on!' Killigrew said impatiently. 'I want someone to help me hitch them to the carriages, not to go bareback riding at Astley's!'

'What about me?' Araminta reminded him. 'I can ride.'

'Very kind of you to offer, Miss Maltravers, but there are going to be people shooting at us. This really isn't a job for a woman. Come on, damn it, surely one of you can hitch a horse to a carriage?'

When no one said anything, Lady Bullivant started to climb the stairs. Her husband caught her by her arm. 'Hester! What are you doing? You heard what he said: this is no job for a woman.'

She jerked her arm free of his grip. 'Unfortunately, it seems there are no men capable here at present. Come along, Araminta.'

The two ladies climbed the stairs. 'I'm afraid you're stuck with us, Mr Killigrew.'

He sighed. 'It seems I have no choice. All right: on the word go, Vowles, Endicott and Iles will go first. Then, the two ladies will come with me to the stables: walk, don't run, understand? Then Burgess and his crew can get to work on the other carriages while we hitch the horses to the two on the right. Charlton, you look after Dahlstedt: without him, we'll never get back to the fleet. Hughes, stay with Lord Bullivant and the maid. Thornton, you and the rest of your men help Vowles, Endicott and Iles keep the guards back. Divide your men into three teams, one for each door.'

Thornton nodded. 'Mr Mackenzie, take Ogilby and Todd and help Vowles; Mr Uren, you take Doc and Searle and help Mr Iles; O'Leary, you're with Endicott and me.'

'Molineaux, you can help Captain Thornton and O'Leary,' said Killigrew. 'Now, does everyone know what he's doing? Speak now, or for ever hold your peace. Right, let's go! Molineaux, your team first.'

The petty officer ran out of the door with Endicott, Thornton and O'Leary. As they pressed themselves up against the wall on either side of the door leading into the keep, Vowles' and Iles' teams followed, mounting the wooden stairs to the gallery. Iles turned right at the top and dropped to one knee immediately outside the door leading into the round tower at the end of the keep, with Uren, Doc and Searle at his back, while Vowles, Mackenzie, Ogilby and Todd raced the length of the gallery to the door at the other end. So far, the Russians seemed to have their hands full fighting the blaze in the keep.

'Ladies, if you'll come with me?' Killigrew stepped out of the doorway and strolled casually across to the stables with Araminta and her mother. 'If you two can start bringing the horses out in pairs, I'll hitch them to the carriages.'

They nodded, their faces pale in the orange glow of the fire.

'When the shooting starts, just drop to the ground and stay there,' Killigrew instructed them.

'Drop to the ground?' Lady Bullivant said indignantly.

'I'm sure you can buy new gowns once you're safely back in England.'

'It's not our *gowns* that concern me, Mr Killigrew. Do you really think it's *wise* to lie on the ground in a courtyard full of horses when there's shooting going on? The horses are certain to be frightened and skittish. I hardly think we can rely on them to look where they're putting their hoofs, do you?'

She had a point, damn her. 'All right, just . . . duck behind the carriages. The side away from the keep: that's where the shooting will be coming from.'

'Really, Mr Killigrew?' Lady Bullivant said acerbically. 'I would never have guessed.'

Flinching under her sarcasm, Killigrew left to fetch the horses and crossed back to the *telezhki*. Burgess, Fuller and Yorath were already hard at work, sabotaging the far two. Araminta brought out the first pair of horses, and Killigrew began to hitch them to the second *telezhka*. 'Get back inside and bring out two more horses,' he told her, his fingers fumbling with the traces. 'The less time you spend out here, the happier I'll be.'

'Is my company really so objectionable?'

'All I'm thinking about right now is your safety.'

She smiled. 'I was aware of that, Kit.' She turned and hurried back to the stables.

Kit. It had been a long time since she had called him that: two and a half years ago, the two of them lying in one another's arms in his seedy rooms in Paddington – hardly a fitting venue for a viscount's daughter, but one of the few places they could be alone together – while her parents thought she was out riding in Hyde Park; her maidservant, acting as her chaperone, was happy to be complicit to the deceit, as she had a sweetheart of her own to spend time with. Realising that perhaps he had underestimated Araminta, Killigrew stared after her . . . and then remembered this was hardly the time for staring at pretty girls.

191

He had resumed hitching the horses when Lieutenant Kizheh ran out of the keep carrying two empty pails. Seeing Killigrew, he stopped halfway to the well. He dropped his pails and tried to draw the sword scabbarded at his hip.

Endicott stepped up behind him and smashed the stock of his musket into the back of his neck. Kizheh crumpled.

Endicott unbuckled the lieutenant's sword belt. 'Sir?'

Killigrew broke off from hitching the horses to see what the Liverpudlian wanted.

'Look familiar, sir?' Endicott tossed belt, scabbard and sword across to him.

The commander caught it by the scabbard: his own scabbard, his own dress-sword. 'That it does, Endicott. Much obliged!' He buckled the belt over the Third Section greatcoat he was wearing and resumed hitching the horses.

Endicott took Kizheh's pistol and tossed it to Molineaux, who caught it deftly. 'Get him out of sight, chop chop!'

Thornton and O'Leary grabbed the unconscious Kizheh and dragged him to one side. 'Tie him up and gag him!' ordered Killigrew. 'We'll need to take him with us.'

'What for?' demanded Thornton.

'Do *you* know the way back to Ekenäs from here?'

Lady Bullivant was patiently waiting with two more horses by the time Killigrew had finished hitching the first pair to one of the *telezhki*. He yoked those two in front, and she headed back to the stables.

Killigrew saw Araminta appear with the next pair. He signalled for her to stay put at the door to the stables. 'Wait until I'm ready for them!' he hissed. Understanding, she nodded.

Above the gate, another gendarme tumbled over the railing of the gallery and fell to the courtyard with a scream that was sharply cut off when his head smacked against the cobbles: Iles' handiwork.

'Get that gun!' the seaman hissed at Attwood, who nodded and hurried down the steps to retrieve the gendarme's musket.

Two more gendarmes appeared in the doorway facing Iles. He shot one in the chest, and the other levelled his musket at him. Iles, Uren and Searle all raised their hands. Then Attwood threw the musket up to them. Iles snatched it out of the air and fired a moment after the Russian did. When the smoke cleared, Iles was standing, but Uren crouched over Searle, who seemed to be wounded.

No more Russians appeared at the door opposite Iles. He quickly reloaded the musket he was holding, and passed the other two he had now acquired to Attwood, who had climbed back up the stairs. 'Know how to load these?' he asked, pointing his own musket at the door ready for the next gendarme to show his face.

Attwood shook his head.

Uren took the muskets from him. 'I'll do it. See what you can do for Dick.'

Killigrew signalled for Araminta to bring the next pair of horses, and began to hitch them to the second *telezhka*. As he did so, Lady Bullivant arrived with the last pair of horses and began to hitch them in front of the first pair.

'I can do that,' said Killigrew. 'Get back out of sight.'

'Many hands make light work,' she retorted. 'And I believe that time is of the essence?'

'You know what you're doing?'

'I should hope so. I've seen my coachman do it enough times. Give me a hand, girl,' she added to her daughter. 'Pass me that trace . . . no, not that one, the one next to it . . . good girl. Now fasten this buckle . . .'

Startled by the sharp reports of the muskets, one of the horses reared, neighing. Stepping to one side to avoid its forelegs, Lady Bullivant managed to catch it by the bridle. She hauled it back down, calming it, with the aid of her daughter, before it could spook the others.

Half a dozen gendarmes charged out of the keep on to the gallery above them. Vowles shot one in the chest, then took a bullet in the face and sprawled on the planks. Mackenzie grappled another gendarme, while Ogilby turned and ran, with Todd hard on his heels. Mackenzie was pushed over the gallery rail to fall to the cobbles below with a yell, and the five remaining gendarmes pursued Ogilby and Todd around the gallery. The foremost of them raised his musket and fired: Todd flung out his arms and stumbled, falling to the boards without so much as a cry.

'Molineaux!' yelled Killigrew. 'We've got a situation developing on the gallery!'

'Leave it to me, sir.' The petty officer ran across to where Burgess, Fuller and Yorath were sabotaging the wheels of one of the unhitched *telezhki*, and pointed to the other. 'Push that one up against the door!' he snapped, pointing across to where Endicott stood on guard with Thornton and O'Leary.

Burges, Fuller and Yorath put their backs to the *telezhka* and, seeing their intention, Thornton and O'Leary ran to help them while Endicott kept the door covered with his musket. Molineaux was already halfway across the courtyard, running to a point below the gallery where Ogilby was still fleeing from the Russians.

'Charlie!' yelled Molineaux.

Ogilby looked down, and the petty officer threw Kizheh's pistol up to him. Ogilby fumbled the catch, and the pistol fell to the boards.

'Bloody lubber!' Molineaux climbed on to a low wall and scrambled up on to the roof of the stables.

As the gendarmes bore down on Ogilby, he managed to grasp the pistol and whirled, firing. One of the Russians clapped a hand to his head and staggered back with blood running between his fingers. The other four charged on.

Molineaux jumped from the roof of the stables, caught hold of the bottom of the gallery and swung there for a moment, before pulling himself nimbly up and over the railing to stand between Ogilby and the gendarmes. The leading gendarme did not see him land on the gallery until it was too late. Molineaux caught the muzzle of his musket, forced it aside, and then gripped it in both hands. He pressed the barrel against the Russian's throat, choking him against the railing. His left hand found the trigger guard and he slipped his thumb through it, pulling the trigger to shoot the next gendarme in the belly. He jerked the musket out of the half-strangled gendarme's hands and swung it like a club to bring down a third, who was too busy stumbling over the body of his fallen comrade to pay attention to what Molineaux was doing.

The last gendarme stopped and backed off. He raised his musket to his shoulder and aimed at Molineaux. The petty officer froze, helpless. A musket barked. The gendarme twisted sharply and crumpled against the railing.

Molineaux glanced down to where Endicott stood in the courtyard below, the muzzle of his musket wreathed with smoke. The petty officer waved his thanks, and then the half-strangled gendarme tried to grapple him. Molineaux rammed the muzzle of the musket he was still holding into the gendarme's stomach. The Russian doubled up in agony, and Molineaux pushed him over the rail with minimal effort.

'Nice work, Molineaux!' Killigrew called up. 'Look to Todd and the cox'n!'

'Aye, aye, sir.' Keeping one eye on the door at the far end, Molineaux ran along the gallery to where Bullivant's steward had fallen. He crouched over him for a moment, and then stood up and continued the rest of the way around to where Vowles lay.

Killigrew and the two ladies had almost finished hitching the team of horses to the second *telezhka*. 'Captain Thornton! Would you be so good as to bring the others up from the dungeons?' he asked.

With one of the unhitched *telezhki* now up against the door of the keep, Thornton nodded and ran across to the doorway leading down to the cellars. He gestured frantically for Charlton and Iles to bring up Dahlstedt, Lord Bullivant and the maid.

A gendarme clutching a musket tried to crawl out between the wheels of the *telezhka* up against the door of the keep. O'Leary snatched the gun from him, tossed it to Endicott, then grabbed the gendarme by the collar and dragged him out. He punched the Russian in the stomach, and kneed him in the face.

'Sir!' Molineaux was standing over Vowles at the far end of the gallery. 'Andy and the steward have both slipped their cables, but I think Mr Mackenzie is still with us.' He pointed down to where the *Milenion*'s mate sat at the foot of the keep immediately below him, nursing an injured arm.

'Mr Charlton, look to Mr Mackenzie,' ordered Killigrew.

The assistant surgeon nodded and ran across to where the mate lay, while Molineaux swung himself over the rail of the gallery and dropped down beside him.

Iles came down the stairs from the gallery at the other end, followed by Uren and Attwood, supporting Searle, who had a bloody handkerchief pressed to the side of his throat. 'Not much point us stayin' up there, sir,' said Iles.

Killigrew glanced up at the door leading into the round tower from the gallery and immediately saw what Iles meant: flames roared out of the doorway, hungrily searching for air. Indeed, the whole keep was ablaze now: if there were any more Russians left alive in there, they were not coming out that way.

'Anything else I can do, sir?' asked Iles.

'Yes! Nip down to the dungeons and fetch a couple of lamps from the wall niches.'

'Aye, aye, sir.'

As Iles hurried away, Killigrew turned to the Bullivants and their maid. 'You'd best climb aboard, ladies.'

'And who's going to drive the carriages?' asked Lady Bullivant.

'Well, I thought I'd drive the first . . .'

'And?'

He sighed. 'Think you can drive one of these, Lady Bullivant?'

'I can drive a pony-chaise.'

'This is a little larger.'

'As you said to me before, I'm afraid you don't have much choice.'

'Your logic is impeccable, ma'am. All right, you get on the driving board of that one. Help her up, Endicott. Leading Seaman Endicott will look after you, ma'am.'

'Come on, missus.' Endicott clasped his hands together before him to make a step-up for her. 'Put your foot here and I'll give you a bunk-up.'

'Do you mind?' she snapped back. 'I'm Viscountess Bullivant: you address me as "my lady" or "ma'am", not "missus". I'll have you know my ancestors came across from Normandy with William the Conqueror.'

'Oh, aye?' Endicott was singularly unimpressed. 'Bloody immigrants, eh?'

Killigrew chuckled. 'Molineaux?'

'Sir?'

'I'll drive. Once we're through the gateway, I want you to get the roof. Your job is to keep an eye on Lady Bullivant. If anything happens to her – if she falls so much as fifty feet behind us – you tell me at once, hoist in?'

'Aye, aye, sir.'

Killigrew turned to Lady Bullivant's maid. 'What's your name, miss?'

Terrified by the heat, smoke and bloodshed all around her, she curtsied in confusion. 'Nicholls, sir.'

'How do you feel about the sight of blood, Nicholls?'

'Can't say I'm over-partial to it, sir.'

'Do you think you could help Mr Charlton with the wounded?'

'I'll try, sir.'

'It's all right, Nicholls.' Smiling, Araminta took the maid's hand and gave it a comforting squeeze. 'I'll help you.'

'God bless you, miss,' said Killigrew. 'You'd best climb up now. You too, my lord.'

'I just want you to know this is an absolute shambles,' snorted Bullivant. 'You're a disgrace, Killigrew, an utter disgrace.'

'Feel free to write a formal complaint to Sir Charles Napier if we manage to get out of here alive,' Killigrew told him cheerfully. 'Mr Charlton! Could you bring the wounded over here? Do what you can for them on the drive back to Ekenäs.'

The assistant surgeon ran his fingers through his hair in agitation. 'Sir, I've got one man bleeding like a stuck pig, another with shattered hands and a third with a compound fracture of the left forearm. May I ask what you expect me to do without surgical tools or bandages while I'm being bounced about in the back of one of these damned filthy carriages?'

'Improvise, Mr Charlton. That's what the navy's best at.' As Iles arrived with two oil-lamps, Killigrew took one from him and handed it to the assistant surgeon. 'You may need this.'

Charlton took the oil-lamp and stared at it, shaking his head.

'What 'bout this'n, sir?' asked Iles, holding up the other.

'Back of the other carriage. Once we've cleared the gate I want you on the roof, keeping a lookout for pursuers.' Killigrew took up a musket from a dead Russian and handed it to the seaman. 'You see them coming, signal Molineaux, who'll be on the roof of my carriage.'

'Aye, aye, sir.'

'The rest of you, grab all the muskets and cartouche boxes you can and get in the back of the other carriage!' Killigrew shouted to the men who still milled about in the courtyard. 'I want them loaded and primed by the time we get to Ekenäs. No, not you, Hughes. You can ride in front with me.'

'Aye, aye, sir.'

Killigrew strode across to where Thornton and O'Leary had left Kizheh bound hand and foot. He hauled the lieutenant to his feet and pulled off his gag.

'You really think you're going to get away with this?' demanded Kizheh.

'See for yourself, if you don't believe me. You're coming with us. You do know the way back to Ekenäs, don't you?'

Kizheh sneered. 'Hum it, and I'll join in on the second chorus.'

'Musket, Hughes!'

The Welshman threw his musket across to Killigrew, who levelled it at Kizheh's head.

The lieutenant sneered again. 'You're not going to shoot me.'

'No?'

'If I'm dead, who'll show you the way to Ekenäs?'

'If you refuse to help us, you're not much use to me, so I might as well shoot you. But no one said anything about killing you. Where's the nearest surgeon?'

Kizheh grinned. 'Ekenäs.'

'Thought so.' Killigrew lowered his aim and shot him through the foot.

'*Chert!*' Sobbing in agony, Kizheh hopped up and down, clutching his wounded foot as blood dripped from the hole in his boot.

'*Now* you will show us the way to Ekenäs?'

'You . . . you *drachevo*!'

'To tell the truth, there always was some question as to whether or not my parents ever actually married, not that it's any of your business. Help him up on the driving board, Hughes. If he gives you any trouble, feel free to hurt him.'

'Just so long as he can still show us the way to Ekenäs, sir?'

'Precisely so.' Killigrew looked around to make sure no one was being left behind, and crossed to where Lady Bullivant and Endicott sat on the driving board of the other *telezhka*.

'Follow me,' he told Lady Bullivant, 'and don't stop for anything. If you get into difficulties, Molineaux will be

199

watching you; he'll let me know. Ready?'

She nodded.

'Let's go.' Killigrew crossed back to the other *telezhka* and climbed up on to the driving board so that Kizheh was wedged between him and Hughes. The commander lashed the reins across the horses' backs, and drove out through the gateway. On the bridge beyond, he reined in long enough for Molineaux to scramble up on the roof. They then rumbled across the wooden bridge, pausing on the other side until Molineaux reported that Iles was on the second *telezhka*. Killigrew drove on.

Beyond the bridge, they came to a fork in the road. 'Left or right?' Killigrew asked Kizheh.

'Left.'

'You quite sure about that, Ivan?' asked Hughes, pressing the muzzle of his musket to Kizheh's ear.

'Yes! Left, left!'

'It took us about three-quarters of an hour to get here from Ekenäs this afternoon.' Killigrew fumbled in Kizheh's fob pocket for his watch, and glanced at it. 'If we don't get there by ten o'clock, Hughes is going to shoot you in the other foot. If we're not there by quarter past, he'll start on your knee-caps. Do you understand?'

Kizheh hung his head. 'Right,' he muttered sullenly.

Killigrew whipped up the horses, and turned right.

Hughes grinned. 'Looks like we've got ourselves a pilot, sir.'

X

The *Milenion*

8.55 p.m.–10.05 p.m., Thursday 17 August

It was dark by the time the second cutter reached Ekenäs. Even at dusk, the gunners in the battery at Vitsand Sound had had no difficulty in spying the white flag flown by the cutter, and Lieutenant Masterson had no reason to suspect that anything different had happened when Killigrew had passed this way with the first cutter twelve hours earlier.

A section of Russian infantrymen awaited the cutter's crew when they tied up at one of the jetties. Using French, Masterson was able to convey to the young officer in charge of the soldiers that he wished to speak to the district commander.

'You may come alone and unarmed. Your men will have to wait here.'

Masterson nodded and turned back to the men in the cutter. 'Got your watch, Mr Saunders?'

The midshipman who had accompanied him nodded. Masterson checked his own watch. 'It's now two minutes to nine precisely. If I'm not back within an hour, try to slip away and get back to the *Ramillies*, tell the captain what's happened.'

'Yes, sir. Sir . . .?'

'Yes, Mr Saunders?'

'What *has* happened, sir?'

Masterson glanced around the harbour. There was the *Milenion*, tied up at the quayside a short distance away, but there was no sign of the first cutter. 'Damned if I know,' he admitted ruefully.

He was escorted through the streets of Ekenäs to the town hall, where he was made to wait in an annexe with two soldiers standing over him. A clerk sat at a desk, stamping papers. As the minutes ticked past, he watched the clock on the mantelpiece reach quarter-past nine, then half-past. Finally, he heard a carriage pull up on the cobbles outside and presently a man in a sky-blue uniform marched in. The clerk leaped to his feet to salute, and said something in Russian with a nod at Masterson, who also stood up.

The newcomer looked the lieutenant up and down. 'You came here under a flag of truce?' he asked in excellent English.

Masterson nodded. 'Lieutenant Matthew Masterson, HMS *Ramillies*. You are the military commander of this district?'

The newcomer proffered a kid-gloved hand. 'Colonel Radimir Fokavich Nekrasoff, at your service. Please come with me.' He stepped through a door and held it open for Masterson to follow. 'Do take a seat, Mr Masterson,' he said, gesturing to a chair in front of the desk in the office.

Masterson sat down and crossed one leg over the other with a display of nonchalance he was far from feeling. 'I had been given to understand that Lieutenant-General Ramsay was the military governor?'

Smiling, Nekrasoff moved to sit behind the desk. 'General Ramsay is away from headquarters at the moment, on a routine inspection of troops at Karis. May I be of assistance?'

'We'll see,' Masterson replied drily. There was something about Nekrasoff that set his teeth on edge, and he instantly distrusted the man. 'The yacht tied up in the harbour . . .'

'Ah, the *Milenion*. I should have guessed. You must understand that Captain-Lieutenant Count Pechorin captured her as a legitimate prize of war. I should not need to tell you that the merchant ships of an enemy power are fair game, as the depredations of your own navy against this very town have shown. I do not see that the rules of war should apply any differently to a civilian yacht.'

'No one in the British navy would dispute that, Colonel. However, I have been instructed to inform you that Vice Admiral Sir Charles Napier is willing to exchange General Bodisco for Lord Bullivant and his family.'

'I regret to inform you, it is impossible.'

'Impossible? Why? It seems a more than fair exchange to me: a senior-ranking prisoner of war for four civilians.'

'Civilians.' Nekrasoff chuckled, and produced a cigarette case, snapping it open and proffering it to Masterson. 'Cigarette?'

'No, thank you.'

Nekrasoff shrugged, took out a cigarette, and snapped the case shut. He tapped the cigarette against it twice before putting the cigarette in his mouth and returning the case to an inside pocket. He struck a match to light the cigarette, and shook it out before dropping it in the ashtray on the desk. He took a drag and blew a long stream of smoke into the air above Masterson's head.

'Lord Bullivant and his family were arrested on Russian territory. Lord Dallaway was taking photographical pictures. In the chart-room of the *Milenion* were found charts of Russian territorial waters. More than enough to convict Lord Bullivant and Lord Dallaway on charges of espionage, I would have thought.'

Masterson laughed. 'Surely you can't suspect they're spies? All right, they may have acted foolishly. They're what we call "war tourists", the fleet's plagued by them, and if they've got into trouble it's their own damned fault. But to execute them for espionage? Isn't that going a little too far?'

'It is not for me to say, Mr Masterson. The orders have come direct from St Petersburg; my hands are tied. If General Ramsay were here, he would give you the same answer.'

Masterson sighed. He was obviously wasting his time.

'I am sorry to have to send you back to your ship empty-handed, as it were,' said Nekrasoff.

'There is one other thing,' said Masterson. 'Mine isn't the first boat to be sent to negotiate the release of the Bullivants. Commander Christopher Killigrew was sent earlier today, in another cutter. He would have passed Vitsand Sound at about nine o'clock this morning?'

Nekrasoff frowned. 'There was a boat that tried to slip past the battery at nine o'clock, rowed by seamen of the British navy. One of the bodies subsequently dragged from the water was found to be wearing the uniform of a British naval officer—'

Masterson's blood ran cold. 'What do you mean, "dragged from the water" . . .?'

Nekrasoff looked surprised. 'Well, naturally the battery opened fire as soon as the boat was within range. There were no survivors.'

The lieutenant leaped to his feet. 'Do you mean to tell me that your gunners opened fire on a boat flying a flag of truce?'

'Calm yourself, Mr Masterson! I heard nothing about any flag of truce. Indeed, that was my first thought when I heard that a boat had attempted to enter the inlet this morning. But I've spoken to the commander of the battery on the subject and he swears on his mother's soul that the boat flew no such flag.'

'Then the battery commander is a liar, Colonel. I watched the cutter leave the *Ramillies* at eight this morning, and I can assure you that she was flying a white flag plainly enough.'

'Then perhaps the officer in command took it down before he reached Vitsand Sound? What sort of man was he, Mr

Masterson? A daring, reckless fellow? Perhaps he thought he and his crew could rescue the Bullivants without negotiating?'

Masterson frowned. Killigrew certainly had a reputation for being reckless and daring. But surely even he would not be so foolish as to disobey orders in the way that Nekrasoff suggested? He shook his head: reckless, perhaps, but not stupid; and only a stupid man would try to row past a battery of guns at point-blank range in broad daylight without a flag of truce flying.

'I'd like to see the bodies of any of the cutter's crew that may have been recovered.'

'That is not convenient at this time. Rest assured, Mr Masterson, the bodies of any officers that are recovered will be returned to your navy at the earliest convenience.' Nekrasoff rose to his feet and gestured to the door. 'Now, unless there was anything else . . .?'

Masterson was escorted back to where the second cutter was tied up. 'Any news of Mr Killigrew, sir?' asked Saunders.

The lieutenant shook his head and climbed down to take his place in the stern sheets. 'Cast off. Back to the *Ramillies*, lads.'

Hughes was toying hopefully with the trigger of the musket when the first houses at the edge of Ekenäs came into view a few minutes before ten o'clock.

'Which way to the surgeon's house?' Killigrew asked Kizheh.

'Take the next left.' Kizheh's face was screwed up in agony as he clutched his wounded foot. 'Now right . . . it's the last house on the left.'

Killigrew slowed as he passed the house. Grabbing Kizheh by the collar, he threw him from the driving board. As Killigrew lashed the reins and the *telezhka* rattled away, the Russian picked himself up and hobbled about in agony.

'Lady Bullivant and the others still with us, Molineaux?'

Killigrew called over his shoulder.

'Yes, sir,' the petty officer replied. 'In fact, if she's not careful, she's going to run over the Russki . . . oh, bugger! He's seen her, and jumped out of the way.'

It was easy enough to find the harbour from there: in Ekenäs, all roads led to the waterfront. Killigrew drew up in a side street not far from where the *Milenion* was moored, and jumped down from the driving board. He crept forward to the end of the street, and peered around the corner. It was a dark night, with the moon not yet risen and only a faint luminescence in the sky to the north to remind him how close they were to the Arctic Circle, but the deck lamps of the *Atalanta* silhouetted the schooner tied up at the same quay where she had been all day, just beyond the rows of upturned fishing boats and nets drying on frames on the wharf.

Killigrew turned back in time to flag down Lady Bullivant's *telezhka*. 'Still with us, my lady?'

'You'll have to drive a good deal swifter than that to lose me, Mr Killigrew.'

'That's the spirit, ma'am!'

Molineaux jumped down from the roof of the first *telezhka*. 'Now what, sir?'

'Get everyone out of the carriages and keep them here until I signal. Then bring them across in groups of two or three. The ladies first, then Mr Charlton and the wounded. The *Atalanta* isn't moored too far away, and I can see the anchor watch from here. I'd rather not arouse their suspicions if we can avoid it.'

'I'm with you on that one, sir. What about the *Milenion*? Isn't there an anchor watch?'

'No, just a couple of guards at the top of the gangplank, by the look of it. I'll deal with them.'

'Right you are, sir.' The petty officer turned to help Araminta down from the first *telezhka*.

Still dressed in the Third Section uniform he had taken from one of the guards, Killigrew slung a musket over one shoulder and sauntered out of the alley with his hands in his pockets, whistling '*Kalinka*'. In a small, sleepy, respectable town like Ekenäs, the waterfront was deserted at that time of night. The two men on guard at the top of the gangplank – probably *matrosy* from the *Atalanta* – watched him curiously as he crossed the quayside.

Killigrew broke off whistling to hail them as he ascended the gangplank. '*Zdorovo, muzhiki!*'

'*Dobryi vecher, szr,*' said the *matrosy*.

'*Kak dela?*'

'*Spasibo, khorosho, szr.*' They saluted him as he reached the top of the gangplank. He touched the brim of his gendarme's shako-*képi*, and then brought the edge of his hand down against the neck of the *matros* on his right, before driving his fist into the other's jaw with a right cross. They hit the deck within seconds of each other.

Killigrew glanced about the deck to make sure no one had seen him deal with the guards. At least all the rigging was still in place, the sails neatly furled, but there was no sign of the four brass guns that had been on the deck when he had boarded the *Milenion* in Ångholmsfjörd: the Russians must have taken them already. Killigrew grimaced: compared to the long gun on the *Atalanta*'s forecastle, the six-pounders had been mere popguns, but popguns were better than no guns at all.

He was about to signal Molineaux to start bringing the others across when he heard a loud thump coming from below decks aft. Taking one of the guard's muskets, he crept cautiously down the after hatch. At the far end of the passageway, he could see light showing under the door to the saloon. He tiptoed to the door, and threw it open.

An attractive blonde woman he did not recognise stood there, her hair rumpled alluringly, clad only in her petticoats, her arms clamped protectively over her ample breasts.

'Who are you?' Killigrew demanded in Swedish. 'What are you doing here?'

'She's with me,' Pechorin said behind him, laying the blade of his sabre against Killigrew's neck. 'And as to what we're doing here . . . that's a question I might well ask you. The musket . . . on the deck, if you please.'

The commander shrugged off the musket and lowered it by its strap.

'Now, kick it over there.'

Killigrew shoved the musket across the far side of the saloon.

The woman dashed into one of the adjoining staterooms and slammed the door, bolting it.

'Using Lord Bullivant's yacht for a private assignation?' Killigrew asked with a smile.

Pechorin gestured at the opulent surroundings. 'Now what woman could say no to a man in surroundings like these?'

'I think I know one. I'll introduce you to her, if you like.'

'No, I think we'll keep this between ourselves for now. Two's company, and all that.' Pechorin moved to stand in front of Killigrew and with the tip of his sabre he indicated the hilt of the dress sword at the commander's hip. 'You do know how to use that thing, I take it?'

'Finest swordsman in all the Russias, eh?' Killigrew asked nervously.

Smiling, Pechorin nodded.

Killigrew drew Leong's pistol from his pocket and levelled it at the Russian. 'Drop the cutlery, Count. I may only have been a runner-up at the East Falmouth Junior Pistol Shooting Championship in 1835, but at this range even I can't miss.'

'Come now, Mr Killigrew! Where's your sportsmanship?'

'I'm afraid Colonel Nekrasoff confiscated it.'

'Ah, how is the good colonel?'

'Still alive, alas. The sword, Count.'

Pechorin threw the sabre down on the rug.

Killigrew retrieved the musket and gestured to the door. 'After you.'

'You're too kind.'

Killigrew marched him up on deck. The two *matrosy* at the entry port were slowly coming to, one of them rubbing his neck, the other his jaw.

'Idiots!' muttered Pechorin. 'Is this your notion of standing guard?'

'I hope they're better at tying knots, for your sake.' Killigrew signalled for Molineaux to start sending the others over. He pointed to a coil of rope hanging from a belaying pin. 'Tie him up,' he ordered one of the *matrosy*, indicating Pechorin.

'Now your friend,' he ordered, once he was satisfied the count was securely bound.

By the time the *matros* had finished binding his shipmate, Endicott had come on board with the Bullivants.

'I thought I told you, only the women at first?' said Killigrew, seeing Lord Bullivant.

'He kind of insisted, like, sir,' Endicott said ruefully, waving to where Molineaux stood at the mouth of the side street.

'Well, now you're here, my lord, you can make yourself useful.' Killigrew tossed him the musket. 'Keep them covered,' he ordered, indicating Pechorin and the two *matrosy*. 'Endicott, tie that one up. Then check the knots on the other two.'

'Aye, aye, sir.'

Bullivant clutched the gun awkwardly to his chest. 'Now look here, young man. You can't order me about as if I was one of your men, you know!'

Charlton came on deck with the maid, the two of them supporting Dick Searle between them. The assistant surgeon had tied a makeshift bandage around Searle's neck, but it was already soaked with blood. 'He's in a bad way, sir,' said Charlton.

'Nicholls, is there such a thing as a sick-berth on board?' Killigrew asked the maid.

She shook her head. 'No, sir.'

'Attwood keeps a medicine chest in the galley,' said Araminta. 'It's got dressings and everything in it. Nicholls, help Mr Charlton take Searle down to my stateroom while I fetch the chest.'

'Yes, my lady.'

Hughes arrived next, with Mackenzie – who had his arm in a makeshift sling – and Dahlstedt. 'Take them down to Miss Maltravers' stateroom, Hughes,' ordered Killigrew. 'You'll find Mr Charlton down there, attending to Searle.'

'He won't be able to fit them all into Araminta's stateroom,' said Lady Bullivant. 'I'll go with them; we can use the main stateroom and one of the other cabins for the wounded.'

'Thank you, my lady.'

She followed Hughes and Mackenzie down the after hatch.

Thornton, Uren and Burgess came on board next. Killigrew glanced anxiously across to where the *Atalanta* was moored. This was taking far too long, and sooner or later someone on the paddle-sloop was going to notice the people emerging from the side street to board the *Milenion*. 'Mr Uren, can you start making ready to get her under way? The others will help you as they come on board. Just don't hoist the sails until I say so.'

'Now just a minute!' protested Thornton. 'You're on my ship now, Killigrew. I give the orders around here.'

Killigrew did not have time for this. 'My sincerest apologies, Captain Thornton. I've just commandeered this yacht in the name of the Queen. Now, are you going to help me sail it out of here, or should I order Leading Seaman Endicott to lock you up in the lazaretto, assuming there's one on board?'

Thornton glanced at Lord Bullivant.

'What do you think you're going to do?' the viscount sneered at Killigrew. 'Sail her out of here and right back to the fleet, just like that?'

'That's the general idea.'

'In case you hadn't noticed, there's a Russian naval steamer tied up not three hundred yards off. Surely you don't

210

think they're going to just sit there and let us sail off without giving chase?'

'Do you see any smoke coming from the *Atalanta*'s funnel, my lord? They're not expecting trouble. I'll lay odds her fires are banked. It'll take them at least two hours to get steam up, and we can be well on our way by then. I served on a paddle-sloop not unlike the *Atalanta* for five years, and I'll lay odds that even under steam she can't make more than nine knots . . . probably less, knowing the quality of Russian engineering. What can the *Milenion* make under full press of canvas, Captain Thornton?'

'I've known her make ten with a following wind, if the breeze is strong enough.'

Sitting with his back to the gunwale, his hands tied behind his back, Pechorin scowled to hear his beloved paddle-sloop spoken of so lightly. 'But you won't be sailing with a following wind, will you, Killigrew? You'll be tacking down a narrow channel. And my second-in-command is no fool. He'll sail after you until he can get steam up. Once he does, he'll catch you and blow you out of the water.'

'With his captain a hostage on board the *Milenion*? I doubt it. And I doubt a brig-rigged paddle-sloop like the *Atalanta* can sail as close to the wind as the *Milenion* can.'

Iles came on board with Fuller and Attwood. 'What can us do to 'elp, sir?'

Killigrew indicated the fishing nets ashore. 'Roll up those nets and bring them on board. Stow them on deck amidships.'

Uren glanced at Thornton. The master hesitated, and then nodded. The three seamen made their way back down the gangplank and started to take down the nets.

Hughes came back on deck. 'The pill-roller's just tucking his patients up in bed now, sir. Anything I can do to help?'

'Yes, you can put these two ashore.' Killigrew indicated the two Russian sentries they had captured.

'Aren't you worried they'll warn their mates on the Russki paddle-sloop, sir?'

211

'It's no good having their captain a hostage on board, if they don't know about it. The first lieutenant on the *Atalanta*'s going to realise something's up as soon as the officer of the watch sees us hoist sail, which will be any moment now . . .'

'Eh, I don't want to worry you, sir,' said Endicott. 'But it looks to me as though the Ivans have already worked out there's summat going on, like.'

Killigrew glanced across to the *Atalanta* and saw that two dozen *matrosy* in green jackets and forage caps, armed with muskets, had descended the paddle-sloop's gangplank. They marched along the waterfront to where the *Milenion* was moored.

'Oh, hell!'

He looked over to the side street, and was pleased to see the last four men – Molineaux, O'Leary, Ogilby and Yorath – were already running across the quayside towards the yacht. They would reach the gangplank ahead of the Russians, but it was going to be a damned close-run thing. 'Hughes, get the Ivans ashore, chop chop! Bear a hand, Endicott!'

'Aye, aye, sir.' Endicott and Hughes each picked up one of the *matrosy* and carried them down to the quayside. Uren, Fuller and Attwood were bringing the nets on board.

'Mr Uren, can you have men standing by to bring the gangplank on board and cast off the mooring ropes as soon as Molineaux and the others are aboard?'

'Aye, sir. Stations for stays!'

'Lord Bullivant, perhaps you would be good enough to go below and keep the ladies there until I tell you otherwise?'

Bullivant seemed inclined to argue, but he looked over the gunwale at the tramp of booted feet on the cobbles. Seeing the Russians charging along the quayside towards them, he hurried below.

Molineaux, O'Leary, Ogilby and Yorath pounded up the gangplank only a few seconds after Endicott and Hughes came back aboard. 'All ashore that's staying ashore!' yelled Molineaux, dodging through the entry port. Burgess and

Attwood dragged the gangplank aboard behind them.

The Russians reached the side of the quay. One of them kept running, leaping out into space and hooking his hands over the edge of the entry port. As he tried to pull himself up, O'Leary stamped on his fingers and the man dropped into the water with a cry.

'Let go the head rope!' ordered Killigrew. 'Take the wheel, Endicott.'

'Aye, aye, sir.'

The Russians on the quayside formed a firing line. Killigrew tossed his musket to Molineaux. 'Put that to good use. Hoist the jib sails, Mr Uren!'

As the jib sails rose above the foredeck, Molineaux aimed the musket over the gunwale. The officer commanding the Russians ashore shouted an order, and Molineaux ducked down behind the gunwale. A ragged fusillade of musketry rattled out from the quayside, a great cloud of smoke billowing from the Russians' muzzles. Bullets smacked into the *Milenion*'s side, or soughed over the heads of the men on deck.

Molineaux straightened and took his time lining up his shot, while the Russians struggled to reload. He fired, and the officer commanding the Russians was thrown on his back with a fair-sized chunk blown out of his skull.

The schooner's bows were already moving away from the quayside. 'Let go the stern fast!' yelled Killigrew. 'Fore braces, tacks and sheets!'

The non-commissioned officer left in charge of the Russians shouted the order to fire, and another ragged fusillade rolled out across the docks. Molineaux had already reloaded: his next shot took the NCO in the shoulder and spun him round.

'Port the helm, Endicott!'

The Liverpudlian spun the wheel. 'Port it is, sir.'

'Haul up the fores'l and mains'l!'

The men stationed at the fife rails heaved on the halyards,

213

raising the gaffs so that the sails were unfurled. They bellied with wind, pushing the schooner's stern to port so that her head came round towards the harbour mouth. Without any leaders to guide them, the Russians on the quayside were firing at random. Killigrew heard a couple of bullets smash through the gallery window, but the *Milenion* was already moving well out from the quay, in danger of running aground on the other side of the narrow harbour. Ashore, the Russians realised they were wasting their time, and started to head back to where the *Atalanta* was moored. Killigrew took a telescope from the binnacle and glanced across at the paddle-sloop. The men on the deck were clearing for action, getting ready to unmoor.

'Right the helm, Endicott,' he said.

''Midships it is, sir.'

'Make for the channel between that island and the shore to port.'

'Aye, aye, sir.' The Liverpudlian looked dubious. 'Eh . . . I don't like to question your orders, sir, but are you sure there's enough water there?'

'No.' Killigrew smiled at him brightly. 'Only one way to find out, though, eh?'

'Apart from stopping to sound the lead,' said Endicott. 'And I don't suppose we've got time to do that.'

'I'm afraid not,' agreed Killigrew. 'Sorry.' The only alternative was to sail to leeward of the island, right under the *Atalanta*'s guns, and there was no guarantee that the first lieutenant was aware yet that Count Pechorin was on board the *Milenion*.

'Never mind, eh?' said Endicott. 'Here goes nuttin'.'

From the lie of the land on either side of the narrow channel – Killigrew had to strain to make it out in the darkness – and judging from the *Milenion*'s lines, he guessed there would be enough water to carry her through, although it was going to be touch and go. But they were either getting out of the harbour this way, or not at all.

Killigrew glanced across to where Pechorin sat against the gunwale, smirking, as if he knew something Killigrew didn't. Nothing for it but to brazen it out and hope for the best. His hands clasped behind his back, he surreptitiously crossed two fingers.

'Is this really necessary?' Lieutenant-General Ramsay asked Nekrasoff as Chernyovsky and his men trooped through his office, carrying out boxes of papers.

'Yes,' Nekrasoff told him curtly.

'But most of those papers are due to be archived . . . I've already given you everything which mentions the *Milenion* and Lord Bullivant and his family.'

'So say you.'

'Are you accusing me of lying?'

'I'm saying you could have made a mistake. Once it is confirmed that they contain nothing that might embarrass the Tsar . . . You should be grateful. Were this whole affair to come out, the government would be in need of a scapegoat.'

'If it's a scapegoat you're after, you might like to think about Captain-Lieutenant Count Pechorin. He was the one who captured the *Milenion*.'

'He had his reasons.'

'Oh? And what were those reasons?'

'No concern of yours, Lieutenant-General.' Nekrasoff took his leave of Ramsay and went outside to watch as Chernyovsky's men loaded the files into the cart parked in the street in front of the town hall by torchlight.

Seeing him, the *starshina* approached. 'Why can't you get your own men to do this? My men are Cossacks, Colonel, not clerks.'

'My men are otherwise engaged at the castle.'

'Well, as long as you don't expect my men to go through all these papers . . .'

'Don't worry. I'll leave that task to men who can read.'

Chernyovsky glowered at him, but said nothing. Feeling

215

pleased with the witticism – and with the day's work in general – Nekrasoff took out his silver-plated cigarette case and selected a cigarette. He struck a match to light it, and hesitated as a strange popping sound reached his ears from some way off. He frowned.

'Hear that?'

Chernyovsky cocked his head on one side. 'Sounds like . . . musket fire!'

The two of them stared at one another for a split second. 'Tell your men to drop everything and bring their carbines!' ordered Nekrasoff, throwing down his cigarette as he broke into a run.

Although he got a good head start on the Cossacks, he was out of condition, and they caught him up just as he emerged from a side street on to the waterfront. They were just in time to see the squad of men from the *Atalanta* firing sporadically after the *Milenion* as she faded into the evening gloom.

Nekrasoff grabbed one of the other *matrosy*. 'What's going on?'

'Someone's stealing the yacht, sir. Lieutenant Lazarenko told us to stop them.'

'Who?'

'Lieutenant Lazarenko, sir. He's the senior lieutenant on board the *Atalanta*—'

Nekrasoff rolled his eyes. 'I don't care about Lieutenant Lazarenko, fool! Who's stealing the *Milenion*?'

'Don't know, sir.'

'It couldn't be the English sailors, could it?' Chernyovsky suggested with a frown.

'Impossible,' spat Nekrasoff. 'All the English sailors are prisoners at the castle with Lord Bullivant and his family and crew.' He saw two men tied up next to one of the stone bollards where the *Milenion* had been moored. 'Who are those men? Bring them to me!'

One of the *matrosy* produced a bayonet and cut through the bonds of the two men. 'It's Malinoff and Klossovsky!'

'You know them?'

'Yes, sir. They're sailors in our crew. They were guarding the English yacht.'

'Bring them here.'

Unsteady on their feet, the two *matrosy* were brought before Nekrasoff, rubbing chafed wrists. 'You two were guarding the *Milenion*?' Nekrasoff asked them.

'Yes, sir,' they chorused.

Nekrasoff held out a hand to Chernyovsky. 'Nagaika.'

The *starshina* took his Cossack whip from his belt and handed it to the colonel. Nekrasoff uncoiled it, and then lashed it across the face of first Klossovsky, then Malinoff.

As Russian seamen, they were used to taking blows, and stood there and took them – flinching when the whip scored lines of blood from their cheeks – but quickly standing to attention again with the gore dripping down their faces. 'Thank you, sir!' they chorused.

'Did you see who it was that stole the *Milenion*?'

'I think they were English, sir,' said Malinoff.

Chernyovsky smirked. 'Perhaps these were different Englishmen from the ones you have secured at the castle.'

'Come on!' Nekrasoff told him irritably. He ran along the quayside to where the *Atalanta* was moored, followed by Chernyovsky and his men and the surviving *matrosy* from the squad sent to stop the *Milenion*. The two men on guard at the top of the gangplank saluted him, and he strode to where the officer of the watch stood on the quarterdeck.

'I need to speak to Captain-Lieutenant Pechorin at once.'

The officer took in Nekrasoff's Third Section uniform with a distinct hint of a sneer of distaste. 'It's customary to ask permission of the officer of the watch before you board one of the Tsar's ships.'

'I haven't got time for formalities, Lieutenant! It may have escaped your attention, but someone is stealing the *Milenion*. Now, where is Pechorin?'

'I don't know, sir. He went ashore a couple of hours ago.'

'Excuse me, sir—' ventured Malinoff.

Nekrasoff rounded on him furiously. 'Be quiet, you! Your stupidity has caused enough trouble for one night!'

'But, sir—'

'Didn't you hear me? I said, hold your tongue, or your next posting will be to the White Sea Squadron!' Nekrasoff turned back to the officer of the watch. 'Who is second-in-command of this vessel?'

'I am, Colonel. Lieutenant Mstislav Trofimovich Lazarenko, at your service.'

'You have seen that the *Milenion* is getting away?'

'It has not escaped my notice, sir, yes.'

'Then may I ask why you are not steaming in pursuit?'

'Our boilers are cold . . .'

'Then fire them up at once!'

'Our stokers are working on it, sir.'

'How long will that take?'

'From cold?' Lazarenko shrugged. 'Two hours.'

'Two hours!'

'Perhaps more.'

'And meanwhile the English are getting away!'

'They won't get far, sir.'

'You seem very sure of that, Lazarenko.'

'It's perfectly simple, sir. If you would check the weather vane at the truck of our mainmast, you would see that the wind is from the south-west. The inlet runs in a south-westerly direction for four *vehrsty*. Even a fore-and-aft rigged schooner like the *Milenion* can sail only within four points of the wind. That means they've got to tack against the wind.'

'And what does that mean in plain Russian?'

'That it will take them at least two and a half hours to reach Vitsand Sound. Once we have steam up, we can cover the distance in about twenty-five minutes.'

'You have sails, don't you? Why not pursue under sail until you have steam up in your boilers?'

'Hardly seems worth the effort, sir.'

218

'What?'

'The *Atalanta* is square-rigged, sir; she can't sail closer than within six points of the wind. Even if we did set out under sail, we'd make so little progress tacking, it wouldn't make much difference.'

'It could make all the difference. If there's only a five-minute margin for error, we're going to be cutting it damn fine.'

'Not really, sir. You see, there's a chain cable across the channel at Vitsand Sound. It's impossible for them to get past.'

Nekrasoff shook his head. 'If Killigrew could escape from the castle, he can find a way to get past that chain cable.' He turned to Chernyovsky. 'There's a coastal battery at Vitsand Sound, isn't there? How long will it take one of your men to reach it?'

Chernyovsky shrugged. 'It shouldn't be too difficult to get a man and a pony across the inlet to Leksvall. From there he can ride to the battery at Vitsand in a matter of minutes.'

'Send your best man at once! Tell him to make sure the battery commander has his men on stand-by, cannon loaded and ready to fire, looking out for the *Milenion*. They're to open fire on it at once. Then you can take the rest of your men to the opposite side of the channel and wait. Killigrew will probably try to send men ashore to break the cable on the east side of the channel. Be ready to ambush them.'

Chernyovsky grinned. 'With pleasure, Colonel.' He saluted, then wheeled and marched back down the gangplank to where his men waited on the quayside, calling for them to fetch their ponies.

Nekrasoff took out another cigarette, tapping it twice against his cigarette case before putting it in his mouth. Confident that there was no way for the *Milenion* to escape the inlet, he felt calm and in control of the situation once more. Let Pechorin and his men take the blame for the escape of the English on board the *Milenion*: he'd worry about how he was going to explain their escape from the castle when Kizheh had told him what had happened there. It would be his own prompt and efficient response to the crisis that would avert disaster, and it would be him – Colonel Radimir Fokavich Nekrasoff – who took the credit.

He might even get the Cross of St George for this.

He noticed Lazarenko talking to Private Malinoff. The lieutenant nodded, and ordered Malinoff below to get his face stitched up by the ship's surgeon.

Lazarenko crossed back to where Nekrasoff stood. 'It seems we've located Count Pechorin, sir.'

'Oh?'

'He's on board the *Milenion*.'

Nekrasoff stared at him in disbelief. 'You mean . . . he's actually helping them to escape?'

Lazarenko smiled, clearly pleased at the invidious position his superior now found himself in. Evidently there was no love lost between the lieutenant and the count. 'Oh, that I very much doubt, Colonel. It seems he was entertaining a young lady in the *Milenion*'s saloon when Commander Killigrew took him hostage.'

'Entertaining a lady on the *Milenion* . . .' echoed Nekrasoff, disgusted. 'At a time like this!'

'Does this mean we cannot open fire on the yacht?' asked Lazarenko. 'I mean, if we hull her, there's a chance the count could be killed.'

'That's not our concern.'

Lazarenko smiled like the cat that got the cream. 'As you will, sir.'

XI

Flight from Ekenäs

10.05 p.m., Thursday 17–12.05 a.m., Friday 18 August

The deck lurched slightly as the *Milenion*'s keel touched bottom, and Killigrew's heart leaped into his mouth. He could feel the keel scraping over rocks below, but hardly enough to slow her. It was just a touch; but enough to throw her head off, off a windward shoal where they did not have much space to spare. And since they were now sailing on the starboard tack, they would be going about at the same time.

'Steady as she goes, Endicott.'

The Liverpudlian wrestled with the helm. 'Steady it is, sir.'

The channel made a sharp dogleg round the south side of the island.

'Ready to go about!' ordered Killigrew.

'It's going to be bloody tight, sir,' warned Endicott. 'Tighter'n a crab's bum-hole, like, if you'll pardon the expression.'

'I have every confidence in you, Endicott. Haul of all!'

'I just hope it isn't misplaced.'

'Hard a-lee!'

Endicott spun the wheel once more. 'Helm's a-lee!'

221

The schooner's bows came round on to a new heading, along the south-west side of the island and the angle of the rocky coast. The men hauled the sheets to bring the foresail and mainsail round to catch the wind from the other side, and Killigrew and Endicott ducked as the mainsail boom swung low across the quarterdeck. The breeze filled the sails once more.

'Ease the helm.'

Endicott brought the rudder amidships, but he was not used to steering a ship that responded as lightly as the *Milenion* seemed to. The bows came round too far, and they were in danger of running aground on the island.

'Meet her! Handsomely does it!'

Endicott spun the wheel back to compensate.

'Right the helm. Luff and touch her.'

'Aye, aye, sir.'

And suddenly the island and the narrow channel were fading astern, and Pechorin was no longer smirking but regarding the commander with a cool and thoughtful gaze.

Killigrew remembered to keep breathing. 'Handsomely done, Endicott.'

The Liverpudlian grinned. 'Nuttin' to it, sir,' he said, wiping sweat from his forehead with his sleeve.

'Steady as she goes.'

'Steady it is, sir.'

With the far side of the channel about a mile off, Killigrew judged he had a few minutes before they would have to tack again. 'Iles! Spell Endicott at the wheel. He's earned a break. Hughes, go for'ard and keep a sharp lookout for shoals and skerries.'

'Aye, aye, sir.'

Araminta emerged on deck.

'What are you doing here?' Killigrew demanded. 'Didn't your father tell you to stay below?'

'I thought that was just until we were clear of the harbour.'

'I'd prefer it if you could remain below until we're out of the inlet. We should be safe enough once we reach the open sea. A couple of hours, that's all.'

'I wouldn't count on that if I were you, Mr Killigrew,' said Pechorin. 'You've still got to get past the chain at Vitsand Sound.'

'I hadn't forgotten,' said Killigrew. It was true: he just had not worked out what the hell he was going to do about it. 'Molineaux, perhaps you'd be so good as to secure Count Pechorin below?'

'My pleasure, sir.' When Molineaux secured someone, they stayed secure.

'Oh, and while you're down there, you'll find a scantily clad young blonde woman has locked herself in the stateroom adjoining the saloon . . .'

Araminta regarded Killigrew with an arched eyebrow.

'His friend, not mine.' The commander jerked his head at Pechorin. 'Secure her also, Molineaux. Who is she, Count? Daughter of one of the local burghers?'

'Er . . . something like that.'

'Wife?'

Pechorin scowled.

Killigrew grinned, and tutted. 'Naughty boy. How in the world is she going to explain this to her husband?'

'Is it my fault if these damned Finns cannot keep their womenfolk at home?' demanded Pechorin. 'I was just bringing some adventure into her life.'

Araminta smiled. 'I'm afraid your notion of adventure doesn't compare with Mr Killigrew's.'

'Don't denigrate what you haven't experienced, my lady,' Pechorin retorted archly. 'Oof!'

'Sorry, Ivan, did I get you with my elbow there?' asked Molineaux, helping the count to his feet. 'Still, serves you right for using smutty talk in the presence of a lady. Come along, now.'

As Molineaux marched Pechorin below decks, Killigrew turned to Araminta. 'Please, miss, I'd much prefer it if you went below.'

She smiled. 'You do seem to have an aversion to my company, Kit. But seriously, is there nothing I can do to help? Mr Charlton seems to have made the injured men comfortable, and I'm afraid I'm really not much of a nurse. Perhaps I could make coffee for you and your men?'

'The way you did on board the *Lightfoot* at Cowes that day?' he reminded her.

She grimaced. 'I'm never going to hear the end of that, am I? I've already told you, I'd never made coffee before.'

'Try not to set the galley on fire this time!'

She gave him a disparaging look, and went below.

Killigrew chuckled to himself.

Charlton came on deck, looking very pleased with himself. 'I've made the wounded comfortable, sir. I'm afraid the sailor who got shot is in a bad way, but there's nothing more I can do for him.'

'What about Mr Dahlstedt?'

'He'll be fine. His hands looked worse than they were. I've splinted his fingers; given time, I'm sure he'll live to play the piano again. If he ever could in the first place. Sleep's what he needs now. I gave him an opiate, and he went out like a light.'

'Good . . .' Killigrew turned away, and then the implication of Charlton's words sank in. He turned back to face the assistant surgeon. 'You . . . did . . . *what*?'

'Gave him an opiate. He was in a good deal of pain, I thought it would be best if he could sleep through it.'

'*You stupid great nincompoop!*' exploded Killigrew. 'He's the only one who knows these waters! How the devil's he going to chart us a course to safety if he's drugged to the eyeballs?'

Charlton looked crestfallen. 'Sorry, sir. I didn't think of that. Do you want me to try to wake him?'

Killigrew shook his head wearily. 'Let him sleep for now. You'd better get your head down too; I think we can manage without you for now.'

'Maybe you should rest as well. Remember what Mr Dyson said: you should be taking it easy.'

'That isn't an option at this moment in time.'

'Are you sure? You do look rather peaky.'

'A little tired, that's all,' he assured Charlton with a wan smile. 'It's been a hard day.' But the truth was, he felt ready to collapse on the deck. The last thing he needed was another fainting fit, not now.

Charlton headed below, passing Molineaux, who was on the way back up. 'Come back, Mr Strachan, all is forgiven, eh, sir?' said the petty officer.

'Mr Charlton's doing the best job he can under difficult circumstances,' Killigrew chided him gently.

'Yes, sir. Sorry, sir.' The petty officer looked suitably abashed.

'Listen, Molineaux: I need you to take an inventory of all the guns on board. Gather together all the muskets and pistols we brought with us, make sure they're all loaded and primed, and make an inventory of all the ammunition we have spare.'

'Aye, aye, sir. Although – with all due respect – I don't reckon barking irons will do us much good if that Russki flapper catches us. Maybe I should have a look round below, see if there's anything else we can use.'

'Such as?'

'Won't know till I've taken a look-see, will I, sir?'

'You're right, I suppose. All right, Molineaux, see what you can come up with.'

'Aye, aye, sir.' Molineaux made his way along the deck, gathering up muskets and cartouche boxes.

'Captain Thornton!' called Killigrew.

The master crossed the quarterdeck to meet him.

'All our lives depend on us getting this ship out of the inlet,' Killigrew told him. 'That means we've got to work together, do you understand me?'

'Yes.' Thornton's face made it clear that understanding the situation and liking it were two very different things.

'I need you to be my second in command. That means when I'm not on deck, you're the officer of the watch.'

Thornton nodded. 'So, what's your plan for getting past the chain cable at Vitsand Sound?'

'It'll still be dark when we get there. With any luck we'll catch the battery napping. All we have to do is send a boat ashore to break the cable on the south side of the channel, and we can sail straight through.'

'I wouldn't count on our catching the gunners napping. I'll wager the Russians will have sent someone ahead to alert them.'

'Well, we'll just have to worry about that when the time comes.'

Thornton did not look reassured.

'I'm going below,' Killigrew told him. 'Keep her on this heading for as long as you can, until we're in danger of running aground on the far side of the inlet. Then put her about on to a southerly heading.' The inlet was over a mile wide opposite Ekenäs. Sailing close-hauled, the schooner was making about a knot and a half: Killigrew reckoned he had a good half an hour before they had to tack.

He made his way below and found Lord Bullivant in the saloon, helping himself to his own brandy. Molineaux had left Pechorin seated on the deck, his hands tied behind his back and his ankles bound.

'What the devil do you want?' the viscount asked Killigrew testily.

'I need to take a look at the charts.'

'Try the chart-room.' Bullivant gestured towards the door with his brandy balloon, spilling some of the liquor on the rug. 'Fifth door on the left.'

Killigrew left the saloon and made his way for'ard. He was about to enter the chart-room when Araminta emerged from one of the staterooms. Seeing him, she followed him into the chart-room, closing the door behind her.

'I think you owe me an explanation,' she said.

'As to what?'

'As to why you broke off our engagement. At least, I *assume* you broke it off. You never had the decency to tell me about it: the first I heard of it was when Papa showed me an article in the newspaper, in which your name was listed as one of the officers sailing with Sir Edward Belcher's expedition to the Arctic. What happened? Did you get cold feet?'

He grinned. 'Only when my sealskin boots wore out.'

She scowled. 'You never could be serious for five minutes at a time. After all the things that we said and did together, I would have thought I deserved better than your flippant remarks.'

'You're right. I'm sorry, truly.'

'Was it something I did? Or did Papa try to pay you off?'

'He did.'

'And what price did he put on me?'

'Two hundred pounds.'

Her jaw dropped. 'Is that all?'

'More than a year's salary for me, at the time.'

'I see. And when you said you loved me, I was foolish enough to believe it. I had no notion you could be bought so cheaply.'

'I hope I can't. I turned him down. That was a couple of months before I left.'

'Then why did you leave? I dare say I'm not the first woman who's ever been jilted, but am I the first who drove a man as far as the Arctic to get away from me?'

'It had nothing to do with you. To tell the truth, I never thought you'd go through with the marriage . . . or that you'd be able to cope on a lieutenant's half-pay for an income.'

'But we talked about this. I said I loved you, didn't I? I can only suppose that, having had your wicked way with me, you lost all interest in me.'

'That's what I wanted you to think.'

'I'm not sure I understand.'

227

'I'm not sure I do either.' He grimaced. 'Miss Maltravers . . . may I still call you Araminta?'

'You used to call me Minty.'

'Araminta . . . Minty . . . all my life I wanted to go on an Arctic exploring expedition. I applied to sail with Franklin, but I was turned down. When Captain Pettifer offered me a berth on the *Venturer*, I could hardly say no.'

'You might have told me. I would have waited. Or we could have brought the wedding forward.'

'I thought you'd say something like that. Which is why I didn't discuss it with you.'

'Thank you very much! I thought I told you I was fed up with men making all my decisions for me?'

'It was for your own good, Minty. Arctic expeditions can be dangerous; the fate of Franklin and his men proves that, and I learned for myself the hard way. Even before I left, I had some inkling I might never return. In that event, I didn't want to make you a widow.'

'Didn't I get a say in the matter?'

'I was afraid you'd talk me out of going on the expedition. I just thought it was best to break it off. I couldn't see any future for us.'

'You might at least have given me an explanation, instead of simply disappearing from my life.'

'I thought it would be easier for you if you could bring yourself to hate me. Treating you shamefully seemed the simplest way to do that.'

Her face softened. 'That's sweet. Incredibly foolish, but sweet. Do you know what I think?'

He shook his head.

'I think you were afraid.'

'Afraid? Of what?'

'Of letting a woman get close to you. The great Kit Killigrew: fearless fighting pirates, slavers and polar bears, passionate seducer of helpless young females—'

'Whatever else you were, you were never helpless.'

228

'But when it comes to more tender feelings? Why *do* all men find it so difficult to say those three little words? Was there someone before me, perhaps? Someone who made you reluctant to risk having your heart broken a second time?'

'I'd rather not talk about it.'

'Ah! So there *was* someone. Don't you understand? I would never have broken your heart.'

'The woman I once lost would never have broken my heart, if it had been up to her. But that's all in the past.'

'Then why didn't you get in touch with me when you returned?'

'Lord Hartcliffe told me that Lord Dallaway was courting you; I thought it was for the best. Besides, I'd . . . um . . . acquired someone else by then.'

She stared at him. 'In the Arctic?'

He nodded.

'You mean, you jilted me for an Esquimaux squaw?' she exclaimed indignantly.

'She wasn't an Esquimaux squaw, she was the widow of a whaling captain. Surely you read about my adventures in the newspapers?'

'I couldn't bring myself to. Every time I saw your name in print, I just felt my hatred of you well up inside me. What about this whaling captain's widow? Is she waiting for you back in England, or have you married her already?'

Killigrew shook his head. 'We broke it off.'

'You mean, you jilted her too?'

'No, she jilted me, if you must know.'

'Good for her. No more than you deserve.'

He nodded, smiling ruefully. 'I found myself caught between two women, and ended up with neither. So you see, if I wronged you, then I've suffered for it.'

'Perhaps, but not nearly enough,' she assured him. 'What happens now?'

'Now I've got to get us safely back to the fleet, otherwise none of us will have any future.'

She took his hand and intertwined her fingers with his. 'A future together?'

'You mean, you'd still marry me?'

She regarded him with mock-sternness. 'I don't think I should let you off the hook that easily, Kit. Not after the shameful way you've treated me. No, I mean to make you suffer, first. You've got a lot of work to do if you're going to regain my trust.'

'If you want someone you can put through hoops, might I suggest a performing dog?'

'That's not such a bad notion. At least dogs are loyal.'

'*Touché*. If I get you and your family back to safety, will that convince you?'

'It would be a good start. But you've got to do it, first.'

'I'm working on it,' he told her, and added: 'Trust me.'

'This from the man who ran away to the Arctic rather than marry me!' Shaking her head, she slipped out of the chart-room.

Grinning idiotically, he turned his attention to the chart lockers. When he opened them, the smile quickly faded from his face.

The lockers were all empty.

He emerged from the chart-room to meet Lord Bullivant coming from the direction of the saloon, with a brandy balloon in one hand and a full bottle in the other.

'The Russians have taken the charts,' Killigrew said heavily.

'Damme! The light-fingered devils! I'll have something to say to Lord Aberdeen about this, I can tell you.'

'Yes, I'm sure that with Britain at war with Russia, the theft of your charts is really going to exercise him.'

'Impertinent young—'

'Pup?' suggested Killigrew.

'Yes, blast your eyes! By God, you go too far! When we get out of this, I'll see to it you never get another posting in the navy for as long as you live.'

'If I might remind you, my lord: we're three miles up a channel with a chain barrier ahead of us and a Russian paddle-sloop behind, with no charts and a drugged pilot. If by some miracle we can get out of this alive, perhaps then I'll worry about how you're going to ruin my career. But in the meantime, I'm more concerned about what we're going to do when we reach Vitsand Sound.'

'This is all your fault! If we'd stayed at the castle and left this mess to the diplomats to sort out—'

'We'd all be dead,' Killigrew finished for him.

'Don't be ridiculous! What could the Russians possibly gain from my death, except to create an international scandal that would turn the opinion of the world against them?' Bullivant stepped into the master stateroom, slamming the door behind him.

Killigrew rubbed his jaw. He had to admit to himself, Bullivant had a point: it would have made far more sense to exchange the Bullivants and their crew along with Killigrew and his men at the first opportunity, instead of secretly murdering them. Unless there was some other reason Nekrasoff wanted Bullivant dead, something he had not revealed during the interrogation at the castle. Lord Bullivant himself must know; but Killigrew was in no mood to ask him, not now. It would have to wait.

Molineaux was nothing if not thorough. 'Leave no stone unturned,' his mentor had always taught him when training him to burgle houses back in London when he had been a child. 'You don't walk through the front door just because it's open; there's probably a better way, if only you look for it.' Words of wisdom, and over the intervening years Molineaux had learned that the principles could be applied to endeavours other than burglary. So once he had gathered up all the muskets and made his inventory of the ammunition, he proceeded to search the *Milenion* from stem to stern, deck by deck.

He was in Bullivant's day-room, making a tally of the shotguns in the gun rack there and checking the drawers for cartridges. Evidently his lordship had been intent on doing some hunting while he was in the Baltic; doubtless it had never occurred to him that he might end up being the one who was hunted.

Someone knocked on the open door behind Molineaux. He turned and saw Miss Maltravers standing there.

'Hullo, miss. No need to knock: I reckon you've as much right to be in here as I have.'

'Actually, I wanted a word with you.'

'With me?'

She nodded. 'About Mr Killigrew. You're pretty close to him, aren't you?'

'You could say that. Mr K's got some fancy Latin phrase for it . . .'

' "*Amicus usque ad aras*"?'

'That's the one.'

'A friend as far as the altars,' she explained. 'No impropriety.'

Molineaux grinned. 'He's not my type.'

'Does he confide in you?'

'Sometimes. As much as he confides in anyone, I reckon. You're wondering why he jilted you, I s'pose?'

'You always were an impertinent rogue, Mr Molineaux,' she said with a smile.

He grinned. 'Thank you.'

'So why did he jilt me?'

'He never said. But I reckon I can guess.'

'Oh?'

'He's a bloody fool, miss, if you'll pardon my French.'

She thought about it, and nodded. 'Thank you, Mr Molineaux.'

'Any time.'

She withdrew, leaving him to continue his search for arms. Having finished in the day-room, he moved on to the next cabin aft and knocked on the door. Hearing an indistinct grunt from within, he took it to be an invitation to enter.

Lord Bullivant sat on the edge of the bunk while the maid stood facing him, her bodice open, so he could nuzzle her breasts. The maid did not look as if she was enjoying it much, and Bullivant did not look as though he cared much how she felt about it. The dressmaker's dummy that occupied one corner of the cabin looked indifferent.

You had to admire the British aristocracy, Molineaux thought ironically. There they were, trapped in Russian territorial waters with a steam-sloop in pursuit, and Lord Bullivant was more interested in exploring the contents of his maid's bodice. Probably he was too stupid to realise how much danger they were in; and from the flushed look on his face and the smell of brandy-breath in the air, Molineaux guessed that drink had played its part in marring his far-from-perfect judgement.

The viscount realised he was being watched, and glared at Molineaux. 'Well?' he demanded. Molineaux had to admit, you could not beat the British aristocracy for sheer imperturbability. 'What do you want?'

The petty officer grinned. 'I wouldn't say no to some of what you're getting.'

'You black devil!' Bullivant snatched a hairbrush off the dresser and threw it at Molineaux's head. The petty officer quickly slammed the door and heard the brush bang against the inside.

Chuckling to himself, he turned away and found himself facing Lady Bullivant.

'Lady B! Your husband's just . . . er . . . um . . .'

She smiled thinly. 'I'm well aware of what my husband is doing, Mr Molineaux. It's nothing new, I can assure you.'

'And it don't bother you?'

'Frankly, Mr Molineaux, I was never more grateful than the day my husband decided he was less interested in me than he was in the servants.' Smiling regally, she glided on down

233

the passageway, leaving the petty officer staring after her in frank admiration.

When she was out of sight, he turned away and continued down to the saloon. Opening the drawers listlessly, he studied the sterling-silver cutlery, even taking out a carving knife to admire it . . . much use it would be against a paddle-sloop!

'Helping yourself to the silver?' asked Pechorin.

Molineaux waved the knife in front of the count's face before returning it to the drawer. 'I'll help myself to your nutmegs if you don't stow it, cully.'

Leaving Pechorin with a slightly bewildered expression on his face, Molineaux began to search the staterooms. The count's blonde lady friend was still trussed up where he had left her on the bunk in Lord Bullivant's stateroom; there was nothing in there that might be any use as a weapon. The same was true of the next stateroom, where Lady Bullivant sat reading a Bible beside the bunk in which Dick Searle lay sleeping.

'Yes?' Lady Bullivant asked, looking up, when Molineaux thrust his head through the door.

'Beg pardon, ma'am. I'm looking for anything we can use as a weapon.'

'Hatpin?'

'I was looking for something a bit more substantial than that.'

Lieutenant Dahlstedt was fast asleep in the bunk in the next stateroom, while Miss Maltravers dozed in a chair beside him. Molineaux eased the door shut and retreated. The next door on that side of the passage was the maid's cabin; the steward's storeroom on the other side from the stairs leading up to the after hatch was more promising: he found two crates of bottles of lamp-oil.

He made his way forward. The next compartment had been converted into a dark room for developing photographic plates: Molineaux was familiar with the paraphernalia of calotypography, for when he had been an able seaman on board HMS *Tisiphone*, Mr Strachan had frequently converted the sick-berth into a dark room to pursue his own interests in that sphere, when it was not required for the purpose for which it was intended. There were a couple of cameras and different tripods, a crate containing unused glass plates packed in straw, developing trays on a work bench, and racks containing bottles of chemicals. Molineaux read the labels: Canada balsam, collodion, gallic acid, hyposulphite of soda, oil of vitriol, potassium iodide, pyrogallic acid, silver chloride, silver nitrate, sodium chloride solution, and spirits of nitre.

The stateroom opposite belonged to Lord Dallaway; nothing of interest there.

More cabins, the chart-room, then the forecastle with the galley amidships. The galley boasted a huge cast-iron cooking range, and pots and pans of every description. A large medicine chest had been taken out and left open on one of the workbenches. Bandages, scissors, bottles of pills and bottles of lotions and medicines, including – Molineaux noticed with a wry grimace at the illustration on the label – Trubshaw's Cordial.

He made his way up through the forward hatch to report to Killigrew on the quarterdeck. 'You sent me to see if I could find anything we could use as a weapon, sir?'

'Yes?'

'Four double-barrelled barking irons in Lord Bullivant's day-room, with plenty of cartridges; thirty-two bottles of lamp-oil in the steward's stores . . . if we stuff rags in their mouths and set fire to them, they'll make good fire bombs. Oh, and there are about a dozen different kinds of acid in the dark room.'

'The dark room?'

'Yur. Someone on board must be into photography in a big way. Dunno how we can use the acid, though. I suppose it would be too much to hope it might dissolve the *Atalanta*, although we might throw it in the Ivans' phizogs to put out their glims. Have to get close, though.'

'Is that the best you could do?' the commander asked in a disappointed tone.

Molineaux bridled somewhat. 'Did you expect me to find a ten-inch long gun, sir?'

Killigrew rubbed his forehead wearily. 'All right, it's not your fault. You did your best. We'll just have to think of a way to—'

'Killigrew!' Lord Bullivant emerged from the after hatch, his face suffused with rage and brandy. 'Killigrew! I've a complaint to make!'

Standing with his back to the viscount, Killigrew rolled his eyes so that only Molineaux could see. The petty officer grinned, and the commander turned to Bullivant with a thin smile pasted on his face.

'A complaint, my lord?'

'Yes! Against that damned blackamoor!' He indicated Molineaux.

'He has a name, my lord.'

'His name is no concern of mine,' sniffed Bullivant. 'All I know is, he's an impertinent rogue.'

'On that account I would have to agree with you, my lord. What did he say this time, precisely?'

'He said—' Bullivant broke off, looking trapped. 'Never mind what he said! He was impertinent, that's all!'

'If you wish him to be punished when we get back on board the *Ramillies*, my lord, I shall need to know the full details of the incident when I take him before Captain Crichton. Were there any witnesses?'

'Witnesses?' Bullivant looked shifty. 'What do you mean, witnesses?'

'Was there anyone else there who can corroborate your story?'

'Are you accusing me of being a liar?'

'Not at all, my lord. But Molineaux is a British citizen, and as such he's entitled to a fair hearing; that's what makes

Britain different from Russia, and I'd like to think that's what I'm fighting this war for. Otherwise, you see, it's just a question of your word against his.'

'Surely the word of a peer of the realm should count for more than that of a nigger petty officer?'

Molineaux clenched his fists and took a step forward. Killigrew stretched out his arm to bar his way to where Bullivant stood, but the petty officer had already caught himself.

'With all due respect, my lord, I have always considered that true nobility means treating all men and women with courtesy, regardless of their rank or social status,' Killigrew said tightly.

'Evidently that's something you and I disagree on,' sneered Bullivant.

'Then I fear your manners do you little credit, my lord.'

'How dare you criticise my manners? Am I to take it, then, that you do not intend to do anything to punish this man?'

'Unless you can be a little more precise about the nature of Petty Officer Molineaux's offence, I'm afraid there's nothing I can do.'

'You're a disgrace, Killigrew! A disgrace to the uniform!' Crimson with rage, Bullivant turned and descended the after hatch.

'Thank you, sir,' murmured the petty officer.

'Nothing to thank me for, Molineaux. I will not have the men under my command treated with such discourtesy by anyone, be they a viscount, an earl, a baronet, or a bow-legged conductor of a tuppenny 'bus. Carry on.'

'Aye, aye, sir.' Molineaux made his way forward to where Endicott and Hughes stood in the waist.

'What were all that about?' asked Endicott.

'I walked in on his lordship and found him nuzzling the dollymop's bubbies.'

Endicott and Hughes laughed.

'Jesus!' said the Welshman. 'Can't say I think much of her taste in men.'

'I don't reckon she had much choice in the matter, Red,' said Molineaux.

'What . . . you mean, he was trying to rape her?'

Endicott shook his head. 'It's only rape when coves like us do it. When gentry coves take advantage of judies, it's called "seduction": "If you want to keep your job, keep me happy".'

Hughes thrust his jaw out aggressively. 'You know what that is, don't you?'

Molineaux and Endicott exchanged glances. 'Exploitation of the working classes?' they chorused.

Hughes stared at them in astonishment. 'How did you know I was going to say that?'

'Everything's exploitation of the working classes to you, Red,' Endicott explained wearily. 'The bosun orders you to clean the head, it's exploitation of the working classes. You get overcharged for a tot o' rum by a bum-boat boy, it's exploitation of the working classes. There's weevils in the hard tack, it's exploitation of the working classes.'

'Yur,' agreed Molineaux. ''Ceptin' just this once – for the first time in my life, and hopefully the last – I'm inclined to agree with Red—'

'Jesus!' exclaimed Endicott, staring past Molineaux to the quarterdeck. The petty officer turned to see Killigrew sprawled on the deck, while Iles stood at the wheel oblivious to what had happened behind him. The three of them ran across to where the commander lay and crouched over him.

'What happened?' Molineaux asked Iles.

'Eh?' The seaman glanced over his shoulder. 'Dunno. 'Ee seemed fine a moment ago.'

'He must've had another of his funny turns,' said Molineaux. 'Red, go fetch the pill-roller.'

Charlton came on deck and directed them to carry the unconscious Killigrew below to one of the staterooms.

'Is he going to be all right, sir?' Hughes asked in concern.

'I expect so,' said Charlton. 'Molineaux, would you be so good as to ask Lady Bullivant's maid if she has any sal volatile on board?'

'Aye, aye, sir.' Molineaux hesitated before leaving, and nudged Endicott. 'Make sure he don't go giving him none of his fancy homeopathic remedies.'

Charlton bridled. 'Are you questioning my medical expertise, Molineaux?'

'No, sir. I were just saying, it's a bit rum, like.' He turned back to Endicott. 'T'other day he gave me some explosive chemicals for a headache! Last thing we want right now is Tom Tidley suffering from an attack of spontaneous yooman combustion.'

Molineaux made his way to the maid's cabin and knocked on the door.

'One moment!' she called.

'It's kind of an emergency, miss.'

She opened the door and looked out. Her face was dry, but her eyes were still red-rimmed from crying. 'Have you got any sal volatile, miss?'

'Sal volatile?'

'Hartshorn.'

'Oh! Yes, one moment.' She rummaged through one of the drawers of the dresser and produced a small, brown bottle.

'Thanks.' Molineaux took it from her and raced back to the stateroom where Charlton was attending Killigrew. Endicott and Hughes still crowded the doorway. 'You two best get back on deck,' he told them. 'I'm sure Mr Charlton can manage without you.'

They nodded and made their way to the companion ladder.

Entering the stateroom, Molineaux gave the sal volatile to Charlton, who removed the stopper from the bottle and wafted it under the commander's nose. Killigrew opened his eyes and blinked, turning his head away from the bottle.

'Charlton! What the devil are you doing?'

'You fainted again, sir. Hardly surprising, under the circumstances. It's been a long day, and you're under a good deal of strain.'

'I've got to get back on deck.' Killigrew tried to move Charlton out of the way, but with Molineaux's assistance he was pushed back down to the pillow.

'You need rest, sir, and plenty of it,' said Charlton. 'You're no good to anyone if you're going to keep fainting.'

'The pill-roller's right, sir,' said Molineaux. 'You get your head down for a couple of hours and have a doss. We can manage without you for a spell.'

'You'd best get back on deck too, Molineaux,' said Charlton.

'Aye, aye, sir.'

The petty officer returned on deck to find Bullivant, Captain Thornton and Mr Mackenzie conferring on the quarterdeck.

'Killigrew made me his second in command, sir...' Thornton was saying.

'And you take your orders from me,' Bullivant reminded him. 'That's what I pay you for.'

'Perhaps we should let one of the navy seamen take command,' suggested Mackenzie. 'This is a military situation, after all.'

Bullivant glowered at the mate. 'The fact had not escaped my attention, Mr Mackenzie. I'm not a complete amateur in military matters, you know.' He puffed himself up. 'You may not be aware of the fact, but I happen to be the colonel of the East Rutland Yeomanry.'

'Yeomanry, eh?' said Hughes, joining Molineaux at the edge of the quarterdeck. 'That'll come in handy, if we meet any Chartists that need riding down.'

'Boat ahoy!' the marine sentry at the *Ramillies*' entry port cried.

'No, no!' the coxswain of the second cutter replied.

'Second cutter coming in, sir!' the sentry called across to the quarterdeck.

Lieutenant Lloyd, officer of the watch, nodded. 'Inform the captain that Mr Masterson has returned,' he ordered one of the midshipmen standing on deck. The midshipman nodded and went below. Presently Crichton emerged on deck in time to meet Masterson climbing up through the entry port.

'What news?'

'The *Milenion*'s there right enough, sir, but there was no sign of Killigrew or the first cutter. The officer I spoke to – an over-smooth fellow called Colonel Nekrasoff – told me that the battery at Vitsand Sound had blown them out of the water.'

Crichton turned puce. 'They opened fire on a boat sailing under a flag of truce?'

'Nekrasoff claimed there was no flag of truce, sir.'

'That's a damned lie!'

'I know, sir. But what could I do in the face of the fellow's bare-faced dishonesty?'

'Russians!' snorted Crichton. 'What more could one expect? What about the Bullivants and Lord Dallaway?'

'Nekrasoff said they were to be tried for espionage.'

'Dear God! Have these people no conscience?'

'It would seem not, sir. What are we to do now?'

'Do? What can we do? I know what I'd like to do – sail right up the inlet and blow Eckness to the devil! But we're too deep-draughted for that. So we'll have to take General Bodisco back to the fleet, and inform Old Charlie of what's happened. Weigh anchor, Mr Pemberton! Lay me a course for Hangö Head, Mr Shearsmith.' To reach Ledsund, first they would have to round Hangö Head, the tip of the promontory that jutted out from the south-west corner of the Finnish coast.

'Aye, aye, sir,' responded the master. 'We should be able to fetch it on a course of south-west by west, sir.'

'Very good. All plain sail, Mr Lloyd, course south-south-east. After ten miles, we'll tack north-west.' Crichton disappeared below, shoulders hunched in defeat.

By the time the ship's bell tolled midnight, the *Ramillies* was under way once more, with all sails drawing. Lloyd took the logboard down from the easel and Adare replaced it with the one he had brought up from the log room.

Lloyd shook his head. 'Mr Killigrew dead . . . I can't believe it.'

'Me neither,' Masterson said grimly. 'You heard what the Old Man said: these Russkis are nothing but a bunch of bare-faced liars. Colonel Nekrasoff told me the body of a British officer had been dragged from the inlet, but when I asked to see it he fobbed me off.'

'You think Killigrew and the others might still be alive?'

'God knows, Lloyd. But if he is, he's certainly a prisoner of the Russkis . . . in which case, heaven help him.'

XII

No Way Out

12.05 a.m.–12.48 a.m., Friday 18 August

On board the *Atalanta*, Colonel Nekrasoff had commandeered Pechorin's quarters. He had intended to rest, but the
truth was he was too anxious to sleep, and too impatient to
get under way in pursuit of the *Milenion*. If he prevented Lord
Bullivant's escape, he would be awarded the Cross of St
George; if he failed, however, he could expect a one-way
ticket to Siberia.

Pechorin's quarters were luxuriously appointed, presumably at the count's own expense. A silver filigree cigar box
– stuffed full of fat Havanas – stood on the desk, and four
decanters – containing port, brandy, Madeira and sherry –
stood on the sideboard. In the cramped cabin, the shelf
above the bunk was cluttered with fencing trophies, and
there was a daguerreotype of Anzhelika Orlova, the prima
ballerina of the Marinsky Ballet Company, framed on the
bulkhead.

There was a knock on the door to the day-room at ten
minutes past midnight. 'Enter!' Nekrasoff called, emerging
from the cabin.

The door opened and one of the sloop's beardless *michmanis* entered, saluting. 'Lieutenant Lazarenko asked me to inform you that we now have a sufficient head of steam to get under way, and we're casting off.'

Nekrasoff nodded curtly and followed the *michmani* back on deck, where the hands were casting off the mooring ropes.

Lazarenko stood on the quarterdeck. He saluted Nekrasoff smartly, and turned to one of the *michmanis*. 'Pass the word to Inzhener Nikolaishvili: turn astern, slow.'

'Yes, sir.' The *michmani* hurried below.

'We should reach Vitsand Sound within twenty-five minutes,' said Lazarenko. 'Unless we overtake the *Milenion* first. Even with her fore-and-aft rig, I doubt she'll have made much headway against this south-westerly breeze.'

The deck throbbed beneath their feet as the engineer started up the engines, and the paddle-wheels plashed slowly at the waters of Ekenäs Harbour, reversing the *Atalanta* out of her berth.

'Ahead half,' ordered Lazarenko. 'Port the helm.'

The helmsman spun the wheel, and the sloop emerged from the harbour into the main channel.

'Helm amidships! Full ahead!'

As smoke streamed from the funnel into the black night sky, the sloop surged ahead, clipping down the channel at a good eight and a half knots.

'Remember, Lazarenko,' said Nekrasoff. 'I want the *Milenion* blown out of the water.'

The lieutenant nodded. 'Clear for action! Gun crew to the bow chaser!' Smiling, he turned to Nekrasoff. 'We'll make kindling of her, sir.'

'Ready to go about!' Thornton ordered as the eastern side of the inlet loomed out of the night off the port bow. In the two and a quarter hours since the *Milenion* had sailed from Ekenäs harbour she had been forced to tack five times already, the runs between each tack growing shorter as the inlet narrowed towards its mouth at the Vitsand Sound. The moon had risen, a silvery crescent hanging low in the sky above the black silhouette of the trees on the shore.

'Haul of all! Hard a-lee!'

Ned Yorath spun the wheel. 'Helm's a-lee!'

The schooner's bows turned away from the approaching shore, and the men at the halyards hauled to bring the foresail and mainsail around to catch the wind from the other side.

'Ease the helm,' ordered Thornton. 'Luff and touch her.'

'Aye, aye, sir.' Yorath brought the rudder amidships and the *Milenion* settled on her new heading, due west, diagonally across the narrowing channel. In another ten minutes or so, they would have to tack again when they approached the opposite shore.

'We should reach the chain cable in twenty minutes' time, my lord,' Thornton reminded Bullivant. 'Should I have the gig hoisted in the davits?'

'Eh?'

'The gig, sir. So we can send men ashore to try to break through the cable at the eastern side.'

'Oh! Yes, yes, I suppose so. Who will you take?'

'I thought we'd send some of Killigrew's men.'

'And some of your own men, Cap'n Thornton,' said Molineaux, who stood close enough to overhear. 'Or were you thinking of leaving us behind as soon as we'd cleared the way for the *Milenion*?'

Thornton bridled. 'That's an outrageous suggestion! How dare you?'

'I'm sure there'll be plenty of time to wait for your shore party to get safely back on board, Molineaux,' said Mackenzie.

Fuller hawked and spat. 'Reckon so, do you, sir?'

'No one asked your opinion, Fuller,' growled Thornton.

'Maybe not, but you're going to get it anyways. I don't know 'bout you lot, but I seed the artillery battery on the west side of the channel when they towed the *Milenion* through Vitsand Sound . . .'

'There's a chance they'll all be asleep,' said Thornton.

'And an even bigger one the Ivans will've sent a rider from Eckness to tell 'em to be on the lookout for us,' said Fuller. 'They prob'ly got orders to blow us out of the water. And we'll be under their guns the 'ole time the darky an' 'is mates are ashore seeing to that there cable. It'll take 'em at least ten minutes to break that cable, prob'ly more. Even if there's anything left of the *Milenion* by the time they do, that'll be more'n enough time for the Russki paddle-sloop to catch us.'

'Are you sure?' asked Bullivant.

Fuller jerked his head at Molineaux. 'Ask him if I'm lying.'

Everyone turned to the petty officer. 'It's a long shot,' Molineaux admitted. 'But it's the only chance we've got.'

'Fuller's right, my lord,' admitted Thornton. 'We'll never get through.'

'Enough!' said Bullivant. 'This is madness. I'm amazed I let things get this far. Stop the vessel, Thornton.'

The master looked relieved. 'As you will, my lord. Mr Uren! All hands bring ship to anchor!'

'What the hell are you doing?' Molineaux asked in horror.

'We're going to surrender,' said Bullivant. 'This madness has gone quite far enough.'

'Stand clear of the chain!' called Uren. 'Let go the anchor!'

Molineaux unslung his musket and levelled it. 'I'll shoot the first man who touches that mud-hook!'

'By God!' exclaimed Bullivant. 'Who the devil d'you think you are, giving orders on my yacht? O'Leary, Ogilby – do as you're told.'

The two sailors stood stock-still, eyeing the musket in Molineaux's hands nervously.

'Take that gun off him, Mr Uren,' ordered Thornton. 'Then tie him up below.'

As Uren advanced on Molineaux, the petty officer turned

the musket on him, bringing him up short.

'I'm taking command,' said Molineaux. 'Hughes, run below and fetch the pill-roller.'

'You!' Bullivant exclaimed laughingly as Hughes hurried down the after hatch. 'You're nothing but a blackamoor. You're in no position to give anyone orders.'

'This is a naval operation,' Molineaux told him. 'And I may only be a petty officer, but I'm still the senior man on watch. And I say we run that cable.'

'And I say it's madness,' said Bullivant. 'I outrank you . . . I'm a colonel of yeomanry, that outranks a petty officer any day of the week . . .'

Molineaux told him what he could do with his yeomanry in no uncertain terms.

Charlton emerged on deck. 'What's going on here?'

'Mr Charlton! Be so good as to order your man to put down that musket and surrender himself. He's a mutineer!'

'Is this true, Molineaux?'

'I ain't disobeyed any orders from a naval officer, sir. With Mr Killigrew sick, you're in charge.'

'Then I order you to put down that musket at once, Molineaux.'

'Hear me out, sir. Lord Bullivant and Cap'n Thornton want to drop anchor and surrender to the Russki paddle-sloop when it catches us.'

'Whereas this fool thinks we should try to run the battery at Vitsand Sound,' said Bullivant. 'Really, Mr Charlton! If you cannot control the men under your command, then I suggest you surrender command to me. I *am* colonel of the East Rutland Yeomanry.'

'Stand down, Molineaux,' said Charlton. 'That's an order.'

'Molineaux's right, Mr Charlton,' said Mackenzie. 'We have to run that battery somehow.'

'Be quiet, Mackenzie!' Thornton said angrily.

'Damn it, sir, do ye no' see? We *canna* surrender to the Russians. They'll blow us out of the water as soon as we're within range! They want us deid; that's why we had to escape in the first place.'

'Nonsense!' said Bullivant. 'They wouldn't dare kill me! I'm a peer of the realm.'

'Not this realm, yer lordship,' Endicott reminded him. 'With all due respect, Mr Charlton, Wes is right: it's a slim chance we can get through that cable before the Russki gunners wake up, like, but at least it's a chance. If we drop anchor, the paddle-sloop will just blow us out of the water.'

Fraught with anguish, Charlton looked at Hughes and Iles. 'What do you chaps think?'

'Damn your eyes, Charlton!' exploded Bullivant. 'This isn't a democracy, man! Order your men to desist from this madness, before we're all killed.'

'We're with Wes, sir,' said Hughes, and Iles nodded.

'Your choice, sir,' said Molineaux. 'A slim chance, or no chance at all. What's it to be?'

'Oh, this isn't fair!' Charlton protested petulantly. 'I'm an apothecary, not a damned executive officer! What do I know about batteries and paddle-sloops?' He took off his cap and ran his fingers through his hair in agitation. 'A slim chance, you say?'

'Better than no chance at all, sir.'

'Carry on, Molineaux. I just hope you know what you're doing . . .'

'You're going to be guided by the advice of a blackamoor?' Bullivant spluttered incredulously.

'He's a good man, my lord. He's got years of experience.'

'You little bloody fool! You're going to get us all killed!'

Charlton turned to Molineaux. 'By God, man, you'd better be right about this!'

Molineaux grinned. 'Cheer up, sir. If I'm wrong, in a few minutes it won't matter much either way.'

The assistant surgeon did not look comforted by the thought.

* * *

Starshina Chernyovsky and his men left their ponies tied up in the trees fifty yards back from the shore. They crept down through the undergrowth to where the tree line overlooked the rocks. Below, the east end of the chain cable was securely embedded in a concrete block. On the opposite shore, the Cossacks could see the artillery battery in the moonlight, a little over two hundred yards away.

Chernyovsky glanced up the inlet to his right. There was no sign of the *Milenion* yet, but it could not be long now.

Ordering his men to stay out of sight, he strode down on to the beach and waved a hand over his head to signal the battery. Someone returned his signal by waving a lantern from side to side: the man he had sent down the opposite side of the inlet had reached the battery. The signal indicated that the battery commander had agreed to Chernyovsky's plan: waiting until the yacht arrived, they would pretend to be asleep while the escaping English sent a boat ashore to try to break the cable. Chernyovsky and his men would wait until the Englishmen were ashore and out of the boat before he signalled his men to open fire. Exposed on the moonlit shore, they would be cut down without mercy, and the rattle of musketry would be the signal for the battery to open fire on the *Milenion* herself.

Chernyovsky's only fear was that the *Atalanta* would overhaul the yacht before she reached the cable.

He retreated into the undergrowth to where his men lay in ambush, and made himself comfortable amongst the bracken. Unslinging his carbine, he checked it was primed and loaded, and sighted down its length to the shore below. 'Carbines on half-cock,' he told his men. 'No one fires before I give the order.'

As the *Milenion* rounded the next headland in the inlet's indented coast, Molineaux could see the pontoons supporting the chain cable in the moonlight, a third of a mile off, broad on the starboard beam. On the right-hand side of the inlet, the battery commanding the narrows was dark and silent. With any luck, he thought, the gunners would all be fast asleep and the yacht could slip past unnoticed. But first, they had to break that bloody chain cable.

They coasted into the channel between Odensö and the mainland on the east side of the inlet, furled the sails and dropped anchor out of sight of the battery. They were only a few hundred yards around the coast of Odensö from the east end of the cable, just hidden around the northern tip of the island.

The gig was already hoisted in the davits. 'Away the gig,' ordered Molineaux, hefting his musket on one shoulder.

'Wish you'd let us come with you, like,' said Endicott.

Molineaux shook his head. 'I need you, Red, and Ben to stay on board with the pill-roller to make sure his lordship doesn't try to sail off without us.'

Endicott looked about the deck. 'Where is his nibs, any-road?'

'I don't know,' admitted Molineaux. Bullivant had gone below with Thornton shortly after their confrontation. 'Out of our hair for now, that's all that matters. Mr Uren! Perhaps you'd be so kind as to come with me, Burgess, O'Leary and Yorath?'

'Stay where you are, Uren!' commanded Bullivant.

'Oh Christ,' muttered Molineaux, and turned in time to see Bullivant emerge from the after hatch with a double-barrelled shotgun in his hands.

'My lord!' exclaimed Charlton. 'I must protest!'

'I've had enough of this foolishness,' said Bullivant. 'I'm taking command now. Tell the blackamoor to put down his musket, unless he wants his ugly head blown off.'

'Do as he says, Molineaux,' Charlton said quietly.

'But, sir . . .!'

'That's an order, damn you!'

Beaten – for now – the petty officer unslung the musket and lowered it to the deck. He knew that Bullivant was resolved to surrender himself. Well, that was no skin off Molineaux's nose, but he'd rot in hell before he'd let himself be taken by the Russians. He measured the distance from where he stood to the bulwark, hoping that Endicott, Hughes and Iles would have sense enough to follow him. But running would mean leaving Killigrew for the Russians, and he was damned if he was going to do that.

'What do you propose we do, my lord?' asked Charlton.

'Nothing at all,' Bullivant said smugly. 'We're going to wait here until the *Atalanta* gets here – can't be long now – and then surrender ourselves. I'm sure the Russians will be lenient.'

'I wish I shared your confidence, my lord,' said a familiar voice. Molineaux's heart leaped when he saw Killigrew climbing up out of the after hatch. 'And please don't tell me I'm supposed to be in bed,' he added to Charlton.

'Nothing was further from my mind, sir,' the assistant surgeon assured him with relief.

'You stay out of this, Killigrew,' said Bullivant. 'I'm in command now.'

'Really?' The commander squared up to him, and with a movement like lightning snatched the shotgun from Bullivant's hands. 'I'm resuming command. One more word out of you, my lord, and I'll have you locked in one of the cabins until we're safe.'

'You wouldn't dare!'

'That's three words,' said Killigrew. 'Hughes! Be so good as to escort his lordship below.'

Hughes grinned. 'My pleasure, sir.' He advanced on the viscount.

'You lay one hand on me, my man, and I shall have you flogged to within an inch of your life!'

'Better to be flogged within an inch of my life than shot an inch beyond it.' Hughes tried to take Bullivant by the arm. The viscount sidestepped and tried to strike him across the face, but Hughes caught him by the wrist before the blow landed. Spinning Bullivant around, he twisted his arm up into the small of his back.

'Arrggghhhh! Damn you, Killigrew! I'll have you hanged for this!'

'Look!' Endicott pointed above the trees on the mainland to the north of the channel.

Everyone turned to see a great black plume of cloud rising up behind the trees, silhouetted against the purple night sky.

'The *Atalanta*,' Bullivant surmised with a smile, taking pleasure in Killigrew's defeat even if it meant his own capture. 'She'll be here any moment. You've run out of time, Killigrew.'

Molineaux felt his heart sink. The paddle-sloop could only be minutes away. There was no time left to break the chain cable, no way they could fight back, nothing they could do but wait for the Russians to come and take them.

'We're not beaten yet.' Killigrew looked around in desperation, and saw the channel ahead.

'Odensö Channel,' said Thornton. 'There's no escape that way: it's a dead end.'

Killigrew ignored him. 'Up the gig! Molineaux, Endicott and Iles – heave up the anchor. Loose the sails, Mr Uren! Carry on, Hughes.'

'Aye, aye, sir.' The Welshman marched Bullivant to the after hatch.

The three Ramillies weighed anchor, while the boatswain and the Milenions unfurled the sails.

'Two points to port, Yorath,' said Killigrew.

'Two points it is, sir,' the sailor responded, as smartly as any bluejacket.

With the wind off the starboard beam, the *Milenion* gathered way and plunged deeper into the narrowing channel.

'For God's sake, Killigrew!' protested Thornton. 'You're wasting your time! This channel's a dead end. You'll do no more than buy us a few more minutes.'

'Scylla and Charybdis, Captain Thornton,' said Killigrew.

'If there's one thing I learned from Captain Keppel, it's this: when faced with a choice between two evils, always look for a third: it may be the least of the three.'

'Stop her,' Lazarenko ordered as the *Atalanta* approached the chain cable. The deck ceased throbbing and the paddle-wheels churned to a halt. In the silence that followed, the only sound to be heard was the dripping of water from the paddles and the gentle slop of the waves against the sloop's hull.

'Well?' demanded Nekrasoff. 'Where the devil is the *Milenion*?'

Lazarenko was at a loss. 'I don't understand it, sir. She hasn't had time to get past the chain cable, and if she doubled back we'd've seen her, even in this light.'

'Well, she must've gone *somewhere*,' sniffed Nekrasoff. 'Yachts don't simply vanish into thin air.'

On the shore a hundred yards away, a tall figure that could only be Chernyovsky had emerged from the trees and was waving to the paddle-sloop. Lazarenko took the speaking trumpet from the binnacle to address him.

'Have you seen the *Milenion*?'

Chernyovsky shook his head, and cupped his hands around his mouth to bellow back: 'Haven't you?'

Nekrasoff snatched the speaking trumpet from Lazarenko. 'How long have you been here?'

'Over half an hour!'

'There's no way on earth the *Milenion* could have come so far in two hours,' muttered Lazarenko. 'It simply isn't possible. Besides, the cable chain is still intact, that's plain to see.'

'Then we must have passed her!' insisted Nekrasoff. 'What about that inlet a few hundred yards back, to the left?'

'The Odensö Channel? It's a dead end: there's a low bridge two-thirds of a mile down it.'

'Does Killigrew know that?'

'He must do. He was captured on Odensö yesterday; Chernyovsky and his men would have taken him across that

253

bridge on the way to Ekenäs. Maybe he thinks if he hides in the channel until we've gone past, he'll fool us into thinking he's already got past the chain cable somehow.'

'What kind of a fool does he take us for?' snorted Nekrasoff.

'He *must* be up that channel,' said Lazarenko. 'There's nowhere else he can have gone.'

'Then we've got him trapped!' Nekrasoff said triumphantly. 'Take us after him, Lazarenko.'

'Yes, sir. Michmani Gavrilik! Order Inzhener Nikolaishvili to turn astern, half.'

Nekrasoff raised the speaking trumpet to his lips once more. 'Starshina Chernyovsky! We think they must have sailed the *Milenion* up the Odensö Channel. Take your men and ride through the forest to head him off at the bridge.'

On the shore, the Cossack saluted and strode back into the woods, calling out to his men.

The *Atalanta*'s engines started up once more, and the paddle-sloop backed up the inlet until it had passed the mouth of the channel. 'Stop her!' ordered Lazarenko. 'Starboard the helm, Beregovoi! Turn ahead full!'

The *Atalanta* nosed her way into the channel.

Nekrasoff produced a cigarette, tapped it twice against his cigarette case, and lit it. 'To use an English idiom, Lieutenant, I think we've finally run our quarry to ground.'

'By the mark, four!' Charlie Ogilby called from the chains, reeling in the lead line. As soon as he had gathered it all in, he swung it around and around and let go again. The lead plopped into the water and sank to the depths, as the *Milenion* glided over it. 'Less a quarter, four!'

'The channel's growing shallower,' observed Thornton.

'What's our draught?' asked Killigrew.

'Eleven feet.'

'Plenty of room.' Killigrew tried to sound blasé. He was more concerned about the width of the channel. The deeper into it they sailed, the narrower it became. With less than forty feet on either side of the hull – less, when one took the shallows into account – there was no room to tack from side to side; all they needed was for the waterway to turn more than four points to windward, and they would be unable to proceed. For now they were clipping along at a comfortable two knots, close-hauled with the wind off the starboard bow. Sailing close to the wind off a leeward shore was dangerous enough; sailing close to the wind with a leeward shore to one side and a windward shore to the other, well . . . Killigrew would not have tried it except *in extremis*. Since they had no choice, he tried to look relaxed, as if he did this sort of thing every morning before breakfast.

'And a half, three!' called Ogilby.

'Maybe we should put a reef or two in the sails,' suggested Mackenzie. 'With the shadows from these trees, we can hardly see where we're going. If there's an obstacle ahead, we'll no' have much time to avoid it. Or much room, for that matter.'

'Molineaux knows what he's doing,' said Killigrew. Molineaux had replaced Yorath at the helm as soon as they had run out of room to turn the schooner: in the seventeen years Killigrew had been at sea, he had never known a steadier hand at the wheel than the petty officer's. 'Keep her full, Molineaux.'

'Aye, aye, sir.' The petty officer came off the wind a little – not that he had much choice in the matter, given the restrictions of the channel – to keep their speed up, sailing as close to the left-hand side as he dared, using his own instincts to gauge the depths of the water as much as Ogilby's cries from the chains.

'And a quarter, three!'

'Damn it, man!' insisted Thornton. 'We're going too fast! That bridge can't be far off . . . if we're not careful, we'll run slap-bang into it!'

'That's the general idea,' agreed Killigrew.

Thornton stared at him in the gloom. 'Oh, sweet Jesus! You're serious, aren't you?'

'It's the only way out of here. My men and I crossed that bridge earlier today . . . yesterday, I mean . . .' had it really been only twelve hours since Chernyovsky and his Cossacks had captured them on Odensö? 'It's pretty old and rickety. With any luck we'll go straight through it.'

'You trust to luck too much for my taste, Mr Killigrew.'

'I don't have much choice. Right now it's one of the few weapons we have in our arsenal.'

'By the mark, three . . . bridge coming up, Mr Killigrew!'

'Very good. You'd best come in-board, Ogilby.' Killigrew peered ahead, but he could make out little in the shadows cast by the moonlight on the trees. 'You see it, Molineaux?' he asked anxiously.

'Aye, aye, sir. Clear as day.' That was another good reason for having the petty officer at the helm at a time like this: his night vision was phenomenal, doubtless honed by his adolescent years as a burglar.

'How far off?'

'A hundred yards from the prow and closing fast, sir.'

Killigrew strained his eyes against the darkness, but saw nothing. He was convinced that Molineaux had misjudged the distance in the poor light . . .

And then suddenly the bridge was there, looming up out of the gloom, a flimsy and insubstantial thing, yet an effective barrier to their escape through the channel if they did not break through.

'Pass the word!' called Killigrew. 'Brace for impact! Aim for the middle of the span, Molineaux.'

'Aye, aye, sir.'

With one arm in a sling, Mackenzie wrapped the other round the ratlines leading up to the mainmast.

Two knots: a little over two miles an hour. If a man walking down the street bumped into you at two knots, you would do little more than reel. If a man walking under a bridge at that speed hit his head on it, he'd do more damage to himself than to the bridge.

But the *Milenion* was not a man walking down the street: she was 170 tons of oak and teak, elegantly yet sturdily crafted by the shipwrights of East Cowes and, even at two knots, 170 tons of oak and teak could do a lot of damage.

The bowsprit passed over the railing of the low bridge, followed by the prow. Killigrew heard wood splinter and in the same instant felt the shock through the deck. Even braced for the impact, he found himself flung forward against the binnacle.

And then all was still.

'Anyone hurt?' he called across the deck.

'Just a few bruises this end, sir,' Uren called back.

'How's that bridge looking, Ogilby?'

'Same as she ever was,' the sailor called back sourly.

'Seems I underestimated the work of Finnish chippies,' Killigrew said ruefully.

'That's it, then,' said Mackenzie. 'It's over.' He glanced fearfully over his shoulder as if the *Atalanta* could heave in sight round the last bend at any moment, as well it might.

'*Nil desperandum*, Mr Mackenzie,' Killigrew called over his shoulder, running forward. 'I have a contingency plan.'

In the bows, he climbed on to the ratlines of the foremast and peered into the gloom ahead until he saw what he wanted. 'Ah-ha! Mr Uren? See that outcrop of rock there, about forty yards beyond the bridge on the left-hand side of the channel?'

'Aye, sir!'

'I want a cable run out from the capstan and belayed around that rock, chop chop!'

'Aye, aye, sir. Fuller, Yorath – bear a hand!'

Killigrew turned to the *Milenion*'s carpenter. 'Burgess?'

'Sir?'

'What tools have you got on board? Specifically, saws and axes.'

'A couple of each, sir.'

'Splendid! Run and fetch them. Hughes!'

'Aye, sir?'

'Do you know who built that bridge, Hughes?'

'No, sir.'

'Russian serfs, Hughes, driven to their labour by the crack of the knout.' In fact, Killigrew very much doubted a Russian serf had ever so much as laid eyes on the bridge – more likely it had been built by Finnish carpenters, serfdom being a long-forgotten memory in the Grand Duchy of Finland – but there was no point in confusing the seaman with minor details. 'In fact, you might go so far as to say that that bridge is the product of Tsarist exploitation of the Russian working classes.'

'Reckon you could at that, sir.'

Burgess came back on deck with the tools. Killigrew jumped down from the ratlines, took an axe from him, and handed it to the Welshman. 'Show us what you think of Tsarist exploitation, Hughes.'

The seaman grinned. 'My pleasure, sir.'

'Give the other axe to Ogilby and one of the saws to O'Leary,' Killigrew told Burgess. 'Nothing fancy, don't try to cut a section out; just split it down the middle so we can kedge through.'

'Aye, aye, sir.'

As the four men scrambled over the head to drop down on to the bridge, Killigrew returned aft to the quarterdeck. 'Mr Charlton, perhaps you'd be so good as to fetch Count Pechorin's lady friend from below? Make sure she has a warm coat and a stout pair of boots on her feet, and a bull's-eye.'

'Yes, sir.'

As the sounds of carpentry came from for'ard, Killigrew cast a glance aft. It could only be a matter of time before the officer commanding the *Atalanta* worked out where they had gone: they had only a few minutes to get through the bridge, and he could not help wondering if he was fooling himself into thinking they still had a chance to escape. But he had been in tighter spots than this before now, and he was damned if he would give up while there was still a glimmer of hope.

The boatswain came back on board with Fuller and Yorath. 'The cable's fast, sir.'

'Capital work, Mr Uren. Now go and see if Burgess needs a hand.'

'Aye, aye, sir.'

Pechorin's Finnish friend emerged from the after hatch, glowering at Killigrew.

'My sincerest apologies for incommoding you, ma'am, and for any distress we may have caused,' he told her in Swedish. 'You're free to go.' He indicated the path, just visible off the left-hand side of the channel. 'The ferry to Ekenäs is but a mile and a half down that track. I regret having to put you ashore alone so far from home, but we can hardly carry you any further. The Royal Navy does not make war on women.'

'The devil take your Royal Navy!' she retorted tartly. 'What am I to say to my husband? He expected me home an hour ago!'

Killigrew had no response to that, even though he had to admit to himself that was hardly his problem; although he was not so ungallant as to say so out loud. With further profuse apologies, he ordered Endicott and Iles to rig up a boatswain's chair so she could be lowered to the boards of the bridge next to where Burgess and the others attacked the carpentry, none more enthusiastically than Hughes. Molineaux lit the candle in the bull's-eye and handed it to her so she could find her way home.

'Reckon she'll be oh-kay, sir?' Molineaux asked as they watched her fade into the darkness without so much as a backwards glance at the *Milenion*.

'Oh, I think she'll be fine. Struck me as rather a formidable young lady.'

'What about . . . well, aren't there wolves hereabouts?'

'Oh, they'll be fine, as long as they steer clear of her.'

Molineaux nodded until Killigrew's meaning sank in; then he gave the commander a funny look, and shook his head wearily.

Killigrew leaned against the bulwark to watch the men working on the bridge. No matter how swiftly they laboured, it was not fast enough for the commander's liking. 'Pity we haven't got any gunpowder on board,' he remarked to Molineaux.

'Yes, sir. Or Mr Charlton's headache medicine.'

'Headache medicine?' echoed Killigrew.

'He means pyroglycerin,' explained Charlton. 'It would be just the thing too, if we had enough. Probably wouldn't take much, either. It's deuced powerful stuff.'

'Don't suppose you know how to make it, do you, sir?' asked Molineaux.

'Funnily enough, I do,' said Charlton. 'It isn't complicated: it's simply a matter of adding glycerine to a mixture of concentrated nitric and sulphuric acids. We've even got some glycerine on board: I noticed a bottle of it in the medicine chest. But no sulphuric or nitric acid, alas.'

Molineaux scratched his cheek. 'Sulphuric acid . . . that's a fancy term for oil of vitriol, ain't it?'

'That's right.'

'And nitric acid . . . spirits of nitre?'

'Yes. Why? You don't happen to have a bottle of each on you, do you?'

'No, sir. But they've got both in the dark room below.'

Charlton blanched. 'Oh, no . . .!'

'What is it?' asked Killigrew.

'Mr Charlton's got everything he needs to mix some pyroglycerin right here on board, sir,' said Molineaux.

'What *is* pyroglycerin?'

'It's a chemical,' said Charlton. 'It has a number of uses in both homeopathic and allopathic medicine. But it's also very explosive. A pint of it would be more than enough to blow that bridge apart.'

260

'And you can make it?'

'Steady on, sir! Yes, in theory . . . but I wouldn't like to try. The stuff's deuced volatile. One knock, and the whole lot could explode.'

Molineaux frowned and cocked his head on one side. 'Hear that, sir?'

Killigrew shook his head, although he knew from past experience that just because he could not hear something Molineaux could, that did not mean the petty officer was imagining it. Molineaux's hearing was every bit as phenomenal as his night vision, and had doubtless been honed in the same way.

The petty officer made his way to the taffrail and Killigrew joined him.

And then he heard it. Or at least, he thought he heard it. The sound was difficult to make out, because of the noise that Burgess and the others on the bridge were making with their saws and axes; he might have missed it altogether, had it not been a familiar sound from the years he had spent serving on board HMS *Tisiphone*. A steady, rhythmic, plashing sound, mechanical in its regularity: the beat of wood against water, so many times a minute each splash seemed to merge into one throbbing hiss; distant, but growing louder.

The sound of a paddle-steamer.

XIII

Trapped

Killigrew turned to Charlton. 'How long would it take you to make some of this . . . what did you say it was called?'

'Pyroglycerin, sir,' Molineaux supplied.

'At least half an hour, sir,' said Charlton. 'It's not a process that can be hurried. But I really don't think it would be wise to—'

'Then we'll have to make do without it for now,' Killigrew cut him off, to the assistant surgeon's evident relief. 'That's half an hour we haven't got.'

Followed by Molineaux, Killigrew ran the length of the upper deck. 'All right, lads, that will have to do,' he called down to the men working on the bridge.

'But we're not finished!' protested Burgess.

'We are if we don't get out of here now!' Molineaux retorted. 'Come on, lads, give us your hands.'

They hauled the four men back over the gunwale on to the deck. 'All hands man the capstan!' ordered Killigrew.

The men arranged themselves at the capstan bars and began to push, turning around it, taking up the slack of the cable Uren had tied around the outcrop of rock on the far side of the bridge. The *Milenion*'s bows nosed against the bridge once more, and the timbers groaned under the strain.

'Heave, damn it!' said Killigrew. '*Heave!*'

The sound of a musket shot startled him. He glanced aft, expecting to see the *Atalanta* rounding the bend behind them, but there was no sign of it. Two more shots sounded, one of them splintering the gunwale close to where he stood, and this time he caught sight of the muzzle-flashes through the trees on the right bank of the channel.

'Infantry?' asked Thornton, ashen-faced.

'Cossacks,' spat Killigrew. He was no expert on the sound of muskets, could not tell a rifle from a carbine from an old-fashioned Brown Bess; but some instinct told him that it would be Chernyovsky and his Cossacks. Nekrasoff must have guessed that they would try to break through the chain cable, and had set Chernyovsky and his men ahead to ambush them. When they had realised that the *Milenion* had turned down the Odensö Channel, they had cut through the forest to head them off at the bridge.

'Come on!' Killigrew tore off his coat and joined the men at the capstan; Thornton and Charlton joined him. Only Mackenzie stood idle – his arm useless in its sling – clearly wishing he could do something to help.

They pushed at the bars, fifteen men straining to drag 170 tons of yacht through a rotten, sabotaged bridge. A bridge Killigrew might have admired for its stubbornness could he have viewed the situation objectively, but for now it was barring his only escape, and he hated it more than he had hated anyone or anything in his life; and Killigrew could be a great hater when he had justification.

Feet scuffled for purchase on the teak deck, bones and timbers creaked, men grunted and groaned, but that damned bridge was as strong as ever. More carbines flared in the darkness, barking from the trees, bullets soughing low over the *Milenion*'s deck. Killigrew convinced himself they were

263

wasting their time; the bridge was never going to break. Better to jump over the bows on to that accursed bridge and run for what limited safety the trees on the left bank could offer; or perhaps to surrender, throw themselves on the Russians' mercy.

On Nekrasoff's mercy.

But a man like Nekrasoff had no mercy. It was pointless to waste energy even thinking about it. Every thought in Killigrew's head, along with every muscle and sinew in his body, had to be focused on one objective and one objective alone: breaking that bridge.

'Come on, you bastard!' he hissed through clenched teeth. 'Break, damn you! Break!'

The bullets whistling over their heads only spurred them on to greater efforts, efforts greater than the human body had been designed for; or rather, efforts greater than any of them ever suspected their bodies were capable of achieving. Something had to give: if the bridge would not break, then the cable would snap, but nothing would break these men.

When Killigrew heard the splintering, he assumed it must be the snapping bones of a man who had strained himself too hard: he dared not believe that they might finally have defeated that bridge. But then the *Milenion* was gliding forward, and as the capstan became slack once more the men pushing at the bars stumbled and fell to their knees. The bridge continued to splinter as the bows thrust the broken central section aside, the jagged timbers scratching the paint-work on the hull, and to hell with Bullivant's paint job anyhow, they were through!

No need for all of them to continue pushing at those bars. Killigrew backed away, sizing up the situation. The Cossacks continued to fire sporadically from the woods to their right, but so far did not seem to be hitting anything other than the bulwarks.

'Take the helm, Molineaux! Endicott, Hughes – grab a musket each and give those Cossacks something to think about! Stand by to cut the cable when I say "now", Mr Uren: the rest of you, when I give the order, leave off the capstan and man the halyards!'

Retreating to the quarterdeck, Killigrew waited for the *Milenion*'s stern to clear the breach it had made in the bridge. The splintered ends still jutted out on either side of the hull, scraping along the sides. He glanced astern, and saw the *Atalanta* steam around the corner behind them. It was less than two hundred yards away, close enough for Killigrew to make out the *matrosy* manning the bow chaser. The big gun was angled to fire through the second of the two gunports in the steamer's port bow, but as it rounded the corner in the channel it was still not at the right angle to fire a shot at the yacht.

And then the *Milenion*'s stern was clear of the bridge.

'Now!' roared Killigrew.

As the hands at the capstan left the bars to man the halyards, Uren brought down an axe and chopped through the cable. The sails were unfurled once more, bellying in the stiff breeze that blew across Odensö Island. Beyond the bridge, the channel veered to the left, but the cable had already been drawing the schooner in that direction and Molineaux had to spin the helm to port to compensate. Once the yacht was in the centre of the channel, he angled it to follow the narrow waterway ahead, before bringing the helm amidships.

The Cossacks were still firing from the trees. Charlie Ogilby slumped to the deck.

The bow chaser on the *Atalanta*'s forecastle boomed, shooting flame into the night. Killigrew heard the round shot screech through the darkness, felt the whole ship shudder beneath his feet as the ball smashed into the *Milenion*'s stern, crashing through the bulkheads below, causing God alone knew what kind of carnage, and Lady Bullivant and Araminta were down there with Mr Dahlstedt, and why the hell were the Russians firing round shot into the hull instead of chain shot at the masts?

'Damage report, Burgess!' roared Killigrew, wishing he had some way of striking back at the paddle-sloop. That this was the first time he had ever been engaged with an enemy steamer was a thought that was far from his mind: his only concern was that the enemy was trying to kill him and those sailing with him, and he was powerless to strike back at them. 'Look to Ogilby, Mr Charlton!'

'Yes, sir!'

The *Atalanta* was barrelling up the channel at more than twice the speed of the *Milenion*, closing the gap between them to less than a hundred yards. The gentle curve of the channel to the west would hide the yacht from sight within two minutes, but that was more than enough time for a competent gun crew to put two more shots into their hull.

As the yacht faded into the night, the shooting of the Cossacks in the trees became even more sporadic. The gun crew of the sloop's bow chaser had had more than enough time to reload . . . what were they waiting for? Killigrew found himself almost wishing they would fire, to get it over and done with, and then his prayer was answered and the gun boomed again. He braced himself for the feel of the round shot – thank Christ they weren't using shell! – smashing through his body, or splinters being thrown up from the deck below to lacerate his flesh. The shot shrieked past to starboard, and the trees on the right-hand bank of the channel shivered and splintered as the ball tore through their trunks. A miss, by God, and a wide one at that!

But the paddle-sloop was less than eighty yards astern and had almost reached the gap the *Milenion* had smashed through the bridge. Never mind the incompetence of the Russian gunners; in a minute or two more they would be able to run the schooner down and ram her. The *Milenion* gathered way as the curve of the channel brought her away from the wind and drove her along at something approaching three knots, but still not fast enough to outrun the next shot.

★ ★ ★

'Why don't they fire?' Nekrasoff demanded impatiently, referring to the bow chaser's gun crew.

'The *Milenion*'s out of their line of fire,' Lazarenko replied evenly. 'Once we're through the bridge, we'll be able to line up for their next shot.'

Standing next to them on the quarterdeck, the *Atalanta*'s second lieutenant studied the bridge. 'That gap's too narrow,' he opined.

'I'm well aware of that, Borislav Ivanovich,' Lazarenko replied. 'We will brush aside what remains with our paddle-boxes.'

'The paddle-boxes are too high.'

'Nonsense, man! Are you saying I don't know my job?'

'Bow chaser ready to fire, sir,' reported the gunner.

'Excellent!' gloated Lazarenko. 'Stand by until I give the word.'

The *Atalanta*'s prow came through the gap in the bridge. Once through she would have enough room to turn a couple of points to port to bring the *Milenion* in her bow chaser's line of fire . . .

The sound of wood splintering was loud enough to be heard above the paddles' plashing. 'What did I tell you?' Lazarenko asked the second lieutenant as the sloop ground its way through the debris. 'Plenty of room . . .'

There came more splintering, and the deck shuddered beneath their feet. Something gave, something else refused to give, and there was yet more splintering as the wheel ground to a crunching halt. The *Atalanta* slewed to star-board, slamming her stern into the opposite end of the bridge with a deafening crash, and Nekrasoff was thrown to the deck by the sudden impact. He rolled over and over until he came to rest in the scuppers. He lay there gasping for breath, scarcely able to credit that he might still be alive.

He looked up to see Lazarenko and the second lieutenant

pick themselves up and dust themselves down. Nekrasoff stood up to find the *Atalanta* had become wedged in the debris of the bridge, slewed diagonally across the gap, the remains of the starboard paddle-wheel hopelessly entangled in the timbers of the bridge. Glancing for'ard, he saw the *Milenion* fading into the darkness where the channel rounded a bend a couple of hundred yards ahead . . . then it was gone.

'Damage report, Dubrovsky!' Lazarenko ordered crisply.

'Yes, sir.' The sloop's shipwright hurried below.

Nekrasoff noticed the second lieutenant grinning at Lazarenko. The first lieutenant became aware of the grin, and regarded him sourly.

'Told you the gap was too narrow,' the second lieutenant said smugly.

'Someone coming out of the woods, sir!' one of the lookouts called.

Nekrasoff and Lazarenko crossed to the starboard gunwale to see Chernyovsky and his Cossacks emerge from the trees, leading their ponies by their bridles. Handing his halter to one of his men to hold, Chernyovsky stepped on to the south end of the wrecked bridge and looked up at the *Atalanta*. Then, shaking his head, he chuckled.

'So much for the navy!'

'You were here before we were,' Lazarenko pointed out. 'You failed to stop them!'

Chernyovsky scowled. 'We're Cossacks, not sailors! Catching enemy ships is supposed to be the navy's business!'

The shipwright emerged from the fore hatch. 'No damage to the hull, sir.'

'Check the paddle-wheels.'

'Yes, sir.' The shipwright detailed two of his men to clamber over the side to check the port-side wheel, while he himself clambered down on to the bridge where he could examine the one to starboard. He shook his head and sucked air in between his teeth. 'Half the paddle-boards will need replacing on this one, and some of the spokes are damaged too.'

'We have enough spare paddle-boards on board, don't we? And the carpenter's crew can repair the spokes.'

'Yes, sir. But first we'll have to get clear of this bridge so we have room to work.'

'All right, send some men ashore and find something we can belay a cable to. We'll have to kedge ourselves clear of the bridge. While that's being done, the carpenter's crew can saw off any of the bridge's timbers that are still entangled with the wheel so we can drag ourselves free.'

'And then you'll still be on the wrong side,' Nekrasoff pointed out.

'I would have thought it was patently obvious we cannot pass this bridge,' Lazarenko said coldly.

'I would have thought that was patently obvious from the outset,' said the second lieutenant.

'I did not ask your opinion, Borislav Ivanovich.'

'No, but I gave it to you anyway. Perhaps if you had not ignored my advice, we would not now be in this mess!'

The two men who had gone over the port side to check the other wheel reported. 'Port-side wheel is sound, sir.'

'That's something, at least.'

'How long is all this going to take, Lieutenant?' demanded Nekrasoff.

Lazarenko glanced questioningly at the shipwright. 'About an hour and a half, sir,' the latter answered for him.

'An hour and a half!' exclaimed Nekrasoff.

'Make it one hour, and I'll see to it that you and every man in the carpenter's crew gets a *schtoff* of vodka each,' Lazarenko told the shipwright.

'We'll do our best, sir.' The shipwright made no attempt to disguise that he was affronted by the suggestion they needed to be bribed to work as swiftly as possible. 'But we can't work miracles.'

'And all this time the *Milenion* is getting further and

further away!' glowered Nekrasoff.

'Oh, they won't get far,' Lazarenko told him coolly. 'You see, less than one *verst* further along, this channel turns to the south-west. And there's no way Killigrew and his men can sail that yacht against the wind.'

'One *verst* away, you say? Ten minutes' walk – in broad daylight over open ground, at least.'

Lazarenko nodded.

Nekrasoff crossed to the bulwark. '*Starshina!*'

Chernyovsky looked up at him questioningly.

The colonel paused to light another cigarette. 'How would you and your men like a chance to redeem yourselves?'

'It's a deuce of a mess down there,' Mackenzie reported to Killigrew. 'The shot came through the gallery window of the saloon . . . there's glass everywhere—'

'Never mind that! Was anyone hurt?'

'Apart from Ogilby? No. Mr Charlton's looking at him at the moment.'

Killigrew would have liked to go below himself to see the extent of the damage, and to make sure the ladies had not been too alarmed by the excitement; although in the case of Lady Bullivant, at least, he very much doubted there was much that could alarm her. But his first priority was to get the *Milenion* as far away from the *Atalanta* as possible. They might have lost the paddle-sloop for now, but it could only be a matter of time before the damage was repaired and the chase resumed.

A few minutes later the channel widened to two hundred yards, and he guessed they were approaching the opposite end. But the channel also bore round to the south, forcing the schooner to sail as close to the wind as she could. Before long, the channel forked on either side of an island: the channel to the right was the broader, but the *Milenion* could not sail close enough to the wind to take it and there was still no room to tack. The left-hand channel was much narrower, and did not look deep enough for the *Milenion*'s draught. The island was only about 350 yards long, and beyond it Killigrew could see open water, with more than enough space to tack in; yet for all their chances of reaching it under sail, it might as well have been on Neptune.

'Shorten sail and let go the anchor!' ordered Killigrew.

'Stand clear of the chain!' bellowed Uren. 'Let go the anchor!'

The chain rattled through the hawsehole as the anchor dropped from the bows to splash into the water.

'Mr Uren, take Iles and Hughes and sound that channel,' Killigrew told the boatswain, indicating the right-hand fork.

'Aye, aye, sir. Lower the gig!'

Once the gig was lowered from its davits, Uren, Iles and Hughes shinned down the lifelines and rowed across to sound the channel with a lead line.

Leaving Thornton in charge on deck, Killigrew descended the after hatch. He missed his footing on the companion ladder – because two of the steps had been smashed away – and landed heavily on the deck below. Feeling foolish, but with only some bruises to show for the mishap, he picked himself up and dusted himself down, glad that no one had seen him fall.

One glance told him what had happened to the missing steps: there was a splintered hole in the door leading to the saloon where the round shot had smashed through the louvred panel, and a similar hole in the door at the opposite end of the corridor. He made his way for'ard to peer through the far hole and found himself gazing into the forecastle, where the ball had passed through the companion ladder in the middle of the compartment before coming to a halt, firmly embedded in the stout timbers of the bows. The wood was grazed on both masts where they descended through the deck above: a few inches to starboard, and the yacht would have been dismasted. It was fortunate for them the Russians had not been using shell: the *Milenion* would have been blown out of the water.

He made his way back to the saloon, where he found Burgess surveying the damage. Pechorin still sat on the deck, bound hand and foot.

'His lordship isn't going to like this!' said Burgess.

It was true: had Killigrew been knocked unconscious and woken up in the saloon, he would never have guessed he was on board a luxury yacht. The windows were smashed, the plush velvet curtains torn to shreds by flying glass and splinters, and the glassware, crockery – and just about everything else that was breakable – broken.

'Think you can board up the windows?' he asked Burgess.

The carpenter nodded. 'I'll tack a piece of canvas to the frame; that should keep the draught out.'

'We've stopped,' Pechorin remarked to Killigrew as soon as Burgess had gone to fetch his tools and some canvas and nails. 'I suppose we're at the south-east end of the Odensö Channel?'

'That would be telling,' said Killigrew.

'You've done well,' admitted the count. 'When I realised you must be running down the channel, I never thought you'd get past that bridge. What happened to the *Atalanta*? I presume it was her who fired that round shot?'

'Sorry, Count. I'm afraid she didn't have as much luck as we did in getting through the bridge.'

'She'll catch you,' Pechorin said confidently. 'The wind's blowing from the south-west: there's no way you can sail out of this channel. Even if she has to steam the long way around Odensö and stop to take down the chain cable at Vitsand Sound, she can still head you off.'

'Well, it looked to me as though whoever's in command of the *Atalanta* made a mess of her paddle-wheels; and we've only got five hundred yards to cover to reach the Skärlandet Channel.'

'Five hundred yards!' scoffed Pechorin. 'It might as well be five hundred *vehrsty*. Why don't you make it easy for yourself, Commander, and surrender? I am not without influence; perhaps I can have you all spared.'

Killigrew shook his head. 'You know as well as I that Nekrasoff wants us dead; and even he wouldn't dare try to murder us all without the backing of his superiors in St Petersburg. Now, why do you suppose that is?'

Pechorin feigned disinterest. 'I really couldn't say.'

'Oh, I think you know, don't you? After all, you were the one who brought the *Milenion* into Ekenäs.'

Pechorin just smiled broadly.

Killigrew checked the ropes binding the count's wrists and ankles, but he need not have bothered: Molineaux knew all the tricks a man could employ to break free of bonds; consequently, he knew how to tie him so he stayed tied up. 'Someone on this ship knows something,' he told Pechorin. 'Something important; something you and Nekrasoff don't want our fleet to know. There's no other reason Nekrasoff would risk the international outcry the murder of Lord Bullivant would cause. Oh, don't feel obliged to tell me: I'll find out without your help.'

'It will do you no good,' said Pechorin. 'You'll never make it back to your fleet.'

'You have a lot of confidence in whoever commands the *Atalanta* in your absence.'

'Lieutenant Lazarenko? I should do. I trained him myself.'

Killigrew smiled. 'Pity you didn't train him not to steam a fifty-foot-wide flapper through a forty-five-foot gap. I'll take my leave of you now, but before I go let me give you something to occupy your mind to help you while away the tedious hours of your incarceration: why do you think Lazarenko fired round shot into our hull when anyone else would have fired chain shot at our masts, to cripple us?'

Pechorin scowled, and Killigrew slipped out of the saloon.

As soon as he had gone, the count took his foot off the shard of glass he had been hiding beneath the sole of his boot. He shuffled forward on his bottom until he could grasp the shard in his kid-gloved hands. Clutching it, he squirmed back

273

against the bulkhead, so that when Burgess returned to repair the hole in the windows the count was exactly where he had been earlier. While the carpenter set to work, Pechorin began surreptitiously sawing at his bonds.

'Sorry, sir,' Mr Uren told Killigrew when he reported back on the *Milenion*'s quarterdeck. 'The left-hand channel is simply too shallow.'

'How shallow?'

'Less than a fathom in places.'

Killigrew nodded. 'Then there's nothing for it: we'll simply have to tow her out through the other channel.'

'Tow her!' Thornton exclaimed incredulously. 'Do you have any idea how much the *Milenion* weighs?'

'About a hundred and seventy tons?' guessed Killigrew. The captain scowled. 'There's no other way. Come on – it's only five hundred yards – it shouldn't be a problem for big, strong lads like we've got. There's room for ten men rowing double-banked in that gig. You'll be in charge, Captain Thornton . . . though I'm afraid you'll have to pull your weight.'

The master nodded his acquiescence: this was no time for standing on one's dignity.

'Take Uren, Endicott, Hughes, Iles, O'Leary, Fuller, Yorath and Attwood.'

'And while we're breaking our backs? Where will you be?'

'The chances are there's at least one man on board the *Atalanta* who knows these waters like the back of his hand, in which case they'll know we'll be struggling to get out of this channel while the wind's blowing from the south-west. They're less than half a mile behind us. What would you do, if you were the officer in command of the *Atalanta*?'

Thornton nodded. 'Send men through the woods to head us off.'

'Our best bet is to ambush them before they get here: that

way I'll take them by surprise, instead of vice versa.'

'You're going to take them on single-handed?'

'Lor', no! I'm taking a secret weapon.'

'Secret weapon?'

'Molineaux!'

The petty officer had picked up a couple of muskets and two cartouche boxes. He threw one of the muskets to Killigrew, who caught it. He slung the musket over one shoulder, and took a cartouche box and slung it over the other. The two of them shinned down to the gig, where Iles and Hughes waited for them.

'Where are we going, sir?' asked Hughes.

'Take us over to the west shore,' Killigrew told him, pointing.

From where the *Atalanta* was entangled in the ruined bridge, there was a straight line over the island on that side, whereas anyone trying to follow the channel on the opposite bank would be going the long way around. Besides, if Killigrew had been in Lieutenant Lazarenko's shoes, he would have sent Chernyovsky and his men to catch them, and the Cossacks would have difficulty getting their ponies across to the mainland with the bridge broken.

Iles and Hughes put them ashore on the western tip of Odensö Island, before rowing back to where Mackenzie and Uren were making a cable fast to the *Milenion*'s bows so they could tow her through the channel to the right-hand side of the inlet.

'Hope they don't go without us, sir,' said Molineaux.

'I hope they get the chance,' replied Killigrew. 'Come on.'

Shouldering their muskets, the two of them plunged into the darkness of the forest.

Burgess had cut a square of canvas and tacked it over the hole in the door of the saloon, and was now working on the windows, when Pechorin finally cut through the rope tying his wrists. Outside, the sound of oars plashing and men singing a sea shanty carried faintly back to the saloon: the *Milenion*'s crew trying to tow the schooner out through the mouth of the channel.

The carpenter had almost finished his task, and it was tempting for Pechorin to wait until he was gone before he took any further action. Get off the *Milenion*, swim back to shore and walk along the side of the channel until he reached the *Atalanta* . . . but what good would that do? He could not leave until he had found some way to cripple the yacht.

On the other hand, he doubted he could take on Killigrew and all the men with him single-handed. But at least killing one of them would even the odds in his favour.

Burgess worked with his back to the count, engrossed in his labours. Pechorin brought his hands in front of him, still grasping the shard of glass, and began sawing at the ropes binding his ankles: it was quicker than trying to unpick one of Molineaux's Gordian knots.

Burgess began to hammer the last tack in place. Pechorin strained at the rope around his ankles, and the last fibres snapped. It was the softest of sounds, yet somehow the carpenter heard it above his own hammering. He whirled in time to see Pechorin leap to his feet. After sitting in the same position for over three hours, the count's limbs were stiff with cramp and he swayed on the deck, giving Burgess time to throw the hammer. Pechorin barely managed to jerk his head aside, and the hammer crashed against the bulkhead behind him. Burgess lunged for the door, but Pechorin interposed himself, still gripping the shard of glass like a dagger.

Burgess grinned. 'So, that's the way of it, is it, Ivan? If it's a fight you're wanting, I'm your man!'

He snatched a chisel from his sack of tools and tossed it from hand to hand. Not much of a weapon, a chisel . . . except in the hands of a carpenter up against a Russian aristocrat more comfortable with a sabre than a shard of glass.

The two of them circled one another around the saloon table. Pechorin wondered why Burgess did not cry out for help; and then he saw the wolfish grin on the carpenter's face, and realised he was enjoying this.

The carpenter lunged, stabbing the chisel at Pechorin's eyes. The count jerked his head back, and caught Burgess by the wrist with his left hand, slashing him across the throat with the shard in his right. Blood spilled over Burgess' collar, but the shard had not gone deep enough to sever an artery. The carpenter continued trying to push the chisel's blade into the count's eyes.

Pechorin hooked a booted foot behind one of Burgess' ankles. The carpenter went over backwards and landed on his back, Pechorin on top of him, pinning his arm to the rug. Burgess drove his left fist into Pechorin's side. The Russian gasped in agony, and stabbed with the shard of glass, burying it deep in the carpenter's neck. The death rattle sounded in Burgess' throat as blood gouted from the awful wound.

Pechorin picked himself up, pressing one hand to his side where Burgess had hit him, and glanced down to where the carpenter bled the last drops of his life away, all over Lord Bullivant's fine Persian rug.

The door opened. Pechorin whirled to see Charlton standing there. 'Is everything all ri—' he began, and stared in astonishment when he saw the prisoner standing over Burgess' still-quivering corpse.

Pechorin grabbed the first thing that came to hand – Burgess' sack of tools – and slung it at Charlton's head. The assistant surgeon stumbled back against the bulkhead and sank to the deck with a livid bruise weeping blood on his temple. Pechorin crouched over him and, finding a pulse in his neck, he tore down some of the curtain ropes and used them to bind Charlton's hands and feet, before gagging him with a napkin. Killing a man in hand-to-hand combat was one thing, but he could not bring himself to murder a man in cold blood.

He searched about for a weapon and took the carving knife Molineaux had admired earlier from the cutlery drawer. Slipping out of the saloon, he listened at the first door on his right – Bullivant's stateroom, presumably – and heard someone snoring. He tried the handle, but the door was locked. He tried the door on the other side of the passage: it opened to reveal a woman's stateroom, to judge from all the frills and fripperies that furbished the space, except that the person lying in the bed was a man in his late twenties, the hands above the covers swathed in blood-soaked bandages. He was not snoring, and looked so pale he might be dead. Pechorin felt for a pulse in his neck, and found a strong one. Holding the carving knife to his throat in case he woke up, Pechorin prised back an eyelid to reveal a dilated pupil; the bottle of laudanum resting on the dresser told its own story.

He heard more snores coming from the next stateroom along, and eased open the door to find Lady Bullivant asleep in the chair, a Bible open on her lap. A sailor lay on the bunk, a bloody bandage wrapped around his stomach. Pechorin slipped out, easing the door shut behind him. A companion ladder led up to the upper deck; beyond, the passage continued to the forecastle, with more doors opening off on either side.

He did not have time to search the whole ship: he climbed the companion ladder, taking care to avoid the two broken steps, and peered cautiously over the coaming of the after hatch.

There was no one on deck.

He climbed up through the hatch, looking around. No one in sight. He crept to the bows and peered over the bulwark to see the gig at the far end of a cable, laboriously towing the schooner towards the open water beyond the mouth of the channel. It was tempting to let the cable slip, but that would only bring the men in the gig back on board to investigate. The men in the boat still had three hundred feet to go, and were making slow progress. Better to leave them where they were, for now. He had the *Milenion* more or less to himself.

But how to stop it? Set fire to it, perhaps? But there were women and wounded men on board. Similarly, he could not hack a hole in the keel and sink her: if the channel was too deep, those still on board might drown.

Sometimes, he reflected, being an honourable man could be a pain in the neck. He did not doubt that, had Nekrasoff been in his shoes, he would have done whatever he could to destroy the yacht, and the devil take anyone on board. But Pechorin had no desire to be like Nekrasoff.

The question was, how long until Lazarenko could repair the *Atalanta* and get here? Not before the men in the gig had towed the yacht clear of the channel, he was willing to lay odds. But even a dunderhead like Lazarenko must know that the *Milenion* could not sail out of the mouth of the channel with the wind blowing from the south-west. The *Atalanta* was only half a mile away. Surely even the first lieutenant would think to send some men overland; in which case, Pechorin had only to keep the yacht here long enough for them to arrive.

But how?

He was still pondering this dilemma when he heard someone moving about in the galley below. He crept down the fore hatch, missed his footing on a missing rung and fell to the deck with a thump.

'Who's there?' Miss Maltravers called from the galley.

He picked up the carving knife he had dropped in his fall and crept cat-footed to the door to the galley, pressing himself up against the bulkhead beside it.

'Hello?' she called.

He saw her shadow fall across the threshold, and reached

through the door to grab her, throwing her against the opposite bulkhead. At first, she was too surprised to cry out: then he had pinned her there, one hand over her mouth, the other holding the carving knife to her throat.

'Please don't make a sound, Miss Maltravers,' he said pleasantly. 'It would grieve me to have to kill a woman, hm?'

XIV

The Skärlandet Channel

1.30 a.m.–2.10 a.m., Friday 18 August

Wide-eyed and white with fright, Miss Maltravers nodded her acquiescence. Pechorin took away his hand.

She did not scream. Instead, she said: 'Not as much as it would grieve me to be killed, I'm sure! I thought you were tied up in the saloon?'

'I felt a sudden urge to stretch my legs.'

'Let her go!' a voice commanded imperiously behind him. He looked around to see Lady Bullivant aiming a double-barrelled shotgun through the hole in the door.

Pechorin quickly spun Miss Maltravers round so that she shielded him, still holding the knife to her throat. 'Drop the gun, ma'am, or I'll kill your daughter.'

Lady Bullivant shook her head. 'I hardly think so. You're not the sort who'd murder a defenceless woman in cold blood. Let her go, Count.'

Pechorin felt foolish – being held at gunpoint by a middle-aged woman! – and yet as he looked down those twin muzzles it was like gazing down the maw of Hell. If only there was some way he could disarm the silly old bat . . .

'Don't you think you should take the safety catches off?' he suggested, bracing himself to tackle her the moment she glanced down.

Her gaze did not waver. 'The safety catches *are* off, Count. I'm not a complete fool.'

He shrugged. 'You can hardly blame me for trying.'

'No, indeed! Now, please have the decency to let my daughter go. Don't think I don't know how to use this thing: many's the time I've accompanied my husband grouse shooting in the Highlands.'

Pechorin smiled. 'Then you'll know that if you try to shoot me with that, you'll do as much harm to your daughter as you will to me.'

'I know. Why do you think I haven't pulled the trigger already?'

'Because I don't believe you could kill a man any more than I could kill a woman.'

Lady Bullivant arched an eyebrow. 'Indeed, Count? Then may I suggest you put your theory to the test, and release my daughter?'

Pechorin looked into those cold, grey eyes of hers, and decided against it.

Lady Bullivant smiled. 'It seems we have reached an impasse.'

'It does indeed.'

'Except the advantage is on my side.'

'And just how do you come to that conclusion?'

'Time is on my side, Count Pechorin. All we have to do is wait, and the others will return on board in due course.'

'Before or after the men my first lieutenant is doubtless sending overland from the *Atalanta* get here?'

'*Touché*, Count.'

A couple of shots sounded in the distance outside. Pechorin glanced up at the deck head. 'What's that . . .?'

Miss Maltravers grabbed him by the arm and pulled the carving knife away from her throat, sinking her teeth into his wrist. He screamed in agony and dropped the knife. She broke free, throwing herself across the room. Suddenly nothing stood between Pechorin and Lady Bullivant's shotgun.

He grinned. 'You wouldn't shoot an unarmed man, would you?'

Her knuckle whitened on one of the triggers.

He turned and dived for cover behind a couple of seamen's chests as the shotgun exploded, lighting the compartment up with a bright flash and sending red-hot needles of agony searing through his left leg. Crouching on the deck behind the chests, he examined his calf, which was peppered with shot.

'You shot me!' he moaned. 'I don't believe it! You actually shot me!'

'Stick your head up and I'll prove it was not an accident!'

Pechorin twisted and drew his legs up beneath him, tensed to make a dash for the door of the galley. Grabbing a fistful of small change from his pocket, he flung it in the opposite direction to distract her attention, and launched himself from behind the chests. The coins fooled Lady Bullivant, but only for an instant, and her next shot narrowly missed him as he made his wild dash.

Reaching the temporary haven of the galley, he limped across the deck to the far door that opened out into the corridor behind her. Even if she had thought to bring some spare ammunition with her, it would take her precious seconds to reload. He stumbled out into the corridor, and took the full force of the shotgun's stock in the face.

If she had been a big, strong man instead of a middle-aged woman, the blow would have broken both his jaw and his neck. As it was, it split the skin of his cheek and hurt – a lot. He fell to the deck, sprawled across the threshold of the galley, and looked up to see her swinging back the shotgun to club him again. Rolling on his stomach, he crawled away down the corridor while she followed him, belabouring his back with the stock of the shotgun.

'Brute! Coward! Beastly Russian swine! I'll teach you not

to hide behind the petticoats of a defenceless young woman!'

Defenceless my eye, Pechorin thought sourly, his wrist beginning to throb where Miss Maltravers had bitten him. At last he managed to haul himself up by one of the brass handrails and stumbled to the companion ladder leading up to the after hatch. As he was about to climb up, he glimpsed Lady Bullivant between the broken rungs, taking two cartridges from the pockets of her skirts and inserting them in the breech of the shotgun. As she snapped the breech shut, he scrambled up the ladder on to the deck, dashed across to the side, and dived over the port bulwark.

The water was icy cold; yet pleasantly soothing for his stinging leg. He had taken a deep breath as he went over the side, and he swam down, down into the inky depths, until his searching hands found the slimy rocks at the bottom of the channel. He pulled himself along the bottom, moving more by instinct than any certain knowledge of where he was going, until he could hold his breath no more.

His head broke the surface – how warm the cold night air felt after his immersion in the colder Baltic waters! – and gulped great lungfuls of air down his throat. He twisted in the water, saw the *Milenion* perhaps fifty feet behind him, the men in the gig rowing back to find out what was going on. Lady Bullivant stood at the side, levelling the shotgun over the bulwark at him. He swore, and ducked back beneath the surface as the gun boomed in her hands.

When he broke the surface again, only a few seconds later, he was but a few yards from the rocky shore. He staggered up out of the water and squelched into the trees, sobbing for breath. Lady Bullivant had reloaded again and fired after him, twice, but by then he had been swallowed up by the darkness, and both shots went wide.

Chernyovsky did not mind the dark beneath the forest's boughs where the moon's beams could not penetrate, but he hated the trees. Like his men, he came from the Steppes, a wide-open country where a man could see as far as his eyesight and the earth's curvature would allow. The trees pressing in around him made him feel claustrophobic, as if they were closing in on him. There was no room for a horseman to break into a gallop, even if he could have seen in the darkness.

The *starshina* led the way, a flambeau held aloft in one hand guttering in the breeze, the other holding his carbine, the pony's reins loose across its neck as he guided it with his knees. His eyes darted left and right as he kept a sharp lookout for trouble. He was not expecting any – they were still a good five hundred yards from the mouth of the Odensö Channel, and if the *Milenion* were still there, it was effectively screened by the trees up ahead – but a lifetime of keeping order in the more troubled provinces of the Tsar's empire (read: brutally oppressing Poles, Jews and Chechens) had taught him that trouble could come anywhere, at any time; usually when he least expected it. The rest of the men he had brought with him rode in single file out of force of habit; there was nothing to fear from anyone following their tracks here. A dozen of them would be more than enough to deal with the fugitive English sailors. After all, it had been these men who had captured Killigrew and his men earlier the previous day, and the Englishmen had not had three women to slow them down then.

Chernyovsky was glad the *Atalanta* had failed to capture the *Milenion* at the bridge. Quite aside from the fact that the black petty officer with Killigrew had killed one of his men, the *starshina*'s nose had swollen into one mass of tender, bruised meat, so that he was constantly aware of it. It seemed to fill his vision, and his fingers were drawn to it as if by magnetism. He raised a hand to feel if the swelling had gone down at all, only to be painfully reminded of just how tender it was. Yes, there was definitely a score to be settled there . . .

'Yaahhh!'

Even if Chernyovsky was on the lookout for trouble,

nothing could have prepared his pony for the spectacle of Killigrew suddenly leaping up from the ferns immediately in its path, right under its hoofs, almost. The beast reared up with a whinny. Chernyovsky was unable to do more than stay in the saddle, giving Killigrew time to level his musket at the man immediately behind the *starshina*. The blast of flame and smoke from the muzzle, accompanied by the musket's crack right next to its head, startled the beast. It reared up again, even more wildly this time, and Chernyovsky – still trying to grip the flambeau in his left hand while he raised the carbine to his shoulder with his right – slipped from the saddle. He managed to land on his feet, however, but was blinded by the muzzle flash in the darkness, and the first thing he knew about Killigrew swinging the musket like a club was when the stock connected with his nose. More lights flashed in the darkness, but this time they were behind his eyes, so that when another musket boomed off to the left he was not sure if the flash was real or a figment of his dazed imagination.

He landed on his backside amongst the bracken and fired his carbine instinctively at the spot where Killigrew had been standing. The muzzle flash revealed only the surrounding tree trunks.

Realising the flambeau only made him a target, he flung it away and slung the carbine across his shoulder. He drew a pistol from his sash and crouched amongst the ferns, his eyes searching the surrounding darkness, ears straining to hear a sound that would betray Killigrew's position. Behind him, he could hear the whinnies of ponies and men shouting in alarm as they blundered about in the darkness.

A couple of shots, muffled, sounded in the distance.

'Close up and shut up!' snarled Chernyovsky, and whirled as footsteps crunching on dried twigs sounded immediately behind him. He thrust the muzzle of his pistol into the face of one of his men, barely recognising him before he pulled the trigger.

'Vasilieff!'

Returning the pistol to his sash, he unslung his carbine once more and pulled a cartridge from one of the pouches sewn on the front of his tunic, taking advantage of the lull to reload. The two of them were joined by Cossack Fedyushin.

'Where are the others?' demanded Chernyovsky.

'Um . . . over there, I think, sir. Matiashvili and Shcharbako are down . . .'

Another Cossack was still standing about twenty yards away, holding his flambeau aloft as he turned about in search of his comrades. 'Get down, Iltchenko!' hissed Chernyovsky.

'Sir?' responded the Cossack, turning in the wrong direction. Another musket boomed, and Iltchenko spun around to face Chernyovsky, the flambeau falling from his hand to illuminate the dark trickle of blood running down his face from the hole that had been drilled through his forehead.

But in the muzzle flash, Chernyovsky had caught sight of another figure in the darkness: the black petty officer, standing not thirty yards away. He levelled his carbine where the black had been standing and fired, only for the muzzle flash to reveal one of his own men in the sights. There was a wail, and the sound of a body crashing down amongst the ferns in the darkness.

'Ekomoff?' Chernyovsky called to him. 'Are you all right?'

There was no reply. The woods had fallen eerily silent.

Then a voice barked out into the darkness, in English: 'You there, Molineaux?'

'Right here, sir!' another voice responded, closer to.

Chernyovsky smiled: these English weren't so bright, giving away their positions by calling out to one another. 'You know where he is?' he asked Fedyushin in a whisper.

The Cossack grinned through his beard in the faint light from a dropped flambeau that had fallen from someone's hand. 'Right there, sir. Want me to deal with him?'

'Make sure he dies slowly,' Chernyovsky told him, wincing as he fingered his swollen nose.

Fedyushin nodded and drew a large dagger from his sash before crawling off through the darkness.

A couple more shots sounded in the distance, but less muffled this time.

'Some more over here, sir!' another voice, with a strange accent, called from another direction.

'Good work, Endicott! Try to flush them through to me. Where's Hughes?'

'Right here, sir!' Yet another voice, another accent. 'I think some of the buggers have gone to ground between us.'

More shots in the distance, in the direction of the *Milenion*, perhaps.

'My God!' breathed Vasilieff. 'They've got us surrounded!'

'Idiot!' snapped Chernyovsky. 'There are just two men out there, putting on silly voices to frighten us!'

A ghastly scream sounded in the darkness. Chernyovsky and his men had heard a scream like that once before, when they had been posted to the Caucasus and had been using their daggers to interrogate a captive believed to be an ally of the rebel chieftain Shamyl. They had laughed then; none of them was laughing now.

Chernyovsky could feel cold sweat dripping from his armpits. 'Fedyushin?' he called. 'Is that you?'

'This Fedyushin, Chernyovsky . . .' Molineaux called back to him, 'would he be a big cove with a pointy black beaver and warts? Sorry, I don't think he can hear you any more.'

The *starshina* tugged his pistol from his sash and fired it in the direction of the voice. Mocking laughter echoed eerily out of the darkness to let him know he had missed.

'To hell with this!' muttered Vasilieff. 'I'm getting out of here!' And before Chernyovsky could grab him, the Cossack had risen to his feet and dashed off through the trees.

The *starshina* hesitated, torn between trying to find Fedyushin – or whatever these English bastards had left of him – and going after Vasilieff. He knew that going after Vasilieff was only an excuse for cowardice. But he was not stupid enough to pretend he was not scared: he was a warrior of the Steppes; this close-quarters fighting in the depths of the Finnish forests at night was a new and unnerving experience for him. Maybe Vasilieff had the right idea . . .

The devil take Fedyushin, he told himself. Rising to his feet, he dashed through the undergrowth in what he hoped was the direction of the *Atalanta*.

The forest lit up for a split second as a bullet soughed past his head, attracted by the noise he made blundering through the bracken. He tripped over a tree root and fell on his face, but something soft broke his fall.

Something soft and warm.

And sticky.

He struck a match, cupping a hand around it to hide the flame, and found himself staring into Vasilieff's dead, staring eyes. His throat had been cut from ear to ear.

In his panic to get away from the *Milenion*, Pechorin had made the mistake of swimming to the east side of the channel; or perhaps it had not been such a mistake, for as he made his way along the bank he could hear musket shots and see muzzle flashes amongst the trees on the other side. If people were fighting amongst the trees, it was a fair bet that some of them were Russians, perhaps his own crewmen sent from the *Atalanta* by Lazarenko, and part of him felt in honour bound to go to their assistance. But he was tired and battered, and his leg was bleeding in spite of the handkerchief he had tied about it as a makeshift tourniquet. Besides, he was a naval officer, not a woodsman. Difficult to see what he could hope to achieve, unarmed, in those black and forbidding woods, other than getting himself killed by one of his own countrymen. His duty was to get back to his paddle-sloop, before that fool Lazarenko sank it.

A few minutes later he came to where the *Atalanta* was anchored in the moonlight beyond the wrecked bridge, the sound of hammering and sawing coming across the water from where the carpenter's crew repaired the starboard wheel. He stuck two fingers in his mouth to emit a shrill whistle, and waved when figures appeared at the sloop's port bulwark. A dinghy was sent across to pick him up, and within two minutes he was climbing up on deck through the sloop's entry port.

A man in the uniform of a colonel in the Third Section strode towards him from the quarterdeck. 'Captain-Lieutenant Count Pechorin? What the devil have—'

Pechorin held up a hand to silence him, and turned to one of the *michmani*s. 'Would you ask Herr Juschke to report to me in my quarters?'

'Yes, sir!' The *michmani* hurried below to find the ship's surgeon.

Pechorin crossed to where Dubrovsky and his men were repairing the damage. 'How's it going, *mouzhiki*?'

The shipwright grinned. 'Another ten minutes, sir, and she'll be as good as new.'

'Good work, Dubrovsky. Keep it up.' He strode across to the quarterdeck. 'Lazarenko!'

'Sir?'

'My quarters. Now.'

'Count Pechorin!' insisted the Third Section colonel. 'I really must protest—'

'Who are you, and what are you doing on my ship?'

'I'm Colonel Radimir Fokavich Nekrasoff, of the Third Section of His Imperial Majesty's Chancery.'

'Ah, the Peeping Tom Brigade, eh? The recapture of the yacht *Milenion* is a naval matter, Colonel, so unless you have some advice that will materially assist me in that matter, you will oblige me by waiting until I send for you.' Leaving Nekrasoff turning puce in his wake, Pechorin descended the after hatch to his quarters.

Lazarenko was waiting for him. 'Tell me, Lieutenant, have we run out of chain shot?' Pechorin asked him, kicking off his boots and unbuckling his belt.

'No, sir.'

Pechorin stripped off his trousers. 'Is there no langridge in our shot lockers?'

'No, sir.'

'Then perhaps you could be so good as to inform me why it was you saw fit to fire a round shot into the *Milenion*'s stern? Surely dismasting the yacht would have been more efficacious in terms of crippling it to ensure its capture?'

Herre Juschke entered Pechorin's day-room. Like most medical men in the Russian Empire, he was of German extraction. 'You sent for me, Excellency?'

'Yes.' Pechorin sat down and put his left leg on the desk. 'Tidy up that mess.'

As the surgeon set to cleaning Pechorin's wound, the count turned back to Lazarenko. 'I'm still waiting for your explanation, Lieutenant.'

'I was acting under the orders of Colonel Nekrasoff.'

'Oh, I'm sure it must have grieved you deeply to be ordered to fire upon the *Milenion* with round shot, knowing you were endangering the life of your commanding officer. You cannot wait to supplant me, can you? A word of warning, Mstislav Trofimovich: it will take more than my death to get you promoted to captain-lieutenant.'

Lazarenko flushed.

'Pass me the brandy, and a glass,' Pechorin told him.

The lieutenant fetched decanter and balloon from the sideboard, and the count poured himself a generous measure.

He winced as Juschke plucked another pellet from his leg with a pair of fine surgical tweezers, and the German dropped it with a clink in a metal kidney dish he had produced from his holdall.

'You know, you really should not be drinking when—' the surgeon began, until silenced by a glare from the count.

'Not that I mind you trying to murder me,' Pechorin added pleasantly to Lazarenko. 'All's fair in love and war, eh? But there were civilians on board that yacht, including three women, as well you know. They might have been killed.'

Lazarenko stood ramrod stiff. 'As I have already told you, Captain-Lieutenant, I was acting under the orders of Colonel Nekrasoff.'

'And since when did the navy take orders from a colonel of the Third Section on the deck of one of its own ships? Get out of my sight, Lazarenko. Go back on deck, and ask Colonel Nekrasoff to join me. Then you can tell Lieutenant Yurieff that he is now first lieutenant.'

The colour drained from Lazarenko's face. 'But, sir—'

'What's the matter, Mstislav Trofimovich? Perhaps you feel your honour is impugned? Perhaps you would like to continue this discussion at sabre's edge?'

'No, sir.'

'Then go.'

'Sir.' Lazarenko saluted Pechorin, his eyes full of hate, and retreated from the day-room.

The surgeon had removed all the pellets he could find, and was swabbing the wounds with medicinal alcohol by the time Nekrasoff entered the day-room. 'Leave us,' Pechorin told him. 'I can do that.'

Juschke knew better than to argue with the count when he was in this mood. 'As you will.' He retreated hurriedly from the day-room, leaving Pechorin alone with Nekrasoff.

The Third Section colonel tried to seize the initiative. 'What the devil do you think you were doing, dallying with some Finnish bitch on board the *Milenion* when your duties were on the *Atalanta*?'

'Even a captain-lieutenant of the Imperial Russian Navy cannot be on duty twenty-four hours a day. It would not have mattered, had you not permitted the prisoners to escape from your custody.'

'Where is the *Milenion* now?'

'They're towing it against the wind towards the mouth of the Odensö Channel, not one *verst* from here.' Pechorin began to wrap a bandage around his calf.

'I thought as much! That's why I sent Starshina Chernyovsky and his men to intercept them. Did you meet them?'

Pechorin regarded Nekrasoff with a smile and a sceptically arched eyebrow. 'You thought as much? Or Lazarenko did? As for Chernyovsky and his men, I fancy Killigrew ambushed them on their way to the *Milenion*. I heard shooting in the woods on Odensö so I followed the channel back here.'

'If just one of them escapes back to the Allied Fleet, Count Pechorin, I shall be sure to inform the Grand Duke Konstantin just who was responsible for the failure.'

'Make sure your own name is at the top of your list, Colonel, and I dare say I'll agree with you. Anyhow, it may make no difference.'

'No difference?' exploded Nekrasoff. 'If the Allies find out about the *Ivan Strashnyi*—'

'The English prisoners know nothing of the *Ivan Strashnyi*.'

'You cannot know that!'

'Killigrew wanted to know why you were so keen to kill them all. If he already knew, why ask? If Lord Bullivant or any of his crew knew, surely they would have told him?' Pechorin shook his head. 'It seems I made a mistake in bringing in the *Milenion*.'

'The first of a catalogue of errors.'

'A catalogue of which you are co-author. I had assumed that General Ramsay would merely keep Lord Bullivant and his family and crew captive in Ekenäs, until the reason for their incarceration no longer existed. There was no difficulty, until the Third Section put its dirty galoshes in.'

'Even if Killigrew knows nothing of the *Ivan Strashnyi*, he knows there is a reason we do not want anyone from the *Milenion* to get back to the Allied Fleet. He must surely put two and two together, and come up with four. And besides, after all Lord Bullivant and his family have been subjected to now, we cannot let them get away.'

Pechorin tied off the bandage on his leg. 'So, we're not

murdering them to protect the *Ivan Strashnyi*. We're murdering them to protect you.'

'To protect *us*, Count.'

Pechorin grunted and stood up, pulling on his trousers. 'Any news from Jurassö?'

Nekrasoff shook his head.

'There is another way, you know.'

'Oh?'

'We capture the *Milenion* and all aboard her, hold them in custody until we know the *Ivan Strashnyi* is safe, and then send them back to England unharmed. That will convince the British authorities of our good faith, and dispel any thoughts they may have that we intended to murder them.'

'Convince them of our good faith!' Nekrasoff echoed scornfully. 'We are at war, are we not?'

Pechorin sat down and pulled on his boots. 'Even in war, there are certain niceties to be observed.'

'Not at the price of victory. I begin to doubt your devotion to the Tsar. You would do well to be warned by your father's fate, Count Pechorin.'

'My father was no more a traitor than I am,' Pechorin retorted coldly.

Nekrasoff smiled. 'My fear exactly.'

There was a knock at the door. 'Enter!' Pechorin barked, without taking his eyes off Nekrasoff's face.

One of the *michmani*s entered and saluted. 'Starshina Chernyovsky has returned, Captain.'

Pechorin nodded and stood up. As the *michmani* retreated from the day-room, the count held the door open for Nekrasoff to precede him. Pechorin took a fat Havana from the box on his desk before following. The three of them went up on deck, where they found Chernyovsky waiting with two of his men.

'Where are the rest of your men, *Starshina*?' demanded Nekrasoff.

Chernyovsky glowered. 'We were ambushed.'

Pechorin chuckled. 'It seems you underestimated Commander Killigrew.' He turned to the shipwright. 'How's that paddle-wheel coming along, Dubrovsky?'

'Just finishing off now, sir.'

'Instruct Inzhener Nikolaishvili to stand by.'

'Yes, sir.' The *michmani* hurried below to the engine-room. The shipwright's crew were replacing the boards on the starboard paddle-box. 'Heave up the anchor!' ordered Pechorin.

'Anchor's aweigh, sir!'

'Set on: turn astern, half!'

The engine thumped into life and the *Atalanta* began to reverse away from the bridge. Once he was satisfied that the repaired starboard paddle-wheel was operating as effectively as the undamaged one to port, Pechorin ordered Nikolaishvili to turn astern, full, until the channel was wide enough for the sloop to make a U-turn.

'Full steam ahead,' ordered Pechorin, snipping one end off his cigar with a cigar-cutter.

The sloop began to plough back the way it had come, towards the mouth of the Ekenäs inlet.

'If the *Milenion* reaches the open sea . . .' warned Nekrasoff.

'Once they reach the Skärlandet Channel, Colonel, they will have to sail close-hauled until they reach the straits between Odensö and Danskog. They will make slow progress.' Pechorin struck a match and wafted the flame back and forth across the end of the cigar until it glowed orange. He took a couple of contented puffs of the rich tobacco smoke. 'We can head them off in half an hour.'

As much as Killigrew had been enjoying his deadly game of hide-and-seek with the Cossacks, he knew he would have to curtail it the moment he heard the first of the shots from the direction of the *Milenion*. Nevertheless, he could not withdraw and leave Molineaux in the lurch, and headlong flight would only enable the Cossacks to come after them. So he had stuck at it until he had killed three of them, Molineaux had killed as many, and the rest were retreating in disarray.

But there was no sign of the petty officer. Killigrew dared not call out his name in the darkness – some of the Cossacks might have stayed behind to avenge their comrades – so he headed back to the *Milenion*, knowing that Molineaux would have heard the shots from the direction of the yacht too, and realise that Killigrew had left. The petty officer was a big boy who had proved he could take care of himself on more than one occasion.

He proved it again that night. As Killigrew saw the channel where the *Milenion* had been in the moonlight through the trees up ahead, a shadow detached itself from the trunk of a pine to his right, and before he could defend himself he felt the touch of cold steel at his throat.

'I sincerely hope that's you, Molineaux.'

'This must be your lucky night, sir.'

The two of them emerged from the trees, Molineaux replacing his knife in the sheath in the small of his back. 'I see you got your Bowie knife back.'

'One of the Cossacks had it.'

'Oh?'

'Hushed him quicker than he'd've been scragged for prigging back in England,' Molineaux said defensively.

The *Milenion* was about three hundred yards to their left, past the island at the mouth of the channel; far enough into the open water to be able to sail around the south end of the island. Killigrew stuck two fingers in his mouth and emitted a shrill whistle to attract the attention of the men who still pulled at the oars in the gig. Seeing the commander and petty officer on the shore behind them, they left off rowing and returned to the *Milenion*, where Thornton and his men went back on board to loose the towing cable while Endicott, Hughes and Iles started to row back to fetch Killigrew and Molineaux.

'That was a fine impersonation you did of Endicott, by the way,' Killigrew remarked while they waited for the gig to reach them.

'Eh, a Scouse accent's easy, like,' Molineaux reprised. 'Your impersonation of Hughes were pretty smart, I thought.'

'I've been known to dabble in amateur dramatics, look you.'

The gig had almost reached them. 'What was all that shooting about?' Killigrew called as he and Molineaux waded into the water to meet the boat in the shallows.

'Pechorin escaped, sir,' said Endicott. 'I'm afraid he killed Burgess.'

'How the hell did he get free?' Killigrew could not believe that Pechorin had wriggled free of any bonds that Molineaux had put on him.

'From what's left of the ropes, I'd say he cut through them with a shard of glass.'

'Damn! My fault: I saw the glass all over the rug, should've realised he'd have wit enough to use some to free himself. Was anyone else hurt?'

'Mr Charlton got bashed on the noodle, but I reckon he'll survive. Oh, and Charlie Ogilby lost the number of his mess, but that were from his wound.'

'Well, at least his death's been paid for, with interest. No one else was hurt?'

'Not unless you count Pechorin himself. Lady Bullivant reckons she winged him.'

'Lady Bullivant?'

'She were the one doing all the shooting. It were all over by the time we got back on board.'

Killigrew and Molineaux had climbed back in the gig now, and Molineaux took a spare oar to help row them back across to the *Milenion*.

'Reckon we're better off without 'im, sir,' opined Iles. ''E weren't much of an 'ostage, were 'ee? Din't stop the Russkis from firin' at our hull, anyrate.'

'You're right there, Iles. Still, I'd rather have had him tied up in the saloon than on the quarterdeck of the *Atalanta*. He'll do a better job of commanding her than whoever was in charge in his absence, if I'm any judge of character.'

Charlton was waiting for Killigrew by the time they got back on board the *Milenion*. The assistant surgeon had wrapped a bandage around his forehead and his face was ashen, but his eyes were bright enough.

'Mr Dahlstedt's awake, sir. He's been asking for you.'

'Thank you, Mr Charlton. How about you? Are you all right?'

The assistant surgeon grinned ruefully. 'Just about, sir. I'm afraid I'm not cut out for fisticuffs.'

'Never mind, Charlton: that's not what the navy pays you for. You did your best, I'm sure. Hoist the sails, Mr Uren!'

'Aye, aye, sir.'

'What course?' asked Thornton.

'Due west, for now.'

'You realise the Russians will have repaired the *Atalanta* by now, don't you? That they're probably already steaming the other way around Odensö to meet us?'

Killigrew smiled thinly. 'The thought had occurred to me. Once we're past that island over there, we'll tack south through the mess of islands between Danskog and Skärlandet. With any luck we'll be able to lose the *Atalanta* amongst the skerries. You have the watch, Captain Thornton.'

Killigrew made his way below and found the pilot sitting up in the bunk in Lady Bullivant's stateroom. 'Hullo, Dahlstedt! Back in the land of the living, eh? How d'you feel?'

'A bit groggy, sir, but I'll survive. Where are we?'

'Just emerging from the south-east end of the Odensö Channel.'

'And the *Atalanta*?'

'Probably steaming around the other side of the Odensö to meet us.'

'Which way does the wind lie?'

'Sou'westerly.'

'Head east, sir.'

'East?'

Dahlstedt nodded. 'East, down the Skärlandet Channel. There's plenty of water, and we'll be able to run before the wind.'

Killigrew had seen the Skärlandet Channel on charts of the area: ranging between four hundred yards and half a mile in breadth, it ran due east for the best part of ten miles, with the south coast of Finland on one side and two long islands on the other, separated by the tiniest of gaps. Sheltered by the islands, in peacetime it was the main route for shipping travelling between Barösund and Ekenäs.

He shook his head. 'The Skärlandet Channel is out of the question. The *Atalanta* will overhaul us long before we reach the end. I thought we'd sail through the islands between Danskog and Skärlandet.'

'We'll never grope our way through those islands without a chart, sir, not at night. The captain of the *Atalanta* will expect us to head west, to join the rest of the fleet at the Åland Islands. The last thing he'll expect us to do is turn east towards Helsingfors.'

'He'll work out where we've gone sooner or later.'

'But we might buy enough time to reach the Fåfängö Gap between Skärlandet and Svartbäck.'

Killigrew frowned. 'Is there enough water for us to get through there?'

'Nearly two fathoms. What's our draught?'

'Eleven feet.'

Dahlstedt grimaced. 'It's going to be tight. But it's our only chance. And look at it this way: if the *Milenion* can get through, the *Atalanta* certainly won't be able to.'

Killigrew nodded. 'She'll have to sail all the way around Svartbäck.'

'Fifteen miles out of her way,' agreed Dahlstedt. 'By the time she gets back, we'll be on the open sea.'

'Thank you, Herre Dahlstedt. If you'll excuse me, I have a change of course to order.'

Killigrew closed the stateroom door behind him and scrambled up on deck. 'Captain Thornton! Put her about, if you please. We're heading east, not west.'

'East? But Hangö Head is south-west!' To reach the fleet at Ledsund, they would have to sail past the Hangö Peninsula; even if the fleet had moved on since the *Ramillies* had left it – had it really only been the day before yesterday? – Admiral Napier usually kept at least one ship stationed off Hangö Head, to monitor shipping movements into and out of the Gulf of Finland.

'You know that, and I know that,' Killigrew told him. 'So does Pechorin. So we head east. That way we can run before the wind and give the *Atalanta* the slip before we turn south and make for the open sea.'

Thornton shrugged. 'Sixteen points to starboard, Fuller.'

'Aye, aye, sir.' The seaman spun the helm.

'I hope you know what you're doing, Killigrew,' said Thornton, shaking his head.

'So do I, Captain Thornton, so do I. Molineaux!'

'Sir?'

'We need to jettison every ounce of weight we can spare. I want you to take Endicott, Iles and Hughes and root out every useless piece of dead weight on board, and throw it over the side.'

The petty officer grinned. 'His lordship isn't going to like that.'

Killigrew lowered his voice conspiratorially. 'Why do you think I'm asking you and the rest of our lads to do it, instead of the Milenions?'

'If we're getting rid of dead weight, maybe we should start with his lordship?'

'Don't tempt me! But since our orders are to take him back to safety, that would rather defeat the object of the exercise. You might start with that round shot embedded in the timbers for'ard. Then all anchors except the best bower, the bath tub, washstands, any furniture that isn't fixed, all pots and pans in the galley, all crockery, all cutlery, all wine . . . whatever you can find.'

'What about the chemicals in the dark room?'

'Lose them all except the ones Mr Charlton needs to make this explosive chemical he was telling me about.'

'Aye, aye, sir. Seth! Red! Ben! Bear a hand, lads! We've got work to do.'

'Pyroglycerin?' Charlton asked Killigrew as the four ratings made their way below.

Killigrew nodded. 'If it's as powerful an explosive as you say it is, I've a feeling it might come in handy before the night is out. You did say you knew how to make it.'

'I also said it was very volatile.'

'This is a volatile situation, Mr Charlton.'

'Before I agree to this, sir, I think there are four things you should be aware of. One: it involves mixing highly concentrated acids; never something one should take lightly at the best of times, let alone in the galley of a ship at sea—'

Killigrew glanced at the glassy waters in the sheltered channel. 'I'd hardly describe this as "at sea", Mr Charlton.'

'Two: the glycerine has to be added drop by drop, and kept cool, because as soon as I start adding it, nitration will take place. The temperature of the compound rises, and if it goes above eighty-six degrees then a deadly poisonous gas called nitrogen dioxide is produced. Three: as I keep saying, this stuff is highly volatile – one tap is enough to detonate it. And four: this stuff is also the most powerful explosive known to man; nearly fifty times more powerful than gunpowder.'

'Fifty times more powerful than gunpowder,' Killigrew echoed sceptically. He had heard of guncotton, four times more powerful than gunpowder, when a factory producing the stuff in Faversham had exploded, killing twenty-one workers, stripping tiles from the roofs of all buildings within five hundred yards, and shattering the windows of houses a mile away. And Charlton thought this stuff pyroglycerin was twelve times as powerful as that. And if mixing it was as dangerous as all that – and to Killigrew it sounded as though Charlton was over-egging the pudding – well, weren't they all in such perilous straits that a little more peril could hardly make any difference at this stage?

'See what you can do,' he told Charlton.

'I don't think you understand, sir. One slip, and this whole yacht could be blown out of the water.'

'Then don't slip.'

Charlton shook his head in disbelief. 'I'll need someone to help me.'

'All right. Tell Molineaux to leave off helping Endicott, Hughes and Iles and to help you instead.' If the pyroglycerin was as dangerous as all that, then Charlton would need a safe pair of hands to assist him, and he doubted there would be a safer pair on board than those of Wes Molineaux.

Charlton nodded and went below.

XV

Recipe for Disaster

2.10 a.m.–2.33 a.m., Friday 18 August

Molineaux knocked on the door to the maid's cabin. 'Who is it?' she called.

'Wes Molineaux. Can I have a word, miss?'

She opened the door and peered out at him, her eyes red-rimmed from weeping. 'What do you want?'

'Rags, miss.'

'Rags?'

'Tow rags. I thought you might have some.'

She flushed. 'That's hardly the sort of question a gennle-man asks a lady!'

'Yur well, you ain't no lady, and I sure as hell ain't no gentleman!' he grinned. 'Sorry to embarrass you, miss; I wouldn't be asking if it wasn't important.'

She sighed. 'Wait here,' she told him, and retreated into the cabin, closing the door behind her. He heard her moving about within, and she opened the door again and thrust a dozen tow rags into his hands. 'Will those do you?'

'Plummy!'

She was about to close the door, but he blocked it with a foot.

'Was there something else you wanted?' she demanded impatiently.

'Just to know if you're all right.'

'Of course I'm all right. Why shouldn't I be?'

'It's just that, after that scene I barged into earlier . . .'

She grimaced. 'I'd rather not be reminded, if it's all the same with you.'

'When I was on the *Tisiphone*, the first lieutenant was Lord Hartcliffe. Your mistress knows him. His guv'nor owns a big palace down in Somersetshire. If you wanted to leave Lord Bullivant's service, I reckon I might be able to find you alternative employment.'

She softened. 'It's very kind of you to offer, but I doubt it would make much difference. I've been in service since I were twelve, and if there's one thing I've learned, all men are the same.'

'Not Lord Hartcliffe. He's a straight-up cove; he wouldn't take advantage of you.'

'What makes you so sure?'

'Believe me . . . you ain't his sort.'

'Backgammon player?' she asked knowingly.

'You didn't hear it from me. But he's as decent a cove as you could ever hope to meet.'

'I'll think about it.'

He nodded, and turned away.

'Molineaux!' she called after him.

'Wes, to my pals.'

'Thanks, Wes.'

'What for?'

'For showing an interest. In something other than my body, I mean.'

He grinned. 'Now, what makes you so sure I ain't interested in that as well?'

'Good night, Wes,' she told him, smiling, and closed the cabin door.

Molineaux dropped the tow rags in the steward's store next

to the bottles of lamp oil and emerged to help Endicott, Hughes and Iles, but met Mr Charlton coming down the companion ladder. 'Ah, Molineaux – Mr Killigrew says you're to stop what you're doing and help me mix this pyroglycerin.'

'The explosive stuff?' The petty officer grimaced. 'Very kind of him to volunteer my services like that. All right, how can I help?'

'I need a saucepan, a basin big enough to rest it in, a spoon, and a thermometer. I'll fetch the chemicals. Where did you say they are?'

'Dark room, sir.' Molineaux indicated the door. 'Reckon you'll find most of the things you're after in the galley. I'll see if I can find a thermometer.'

'We'll also need some cold water . . . sea water will have to do. Bring me a bucketful.'

'Aye, aye, sir.'

Molineaux found a bucket and a coil of rope in the stores and carried them both on deck, where he approached Captain Thornton. 'Begging your pardon, Mr Thornton, but could you tell me where I could find a thermometer?' he asked, tying one end of the rope to the bucket's handle.

'A thermometer? What the devil d'you need with a thermometer?'

'It's for Mr Charlton, sir.'

'Oh, all right. There's one in the chart-room, hanging on the wall next to the barometer.'

'Thanks.' Molineaux made his way to the side and threw the bucket over, drawing it back on board once it was full of water. Coiling the rope, he carried the bucket below to the galley, where he found Charlton had assembled everything else he needed.

'There's your sea water, sir.'

'Thermometer?'

'Getting it now, sir.' Molineaux made his way to the chart-room and took the thermometer down from the wall.

Returning to the galley, he presented it to Charlton, who eyed it unhappily.

'This is a weather thermometer.'

'What other kind is there?'

'Never mind, it will do. Can you take the wooden bit off the back of it for me? But be very careful not to break the glass tube!'

Molineaux rolled his eyes. 'I'll try not to, sir.' He found a knife he could use as a screwdriver and removed the screws from the brass brackets that held the thermometer in place. Charlton, meanwhile, half-filled the basin with sea water, and then placed the pan inside it. He put the bottle of glycerine in the bucket, still more than half-full with water. He took off his tailcoat, rolled up his sleeves, and carefully mixed the oil of vitriol and the spirits of nitre in the saucepan, using a measuring cup to get the proportions correct.

'Be very careful with this stuff, Molineaux,' he said, stirring the mixture gingerly with a long-handled spoon. 'It's acid. If any splashes on you, wash it off at once, d'you hear?'

'I'll try to bear that in mind, sir.'

Charlton took the dropper from the medicine chest and filled it from the bottle of glycerine, adding it one drop at a time to the acid mixture, still stirring gingerly with the spoon.

'Why not dump it all in at once?' suggested Molineaux.

'Because it will blow up in our faces,' Charlton told him.

'Fair enough.'

His face a picture of concentration, the assistant surgeon continued to add the glycerine drop by drop to the acid mix. Every now and then he would break off and carefully dip the thermometer's bulb into the concoction.

'Fifty-nine degrees,' he said, holding the thermometer out to Molineaux. The petty officer reached for it, but Charlton held it back. 'Be sure you only hold it by the dry part at the top . . . and rinse it off at once.'

'Aye, aye, sir.'

Charlton let him take the thermometer and resumed dropping in the glycerine.

'This reminds me of how I used to help Mr Strachan with his experiments on board the *Venturer*,' said Molineaux.

'Did Mr Strachan ever complain about your talking when he was trying to concentrate on a particularly tricky and dangerous experiment?'

'No, sir. As a matter of fact, he used to talk me through it. You know, explain what he was doing, and why, and what the science was behind it. And he always made it easy to understand, without being patronising. Reckon I learned a lot from Mr Strachan, I did.'

'Yes, well, I'm not Mr Strachan,' Charlton said in the terse tones of a man sick and tired of being constantly compared with a predecessor, to his own detriment.

'You saying you'd like me to stow it, sir?'

'I'd appreciate it ever so much.'

Molineaux watched in silence as the assistant surgeon continued to add the glycerine to the mixture.

Hughes bustled noisily into the galley with a sack, and Charlton crumpled. 'You need any of this stuff?' asked the Welshman. 'Only, Mr Killigrew says it's all got to go over the side.'

'Just this stuff here,' said Molineaux, gesturing to the makeshift apparatus. 'Anything else you need, sir?'

'Yes: we'll need a second saucepan, a funnel, three pint bottles and some baking soda. The rest can go.'

Molineaux rummaged about and managed to find everything else Charlton needed. The assistant surgeon resumed dropping the glycerine in the mixture. Sweat dripped down Charlton's face, and he broke off to wipe his forehead with his sleeve.

Hughes was reaching up to take the remaining pots and pans down from an overhead rack when the whole lot broke away and crashed to the deck behind Charlton.

The assistant surgeon jumped a foot in the air and

responded with language Molineaux had never dreamed a gentleman might be familiar with. He rounded furiously on Hughes. '*Do you mind?*'

The Welshman looked hurt. 'Sorry, sir. It was an accident.'

'One more accident like that, Hughes, and we'll all be blown sky high!'

Hughes pulled a face at Molineaux, who shrugged. 'Cut along, Red. Mr C needs to concentrate.'

'Aye, aye, Wes.' Having stuffed the pots and pans in his sack, Hughes beat a hasty retreat from the galley.

'Any drinking water?' asked Charlton.

'Reckon there's some in this cistern, sir.'

'Right: run some off into the second saucepan and let it stand. We'll need it later.'

'How much do we need?'

'No point in filling it above halfway: if that's too much, we can tip some out when the time comes.' Charlton laid the medicine dropper to one side. 'Thermometer,' he said, holding out one hand. Molineaux passed it to him. Charlton dipped it in the mixture, and frowned as the mercury rose up the tube. 'Uh-oh.'

' "Uh-oh"?' echoed Molineaux. 'What do you mean, "uh-oh"? I don't like the sound of that "uh-oh"!'

'Temperature's up to sixty. We've got to keep it cool.'

'What happens if we don't?'

'If it rises above sixty-seven, then the mixture reaches saturation point: no more pyroglycerin can be made, and there's a good chance that the layer of pyroglycerin that's already floating on top will explode in our faces. If it rises too quickly, it'll start giving off nitrogen dioxide.'

'How will we know if that happens?'

'You'll see it give off a dull red gas. You'll also asphyxiate, as nitrogen dioxide is deadly poisonous.'

'Better keep the temperature down then, eh, sir?'

'Well, don't just stand there, man! Get some fresh sea water!'

'Aye, aye, sir.' Taking the coil of rope, the petty officer sauntered towards the door.

'Molineaux?' Charlton called after him.

'Sir?'

'*Run.*'

Molineaux ran. He stopped at the boatswain's store to help himself to another bucket, tying the rope around the handle as he took the steps of the companion ladder two at a time. He dashed across the deck, threw the bucket over and drew it in as soon as it was full. Slopping water everywhere, he dashed below, almost slipping on the steps and barely saving himself from spilling the whole lot.

He ran into the galley and skidded to a halt, mindful not to startle Charlton. 'Fresh sea water, sir.'

'Right. I'll lift the saucepan; you take out the basin from below, tip out the water that's already in it, then pour in the fresh sea water and replace it under the saucepan. And . . . Molineaux?'

'Sir?'

'Once I lift the saucepan, speed is of the essence.'

'I think I've got the gist of it, sir.'

With sweat running from his hairline, Charlton lifted the saucepan. Molineaux removed the basin, tipping the old water into the first bucket, pouring sea water from the second in its place, and slid the basin back beneath the saucepan. Charlton lowered it again, and dipped the thermometer in the mixture once more. He watched the mercury rise.

'Sixty-four, sixty-five, sixty-six . . . sixty-seven . . . sixty-seven . . . it's holding at sixty-seven . . . Christ, why isn't it dropping? It should be dropping!'

'Give it a chance, sir,' said Molineaux, trying to keep calm. The panic in Charlton's face was infectious.

'Sixty-seven . . . sixty-seven.'

'It's dropping, sir.'

'So it is! Thank Christ for that! Sixty-six, sixty-five, sixty-four . . . oh, thank you, God! Jesus, that was a close one! Rinse,' he added, handing the thermometer back to Molineaux. He slumped down on one of the chairs.

Molineaux dabbled the thermometer in the first bucket and turned to look at Charlton. The assistant surgeon seemed to have shrunk six inches. He sat motionless, staring at the deck.

'You oh-kay, sir?'

'Hmph?' Charlton was not used to the slang Molineaux had picked up while working on an American slave ship.

'All right, I mean.'

Charlton shook his head. 'I can't do it,' he whispered.

'Do what, sir?'

'This!' The assistant surgeon took in the saucepan, basin and buckets with a sweep of an arm. 'Damn Killigrew! When I accepted a post on a naval ship, no one said anything about having to make explosives. I'm an apothecary, damn it, not a chemist!'

'Mr Strachan used to be just an apothecary, but he used to do all kinds of things—'

Charlton leaped to his feet. 'Damn your eyes! Will you stop going on about Mr bloody Strachan? From the moment I stepped on board the *Ramillies*, it's been nothing but "Mr Strachan this" and "Mr Strachan that" and "Mr bloody Strachan the other" from you and Endicott and Hughes. How many times do I have to tell you? *I'm not Mr Strachan.* And I'm sorry if that makes me a lesser man in the eyes of you and your shipmates, but I can only be what I am.'

It had never occurred to Molineaux that his constant reminiscing about Mr Strachan might make Charlton feel bad; but then, it had never occurred to him that he talked about Strachan so much. Now he realised that each time he and his friends had mentioned Strachan in passing, it must have been like a knife in the guts of Charlton's self-esteem.

'Sorry, sir. I didn't mean to compare you to Mr Strachan. I mean, for one thing, you're a lot younger than he is. I remember when he started out, he was just as big a booby as . . . as anyone. You'll learn. All I'm trying to say is, that's when the Andrew Miller's all about. We spend so much time cut off from all the conveniences of modern civilisation, whether we're at sea in the middle of the Pacific or frozen in the heart of the Arctic . . . we just have to learn to adapt to our surroundings, to improvise with whatever materials we've got to hand to get ourselves out of whatever pickle we've gotten ourselves into. So sometimes an officer like Mr Killigrew has to be a diplomat, a petty officer like me has to be a sodger, and a pill-roller like you has to be a chemist. Maybe Mr Killigrew ain't no Lord Palmerston, no more'n I'm Harry Flashman or you're Humphry Davy. But what matters is that we're all counting on one another, so we do our best and somehow scrape through.'

Charlton sat down, shaking his head. There were tears on his cheeks. 'Maybe you can live like that, Molineaux. I'm not cut out for it, I tell you. I should never have joined the navy.'

'Well, you're here now.'

'Don't I know it! It's no good, Molineaux. I can't do it. I refuse. So you can just go up on deck and tell Mr Killigrew he'll have to find someone else to mix his pyroglycerin, because I won't do it.'

'That's all right, sir. He'll understand.'

'Will he?' Charlton wiped his face with his hands. 'He always expects so much of the men who serve under him.'

'Only 'cause he's got such a high opinion of us, sir.'

'Well, in me he's mistaken.'

'All I know is, he grannies the risk in making this stuff, and he wouldn't ask you to do it if it weren't important.' Molineaux glanced at the saucepan. 'Maybe I can do it?'

'You? You wouldn't know where to begin.'

'You could talk me through it, couldn't you?' Molineaux picked up the thermometer and dipped it in the mix. 'Temp'rature's down to fifty now, sir. Reckon it's safer to start adding the glycerine again?'

Staring at the deck between his feet, Charlton just shook his head and said nothing.

Molineaux took a deep breath, picked up the medicine dropper, and sucked some more glycerol from the bottle the way he had seen the assistant surgeon do it. 'One drop at a time, eh?'

'What does it matter?' Charlton demanded bitterly.

'That's what I always tell meself, sir. I used to be afraid of croaking, but I don't reckon being dead's so bad. Now, being maimed – winding up with only one foot, like poor Mr Strachan – that scares me. It's all right for him, he's blunted, he don't need both his dew-beaters to make a living; but a cove like me, if I lost a foot? I'd be on the griddle. But if this stuff is half as powerful as you say, I don't reckon there's any chance of that. Don't reckon we'd feel a thing.'

'But that's just it, isn't it? If it was just me, maybe – maybe – I could do it. But it's the responsibility. It's not just our lives in the balance . . . it's the others, as well. One slip, and they'll all die too.'

'We'll all croak anyhow, if the Ivans catch us. Given the choice, I'd rather get blown up than face a Russki firing squad. You ever work as an apothecary ashore, sir?'

'For a while. Couldn't make a go of it. The working-class people didn't trust my homeopathic cures, and I didn't have the right contacts to get any clients from the more open-minded middling sort,' Charlton added bitterly.

'Y'see, that I could never do.'

'What?'

'Be an apothecary.'

'It's not difficult, if you can pass the exams. You're bright enough; with the right training, I'm sure you'd be as good an apothecary as anyone.'

'Maybe so, but I reckon I'd have an even harder time getting clients than you did. It's the skin, see? White folks like you don't trust blacks, you all think we're thick, that we'd get the dosage wrong or prescribe the wrong drugs or something like that.'

'Now, I never said you were thick.'

'Not you personally, sir. White folks in general, I mean.' Molineaux shrugged. He'd got past bitterness about it a long time ago. Bigotry was one of those things in life you had to learn to accept, like cholera, typhus and lawyers. He did not like it, but he was not going to let it control his life; the way he looked at it, if he did, he would be letting the bigots win. Better to get on with his life, and pray that one day the world progressed to the stage where there was no more room in it for bigotry or any of those other unnecessary evils.

'No, prescribing drugs to sick folk: I couldn't do that. I mean, suppose I made a mistake? I might make someone sick; or – worse – kill 'em off altogether.' The medicine dropper was empty. The level of the glycerine left in the bottle had dropped too low for him to be able to draw out any more that way, so he found a clean dish Hughes had missed and poured some into that. 'I couldn't handle that responsibility.'

'It's easy enough, when you know what you're doing. You just have to concentrate on your work and make sure you *don't* make a mistake.'

'Kind of like cooking up this stuff, eh, sir?'

Charlton grimaced. 'Have you checked the temperature of that lately?'

The petty officer dipped the thermometer in again and watched the mercury crawl up the scale. 'Fifty-two degrees. That oh-kay?'

'You're safe enough as long as you keep it below sixty.'

The two of them lapsed into silence once more, Molineaux concentrating on what he was doing, Charlton lost in his own thoughts. After a while, the petty officer looked up. 'That's the last of the glycerine, sir. What do I do now?'

'Tip out the water in the second saucepan until there's an amount left equal to the mixture in the other pan . . . no, use the measuring cup. Here, let me get it.' Charlton stood up and joined him at the worktop. 'Gently does it! You can't see it, but the pyroglycerin should have formed a layer above the remaining acid below.'

'You mean, it's ready to use?'

'Not quite. First we have to decant it, then wash it with a sodium carbonate solution to neutralise the acid left in suspension.'

'Have we got any sodium carbo-whatsit?'

Charlton picked up the tub of baking soda. 'A fancy name for this. Rinse out the first saucepan and dissolve some of the baking soda in ordinary water from the cistern . . . here, let me help.'

'Thanks, sir.'

Charlton realised he was holding the pan with the pyroglycerin in it. 'You're a sneaky bastard, Molineaux, did anyone ever tell you that?'

The petty officer beamed proudly. 'Thank you, sir.'

Killigrew waited until the *Milenion* was on an easterly heading, sailing into the Skärlandet Channel, before leaving Thornton in charge of the watch and making his way below. He unlocked the door to Lord Bullivant's stateroom, but only found his lordship flat out on the bunk, snoring like a pig, two bottles of brandy on the deck, his breath rank with it.

'Don't think too harshly of him, Mr Killigrew.'

He turned to find Lady Bullivant standing in the doorway behind him.

'His father died young,' she explained. 'All his life he's been used to getting his own way. These past few days have . . . well, taken the wind out of his sails, I suppose you'd say.'

Killigrew nodded. As long as Bullivant was asleep, he could not give the commander any trouble; that was something to be thankful for, at least. 'I understand you had a bit of excitement while I was ashore earlier, ma'am.'

She smiled. 'Nothing I was unable to cope with.'

'Endicott tells me you managed to wing Pechorin.'

'I'm only sorry I did not kill the swine. Is that a terrible thing to say?'

'We're in a terrible situation. If we're going to get back to safety, we must take drastic measures. We are at war, after all. And they were the ones who dragged you into this business.'

'It would never have happened if we had stayed in England. I confess, I was against this voyage from the outset. But once Rodney's made his mind up about something . . . he grew up during the Great War with France, don't forget. I think he's always regretted having been too young to fight.'

'Where *were* you, when the *Atalanta* first overhauled the *Milenion*?'

'On an island, out in the Gulf of Finland. I forget its name; Captain Thornton would know. We'd gone ashore for a picnic. It seemed a pretty spot. Lord Dallaway wanted to take some calotypes of Araminta standing in front of the lighthouse. Why do you ask?'

'There has to be some reason why Nekrasoff wants us all dead. The only possible explanation I can think of is that you saw something . . . something the Russians don't want anyone to know about; something they'd go to any lengths to stop Admiral Napier from discovering.'

'I certainly don't recall seeing anything that would be remotely interesting to Admiral Napier.'

He nodded. 'How is Miss Maltravers, by the way?'

'A little shaken. Pechorin held a carving knife at her throat. I don't believe he intended to use it, but I doubt she saw it that way at the time. I had Nicholls make her some camomile tea. She's sleeping in one of the staterooms, I hope; or trying to, at least.'

Killigrew took his leave of Lady Bullivant, and knocked softly on the door of Araminta's stateroom. When there was no reply, he opened the door a crack and peered through to see her fast asleep, her chest rising and falling beneath the covers to assure him she was alive. He smiled, and was tempted to go into the stateroom to kiss her on the forehead, but he was afraid of waking her. She needed her sleep; so did he, for that matter, but he had resigned himself to not getting any this night.

He made his way up on deck. With the wind broad on the starboard quarter, the schooner was clipping along at a good five and a half knots, the fastest rate they had yet attained on the voyage from Ekenäs; but it was still not fast enough to outrun the *Atalanta*. Other than praying for stronger winds, however, there was nothing they could do about that. He checked his watch: incredibly, it was still only twenty-five past two in the morning; twilight could not be far off in these latitudes, although there was no sign yet of the sky lightening in the east.

'Captain Thornton!'

'Yes, Mr Killigrew?'

'What was the name of the island where you dropped anchor when the *Atalanta* caught you?'

'Jurassö, a small island about six miles off the coast of the mainland.'

The name meant nothing to Killigrew. 'What's at Jurassö?'

'Nothing much: a lot of trees, a lighthouse, some iron-works . . .'

'You went ashore?'

'Yes. Miss Maltravers suggested a picnic. I saw no reason not to. Lord Dallaway was taking some photographic pictures and Nicholls was laying out the picnic when the *Atalanta* appeared.'

'What the devil was she doing so far out from the coast? If she was sailing from Barösund to Ekenäs, she could have used this channel, instead of running the risk of falling in with a British ship.'

'Captain-Lieutenant Pechorin did not strike me as the sort of commander who would run shy of an encounter with an enemy vessel.'

'Me neither,' Killigrew admitted. 'All the same, it's damned queer . . .'

316

'Mind your backs!' called Endicott, backing out of the fore hatch and dragging one end of an enamelled bathtub out after him. When it was all the way out of the hatch, Iles was revealed holding the other end. The two of them crossed to the gunwale.

'Hi! You there!' called Thornton. 'What the devil d'you think you're doing with that?'

'They're carrying out my orders,' Killigrew told him. 'We've got to lighten the load.'

'That's his lordship's bathtub!'

'One . . . two . . . three!' With a tremendous effort, Endicott and Iles managed to get the bathtub on the bulwark, from where they could push it over. It hit the water with a terrific splash. For a few moments it floated, but water fountained up through the plughole, until it foundered and sank without trace.

'*Was* his bathtub, you mean,' said Killigrew.

Hughes followed Endicott and Iles on deck, carrying a couple of bulging sacks that followed the bathtub over the side.

'What was in those?' demanded Thornton.

'Hughes!' called Killigrew.

'Sir?'

'What was in those sacks you just threw overboard?'

'Pots, pans, and his lordship's best silver.'

'But this is outrageous!' protested Thornton. 'What the devil do you think you're playing at?'

'We've got to keep our weight down to keep our speed up,' said Killigrew.

'It's all right, Thornton,' said Lady Bullivant, emerging from the after hatch. 'Mr Killigrew has my permission. He is in charge, after all.'

'If you say so, ma'am.'

'Thank you, my lady,' Killigrew said with feeling.

'On deck there!' O'Leary called from the maintop.

'What is it, O'Leary?'

'Sail ho!'

'Where away?'

'Dead astern!'

Killigrew glanced back over the taffrail, but could see only darkness. He swung himself up into the ratlines and clambered up to join O'Leary at the maintop. The Irishman handed him a telescope. 'See it, sir?'

The commander raised the telescope to one eye and levelled it. He could just make out the deck lights.

'Might not be the *Atalanta*, sir,' O'Leary said dubiously, not really believing it himself.

Killigrew handed back the telescope and shinned down a backstay to the deck. 'We've got a steamer coming up astern, about a mile off.'

'The *Atalanta*?' asked Lady Bullivant.

'More than likely,' admitted Killigrew. 'I'm afraid Count Pechorin was more intelligent than I gave him credit for: it seems he's double-guessed me.'

'How long until she overhauls us?'

'About twenty minutes ... but we'll be in range of her bow chaser within eight.' Killigrew's mind raced. There were still more than four miles to cover before they reached the Fåfångö Gap; at their current speed, it would take them about three-quarters of an hour to reach it. The *Atalanta* was going to catch them before they covered a fraction of the distance.

'Is there nothing we can do to escape?' asked Lady Bullivant.

Killigrew's eyes fell on the fishing nets arranged on deck. He took the telescope from the binnacle and gazed forward. He could just make out a low skerry in the channel ahead, fifteen hundred yards off, black against the dark waters that shimmered in the moonlight. The main channel ran to the north of the island, a little over two hundred yards wide.

He handed the telescope to Thornton. 'See that skerry? I want you to make for the north side of it, as close in as you

318

are. Then come hard about to port to the opposite side of the channel, again as close as you dare. Sheer off hard-a-starboard, and resume our present course.'

'All right.' From the tone of his voice, Thornton had finally reached the point where he was prepared to take anything Killigrew told him on trust. 'One point to port, Fuller.'

'One point to port it is, sir.'

Killigrew crossed to the after hatch and bellowed down it. 'Molineaux! Endicott! Hughes! Iles! Belay what you're doing and tumble up! All hands on deck!'

Three of them emerged quickly and smartly.

'Where's Molineaux?' demanded Killigrew.

'Still helping the pill-roller in the galley, sir.'

'Not good enough, Endicott. Tell him I want him topsides chop chop.'

'Aye, aye, sir.' The Liverpudlian went below again. He re-emerged on deck within a minute. 'Begging your pardon, sir, but Molineaux says the process has reached a delicate stage, and he hopes you'll forgive him but he's not going to leave Mr Charlton until they're done.'

Killigrew knew Molineaux would not disobey an order without good reason. 'All right, we'll just have to manage without him. Fetch those nets to the starboard bow.'

'We're going fishing, sir?' asked Hughes.

'That's right.'

'What are we hoping to catch?'

'A paddle-sloop.'

'A paddle-sloop!' the Welshman echoed in disbelief.

'Get one of the nets up on the bulwark, but don't put it over the side until I give the word. Hughes, help me with the first one. Endicott and Iles, I want you two standing by with the second; get ready to put it over the side as soon as Hughes and I put the last of this net over. Remember, we want to string them out across the channel, so pay them out, don't just drop them over the side in one bunch.'

'So that's why you made us bring these nets on board, sir!'

exclaimed Hughes, finally cottoning on.

'It's called thinking ahead, Red,' said Endicott. 'You should try it sometime.'

'Cut off every second float,' Killigrew told them. If the crew of the Atalanta spotted the cork floats before they reached the nets, the attempt to foul them would be in vain; the fewer floats that showed, the less chance there was of being spotted in the moonlight.

'Reckon 'ee's goin' to work, sir?'

'I hope so, Iles. I sincerely hope so.' Killigrew would have been more confident if the *Atalanta* had been a screw steamer rather than a paddler: while being a more efficient means of propulsion, screw-propellers had the disadvantage of seeming to be designed to get caught up in fishing nets, whereas a paddle-wheel was more likely to thrust a net under and astern than it was to get caught. Yet sometimes paddle-steamers *did* get caught up in nets: it had happened to the *Tisiphone*, once, and it had taken the crew an hour to untangle them.

But that was the least of Killigrew's worries: at the rate the steamer was gaining on them, there was a good chance Pechorin would be able to blow the *Milenion* out of the water before the *Atalanta* even reached the nets.

XVI

The Fåfängö Gap

2.33 a.m.–3.25 a.m., Friday 18 August

'*Milenion* in range, sir,' the *Atalanta*'s gunner reported to Pechorin on the quarterdeck.

'Load the bow chaser with chain shot and stand by to aim for her mainmast; but don't fire until I give the word.'

'Yes, sir.' The gunner saluted, made an about-face and headed forward.

'If they're in range, why not fire?' demanded Nekrasoff.

'Extreme range, Colonel. No point in wasting shot. Don't worry; they're not going anywhere. They're hemmed in: this channel continues for another twelve *vehrsty*. We'll be alongside them in fifteen minutes.'

Lieutenant Yurieff was watching the *Milenion* through a telescope. 'Why are they sailing so close to the southern side of the channel?' he wondered out loud.

'Trying to tempt us into the shallows, I expect, in the hope we run aground. Maintain your present course,' Pechorin added to the helmsman.

'Yes, sir.'

'She's putting about,' warned Yurieff. 'Turning to port . . .'

Pechorin frowned. 'What the devil are they playing at?'

'Zigzagging, sir?' suggested Yurieff. 'Trying to make themselves a harder target to hit?'

'Presenting us with their side!' Nekrasoff said triumphantly. 'You could hull her with round shot.'

'I could,' agreed Pechorin. 'But I'm not going to; not while there are innocent women on board.' Which seemed an odd thing to say when one of the women had recently filled his leg with buckshot, but he had to admit he had been asking for it. 'May I remind you that as long as the fugitives are on board the *Milenion* this is a naval matter, Colonel, and as long as it remains so we'll do things my way. What you do with the prisoners once you get them ashore is your own affair.' Which was not to say he did not intend to lobby every senior official to make sure that no harm came to the Bullivants.

'We'll wait until they're within four hundred *sazhen*, and then open fire with chain shot and dismast them,' decided the count. 'Once they're crippled we'll have no difficulty running alongside and boarding them.'

'They're putting about again, sir,' said Yurieff. 'Turning to starboard now.'

'Range?'

'About five hundred *sazhen* I should say.'

Pechorin took out a cigar, snipped off the end and lit it with a match, the epitome of calm. He puffed away contentedly, the only thing that troubled his spirit a strong feeling that this was hardly a worthy opponent. In Killigrew he had a worthy adversary, that much he did not doubt; but a paddle-sloop against an unarmed schooner? For as long as he could remember, he had wanted to prove his mettle in a battle at sea. Now Russia was finally at war with another European power – and he had been given command of his own ship – first he had been ordered not to leave port; and now that he had finally been let off the leash, it was to hunt down a yacht!

'Range, four hundred and fifty *sazhen*,' said Yurieff.

'Steady as she goes,' said Pechorin. 'Tell the gun crew to

stand by for my word of command.'

The deck thrummed beneath their feet as the *Atalanta*'s paddles churned the water to a millrace on either side of the sloop. The gap was being closed inexorably.

In spite of the cold weather, Nekrasoff took out a handkerchief and mopped sweat from his brow. 'Damn it, why don't you fire?' he hissed.

'Everything comes to he who waits,' said Pechorin, and held out his hand to Yurieff. The lieutenant gave him the telescope, and the count raised it to one eye. The gap had closed to four hundred *sazhen*, just under a thousand yards: close enough to be reasonably confident of a shot. There was no point in holding off now, except to exasperate Nekrasoff.

The telescope pressed to his right eye, Pechorin waited . . . and waited . . .

'And . . . *fire!*'

The captain of the gun hauled on the lanyard and the bow chaser boomed, belching flame and smoke into the night. The chain shot whirred into the air. Pechorin strained to see through the cloud of smoke that now wreathed the bows, and was rewarded with the sight of a spray of water, dingy blue-grey in the moonlight, slicing up from the surface of the channel some fifty yards beyond the *Milenion*, and a little to port.

'*Chert!*' exclaimed Pechorin.

'Who taught your men how to shoot?' scoffed Chernyovsky. 'Louis Braille?'

Pechorin ignored him. 'Reload!'

'Run in!' ordered the gunner. The gun crew manned the side tackles, drawing the bow chaser back from the gun port. Once the gun was laid in for loading, the right rearman choked the luff of the preventer tackle and the men closed up.

'Sponge!'

The captain of the gun stopped the vent. Water was sprinkled over the sponge before it was rammed to the bottom of the bore, given a twist and withdrawn.

'Load!'

A quill tube was inserted in the vent. Cartridge, wad and chain shot were all loaded into the bore and thrust home with the rammer. The captain of the gun pricked the cartridge through the vent with a priming wire.

'Run out!'

The muzzle of the bow chaser was run out through the gun port. Two of the gun's crewmen adjusted the sights.

'Point!'

The gun was lined up on the *Milenion*'s mainmast, now no more than 750 yards away.

'Elevate!'

'Lower.' The captain of the gun brought the top of the fore sight in line. 'So!'

'Ready!' called the gunner.

'*Fire!*'

In the galley, Molineaux heard the first boom of the *Atalanta*'s bow chaser and knew what was coming next. 'Better put that saucepan down, sir.'

Charlton complied. They heard the shot slash into the waves.

'Dear God!' the assistant surgeon exclaimed, looking sick. 'They're shooting at us!'

'They tend to do that when there's a war on, sir,' said Molineaux. 'I'd decant that pyroglycerin now if I were you.'

'But what if the next shot comes through the galley?'

'If a round shot comes through the galley right now, reckon it'll blow up the pyroglycerin whether it's resting on the worktop or in your hands. But it takes a British gun crew at least a minute to reload a gun, and from what I've seen of Russian gunnery so far, they ain't a patch on the likes of us . . . so you've still got at least thirty seconds, if you look lively.'

Charlton started to decant the pyroglycerin from one saucepan to the other. His hands shook so much that Molineaux had to reach out and steady them.

'What if they fire one of their other guns?' asked the assistant surgeon.

Molineaux shook his head. 'No can do, sir. They've only got three guns, and two of them point out at the sides. They're coming up from astern, so they can only use the bow chaser.'

Charlton had barely finished decanting the pyroglycerin when they heard the muffled boom of the *Atalanta*'s bow chaser. The assistant surgeon whimpered.

'We got an official term for times like this, sir.'

'Yes?'

'Yur: sweaty-bum time.'

Charlton laughed in spite of himself, and they heard the rip of canvas above them.

Molineaux glanced up at the deck head. 'It's all right: that one went through one of the sails. It means they're going for the masts; using chain shot, by the sound of it.'

'That's good?'

'It means they're not aiming for the hull.'

Charlton nodded soberly. 'That's good.'

'Yur. Unless they succeed in dismasting us: then we're scuppered.'

Pechorin levelled his telescope. When the smoke cleared, he saw a great rent had been torn through the *Milenion*'s mainsail, the ragged canvas flapping in the breeze, but the mainmast remained intact.

'That should take a couple of knots off their speed,' he remarked with satisfaction. 'Reload!'

The bow chaser was run in, sponged, loaded, run out, pointed and elevated once more.

'Ready!' called the gunner.

Pechorin took a deep breath, and—

A strange groaning noise from the starboard paddle-wheel distracted him. Even as he looked across at the sponson, there came an odd rending sound, like giant stitches popping, followed by something snapping and splintering, and a God-awful crunching sound. A shudder ran through the deck, making Nekrasoff and Chernyovsky stagger.

'What the devil was that?' demanded the Cossack.

Pechorin did not reply, as much at a loss as Chernyovsky, but he had a sick feeling in the pit of his stomach. He turned to one of the *michmani*s. 'Stop engines!' he barked.

The *michmani* hurried down the hatch and the throbbing of the deck died beneath their feet. The paddle-wheels had already stopped turning. An eerie silence descended over the sloop.

'What the devil happened?' demanded Nekrasoff.

'I don't know!' Pechorin snapped at him, crossing to the after hatch. 'Nikolaishvili!' he roared.

'Sir?' the engineer's muffled voice came back.

'What in God's name just happened?'

'Something must've jammed one of the paddle-wheels.'

'Yurieff! Check the port-side paddle-wheel!'

'Sir!'

While the lieutenant climbed on to the port-side paddle-box to peer over, Pechorin mounted the one to starboard, and saw the net entangled with the paddles. '*Chert!*' He stood up, whipped off his cap, and threw it down to the deck in fury.

'This one's clear, sir!' Yurieff called across the deck.

'This one isn't,' Pechorin responded heavily. 'A fishing net!'

Yurieff frowned. 'A fishing net, sir? But this is a major shipping lane . . . who would be stupid enough to lay a fishing net across this channel?'

'Who do you think, numbskull? Killigrew, damn him!' Pechorin noticed the gun crew standing by, awaiting further orders. 'What the devil are you waiting for?' he roared. 'Fire, damn you!'

The captain of the gun hauled on the lanyard and the bow chaser boomed, but the *Milenion* had already moved out of its line of fire and the shot went wide.

'Reload!' Pechorin jumped back down to the deck. 'Away the dinghy, Vasyutkin! I want those nets cut away, at the double!'

The gun crew reloaded, but by the time they were ready to fire again the *Milenion* was already more than a thousand yards away. Even with the mainsail flapping limply in the breeze she was able to widen the gap with every passing moment. The fourth shot went wide, the fifth fell short, and after that she was out of range.

'Damn that son of a gun!' Pechorin said, almost to himself, the ghost of a smile creeping across his features as he shook his head in rueful admiration. One of the most advanced vessels in the Russian navy . . . crippled, by a fishing net! 'Damn him to hell!'

'Enough of this foolishness!' spat Nekrasoff. 'I'm taking command of this vessel.'

Pechorin looked him up and down contemptuously. 'You? Don't be ridiculous! You don't have the authority.'

Nekrasoff showed him his warrant card and his orders from the Grand Duke Konstantin. 'These give me all the authority I need, Count. Stand down. I'm replacing you as commander of this vessel. Lieutenant Yurieff! Fetch Lieutenant Lazarenko and inform him he is now acting captain of the *Atalanta*.' He turned to Starshina Chernyovsky's two men. 'Escort Count Pechorin to his quarters and keep him there under guard.'

As the two Cossacks seized Pechorin, several of the *matrosy* on deck left off what they were doing to go to their captain's defence. Chernyovsky pulled his pistols from his sash and levelled them.

'To whom do you owe your loyalty?' Nekrasoff asked the *matrosy* mildly. 'Count Pechorin? Or the Tsar? As a full colonel of the Third Section, I am the senior officer on board. Anyone refusing my orders is a mutineer. Do I make myself plain?'

The situation was so ridiculous, Pechorin would have

laughed if he had not been so angry. 'Do as he says, *mouzhiki*,' he told his men. 'Obey his instructions to the letter.' He turned his contemptuous gaze back on Nekrasoff. 'Let's see just how big a mess of things Lazarenko and this Third Section turd can make.'

Killigrew stared up at the ragged sail above him. 'Mr Uren!'

'Sir?'

'Please tell me you have another mains'l in the stores?'

'Yes, sir. O'Leary, Yorath, Attwood! Help me get that rag unbent from the mains'l gaff!'

As the boatswain and the three sailors loosed the halyards to lower the gaff, Killigrew turned to where Fuller stood at the wheel. 'I'll take the helm, Fuller. You fetch the spare mains'l. Iles, Hughes – give him a hand. Help Mr Uren and the others unbend that mains'l, Endicott.'

'Aye, aye, sir!'

The men went to work with a will. The crippled paddle-sloop was fading into the darkness astern, but not fast enough: the ruination of the mainsail had knocked a couple of knots off their speed – knots they could ill afford to lose – and the *Milenion* crept along at three and a half knots now.

Mackenzie levelled his telescope astern, holding it awkwardly in one hand. 'Looks like we've lost them,' he said, trying to sound chirpy.

'For now,' agreed Thornton. 'But it won't take them for ever to untangle those nets.'

'One hour,' said Killigrew. His palms were damp inside his kid gloves where they gripped the helm. 'That's all I ask. One hour.'

But even he knew that was too much to expect.

By the time Fuller, Iles and Hughes came back on deck with the spare mainsail, Uren and the others had removed the ruined one from the gaff and boom. The throat-rope was rove through the hole under the jaws of the gaff and secured. They hauled out the head of the sail by the peak-earring.

328

Once it was taut, the lacings were passed through the eyelet holes and round the jack-stay. They seized the bights of the throat and peak brails to the leech and rove them through the blocks on the gaff. The foot brail was seized to the leech just above the clew, and the luff of the sail seized to the hanks around the mainmast. Once the tack was seized to the boom, they hooked on the outhaul tackle with an eye round the boom, reeving through a single block at the clew and then through a sheave-hole in the boom. Within a few minutes, they were hauling the new mainsail back up the side of the mainmast, and Killigrew was pleased to see them working as a team for once.

'Good work, lads. I'd give the order to splice the main-brace, but we're going to need clear heads . . . for the next hour, at least. You have the watch, Captain Thornton.'

'Aye, aye, Mr Killigrew.'

The commander made his way below decks to look in on Charlton and Molineaux. He found them in the galley, decanting an oily, yellow-tinged liquid from a saucepan into a wicker-covered bottle with the aid of a funnel.

'Thought you might like to know the danger's past,' Killigrew told them.

'I wouldn't go that far, sir,' replied Molineaux, while Charlton concentrated on what he was doing, the tip of his tongue thrust between his lips.

'Sorry about the fireworks. If you've got any complaints, you'll have to address them to the Russian Admiralty. Must have been pretty damned nerve-racking for the two of you down here with this stuff, not being able to see what was going on, and wondering if a shot was about to come smashing through the bulkheads.'

'Molineaux guessed what was happening,' said Charlton, handing the empty saucepan and funnel to the petty officer. 'He talked me through it.'

'Not that he needed it,' said Molineaux. 'Nerves of steel, this one, sir. Me, I was wetting myself.'

Molineaux and Charlton exchanged glances, and Killigrew was aware of something unspoken between them that he guessed he would never hear about. He let it pass. 'You never wet yourself, even when you were a babe in arms, Molineaux.' He indicated the bottle. 'Is it ready?'

Charlton nodded.

'Does it work?'

'There's one way to find out.' Charlton wiped the blade of a knife with a tea towel and put it on the table, away from the bottles. Then he used the medicine dropper to place a single drop of the liquid on the flat of the blade. 'Anyone got any matches?'

Killigrew patted down the pockets of the Third Section tunic he was still wearing and found the matches he had taken from Leong. He handed the box to Charlton, who struck one and touched it to the drop on the knife. The liquid burned briefly with a clear, blue flame.

Charlton's face fell. 'Just what I was afraid of.'

'Ain't it no good?' Molineaux asked plaintively. 'After all that?'

'It's good.' The assistant surgeon handed back the box of matches.

'How much have we got?' asked Killigrew

The assistant surgeon indicated the two bottles. 'Two and a half pints.'

Killigrew frowned. 'Will that be enough?'

'Depends what you want to do with it. If you were planning to move any mountains, you can forget it. But if you want to blow a hole in the side of the *Atalanta* . . . well, I think what's in those bottles will give you a good start.'

The commander eyed the two bottles warily. 'Perhaps we'd best put them somewhere safe for now. Molineaux, do you think you could find something we could use to pack them? Horsehair from a mattress or something like that?'

'I know just the thing, sir.' The petty officer hurried from the galley.

'Sir . . . there's something I think you ought to know,' said Charlton.

'Oh?'

'If we ever make it back to the *Ramillies*, I'm going to offer my resignation to the Old Man.'

'I'm not sure that's allowed, in wartime. Why? What's brought this on?'

'I'm not cut out for this, sir. Molineaux was lying – with the best intentions, I know – but he was lying. I haven't got nerves of steel. I lost control, panicked . . . if Molineaux hadn't been here, I'd've given up.'

Killigrew had been in the navy long enough to have heard plenty of confessions like this from young men new to active service, and by now he thought he had a good idea of what to say, 'You're afraid you're a coward? Courage isn't absence of fear, Mr Charlton. We all get scared. Courage is finding the strength to go on in spite of our fears.'

Charlton smiled. 'Molineaux said how your expecting so much from him and his shipmates made them reluctant to let you down. I suppose that's why you push them all the time?'

Killigrew shook his head. 'War pushes us all, Mr Charlton. I just rely on them to do their duty, because I know they will. If anything, knowing that pushes *me* . . . because I'm just as frightened of letting them down as they are of disappointing me. At least think it over before you make any decision. We will get back to the *Ramillies*, I promise you that. When we do, I'll have a discreet word with the Old Man . . . and I'll have nothing but praise for your conduct thus far.'

'Even though I drugged Mr Dahlstedt?'

'It was the right decision medically, if not militarily. Medical decisions are your department, military ones mine.'

'Meaning?'

'It was my responsibility. I should have known you'd give Dahlstedt something to help him through the pain, and asked you not to. If you're definite you can't take the strain any longer, I'm sure the Old Man will understand; he may be as

331

mad as a hatter, but he's a decent old stick. We can have you transferred to the *Belleisle* until the fleet sails back to England, get you an appointment ashore if this nonsense drags into a second year, and when the war's over you can tender your resignation. No blame will attach to you.'

Charlton nodded. 'Thank you.'

Molineaux returned carrying a crate full of straw. 'Is this what you had in mind? Lord Dallaway was using it to keep his photographic plates in.'

'Perfect,' said Charlton.

They packed the bottles in the straw as tenderly as if they had been tucking a baby up in its cot. 'Stow it in the bilges, Molineaux,' said Killigrew. 'Get Endicott to help you. And make sure it's secure! We don't want it shifting every time the boat heels.'

'You can say that again, sir!' Molineaux hurried out.

'The bilges?' asked Charlton.

'Below the waterline,' Killigrew explained. 'If the *Atalanta* manages to catch us again and starts lobbing round shot into our hull, that's where it'll be safest.'

Once Molineaux had returned with Endicott to stow the crate, Killigrew and Charlton made their way up on deck. With the new mainsail bellying with wind, the *Milenion* was clipping along at a handsome five and a half knots once more. Three o'clock approached, and already the first traces of the coming dawn were in the sky ahead of them. Killigrew suddenly realised how tired he was. He had reached that peculiarly light-headed feeling a man gets when he has left the familiar realm of exhaustion behind him and entered into the *terra incognita* that lay beyond. It was incredible to think it was only twelve hours since Kizheh had fetched him from Herre Grönkvist's house; so much had happened since then, it seemed more like twelve years. Once he got back on board the *Ramillies* – he could not afford to consider failure as a possibility – he knew he was going to sleep for a month; and if Crichton did not like it, he could lump it.

Once the crate of pyroglycerin had been stowed, Molineaux and the others continued to jettison everything that could be jettisoned, leaving a trail of jetsam in their wake. They rounded the north-eastern corner of Skärlandet Island at six minutes to three, and there was enough light from the rising moon for Killigrew to see the narrow strait between Skärlandet and Svartbäck less than six hundred yards off the starboard bow.

'Three points to port,' he told Fuller.

'Three points to port it is, sir.'

'Sweet Jesus!' exclaimed Thornton, realising the commander's intention. 'You're not seriously going to try to take us through there, are you?'

'It's our only hope,' Killigrew told him. Because if they could not get out of the channel here, it would make no difference if it took the crew of the *Atalanta* one hour or five to untangle the nets tightly entwined about the paddle-wheel: they would still catch the *Milenion* before she reached Barösund.

'Heave to, Mr Uren!' Killigrew ordered when they were a hundred yards off the gap. 'Away the gig!'

He shinned down the lifelines to the boat, and was rowed through the gap by Iles, Yorath, Hughes and O'Leary. He plumbed the depths with a lead line, never recording more than a fathom and three-quarters – ten and a half feet – marking the shallowest channel with empty bottles anchored with ropes and makeshift weights.

Once back on board the *Milenion*, he summoned everyone on deck, including Dahlstedt and Lord Bullivant, who had to be supported by his daughter. 'Now listen carefully, everyone! I'll keep this short and simple, if by no means sweet. Our staying alive depends on us reaching the open sea. And our reaching the open sea depends on our getting through that channel.' He pointed past the bows. 'There is *no other way*. If there were, we'd take it. There's one small problem, however . . .'

'Ain't there always?' muttered Fuller.

'The *Milenion*'s draught – under normal circumstances – is eleven feet. The depth of that channel is ten and a half.'

'The words "camel" and "eye of a needle" spring to mind.'

'Indeed they do, Captain Thornton. But we *can* do this. All we have to do is make the *Milenion* lighter, so she doesn't sit so deep in the water. Now, some of you have been hard at work for the past forty minutes, throwing overboard everything that could be jettisoned; enough – at a guess – to reduce our draught damned close to ten and a half feet. But we can't run the risk of running aground. If we do, the *Atalanta* will catch us, and . . . well, I leave it to your own imaginations to guess what happens then. But there's something on board this yacht that we can still jettison . . .'

They looked at him blankly.

'You lot,' said Killigrew. 'Molineaux, Endicott and I can sail this ship through the gap without help; the remaining sixteen of you are – assuming an average of a hundred and forty pounds each – a ton of deadweight.' He grinned crookedly. 'Nothing personal . . .'

'So here's what we're going to do. Everyone's going to be shipped to the shore over there until we've got the *Milenion* through the gap. Two trips should do it. When the *Milenion*'s reached deeper water, we'll ship you back on board and be on our way. Once we get through the gap, there's no way the Russians can follow us. It's more than five miles to the far end of the island to port; by the time the *Atalanta* has sailed around it, we'll be safely out to sea.'

Grumbling, everyone clambered down to the gig via the accommodation ladder, or was lowered to it by a hastily rigged boatswain's chair. As Killigrew leaned over the bulwark to watch Iles and Hughes shove the gig away from the *Milenion*'s side, Molineaux joined him.

'What about Burgess and Ogilby?' the petty officer asked in a low voice. 'Pardon my graveyard humour, but they really *are* dead weight.'

'Wait until Iles and Hughes have taken off the second boatload, and quietly ditch their bodies over the side,' murmured Killigrew. 'We haven't got time for an argument about how they deserve a decent Christian burial. Christ knows, no one would like to give them a proper funeral more than I; but the living must take precedence over the dead, even if some of the living don't appreciate just how precarious their position is.'

Searle was too badly injured for Charlton to be prepared to permit him to be moved about, so they left him in Araminta's stateroom, but everyone else still on board apart from Killigrew, Molineaux and Endicott was put in the second boat. While they were being taken off, Molineaux and Endicott brought the two corpses on deck and dragged them to the port bulwark.

'We ought to say something,' said Molineaux.

Endicott thought for a moment and whipped off his bandanna, clutching it to his chest. 'Oh Lord, we commit to Yer care the souls of our . . . acquaintances . . . now departed, as we commit their bodies to the deep, like. Take care of them, but not so much that it distracts Yer attention from takin' care of us, on account of how our need is the greater, as I'm sure Yer'll appreciate.'

'Amen,' said Molineaux.

The two corpses hit the water with a splash.

'All right, lads,' Killigrew called from the helm. 'Loose the headsails!'

The jib and flying jib snapped at the wind, and the *Milenion* began to creep forward through the gap. Everyone else who had been on board watched from the rocky shore to starboard. The headsails loosed, Molineaux made his way to the bow to shout steering orders to Killigrew at the helm, while Endicott manned the halyards in the starboard waist.

'Half a point to windward, sir . . . bit more . . . that's it! Keep her steady . . . steady . . . handsomely does it . . .'

Killigrew felt the keel touch bottom through the deck

boards beneath his feet. His heart was in his mouth; they *had* to make it.

The scraping of the keel on the rocks below became more pronounced. He thought about the pyroglycerin in the bilges and wondered if it had been such a good idea to stow it so close to the keel after all. 'Come on, you bitch,' he hissed through gritted teeth. 'You can do it . . .'

And then the scraping was gone and they were running free.

Endicott grinned at him with relief. 'Touch and go there, sir, eh?'

A shudder ran through the schooner as they touched bottom again, more firmly this time. Endicott grabbed a backstay to support himself while Killigrew was thrown against the helm.

They were aground.

'Touch and stay, more like,' Killigrew said bitterly. 'Never mind. Perhaps we can kedge her through.' He took the speaking trumpet from the binnacle and crossed to the starboard bulwark. 'Bring the gig back across, Captain Thornton! We need eight big, strong lads.'

Thornton brought the boat back out to the *Milenion* with Uren, Iles, Hughes, Fuller, O'Leary, Yorath and Attwood. 'Everyone up on deck except Mr Uren, Iles and Yorath,' Killigrew called down from the entry port. 'We need to kedge through. Row for'ard, lads, and we'll lower the anchor to you.'

Once the anchor was on board the gig, Iles and Yorath rowed it out in front of the *Milenion*, as far as the cable would allow, and dropped it into the water.

'Man the capstan!'

The men on deck gathered around the capstan and turned it, drawing in the slack of the cable. The anchor scraped along the bottom until it became caught on the seabed. By then Iles and Yorath had rowed the gig back to the schooner's side. Tying the boat to the side ladder by its painter, they followed

Uren up on deck and joined the others at the capstan. They heaved at the bars, feet scraping on the deck, grunting with effort. The cable became taut and the timbers groaned under the strain.

'Come on, lads!' urged Killigrew, joining them at the capstan and pushing all his might. 'We can do it! Just a few feet!'

He pushed until he thought his heart must burst and his sinews split. But the *Milenion* would not budge an inch, never mind a few feet. He left off pushing, sinking to the deck with a gasp. 'All right, lads, belay pushing.'

'Any more bright ideas, sir?' asked Endicott.

'We're still too heavy,' said Killigrew. 'There must be something else we can throw overboard to lighten her.'

Molineaux shook his head. 'We jettisoned everything but the kitchen sink. And if there'd been one of them on board, we'd've jettisoned that too.'

Killigrew nodded. He knew Molineaux would not have missed a trick.

And then he looked up. 'What about the cooking range?'

'The cooking range?' echoed Hughes. 'It's cast iron. It's got to weigh at least a ton.'

'Exactly,' said Killigrew, jumping to his feet. 'Come on, lads!'

They trooped down to the galley, where Killigrew surveyed the scene.

Hughes shook his head. 'No way, sir. No way. It's impossible.'

'You're in the navy now, Hughes. Nothing is impossible. If Archimedes was ready to have a stab at moving the world, I don't see why we should be defeated by a cooking range. Fetch Burgess' tools from the saloon.' Killigrew pointed to the deck head. 'I want those deck boards removed. Molineaux, go aloft and rig as many blocks and tackles as you think we'll need to hoist that stove on the fore gaff.'

Molineaux sucked his teeth in. 'We'll need a couple of preventer stays on the fore mast.'

'Make it so. Give him a hand, Iles. The rest of you, start taking up those deck boards.'

It was the work of a few minutes to make a hole in the deck immediately over the cooking range, while Molineaux and Iles brailed the foresail and rigged up their blocks and tackles. Supervising the work in the galley, Killigrew's gaze fell on the medicine chest open on one of the worktops, and the bottle of Trubshaw's Cordial caught his eye. He took it out and stared at the label. At the top it bore the legend: 'Trubshaw's Cordial', and below that was a picture of a Negro petty officer carrying an unconscious man on his back across a snowy wasteland while a polar bear eyed them both from a ridge of ice. Beneath this, in quotes, the words: 'I can keep going for ever . . . on Trubshaw's Cordial.' And just beneath that, a facsimile of a familiar signature.

'Molineaux!' roared Killigrew.

The petty officer's face appeared at the hole in the deck head above. 'Sir?'

Killigrew merely showed him the bottle. Recognition showed on Molineaux's face at once; he might even have blushed.

'Is that how you paid for your new boots?' asked Killigrew. 'And your repeater?'

'Advertising endorsements,' said Molineaux. 'It's a prime lay. I wonder you haven't been asked yourself.'

'A gentleman does not endorse commercial products, Molineaux.'

'Your loss, sir.'

Killigrew squinted at the bottle again. 'Is this stuff any good?'

'Wouldn't touch it with a barge pole, sir.'

The ropes were lowered through the hole, where Killigrew and Endicott made them fast to the range. They passed up the guy ropes to Fuller and O'Leary before making their way on deck and grasping the heaving lines. Killigrew took off his gloves.

'Everyone ready? On the count of three: one . . . two . . . three, *heave*!'

They hauled on the ropes. The blocks creaked, and the fore gaff groaned.

'And again . . . *heave*!'

The cooking range rose from its brickwork bed on the galley floor: only an inch, but it was a start.

'And again . . . *heave*!'

They hauled on the ropes, hand over hand, hoisting the range out of the galley an inch at a time. The blocks squealed in protest.

'That tackle isn't going to hold,' Hughes muttered dubiously, gazing aloft.

'It'll hold!' insisted Molineaux. 'Heave, damn you!'

At last the bottom of the range was level with the deck, then a few inches above it. Fuller and O'Leary took up the slack on the guy ropes to steady it as it swung from side to side.

'Heave! Heave! *Heave!* That's it, my buckoes . . . nearly there . . .'

They hauled it up until the bottom was clear of the bulwarks, and then swung it towards the side. The gaff jaws groaned in protest . . . and the peak span snapped.

The gaff jerked down, slamming the range against the top of the bulwark, which splintered under the massive weight. The whole ship rocked under the impact. It was too much for the preventer stays to hold. They parted, and the range tumbled from the side to hit the water with a terrific splash. The gaff whipped down like an executioner's axe. Killigrew saw Molineaux standing directly beneath it and launched himself across the deck. Catching the petty officer around the waist in a rugby tackle, he knocked him clear a split-second before the gaff chopped down on the deck.

Molineaux sat up and gazed across at the gaff that had

339

come so close to squashing him. 'Thanks, sir.'

'No more than I owe you a dozen times over,' Killigrew told him. 'Besides, I need every man available to get us out of here. Anyone else hurt?'

The others shook their heads, some still standing, others sprawled where they had thrown themselves clear of the falling spar. Killigrew and Molineaux picked themselves up and dusted themselves down. 'Right, cut those ropes and tidy up this mess.'

'Eh, I don't want to worry you, sir,' said Endicott. 'But we're still touching bottom.'

Killigrew thumped his fist against the bulwark. 'Damn it to hell!' All that effort . . . for nothing!

'That ain't the half of it, boys,' said Hughes, pointing off the starboard quarter to where a plume of smoke was visible above the tops of the pine trees crowding the north-east end of Skärlandet Island, black against the dingy blue-grey sky.

'The *Atalanta*!' groaned Attwood.

XVII

Out to Sea

3.25 a.m.–8.30 a.m., Friday 18 August

Mackenzie smiled ruefully at Killigrew. 'Never mind, sir. It was a brave effort. We did our best.'

Killigrew stared at him. 'What the hell are you doing, still on board?'

'Sir?'

'Get back in the gig, damn it! All of you! Back in the gig!' He dashed for the helm while they scrambled to the entry port, swarming down the side ladder to the boat.

And ever so slightly the deck began to roll beneath Killigrew's feet. He could feel each gentle thud as the swells rolling through the gap lifted the keel off the bottom and dropped it down again. But the headsails and mainsail were still full, and each time the *Milenion* was lifted, she was put down again a couple of inches further along. Slowly she juddered her way forward, and as the bottom shelved away the bumps became fewer and further between, until once again the schooner was floating free.

Killigrew threw back his head and let out a wild whoop of exultation. 'We did it!' He belayed the helm, and ran across to the entry port. 'We're through! We did it!'

The men in the boat huzzahed lustily.

'Everyone back on board except Yorath and O'Leary – you two, row back ashore and collect the others! Take the helm, Fuller. Molineaux, Endicott, Iles and Hughes . . . get that gaff repaired, chop chop!'

The Bullivants were climbing back on board by the time the *Atalanta* steamed into view around the headland off the starboard quarter, less than nine hundred yards off. With only the headsails and mainsail drawing, the *Milenion* was creeping along. 'Two points to starboard, Fuller!' ordered Killigrew, as they breasted the headland at the west end of Svartbäck. 'Make for the channel between those two islands.'

'Aye, aye, sir!'

The *Atalanta*'s bow chaser fired, hurling a shot towards the *Milenion* with a shriek like ripping canvas. The shot hit the water fifty yards off the schooner's starboard bow: the Russians were using round shot again, and aiming at the hull. Thinking of the bottles of pyroglycerin sitting in the bilges brought Killigrew out in a sweat: he had told Charlton they would be safe enough below the waterline, but the truth was that a round shot could be an unpredictable thing once it started bouncing around inside a hull.

The *Milenion* was running before the wind, but making slow progress without her foresail, while the *Atalanta*'s paddles powered her forward to close the gap. The paddle-sloop fired again, this time at a range of seven hundred yards. They could not miss. But they did, putting a ball in the water only a few feet from the stern and drenching everyone on the quarterdeck with spray.

The *Atalanta* was still nearly three hundred yards from the gap when she fired again. Killigrew braced himself, and this time felt a sickening lurch in his stomach as another shot slammed into the schooner's stern, making the deck shudder. It was as well Dahlstedt and the Bullivants were still on deck, crouching ashen-faced in the lee waist.

As the seconds ticked by, the feeling of helplessness was overwhelming. The gap between the two vessels was still closing. Killigrew could picture the crew of the sloop's bow chaser working the gun, sponging, reloading and running it out through the port. The sloop was barely four hundred yards astern.

And then . . . was it his imagination, or was the gap between the two vessels widening at last? Taking the telescope from the binnacle, Killigrew strained his eyes against the gloom and saw the bottles he had used to mark the channel, bobbing around the *Atalanta*'s sides. The sloop was stationary: the fools had run her aground!

But before he could whoop a second time, the sloop's bow chaser roared again. Another shot slammed into the *Milenion*'s stern. The schooner could not take much more of this pounding.

Clear water was opening up to port. 'Two more points to starboard, Fuller!'

'Two more points it is, sir!' At least the steering gear was still working.

The gap was still only five hundred yards, but the *Milenion* was gathering way as she came off the wind. The next shot skipped across the waves and smashed into the port quarter: the Russians were trying to hull them below the waterline.

'Damage report, Mr Mackenzie!'

'Aye, aye, sir.' The mate hurried below.

'For God's sake, man!' protested Bullivant. 'This is madness! You're going to get us all killed!'

'You have any better suggestions, my lord?' Killigrew snapped back. 'I would have thought it was plainly obvious that the Russians mean to destroy us; I don't intend to make their work any easier for them by surrendering!'

Mackenzie came back on deck. 'We're hulled at the waterline, sir. Must be two foot of water in the well already, and rising fast.'

'Damn it!' hissed Killigrew. 'Did you find the hole?'

'Yes, sir. Port quarter.'

'Can we fother it?'

'I think so, sir.'

'Make it so. Iles, Hughes – man the pumps!'

Uren, O'Leary and Yorath fetched a spritsail from the sail locker and worked it into a thrummed mat, greasing and tarring it well. They worked swiftly but, with water flooding into the hold, every second counted.

Another two minutes passed, another shot was fired. Killigrew exhaled with relief when it splashed into the waves several dozen yards to starboard. The Russians were firing the bow chaser through the sternmost port in the port bow, but the next shot fell even wider: they could not angle the gun any further round.

'One point to port, Fuller!'

Fuller gave the helm a twitch. Killigrew gazed amidships, until the *Atalanta* was in line with the centre of the taffrail.

'Helm amidships!'

''Midships it is, sir.'

A second gun crew now worked the thirty-two-pounder abaft the sloop's port-side paddle-box. It belched flame, and the ball skipped across the waves to port.

Killigrew wiped his brow with his sleeve. 'We're in their blind spot.' The bow chaser could not be angled any further aft, the port-side thirty-two-pounder no further forward, and with her keel wedged on the bottom the sloop could not manoeuvre to correct the problem.

Uren, O'Leary and Yorath finished thrumming the spritsail, and Molineaux and Endicott passed a couple of lines under the keel so they could drag it in place and heave it tight against the schooner's side where she had been holed. The water pressure would force the tarred oakum into the hole and slow the flood of water. That was the theory, at any rate.

Once the thrummed mat was in place, Mackenzie went below to see how well it was keeping the water out. He re-emerged, soaked to the chest. 'It's a shambles down there,

I'm afraid Searle's dead. I don't suppose he felt much: one of the shots slammed right through his bunk. We'll be scraping him off the bulkheads for weeks; what's left of him.'

'Mr Mackenzie!' Killigrew chided him, flickering his eyes to where the Bullivants stood; but they all looked dazed, they hardly seemed aware of anything that was going on around them, let alone anything that the mate had to say. 'Any other casualties?'

'No, sir.'

That was something, at least. 'What about the fothering?'

'Seems to be working.'

'How much water in the well?'

'Six feet,' the mate said grimly.

The commander could well believe it: the schooner was visibly lower in the water. 'Check the well at five-minute intervals,' he told Mackenzie.

'Yes, sir.'

Killigrew crossed to the taffrail and watched the grounded *Atalanta* slowly fade astern. The sky was lightening rapidly. He checked his watch, and was mildly surprised to discover it was still only half-past three in the morning. He rubbed his face wearily.

Araminta came across to stand next to him. 'Can I talk to you?'

He managed a wan smile. 'I don't see why not.'

'We're damaged badly, aren't we?'

'Not necessarily.' He tried to sound chipper. 'It all depends on whether or not the men working the pumps can keep pace with the water leaking in through the fothering. Of course, the water already on board will slow us . . .'

'Can we make it to the fleet? And please, I don't want to hear any lies meant to reassure me,' she added.

'In that case, ask me again in half an hour. I'll have a better idea of how badly we're hurt by then.'

'We're in a tight spot, aren't we?'

'I've known tighter,' said Killigrew. 'No, really,' he added, seeing the look on her face. 'We've been in spots tighter than this before now, haven't we, Molineaux?'

'You can say that again, sir. Back in the Arctic for one, the winter before last, stranded a thousand miles from civilisation with a polar bear nipping at our heels.'

'Or that time in the New Hebrides,' said Killigrew. 'Marooned on a desert island, hunted by a tribe of savage cannibals, and up to our necks in a quagmire,'

'Hoo, yur! I forgot about the cannibals and the quagmire. That were a tight spot and no mistake.'

Araminta looked at Killigrew. 'You're actually enjoying this, aren't you?'

He ran his fingers through his hair. 'Well, perhaps not *enjoying* it *per se* . . . but if the djinn of the lamp could whisk me up and put me down in a nice, safe clerk's job in London right now, you can be sure I'd tell him to go to the devil! At least I've got the satisfaction of knowing that in thirty years' time, I'll be able to look back and say I've lived life to the full; which is more than that clerk can say.'

She lowered her voice. 'Something to tell our grandchildren?'

He surreptitiously slipped his hand in hers. 'Exactly.'

The *Milenion* rounded the east end of Fåfängö Island. 'What course, sir?' asked Fuller.

Killigrew thought for a moment. The wind was still south-westerly, and south-west was the course they needed to follow if they were to reach Hangö Head. 'South by east,' he decided. 'We'll make a long tack out into the gulf – more chance of falling in with a friendly vessel out there – before we come about when we're far enough south to make Hangö Head on a heading of west by north.'

'South by east it is, sir.'

As the next half an hour crawled past, the sky lightened from indigo to a dingy blue. The next island they passed hid the *Atalanta* from sight, and the archipelago thinned out before them, the open gulf ahead. The pitching of the deck increased as they moved out into less sheltered waters.

'Six foot of water in the well,' Mackenzie reported at eight bells. 'Maybe closer to six feet and one inch.'

Killigrew nodded, feeling sick. If the water was rising at an inch every half an hour, they had perhaps ten hours before the *Milenion* foundered and sank, maybe not even that much: the more water they had on board, the faster it would pour through the fothered hole in the hull. To get to Ledsund, they would have to tack against the wind, with six feet of water slopping about below decks they'd be lucky to make a knot and a half. They were more than twenty sea miles from Hangö Head, the first place they could be sure of meeting a British vessel. The mathematics of their situation were inescapable: their only chance was to fall in with an Allied vessel out in the gulf before they foundered; or before the *Atalanta* caught up with them again.

'Molineaux, Endicott – spell Iles and Hughes at the pumps,' ordered Killigrew. 'Get a second fothering over the first, Mr Uren. Iles and Hughes, you can bear a hand.'

'Anything we can do to help?' asked Lady Bullivant.

Killigrew nodded. 'Bail.'

'Bail?'

'Find buckets, pails, saucepans, hats if you have to – whatever we didn't jettison last night – and form a human chain from below decks.'

'Will that make a difference?'

'Every little bit helps.'

Captain Thornton organised the human chain with the energy of a man determined not to lose the ship he loved.

Killigrew made his way down the after hatch to see the damage for himself. Mindful of the two steps that had been knocked out of the companion ladder the first time the *Milenion* had been fired upon, he watched his footing this time, which was just as well because the steps ended after three rungs; the rest of the ladder had been blown away.

'A shambles,' Mackenzie had called it. That was putting it mildly. The breeze blew through the holes punched in the sides, bulkheads had been ripped away, a trough in the deck gaped to reveal the dark, flooded hold below, and splintered timbers lay everywhere. Here and there one or two oil lamps still burned in their gimbals, casting eerie shadows of wreckage that shifted with each roll of the hull. With a couple of round shot, the *Atalanta* had taken the well-ordered, spotlessly maintained living quarters of the lower deck and transformed them into a scene of hellish chaos, where the remnants of civilised existence strewn higgledy-piggledy ceased to have any meaning amongst the wholesale destruction.

Gripping the coaming above, Killigrew lowered his legs past the last remaining rung of the companion ladder and swung himself clear of the trough to land on one of the exposed deck beams. He teetered and caught hold of a bulkhead in an effort to right himself, only for it to snap away in his hand. He squatted, putting his hand out to grasp the next beam, and barely stopped himself from falling through into the hold. In the shadows below, he could see the water glinting in the faint light of an oil lamp. There must have been about three feet of water sloshing about the hold. The bilges would be completely flooded; and in there somewhere, the crate containing the two bottles of pyroglycerin Charlton and Molineaux had gone to so much trouble to make.

He headed forward, to where the remaining companion ladder was relatively intact, and waited for Araminta to finish passing a bucket of water up to her mother on the deck before climbing through. He crossed to where O'Leary stood ready to man the braces.

'Know anything about carpentry, O'Leary?'

'Not much. If it's a chippy you're after, sir, you'd be better off talking to Ned Yorath: he's a better man with hammer and saw than me.'

Killigrew thanked him and crossed to where Yorath stood. 'O'Leary tells me you're a carpenter.'

'I wouldn't go that far, sir, but I've been at sea long enough to know how to splice a mainbrace.'

'In which sense?'

Yorath grinned. 'Both.'

'Some of the pillars on the lower deck have been smashed. Frankly, I'm not sure what's holding up the quarterdeck any more.'

'Want me to shore 'em up, sir?'

Killigrew nodded and Yorath headed below.

The commander made his way aft to where Thornton was taking a turn at the helm. 'It's bad, isn't it?' murmured the captain.

'Let's just say I've seen colanders that were more sea-worthy than this schooner is now.'

Killigrew crossed to the bulwark and patted the timbers lovingly. The *Milenion* had got them this far, in spite of all the odds. Maybe she could yet come through for them.

'Don't let me down, sweetheart,' he murmured. 'A few more hours: that's all I ask. Just stay afloat a few more hours.'

Pechorin was lounging with his feet on the desk in his day-room, smoking a cigar, when he felt the *Atalanta* run aground. He checked his watch and had a wager with himself, that the knock would come at the door within ten minutes.

At nine minutes and fifty-one seconds, he was not disappointed. 'Come in!'

Nekrasoff shuffled into the room. 'We're aground.'

'Really,' Pechorin said heavily. He tapped ash from his cigar and watched Nekrasoff with studied insolence.

'And the *Milenion* got away.'

'Did she?'

'Yes.'

'So? That's not my problem. You relieved me of command, remember?'

Nekrasoff took a deep breath. 'I should like you to resume command,' he muttered.

Pechorin cupped a hand to his ear. 'Pardon?'

'I should like you to resume command.'

'Aren't you forgetting something?'

'What?'

'You have to say the magic word.'

Nekrasoff sighed. 'Please.'

'Thank you.' Pechorin stood up. 'To tell the truth, I should like me to resume command too, before that dunderhead Lazarenko sinks my ship.'

'The Tsar's ship.'

'The ship that the Tsar has entrusted to my care. *My* care, Nekrasoff. Remember that. My resuming command is dependent on our doing things my way from now on, do you understand? Any more interference from you, and I'll have you clapped in irons, and use your letter of authority from the Grand Duke Konstantin to wipe my backside. I hardly think His Imperial Highness is going to be impressed with the way you've used the authority he's given you so far, do you?'

'Just get me the *Milenion*,' Nekrasoff growled as they made their way up on deck.

'After the mess you've made of things, I'm not sure that's possible. They must be past Fåfängö Island by now, well on their way out to the open sea.'

'They must *not* reach the Allied fleet!'

'First things first,' Pechorin told him, climbing up through the after hatch. 'Ivanets! You will place Lieutenant Lazarenko under arrest. He will stand trial for incompetence at our earliest convenience.'

'But I was only obeying orders!' wailed Lazarenko.

'You were not obeying any orders given by *me*, Mstislav Trofimovich! Take him below and clap him in irons!' Pechorin turned to Lieutenant Yurieff. 'You've tried reversing the engines,' he said. It was a statement rather than a question: he had felt the note of the engines' vibrations through the deck in the day-room. 'All right. Let's unload all the stores, all the shot, everything it takes to get this barge afloat. If that doesn't work, we'll try kedging astern.'

'Yes, sir.'

'How long will it take to get us under way again?' asked Nekrasoff.

'Not long,' Pechorin told him acidly. 'Just a few hours, that's all.'

The sun rose at a quarter to five to find the *Milenion* sailing close-hauled on the starboard tack beneath a pale blue sky dotted with a few ragged tufts of cloud. That was not good: Killigrew had a feeling that Pechorin would not give up so easily, and he had hoped for a thick fog to mask the schooner. The gaff had been repaired, and the foresail bulged with wind. The *Milenion* was making two knots, as good as could be expected when they were sailing this close to the wind with more than six feet of water in the well.

The Finnish coast was astern, and a few islets and skerries were dotted about to port and starboard, but ahead was only blue water for as far as the eye could see, barring a largish island two and a half miles off the starboard bow. At least now there was more water than land in view. No other ships in sight, either: the depredations of the British fleet were keeping Finnish merchantmen in harbour as well as Russian warships. It was good there was no sign of the *Atalanta*, but it would have been better to sight a British or French frigate on patrol.

'You know where we are?' Killigrew asked Dahlstedt.

The Finn nodded and pointed to a small island less than half a mile to port. 'That's Träskö, there. And that island off the starboard bow? That's Byusö.'

Within half an hour they were level with Byusö, and a larger island came into view beyond. 'That's where it all started,' said Thornton.

'Hm?'

'Jurassö.'

Killigrew took the telescope from the binnacle to survey the island, saw rocks, trees, a tall lighthouse rising up at the west end, no sign of the ironworks; certainly no indication that Jurassö housed any kind of military secret that justified Nekrasoff's determination to stop the Bullivants from escaping from Finland alive. It was tempting to make for the island and send a boat ashore to investigate – Jurassö could not be more than a mile across – but Killigrew's first responsibility was to the civilians on board. Jurassö could wait for another day.

Mackenzie went to check the level of the water in the well. 'Six feet and two inches,' he reported.

An inch in a little less than two hours, despite the efforts of the men at the pumps and the bailing crew. The second thrummed mat was making a difference, but not much. Still, at least now there was a slim hope they might make it as far as Hangö Head before the *Milenion* foundered.

'Listen, Killigrew,' Thornton said awkwardly. 'I know my attitude hasn't been as . . . helpful . . . as it might have been. I . . . well, I just want to say I'm sorry, that's all. We couldn't have made it without you and your men. We owe you our lives; and I'll tell Lord Bullivant so.'

Killigrew managed a wan smile. 'That's very kind of you. But we're not home and dry yet.'

'Difficult to see what can go wrong now. The Russians wouldn't dare risk one of their ships in the open sea, just to catch us . . . would they?'

Killigrew gazed speculatively towards Jurassö, wondering what vital secret the island held. 'That remains to be seen.'

'Man the capstan bars!' ordered Pechorin. 'Stand by in the engine-room.'

'What if it doesn't work this time?' asked Nekrasoff.

Pechorin looked at him. 'Then we're stuck.'

'For how long? It's been nearly two hours!'

'Until the Admiralty sends another steamer to tow us off. And – given that Admiral Rykord will be none too impressed by our running the *Atalanta* aground – I don't imagine he'll be in much of a hurry to spare another ship to free us from our own incompetence, do you?'

'Engine-room standing by, sir,' reported one of the *michmanis*.

'Set on. Turn astern, full speed.'

The *michmani* hurried below and presently the engine throbbed into life. The paddle-wheels turned, churning up the water on either side of the hull, but even with most of her stores ferried to the shore of Svartbäck Island – along with all but enough men to work the engines and the capstan – the sloop still refused to budge.

'Turn the capstan!'

The men heaved at the capstan bars, drawing up the slack of the cable paid out to the anchor dropped in the channel astern of the sloop.

'That's it, *mouzhiki*!' called Pechorin. 'I think I felt something that time – heave, damn you! Heave!'

The engine rattled, the men heaved at the capstan, and then Pechorin really did feel something give. With a scraping the count could feel through his feet – he dreaded to think what damage they had done to the copper sheathing on the keel – the *Atalanta* slid back one foot, then another, and then the movement was constant. She floated free.

'Stop engines!' he ordered. 'We're off!'

The men at the capstan cheered, a cheer that was quickly echoed by the men ashore. Pechorin permitted himself a smile. 'Bring the stores and the men back on board quickly, and we'll get under way again,' he told Yurieff, taking out another cigar.

'Yes, sir!'

Pechorin lit his cigar and made his way below, followed by Nekrasoff and Chernyovsky. In his day-room, he took a chart from the chart locker and spread it on the table, weighing

353

down the corners with four paperweights.

He checked his watch. 'One hour and fifty minutes since the *Milenion* sailed through the Fåfängö Gap. Let's see, she'll have headed west, towards the Allied Fleet at the Åland Islands . . .'

'Is there any chance we can still catch her?' asked Nekrasoff.

'Every chance. The wind's been blowing steadily from the south-west all morning. Even sailing due west, she'd be close-hauled. I doubt even a fore-and-aft-rigged schooner could make more than two knots that close to the wind.' Pechorin picked up a pair of dividers and drew an arc on the chart, based on their current position. 'She couldn't be any further west than Älgö Island. But I doubt they'd even have got that far.'

'What makes you say that?'

'It's a long way to the Åland Islands from here. But Allied warships have been sailing up and down the Gulf of Finland constantly ever since they began their blockade. Killigrew's best chance of safety is to sail south, to the open sea. There they stand a chance of falling in with a British vessel that can protect them. So first, they'll have headed south; again, sailing close to the wind, no more than two knots. I doubt they've got much further than Byusö.' Pechorin tapped at the island on the chart. 'Once they reach the shipping lanes, they'll turn west, somewhere south of Jurassö, and head for Hangö Head.'

'And how do you propose to catch them?'

'We sail east, around the far end of Svartbäck, then turn south-east into the open sea before coming around on a south-westerly heading between Träskö and Nothamn to intercept them. If we get the crew and stores back on board by seven-thirty, under full steam we can reach Nothamn within an hour. I doubt the *Milenion* will be further west than Jurassö: we should be able to see her clearly enough in this weather. We can steam at four times the speed she sails at:

we'll overhaul them before nightfall.'

'And if you're wrong? If Killigrew hasn't gone south and west?'

'Then we lose them. But that's less of a worry than what happens if we should run into a British frigate.'

Pechorin smiled. The *Atalanta* against a British frigate: it would be a dream come true. He'd show the Allies that the Russian navy could fight; yes, and his masters back at the Admiralty in St Petersburg.

'On deck there!' Fuller called from the masthead. 'Sail ho!'

Killigrew looked up from the quarterdeck. 'Where away?'

'On the starboard beam.'

It was eight o'clock in the morning, three-quarters of an hour since the *Milenion* had turned to starboard. Now she sailed westwards, close-hauled, with Jurassö just over a mile off the starboard bow.

Killigrew took the telescope from the binnacle and levelled it. Seven miles off, the plume of charcoal-grey smoke on the horizon jumped into view almost at once, rising up from behind the trees on the long spine of Svartbäck Island, which merged with the mainland behind.

'A steamer,' grunted Thornton. 'Headed due east, by the look of it.'

'Until it reaches the east end of Svartbäck,' agreed Killigrew.

'Is it the *Atalanta*?' asked Araminta.

'Most likely.'

They watched the plume of smoke until it emerged from behind the mass of islands to the north-east of Träskö about fifteen minutes later and was revealed to be a paddle-steamer. The ship must have seen them at more or less the same time, for it put about on a south-westerly heading to intercept them. Now there could be no doubt in anyone's mind.

'How long before she catches up with us, Kit?' asked Araminta.

'An hour, maybe two.' There was no point trying to shield her.

'We could put about on an easterly heading, run before the wind,' said Lord Bullivant.

Thornton shook his head. 'We'd only be putting off the inevitable . . . and sailing deeper into the Gulf of Finland.'

Killigrew nodded. 'We'd best maintain our present heading. Every mile west we sail takes us closer to safety . . . and there's always a chance we'll run into one of our own ships.' He did not really believe this himself.

'And when the *Atalanta* catches us?'

'We fight,' Killigrew said simply.

'For God's sake, man!' protested Bullivant. 'A handful of muskets, against the guns of the *Atalanta*? It's suicide!'

'So is surrendering. Nekrasoff isn't going to let us live. Not now.'

'Better to go down fighting,' agreed Thornton.

'Oh, heavens!' Araminta lowered her gaze to the deck.

'Have courage, Minty,' Killigrew told her. 'We're not beaten yet. I've still got one or two tricks up my sleeve. Molineaux!'

'Sir?'

'Better get our secret weapon ready.'

'Aye, aye, sir.'

'You have the watch, Captain Thornton,' said Killigrew.

Molineaux fetched a coil of rope from a belaying pin and Killigrew was about to precede him down the fore hatch when Charlton caught him by the sleeve.

'You're going to get the pyroglycerin we made last night, sir?'

'You wouldn't want it to go to waste, would you?'

'But I thought Molineaux stowed it in the bilges.'

'That he did, as per my ever-so-brilliant instructions,' Killigrew admitted wryly.

'The bilges that are flooded?'

'Yes, Mr Charlton. The bilges that are flooded.'

356

Killigrew and Molineaux descended to the hold, where they found themselves hip-deep in the water that sloshed back and forth between the bulkheads. 'Can you remember where the hatch to the bilges is?' asked Killigrew.

'Right along here, sir.' Molineaux led the way between the storerooms to a part of the hold where hardly any light reached. He fumbled under the water, at last pulling up a hatch cover. 'Down there, sir.'

Killigrew began to strip off his tunic. 'Don't you think you ought to leave this one to me, sir?' asked Molineaux. 'You're supposed to be taking it easy.'

'Now, you know I'd never ask any man under my command to do something I'm not prepared to do myself.'

'I know it, sir. That's why I don't mind volunteering.'

Someone came down the companion way and waded down the deck towards them. 'Who's that?' called Killigrew.

'It's me: Mr Charlton,' came the reply, and with the next step the figure stepped into a pool of light cast by a hole in the deck head to reveal the assistant surgeon's face. 'I've just thought of something.'

'Is it urgent?' Killigrew asked impatiently.

'I think you'd better hear me out, sir.'

'Go on, then.'

'The bottles of pyroglycerin have been submerged in this water for a few hours now, haven't they?'

'Nearly five.'

'So the pyroglycerin's probably reached the same temperature as this water by now, hasn't it?'

'What of it?'

'Pyroglycerin freezes at fifty-six degrees Fahrenheit. I don't know how cold this water is, but I'll lay odds it's a lot colder than fifty-six.'

'So it's probably frozen in the bottles?'

'I sincerely hope so. Frozen pyroglycerin is actually quite stable. But partially-frozen pyroglycerin? That's even more volatile than pyroglycerin at room temperature.'

357

'He means even more likely to explode if I knock it about too much?' asked Molineaux.

Killigrew nodded. 'Still sure you want to volunteer?'

'I'm sure I don't want to leave a job like this to anyone else, if that's what you mean.' Molineaux handed the coil of rope to Killigrew and stripped to the waist, passing his jacket, guernsey, shirt and bonnet to Charlton. 'Hold on to these for me, would you, sir?'

The assistant surgeon nodded.

Killigrew handed the petty officer one end of the rope, and Molineaux passed it around his waist and tied it in place. 'Is it far to where you left the crate?' asked the commander.

'About thirty feet.'

'What's it going to be like down there?'

'Not too bad: pig iron rather than gravel for ballast, at least.' Molineaux lowered his legs and torso through the submerged hatch, until only his head showed above water.

'If you get into trouble, give the rope three sharp tugs and I'll come in after you.'

'Thirty feet, with nothing between me and the crate but some pig iron and a few timber frames,' scoffed Molineaux, checking his Bowie knife was still in its sheath in the small of his back. 'Easy as caz.'

'Just don't get cocky.'

'At least I won't have to worry about rats: reckon they deserted this ship hours ago.' Molineaux took a couple of deep breaths, and ducked under the water.

'Is he going to be all right?' asked the assistant surgeon.

'Molineaux? You needn't worry about him, Charlton.' Killigrew paid out the coil of rope he held. 'He's indestructible.'

'You've known him a long time, haven't you?'

'Seven years.' Even as Killigrew said it, he realised how those years had flown past. Skirmishes with slavers on the Guinea Coast, battles with pirates in the South China Sea, fights with cannibals and escaped convicts in the South Seas, and a struggle for survival in the desolation of the Arctic. *Happy days*, he thought ironically. 'He says he's going to be a bosun one day.'

'Has there ever been a black bosun in the Royal Navy?'

'I don't know,' admitted Killigrew. 'But if there hasn't, you can rely on Molineaux to be the first. He's a Henson: he can do anything.'

'A Henson?'

'His mother's maiden name. She resumed it after his father walked out on the family when Molineaux was six. He became a petty thief soon after that. Within ten years he was the finest burglar in England and the toast of the swell mob.'

'If he was such a good burglar, why did he give it up to become a sailor?'

'He stole a Grande Amati.'

'What's a Grande Amati?'

'A violin made by the man who taught Stradivarius how to make violins. You don't steal something like that and carry on with your life as normal the next day. One of his accomplices tried to cheat him by tipping off the police, and he picked the navy as a good place to lie low until the hue and cry had died down. There was a time when half the ratings on a ship like the *Ramillies* would have had stories like that, if none quite so spectacular.' Killigrew grinned. 'I don't know: somehow the navy just doesn't seem the same now it's gone all respectable on me.'

'Still, that must have been a few years ago. If the navy was only ever a temporary refuge, why did he stay on all this time?'

'I don't know. I suspect Molineaux wouldn't be able to give you a straight answer either, if you asked him. But I have a theory.'

'Oh?'

'Molineaux likes a challenge. When he'd risen to the peak of his criminal career while he was still in his late teens, the challenge had gone. So he found another career, and now he's working to reach the peak of that one. Wouldn't surprise me if he left the navy after he's been a bosun for a couple of years.'

'I thought he was in for life.'

'I thought I was in for life, when I joined.'

'Don't tell me *you're* thinking of resigning!'

'As I say, it's not the same navy it was when I joined. Not the same world it fights to protect. People had different values then. In those days it was all about ideals: liberty and justice, defending the weak and vanquishing the villains. At least, that's the way it seemed to me at the time. Nowadays it's all about money. Surely you don't think we'd go to war to protect Turkey if our commercial interests in India weren't threatened?'

'I hadn't really thought about it. Are you so sure it's the world that's changed? Are you sure it isn't you?'

'Grown up, you mean? Perhaps.'

'If you don't like it any more, why do you still do it? Or are you waiting for the war to finish so you can resign with honour too?'

Killigrew shook his head. 'The problem I've got is that if I resign from the navy, I'm not sure what else I could do with my life. Not all of us are as in control of our destinies as Molineaux, you know.'

'Speaking of Molineaux . . . he's been gone an awfully long time.'

'Hm? Oh!' Killigrew had almost forgotten about the rope he was holding. 'Well, he hasn't signalled he's in difficulties yet.'

'Maybe the rope got snagged around something,' suggested Charlton.

Before Killigrew could reply, something bumped against the underside of the deck about thirty feet from where they stood. 'Well, he's still alive, at any rate.' He started to draw the rope in, being careful only to take in the slack without dragging Molineaux: trying to push the crate before him in that cold and pitch-black water, the petty officer had enough problems as it was. 'Well, the rope's not snagged, at least.'

Something surfaced through the hatch, and the crate bobbed up, the lid still securely in place. Killigrew grabbed it before the sloshing water could knock it against one of the bulkheads, and Molineaux's head broke the surface. He whooped air into his lungs.

'Are you all right, Molineaux?' asked Killigrew. 'We were starting to get worried.'

The petty officer nodded, still struggling for breath. Killigrew and Charlton waited patiently for him to get his wind back.

'Any chance of a cuppa tea?' was the only explanation they got.

They made their way back on deck, Killigrew and Molineaux taking turns to hand the crate up to one another through the hatches. By the time they emerged on deck, the steamer was less than five miles off, still on a course to intercept them. Killigrew took the telescope from the binnacle and levelled it at the strange ship. One glance told him all he needed to know.

It was the *Atalanta*. If they maintained their present course it would meet them within an hour. This time there was nowhere to run, and nowhere to hide, nothing for it but to stand and fight.

XVIII

Sloop Versus Yacht

___

8.35 a.m.–10.00 a.m., Friday 18 August

The *Atalanta* was still more than four and a half miles from her quarry when the *Milenion* disappeared behind the south side of Jurassö at twenty-five to nine. Pechorin ordered the helmsman to maintain their present course, which would cut across the yacht's bows on the south-west side of the island. While the *Milenion* was out of sight, he half expected Killigrew to turn and run before the wind, but the thought did not trouble him: even running to leeward, the yacht could not outpace the steamer.

But the *Milenion* emerged on the other side of Jurassö almost on the dot of nine, with less than two miles separating the ships. 'One point to starboard,' ordered Pechorin.

'One point to starboard it is, sir.' The helmsman made a fractional course adjustment to intercept the schooner.

'She should be in range of the bow chaser with another twelve minutes, sir,' judged Lieutenant Yurieff.

'Beat to quarters,' Pechorin ordered gruffly. There would be no glory here; he only wanted to get the whole sorry business over and done with as quickly as possible. 'Clear for action.'

Nekrasoff smiled. 'We've got them now!'

'You'd best go below,' Killigrew told the Bullivants. Not that they would be any safer below decks than topsides if the *Atalanta* began to lob round shot at them again. But his plan was to steer clear of the muzzle of her bow chaser, in which case they would have more to fear from muskets fired from the sloop's tops. 'You'd best go with them, Mr Charlton.'

The assistant surgeon nodded and followed the Bullivants down the fore hatch to the forecastle – the one part of the lower deck that was still relatively intact – leaving Killigrew on deck with Thornton, Mackenzie and the sailors. Molineaux, Endicott and Hughes held a musket each, leaving the Milenions to work the sails. Killigrew took the helm himself.

On the bow, Iles had charge of the crates of lamp-oil bottles Molineaux had taken out of the steward's stores and brought up on deck: the other Ramillies present had agreed that Iles had the strongest throwing arm. The two bottles of pyroglycerin were there in their crate too, but Killigrew wanted to hold them in reserve: he was not convinced they would even work, so resorting to those would be a final pitch of the dice.

Iles began uncorking the bottles and stuffing the tow rags into their necks. 'You sure 'ee's gonna work, Wes?' he asked dubiously.

'Can't fail,' the petty officer told him, proud of his invention. He called it a 'Molineaux cocktail'.

'We're gonna 'ave to get gurt close, sir,' said Iles.

'You let me worry about that,' said Killigrew. 'You just make sure you put them on the *Atalanta*'s deck. Aim for the gun crews,' he added. 'Maybe we can't win, but we can make them pay dearly for their victory.'

Whereas a British tar was a jack of all trades who was expected to be able to hand, reef and steer, heave the lead, turn in a deadeye, gammon a bowsprit, fish in a broken spar, rig a purchase, and knot, point, splice, parcel and serve,

Russian *matrosy* were trained to specialise: a man brought on board a ship as a seaman gunner knew how to serve his gun, and that was all. Their seamen gunners even specialised as to what numbers they served as in a gun crew, so that if the number two man was killed, number nine would be at a loss if called upon to take his place. Killigrew and his men might not put the guns out of action, but with any luck they might reduce the enemy to crewing their guns with men who did not know what they were about.

When the two ships were twelve hundred yards apart, Killigrew spun the helm to port, making straight for the *Atalanta*. With the wind now broad on the port quarter, the *Milenion* clipped along at a good two and a half knots, the two vessels speeding to meet one another head on at a combined speed of eleven knots.

There were four gun ports through which the *Atalanta*'s bow chaser could fire, two on either side of the prow, but with the bowsprit in the way it could not fire directly ahead. The steamer turned her bows to starboard, and the bow chaser was run out through the first port-side gun port. Killigrew twitched the helm to starboard, keeping the *Milenion* in line with the sloop's bowsprit.

Another course adjustment brought them back under the bow chaser. Nine hundred yards apart now. Killigrew waited until he saw flame shoot from the gun port, and spun the helm to port. The boom echoed across the water, the shot shrieking through the air. Chain shot: Pechorin was going for the masts again. The shot whistled only feet away to port, slicing into the waves astern.

Killigrew was already spinning the helm back to starboard, bringing them out of the bow chaser's line of fire, in line with the bowsprit once more. On the *Atalanta*'s forecastle, the seamen gunners would be racing to reload: one, maybe two minutes before they fired again. But they would only have time for one more shot before the ships collided, as long as both vessels maintained their current courses.

Pechorin made no attempt to give the bow chaser another shot at the *Milenion*; perhaps he was planning to run the yacht down. Everything depended on whether or not Killigrew could second-guess the count. *What's on your mind, you Russian bastard?* Was Pechorin going to try to take them alive? How come sometimes they fired with round shot at the hull, and sometimes with chain shot at the masts? The first time, Lieutenant Lazarenko had been in command, and he had used round shot regardless of the fact that Pechorin himself had been a prisoner on board. Then, once Pechorin had had a chance to get back on board his ship, they had used chain shot, but then round shot again at the Fåfängö Gap. Now he was back to using chain shot, for the moment at least. The count did not strike Killigrew as the kind of man who would happily fire round shot into the hull of a ship with women on board. Had he even been in command when the *Atalanta* had almost caught them at the gap?

Killigrew watched the paddle-sloop intently. The two ships were only 250 yards apart now, and when the sloop began to turn to starboard again, he was ready. He had guessed that Pechorin would go for the weather gage, even though he had no need of it with his sails furled. Old habits died hard, and a good commander would not rely on steam engines alone. Killigrew turned the schooner to port, but not quickly enough: the bow chaser boomed again; another chain shot, smashing through the mainmast in the blink of an eye. The topmast and mainsail gaff crashed down to the quarterdeck, and he threw himself flat as the debris hurtled down around him. The tattered mainsail crumpled down over the starboard quarter, a tangle of rigging dragging the broken topmast through the water alongside.

Killigrew picked himself up and lunged for the spinning helm to right the *Milenion*'s course. Within seconds, the yacht's neat and orderly deck had been reduced to a shambles of broken spars and tangled rigging. Mackenzie lay beneath one of the spars, pinned to the skylight by the ropes, his shirt stained crimson by the blood that dribbled from his lips with each cough.

With the headsails and foresail still drawing, the *Milenion* continued to make headway, although the wreckage trailing over the side dragged her over to starboard and Killigrew had to wrestle the wheel to compensate. 'Uren, Attwood, Yorath – get that wreckage cut away, chop chop! Fuller, O'Leary – a couple of preventer stays on the mainmast, if you please. Look to Mr Mackenzie, Captain Thornton.'

The *Atalanta* was less than 150 yards away now. Even with the mainsail gone and the main topmast trailing in the water, the *Milenion* was still making one knot, and the two ships raced towards one another at about nine knots, some five yards a second.

Iles struck a match and tried to light the flambeau he held, but the wind blew it out.

The Milenions sawed frantically with their clasp knives at the ropes trailing over the starboard quarter. 'Get that spar free!' Killigrew hissed at them through gritted teeth. In the next few seconds, he was going to need every ounce of manoeuvrability he could squeeze out of the crippled yacht.

A hundred and ten yards, one hundred, ninety . . . would Pechorin sheer off, or just keep coming? There could be little doubt the *Milenion* would come off worse in a collision.

Iles struck another match. This time, the flambeau began to burn.

Seventy yards, sixty, fifty . . .

The last rope attaching the dragging topmast to the yacht was sawn through.

'Clear!' yelled Uren.

Killigrew spun the helm to port. Without the mainsail to push her stern to port, the *Milenion* came around sluggishly. He saw the men on the *Atalanta*'s forecastle run the bow chaser out through the port-side gun port, and that was when he spun the helm to starboard. Even if the gunners had had time to reload, there was no time to push the bow chasers on its brass racers to one of the starboard gun ports.

Standing at the starboard bulwark, Iles applied the flambeau's flame to one of the bottles of oil.

The *Milenion* slipped under the steamer's prow to starboard, less than ten feet away from the bows, in danger of having her stern crushed under the sloop's paddle-wheel.

Iles flung the bottle overarm. It smashed against the gingerbreading on the sloop's prow, ineffectually dousing the side with burning oil. The seaman swore and grabbed another bottle.

The two ships were so close, Killigrew could see the faces of the men at the *Atalanta*'s bulwarks clearly as they stared down at the *Milenion* in blank incomprehension. Molineaux, Endicott and Hughes blazed away with their muskets, and Killigrew saw a man twist away sharply. The three bluejackets hastily began to reload their muskets.

Iles threw another bottle, underarm this time, and it sailed through the air to land on the forecastle behind the bulwark. If it smashed, Killigrew neither saw nor heard it. Iles picked up another bottle, lit the oil-soaked tow rag in the neck, and was about to fling it when the sloop's starboard paddle-box clipped the yacht's starboard quarter with a splintering crunch. The schooner shuddered and rolled, the stern shoved aside by the *Atalanta*'s weight, and Killigrew had to grip the helm tightly to stop himself being knocked off his feet. When he had steadied himself, he saw Iles on his back, a burning bottle of oil rolling in an arc from his hand.

Hughes snatched up the bottle and flung it over the paddle-box.

Killigrew spun the helm to port, bringing the *Milenion*'s prow close in to the *Atalanta*'s stern. Abaft the paddle-box, the muzzle of a thirty-two-pounder projected from a yawning gun port. As the *Milenion* passed beneath, the gun belched smoke with a deafening crack, but it was loaded with round shot; and the *Milenion* rode too low in the water for the sloop to depress her guns far enough to hit the hull at that range. Molineaux snatched up another bottle, lit it from the flambeau, and flung it across the water.

Smoke rose from the sloop's forecastle now: Iles' second bottle had started a serious blaze. Killigrew saw a *matros*, his uniform in flames, hurl himself screaming from the sloop's bulwarks amidships. He hit the water and floated face down in the wake of the paddle-wheel.

The yacht was almost past the *Atalanta*'s stern when an explosion blossomed on the sloop's deck, driving the starboard thirty-two-pounder through the bulwark. It crashed down into the waves below. The bluejackets cheered exultantly. Molineaux's bottle must have ignited some cartridges brought up on deck for the gun.

But Killigrew knew too well they had only scotched the sloop, not killed it. He spun the helm to starboard, sheering away from the *Atalanta*'s stern. Endicott ran aft with another burning bottle in his hand, aiming to lob it over the sloop's taffrail so that it smashed against the quarterdeck, but it fell a few feet short and landed in the water.

The *Atalanta* turned to port, trying to bring one of her other guns to bear on the *Milenion*. Molineaux, Endicott and Hughes picked up their muskets and started to reload.

The sloop was faster than the yacht, but even without the mainsail the schooner had a tighter turning circle. Killigrew kept his turn loose, however: if he could fool Pechorin into thinking the *Milenion* with her mainsail gone was less manoeuvrable than the *Atalanta*, he might be able to get under her starboard side for another run.

Within a couple of minutes, the two ships were three hundred yards apart, circling in to meet one another again. The bow chaser boomed from one of the gun ports in the starboard bows, and the quarterdeck jerked beneath Killigrew's feet as a round shot slammed into the yacht's side.

'Damage report, Captain Thornton!'

The master nodded and raced below.

The Russians had put out the fire on the sloop's forecastle.

Killigrew could see them pushing the bow chaser to one of the port-side gun ports. Pechorin was going for the weather gauge again, hoping to sail past the yacht to starboard on this run. Killigrew smiled – *got you, you bastard*!

On the schooner's forecastle, Molineaux, Endicott and Hughes did not wait until the two ships were alongside. They blazed away with their muskets at the men working the bow chaser.

'Mr Uren! When I give the word, I want you to see how far you can swing the mains'l boom out to starboard!' called Killigrew.

The boatswain looked bewildered. 'The mains'l boom? Without the mains'l . . .'

'Trust me!'

Uren looked at him, and nodded.

The two ships were only yards apart again, the steamer's paddles beating down on the water as she powered herself forward through the waves. Killigrew waited until the last possible moment before spinning the helm to starboard.

The *Milenion* slipped under the *Atalanta*'s prow a second time, sailing past her gunless starboard side. Killigrew spun the helm back to port, bringing her as close in to the sloop's side as he could. Molineaux, Endicott, Hughes and Iles managed to lob two broadsides of burning oil bottles on to the sloop's deck as they passed, but this time the musketeers on the *Atalanta* were ready for them. As bullets slammed down into the deck Endicott fell with blood pumping from a wound in his thigh. Molineaux, Hughes and Iles ran aft to the quarterdeck, each man clutching a burning oil bottle.

As soon as the yacht's midships were level with the *Atalanta*'s stern, Killigrew spun the helm hard-a-port, turning in under the sloop's taffrail.

'Now, Mr Uren!'

Uren, Yorath and Fuller hauled on the boom guy, swinging the mainsail boom out beyond the *Milenion*'s starboard quarter. The *Atalanta* was powering away from them, and

Killigrew thought he had misjudged it. But just as the boom was reaching the end of its sweep, the tip smashed against the sloop's gallery window, shattering the glass and knocking out the leading.

Molineaux, Hughes and Iles were ready. They flung their bottles. One smashed harmlessly against the gingerbreading on the stern, but the other two sailed through the broken window to shatter in the day-room below the quarterdeck.

Killigrew turned the helm to port, running before the wind. Madness to try another pass: they had been lucky to do so much damage as it was. The steamer would soon overhaul them, but for now the Russian crew looked as though it had enough problems of its own: the rigging and sails were all ablaze, and although the engine would be undamaged, smoke poured out of the wrecked gallery window. The sloop was pointed away from them, and showed no signs of turning back.

'Have Mr Charlton come on deck to tend to the wounded!' called Killigrew.

Thornton emerged from the after hatch. 'We're hulled at the waterline,' he reported grimly.

'Fother her, Captain Thornton.'

'Attwood, Yorath! The pump! Uren, Fuller, O'Leary – fetch ropes and canvas!'

'Molineaux, Hughes, Iles – give them a hand,' ordered Killigrew.

While Charlton came on deck to bind the wound in Endicott's thigh, Thornton and the others did what they could to patch the wound in the *Milenion*'s side, running ropes under the keel to brace another thrummed mat over the fresh hole.

'I'm afraid Mr Mackenzie's dead,' Charlton reported to Killigrew. 'I've patched up Endicott: he's lost a lot of blood, but I think he'll live. I've given him an opiate to help him sleep through the pain.'

One dead, one wounded . . . even though he knew it was

nothing short of a miracle they had not suffered worse casualties, it was still too many for Killigrew. Had he been a fool to risk the encounter? He told himself the choice had not been his to make, yet he could not help wondering if there had been some other tactic that might have spared Mackenzie's life.

'Can Endicott walk?' he asked.

'Yes, I'm sure he'll make a complete recovery in the fullness of time, provided the wound doesn't turn gangrenous.'

'That's very reassuring to hear, Mr Charlton, but I was less concerned about the fullness of time than in the next twenty-four hours.'

'Oh! Not a prayer.'

Killigrew nodded. 'Thank you, Mr Charlton. Iles, Hughes – rig up a litter for Endicott.'

Charlton gazed to where the *Atalanta* had stopped, her stern still turned towards the *Milenion*, now slowly falling astern as the stricken schooner limped westwards. The flames were already dying down as the crew assaulted the fires with buckets of water, but a cloud of smoke still wreathed the sloop. 'Why don't they follow?' he wondered. 'Can we have hurt them that badly?'

'The fire we started in the captain's day-room must've burned through the ropes controlling the steering gear,' said Killigrew. 'But it won't take them for ever to repair. And next time, Pechorin won't make the mistake of underestimating us.' The *Atalanta* must have suffered casualties; to know what was on the count's mind, Killigrew had only to look at Mackenzie's lifeless corpse, and multiply the anger he felt – towards himself as much as towards his enemy – by the number of dead and wounded men on the paddle-sloop. 'He'll blow us out of the water as soon as he gets within range.'

'There won't be a next time, sir.' Uren scrambled up through the after hatch. 'We've fothered the hole, but the water's still rising fast in the well. The *Milenion*'s dying sir, and there's nothing we can do to save her.'

'How long?' asked Killigrew.

'Twenty minutes before she founders . . . half an hour, if we're lucky.

Killigrew nodded, and altered course a couple of points to port, making for the nearest land. There was only one road left open to them, and it led to Jurassö.

As the *matrosy* cleared the deck of the *Atalanta* of debris and dead bodies, two of them carried Michmani Gavrilik to the fore hatch on a makeshift litter. The young man reached out to Pechorin as he passed, and the count signalled for them to wait a moment.

Pechorin bent over Gavrilik. The young man's face was hideously burned. 'I'm sorry, sir,' he whispered. 'I let you down.'

The count shook his head. 'You did splendidly, Gavrilik. I'll see to it you get promoted for today's work.'

But Gavrilik could no longer hear him. Feeling sick at heart, Pechorin drew down his eyelids and straightened. 'Take him below,' he told the two bearers.

The senior petty officer approached, picking his way over the debris, and saluted the count. 'Make your report, Vasyutkin,' Pechorin told him.

'At least four dead, probably more: I saw a couple of men go over the side. We won't know until we've mustered the surviving crew. And sixteen wounded, some of them severely. Herr Juschke says at least three of them won't last until nightfall.'

Pechorin nodded. 'Thank you, Vasyutkin. Carry on.' He took the telescope from the binnacle and levelled it to where the *Milenion* was sailing towards Jurassö. The schooner was low in the water, close to foundering: she would not get far. But that was little consolation.

'Count Pechorin?'

He turned to see Nekrasoff standing there.

'Please explain to me how this happened. A fully armed paddle-sloop, pitted against an unarmed yacht . . . and yet we managed to come off worse!'

Pechorin could have pointed out that the damage was only superficial, and that unlike the *Milenion* they were in no danger of sinking, but he knew the colonel had a point. Once again he had underestimated Killigrew, and it had been his men who had paid the price.

'You're a disgrace, Captain-Lieutenant,' Nekrasoff continued. 'Not fit to command a hay barge on the Neva! You'll be kicked out of the navy when St Petersburg hears about this; yes, and sent to Siberia too, I shouldn't wonder—'

Pechorin grabbed Nekrasoff by the lapels of his tunic and slammed him back against the bulwark. 'With half a dozen of my men dead and another three on their way to join them, do you really think I give a damn about my career right now? When this business is done, you may make whatever report you like to your superiors. But I *am* going to catch Killigrew, of that you may rest assured. Until I do, this is still a naval operation and I remain in command, so I'll thank you to keep your opinions to yourself. And stay out of my way!' He spun the colonel round and sent him staggering across the deck.

He turned to Lieutenant Yurieff. 'Report from the engine-room?'

'No damage to the engines, sir. We're ready to get under way just as soon as Dubrovsky's fixed the steering gear.'

Pechorin nodded. 'Where is he?'

'In your quarters, sir.'

The count made his way below and found the carpenter where Yurieff had said he would be, supervising two of his crew as they ran fresh ropes along the underside of the deck head. The day-room was a mess, the timbers blackened and charred glass all over the floor.

'Took the liberty of coming in here without asking permission, sir,' said Dubrovsky. 'Hope you don't object. I thought

373

you'd want me to repair the steering gear as quickly as possible.'

Pechorin nodded. 'You did right, Dubrovsky. How long?'

'Fifteen minutes?'

'Quicker if I stop interrupting you with foolish questions, eh?' Pechorin managed a wan smile. 'I'll leave you to it.'

'Appreciated, sir.'

Pechorin went back up on deck. Most of the crew were engaged in replacing damaged spars, burned sails and rigging. It would be another hour before they could sail again. But Pechorin did not mean to wait that long: he still had steam power, and he intended to use it. He levelled the telescope at the *Milenion* once again, already two-thirds of a mile off and disappearing behind a headland that projected from the south-west corner of Jurassö where a tall lighthouse towered over the island. The yacht was visibly lower in the water than the last time he had looked, the waves lapping beneath the shot holes punched in the lower deck: another half an hour, no more.

At last Dubrovsky came back on deck and instructed the helmsman to spin the wheel, while he leaned out over the taffrail to watch the rudder.

'To starboard . . . now to port . . . that's it. How's she feel?'

'Good as new, sir.'

'Good work, Dubrovsky,' said Pechorin. He resisted the temptation to ask if the jury-rigged steering gear would hold: when the carpenter repaired something, it stayed repaired. 'Ready to go?'

'Ready when you are, sir.'

Pechorin turned to Yurieff. 'Instruct Inzhener Nikolaishvili: set on, full ahead.'

'Yes, sir.' The second lieutenant turned to the speaking tube and relayed the order to the engine-room. The deck thrummed beneath their feet and the paddles plashed into life once more.

'Five points to starboard,' Pechorin ordered the helmsman.

'Five points it is, sir.'

The *Atalanta* altered course until she was steaming for the headland at the south-west corner of the island. It took them seven minutes to pass the headland, and then the *Milenion* was in view again, about half a mile off. Killigrew had not run her into one of the coves on the coast of the island, but was sailing east now. The wind had veered to the west and the schooner was running before it. Pechorin wondered what the hell he was playing at: wherever he was headed, the yacht would sink before he got halfway there. He levelled the telescope and made out a figure in a blue jacket and bonnet standing at the helm.

'Another four points to starboard,' he instructed the helmsman. He would not make the same mistake twice: this time he would stand off and fire chain shot at the *Milenion*'s masts until she was dead in the water, before sending a boarding party across.

'Gun crew to the bow chaser,' he ordered. 'Reload with chain shot.'

'The bow chaser's gun crew are all dead or wounded, sir,' reported Yurieff. 'So's Stachvanyonok.'

'Then you will have to stand in for Stachvanyonok, and transfer the port gun's crew to the bow chaser.'

'Yes, sir.'

Even with the wind full abaft, the *Milenion* crept along with her mainmast gone and her hull so low in the water it was a wonder she had not foundered already. It was a matter of minutes before she was within easy range. She made no attempt to manoeuvre; what the devil was Killigrew playing at? The commander had one last trick up his sleeve, of that Pechorin had no doubt. He waited until the yacht was only five hundred yards ahead of him before giving the order to fire.

One shot was all it took. The chain shot slashed through the foremast and it came crashing down on the deck in a tangle of rigging and canvas. The bow chaser's gun crew cheered lustily: the yacht was dead in the water, completely at their mercy. Pechorin levelled his telescope. The schooner's deck seemed deserted: even the man at the helm was gone, as if borne to the deck under the mass of tangled debris.

Pechorin could tell himself that he would lobby his superiors in St Petersburg for the Bullivants to be treated properly, according to the laws of war, and perhaps they would even listen. But government bureaucracy moved slowly, and by the time anything was done Nekrasoff would already have had them quietly killed, their bodies burned beyond recognition and buried in unmarked graves in a secret location; he certainly had the authority. Killigrew had probably worked that much out for himself, and he realised he would not be doing the Bullivants any favours by surrendering at this stage of the game. He was the kind of man who would fight to the end, no matter how hopeless the odds. Pechorin would do exactly the same, had their positions been reversed. He could well imagine Killigrew and his men crouching below the bulwarks, ready to repel boarders with muskets and cutlasses. It was tempting to lob a few more round shot into the *Milenion*'s hull, smash her to pieces in revenge for the men killed on the *Atalanta*, but he was still mindful there were women on board the yacht. Besides, it was Killigrew he wanted his vengeance on: he wanted to cut it out of him with his sabre, piece by piece, not grant him a quick and clean death that he might risk with round shot.

Yurieff made his way aft to the quarterdeck and saluted Pechorin. 'Permission to lead a boarding party, sir.'

Pechorin hesitated. Sending Yurieff across with a cutter and two dozen of his best men, armed to the teeth, was the obvious thing to do. In fact, he was tempted to lead the boarding party himself, but as captain he knew his place was on the quarterdeck; his days of leading boarding parties were behind him now, he mused sadly.

Still, there was something not right: something about the

dead stillness of the *Milenion* that made the hairs prickle on the back of his neck.

'Not granted. Release Lazarenko from the lazaretto and have him report to me at once.'

Yurieff looked crestfallen. 'Sir?'

'You heard me, Borislav Ivanovich.'

'Yes, sir.' Yurieff saluted and descended the after hatch.

The *Atalanta* was almost level with the *Milenion* now, a hundred yards off her port quarter. 'Stand by in the engine-room to stop her,' he ordered the *michmani* at the speaking tube.

'Yes, sir.' The *michmani* blew into the tube, listened for a response, and said: 'Stand by to stop her.'

'Stop her!' ordered Pechorin.

'Stop her.'

The paddles slowed and stopped, the sloop drifting to a halt.

'Assemble a boarding party,' Pechorin ordered Vasyutkin. 'Two dozen of our best men.' No need to tell Vasyutkin that when he said their best men, he meant the toughest and most ruthless in hand-to-hand combat, not the ablest seamen or the cleanest living. Not that the crew of the *Atalanta* had had any experience of boarding hostile vessels before now, but a few of the men had proved their ruthlessness in hand-to-hand combat in brawls with Finnish jägers in the waterfront taverns of Ekenäs.

As the boarding party gathered on deck, Chernyovsky and his two men approached. 'We want to go with the boarding party.'

'I'm afraid not,' Pechorin told him coldly. 'This is a naval operation, Starshina. Frankly, I don't know why you and your men came on board, or why I let you. Boarding a hostile vessel is dangerous work—'

Chernyovsky grinned. 'My men and I are used to dangerous work, Count.'

'Aye . . . butchering Jews, Poles and Chechens, I suppose!

377

My men work as a team, Starshina; that's the way I trained them. They don't need three strangers getting under their feet.'

Chernyovsky fingered his swollen nose. 'There's a black petty officer on board I've a score to settle with.'

'Your personal vendettas are no concern of the Imperial Russian Navy, Starshina.'

Yurieff returned on deck with Lazarenko, the first lieutenant looking bewildered and a little apprehensive. 'Ready to redeem yourself, Mstislav Trofimovich?'

'Sir?'

'I'm giving you a second chance,' explained Pechorin. 'I want you to lead the party that boards the *Milenion*. Bring me Killigrew alive, and the Bullivants unharmed, and I'll have the unfortunate incident of your mutiny expunged from the log.'

Lazarenko's face brightened. 'You mean, I'll be reinstated as first lieutenant? There'll be no court-martial?'

'If you bring me the Bullivants unharmed, yes.'

'I won't let you down, sir.'

'Just be careful, do you understand? No heroics.'

'Against a handful of sailors?' sneered Lazarenko.

'Don't underestimate them, Mstislav Trofimovich. They've come this far, haven't they? Just watch yourself, keep your eyes and your ears open, and be ready for anything, do you understand me? A man like Killigrew doesn't fight honourably when the odds are stacked against him – he's got too much sense for that – so don't expect him to observe the rules of war. And the moment the *Milenion* founders – which will be any minute now, by the look of it – get your men off there, get clear until she's sunk, and then go back in to pick up any prisoners. I want the Bullivants alive, and Killigrew too if possible. As for the rest of them . . . well, I don't want to hear about any atrocities, but shoot first and ask questions later, do you understand me?'

Lazarenko knitted his brows. 'If we shoot them, sir, we

378

won't be able to ask them any questions if they're dead—'

'For Christ's sake! It's a figure of speech, Lazarenko. The point is, I'm less interested in hearing the answers to any questions than I am in you and every man in your boarding party coming back alive, do I make myself plain? I've lost enough men today as it is. Now get in that cutter, before I change my mind and let Yurieff go in your place; and before the *Milenion* sinks.'

'Yes, sir.'

Lazarenko and his men boarded the cutter and set out across the waves to where the *Milenion* still floated ... barely. She was a ruined hulk, battered beyond all recognition and in her death throes. It was a wonder Killigrew had not already abandoned ship: the yacht was a death trap now. What was the commander playing at?

What would I do if I were in his shoes? Pechorin asked himself. *He can't get anywhere on the* Milenion, *so he needs another ship. The only other ship around here is the* Atalanta ... *has he got some scheme to capture this ship? He can't have more than a dozen men under his command. What could they do? Swim underwater and climb up the port side while two dozen of my men are on board the* Milenion *and the rest are at the starboard bulwark, waiting to see what happens now?*

Pechorin shook his head. It was too far to swim underwater, and even if all twelve of them made it ... even with two dozen men on the *Milenion*, half a dozen dead and sixteen in the sick berth, Pechorin still had about fifty men under his command. Killigrew could not hope to overpower them all.

Perhaps he would try to overpower the boarding party and take Lazarenko hostage. Again, Pechorin shook his head. Lazarenko was an officer of the Imperial Russian Navy: if he were captured, he would have to take his own chances. Lazarenko would know that, and so would Killigrew. Even he could not be desperate enough to think he could get away with an exchange: Lazarenko for the *Atalanta*.

But perhaps it was not Lazarenko he was after: perhaps it was the cutter. After all, there was no sign of the *Milenion*'s gig, and Killigrew and his men could hardly abandon ship without . . .

No sign of the gig.

Stupid, stupid, stupid! Pechorin pounded his forehead in anger with himself. The cutter had already reached the *Milenion* and Lazarenko and his men were climbing through the entry port. Pechorin snatched the speaking trumpet from the binnacle and rushed to the bulwark.

'Lazarenko! Get back here now, do you hear me? Get back here now! It's a trap!'

No one tried to stop Lazarenko and his men as they boarded the *Milenion*, but no one came on deck to surrender either. The ship seemed deserted, all except for the figure trapped and partially obscured by the wreckage on the quarterdeck. Were the rest hiding below decks? Well, it would not be long before the yacht sank: they would show themselves soon enough then.

Lazarenko gestured to the figure on the quarterdeck. 'Find out if he's still alive,' he told Private Malinoff. The *matros* nodded and ran across, clearing away the debris that pinned the figure to the deck.

With a pistol in one hand and a cutlass in the other, Lazarenko glanced down the after hatch. The companion ladder was badly knocked about – some ropes had been lashed around the last remaining step to hold it together – and there were already a few inches of water sloshing about the deck below.

Pechorin shouted across from the *Atalanta*. A trap? What was he talking about? The only danger here was that the yacht would sink before he had time to get off. But where were the survivors hiding themselves? They had to be somewhere.

'Aren't we going back on board the *Atalanta*, sir?' asked one of the *matrosy*.

'In a moment,' Lazarenko told him. 'We've still got time to take a quick look around the lower deck.' He began to descend. The last four rungs of the companion ladder were missing, blown away by one of the shots that had penetrated the lower deck: he would have to jump from there.

Malinoff finally succeeded in revealing the body on the quarterdeck as nothing more than a dressmaker's dummy wearing a British seaman's blue jacket and a bonnet. Malinoff looked up with sadness in his eyes, and a vague sense of injustice, as some instinct told him that Pechorin was right. 'Oh, no . . .'

Lazarenko had seen the ropes that apparently held the bottom-most remaining step together. What he did not see was that the sides of the companion ladder had been sawn through so it would break away at the least pressure. He went down, dropped the last couple of feet to the deck below with the step beneath his boots. The water sloshing about the deck did little to break the impact, and the two bottles of pyroglycerin bound out of sight to the underside of the step shattered beneath his weight.

XIX

Russian Hide and Seek

_____

10.00 a.m.–11.30 a.m., Friday 18 August

The thunderous crack of the explosion carried clearly across to where Killigrew and Molineaux crouched amongst the bracken under the trees on the island of Jurassö. There was surprisingly little smoke or flame, just a brief flash, and the deck boards and the men standing on them were thrown high into the air before splashing down all around the *Milenion*.

'Lumme!' exclaimed Molineaux. 'Looks like the pill-roller weren't exaggerating when he said that stuff was powerful.'

Killigrew nodded. 'If anything, I'd say he understated the case.' He had hoped to get one or two members of any boarding party Pechorin sent on board the *Milenion*, perhaps even the count himself. The booby trap had been no act of spite, but a matter of military necessity. When Pechorin realised Killigrew and the others were on the island, he would come looking for them, and the only chance Killigrew and his men stood then was to take advantage of the cover the trees gave them to pick the Russians off one by one. They had inflicted some casualties on the crew when they had lobbed the burning oil bottles on the sloop's deck – how

Killigrew wished they had used at least one of the bottles of pyroglycerin then, now that he saw its power! – and Pechorin could not have more than eighty men who were not *hors de combat*.

Eighty! Against ten. Killigrew discounted the ladies, of course, and the wounded – Endicott and Dahlstedt, the latter would not be much help with his hands bandaged – and Bullivant and Charlton, neither of whom was likely to be much use in a fight, if for very different reasons. That left himself, Molineaux, Hughes, Iles, Thornton, Uren, Attwood, Fuller, O'Leary and Yorath. Eight to one. But they would stand a better chance ashore, amongst the trees, and they still had muskets. If the cartouche boxes they had taken from the Russians were growing light, they had plenty of ammunition for the shotguns.

And then someone on board the *Milenion* had stepped on the booby trap. It was impossible to believe that any of the boarding party – who had been concentrated around the after hatch, the centre of the blast – could have survived. That reduced the odds to eleven to two, and suddenly Killigrew was grateful he had not used those bottles of pyroglycerin earlier after all. Things did not seem so hopeless now.

He had begun using the gig to ferry the people on board the *Milenion* to the south coast of Jurassö the moment the yacht had been hidden from the *Atalanta*'s sight. The men left on board while the first boatload was taken ashore had got everything ready, Iles sacrificing his jacket and bonnet while Hughes lashed up the helm and Killigrew and Molineaux prepared the booby trap. On both trips, the gig had been dangerously overloaded, but somehow they had made it. Not a moment too soon either, for the *Atalanta* had come steaming around the headland just as Killigrew and his men finished dragging the gig up across the pebbles of a rocky cove and out of sight amongst the foliage beneath the trees. The men on the *Atalanta* might have seen them if their eyes had not all been fixed on the *Milenion* as it sailed away on her final voyage with only a dressmaker's dummy at the helm.

The hull still looked intact, but the concussive effects of the blast must have broken her back, for she began to slip under the waves.

Molineaux took off his bonnet and clasped it to his breast. 'She was a good ship, sir.'

'That she was, Molineaux. But people are more important than ships. She served her purpose.' Even as he said it, it sounded oddly callous: there was more to a ship than timbers, ropes and canvas, and the people that were still with him were only alive because the *Milenion* had served them so well. Still, if sacrificing such a fine schooner saved the life of one of his party, it would have been worth it.

'Speaking of people, I don't reckon his lordship's going to be chuffed when he hears what you've done to his yacht.' They had not told the Bullivants about the little surprise they had been preparing for the boarding party.

'He can't blame me for that. He lost her the moment she became a prize of war. He should never have brought her to the Baltic in the first place. If anything, he can thank us for the few extra hours he had on board her.'

Killigrew watched the *Atalanta* through his miniature telescope, taking care to shade the lens so that sunlight would not reflect from it, giving away his position. The boarding party's cutter still floated in the water, doubtless surrounded by flotsam from the *Milenion*; he could not see any at that distance, but he had seen ships go down before and could well imagine the scene. There was no sign of any survivors from the boarding party.

Even if Pechorin had been killed by the booby trap (Killigrew sincerely hoped so: the count had brains, and that made him more dangerous than any muscle-bound underling), there must have been someone left on board the *Atalanta* who would realise that the fugitives had left the *Milenion* while it was out of sight and rowed for the only land within a mile, Jurassö. Killigrew expected the Russians to send a party of men armed to the teeth to search for them now. If the party was large enough, there was a chance Killigrew and his men could wait until they were thrashing about amongst the trees, overpower the men left to guard the boats, steal two of them, row out to the *Atalanta*, deal with the token anchor watch, and sail her to Hangö Head. Divide and conquer: it was a long shot, but it was their best chance nonetheless.

The *Atalanta* got under way once more, but to Killigrew's surprise she did not head directly towards the island to send a boat ashore close to where the fugitives must have landed. Instead, she steamed around the headland at the south-east corner of the island and disappeared from view, so that all that was visible was the cloud of smoke rising from her funnel above the trees. Was she headed back to Ekenäs? Did they think that everyone who had been on board the *Milenion* had been killed in the blast; that it was over? It was impossible to conceive that the *Atalanta* could have followed them with such determination, only to give up just when they had them cornered.

Killigrew and Molineaux exchanged glances. 'Wait with the others,' the commander told the petty officer. 'I'll be back in a moment.'

He broke cover from the trees, picking his way across the rocky shore to the spine of the ridge on the left. He crested the rise in time to see the *Atalanta* follow the coast round to north, steaming north-west and disappearing from view behind the trees that covered that part of the island.

When he got back to where the others waited amongst the trees, it came as no surprise to discover that Lord Bullivant was furious.

'Congratulations, Killigrew! Not only have you got four of my men killed; not only have you sunk my yacht . . . as if all that weren't enough, you've contrived to leave us stranded without food or water on an uninhabited island in the middle of the Gulf of Finland! Bravo, young man! Bravo!'

385

'Oh, do be quiet, Rodney!' snapped Lady Bullivant. 'We're still alive, are we not? Given the determination to murder us all that the Russians have shown thus far, I consider it nothing short of a miracle that most of us are still alive. The miracle in question is Mr Killigrew, and we owe him our thanks.'

'You're too kind, ma'am,' said Killigrew. 'I think my men deserve their fair share of credit for our having got so far; and we couldn't have done it without the help of Captain Thornton and his crew. But before we all start patting ourselves on the back, we're not out of the woods yet. I don't know where the *Atalanta*'s gone, though I'll lay odds she's not far away.'

'Now what do we do?' asked Thornton. 'We've still got the gig; some of us could get in it and row to Hangö Head for help.'

'All in good time, Captain Thornton. I'm not sure I want to risk the gig on the open sea in broad daylight until I'm positive the *Atalanta* has gone for good. First things first: we need to find shelter; shelter, and perhaps food. I don't know about you, but I'm famished. Molineaux, there are supposed to be some ironworks somewhere on this island. If there are ironworks, there must be homes for the men that worked in them.'

'The ironworks are on the east side of the island,' said Thornton. 'We saw them from the *Milenion* when we were here before this whole business started.'

'Thank you, Captain Thornton. Perhaps you'd like to go with Molineaux and try to find them for us?'

Thornton nodded.

Killigrew threw Molineaux one of the shotguns. 'Be careful: the ironworkers' cottages may still be inhabited.'

The petty officer nodded and headed off through the trees with Thornton.

Killigrew turned to where the assistant surgeon crouched over Endicott. 'How's he doing, Mr Charlton?'

'Not bad, but I haven't got the proper facilities to care for him as I'd like.'

'Do what you can, Mr Charlton. Endicott? How are you feeling?'

'Never felt better, sir,' the Liverpudlian replied with an inane grin.

Killigrew smiled. 'That will be the laudanum talking. You hold on, Endicott: we'll have you back on board the *Ramillies* in a brace of shakes. Mr Charlton, you're in charge here until I get back. Be sure you post sentries to keep a lookout: one-hour watches. Make sure no one wanders off.'

'Yes, sir. Where will you be?'

'I'm going to take a look-see at the north side of the island. Hughes!'

The Welshman looked up.

Killigrew threw him the other shotgun. 'You're coming with me.'

'As you will, sir.'

Killigrew and Hughes made their way through the trees. It was turning out to be a beautifully temperate summer's day, the sunlight filtering down through the boughs overhead, the birds singing in the trees. So soon after the brutal encounter with the *Atalanta*, the war seemed a very long way away indeed; but Killigrew knew only too well that appearances could be deceptive.

They had gone perhaps a hundred yards when he heard the unmistakable sound of someone chopping at a tree with an axe.

'Woodsmen, sir?' murmured Hughes.

'Sounds like it. Come on, maybe we can get some food from them.'

'Won't they be Russians?'

'Finns, you mean. If we offer them money, show them we mean no harm, perhaps they'll help us. It's a risk we'll just have to take.'

A few more steps further on, and they heard a cry of '*Stroevoi les!*' followed by the groan of a falling tree, and the crash of snapping branches.

'Was that Finnish, sir?' asked Hughes.

'Russian, I think.'

The two of them advanced more carefully, creeping from tree trunk to tree trunk until they could see half a dozen *matrosy* at work in a clearing, lopping the branches off the trunk of the tree they had cut down. Killigrew and Hughes ducked down amongst the bracken, but the Russians were too intent on their own work to have seen them.

'They must be from the *Atalanta*, sir,' said Hughes. 'Reckon she must be short of coal, if they're resorting to burning wood in her furnaces.'

'Perhaps,' allowed Killigrew, unconvinced. He watched with the Welshman until the Russians had stripped all the boughs off the trunk, and tied harnesses around it so they could drag it away through the forest, singing some sonorous Russian shanty. That was when Killigrew knew that Hughes was wrong, because if the Russians had only wanted firewood, it would have made more sense to cut up the trunk where it lay, and carry the pieces individually.

It was not difficult to follow the Russians as they dragged the log through the forest: the trail they left was unmistakable, and they moved so slowly Killigrew and Hughes could take their time following them. Indeed, Killigrew grew so impatient with the Russians' slow progress, he decided to move ahead of them, following a parallel course through the trees to find out where they were headed. He had his answer soon enough when he and Hughes breasted the next rise and the north side of the island came into view.

The two of them stopped dead. 'Is that what I think it is, sir?' asked Hughes.

Killigrew nodded. 'Now I understand why the Russians are so keen to stop us from getting back to the fleet.'

A smaller islet lay off the north coast of Jurassö, a few acres in area, thickly covered with trees. An indentation on the coast opposite the islet created a lagoon surrounded on all sides but the west, effectively screened by the towering pines that grew on both islands.

The *Atalanta* was anchored at the mouth of the lagoon, but that did not surprise Killigrew: he had known it would not be far away; the only thing he had not understood was why she had not dropped anchor in the cove on the south side of the island. Now, all was clear.

The paddle-sloop was dwarfed by the massive two-decker that dominated the centre of the lagoon. One of her masts was missing, and to judge from the way she sat low in the water she had been hulled below the waterline and now rested on the bed of the lagoon, keeled over on one side. She could only be the *Ivan Strashnyi*: she must have limped this far after her encounter with the *St Jean d'Acre*. But to judge from the amount of activity going on around her sides, on her upper deck and on the shore below, the Russians had every hope of recovering the second-rate ship of the line. The lagoon formed as perfect a hiding place as the captain of the *Ivan Strashnyi* could have hoped to find in the Gulf of Finland. The trees on the island to the north screened the lagoon so effectively that as the *Milenion* had passed the island a couple of miles to eastward, he had taken the smaller island for part of Jurassö itself, never dreaming it might hide a crippled two-decker.

Small wonder Nekrasoff had been so determined to destroy the *Milenion* and kill all who had been on board her: he must have thought Lord Bullivant or someone in his crew had sighted the *Ivan Strashnyi*. With the bulk of the Russian fleet holed up behind the maritime fortresses of the gulf, the two-decker would have been a gift to any British frigate that chanced to discover her in her present crippled condition. This explained what the *Atalanta* had been doing so far from the Finnish coast when it had encountered the *Milenion* in the first place. How the *Ivan Strashnyi*'s captain had got word of his predicament to the Finnish mainland in the first place would probably remain a mystery, but the *Atalanta* must have been sent from Ekenäs to render what assistance it could, only to find Lord Bullivant's yacht apparently snooping around the island.

And small wonder Pechorin had not bothered to send a boat ashore on the south side of the island, when he had known that less than a mile away on the other side of the island he would find all the men he would ever need to carry out a thorough search of the forest. Forget eleven to two: seventy to one was now closer to the mark.

Even as Killigrew watched, the *Atalanta* put a gig into the water. It rowed past the listing *Ivan Strashnyi* to where the *matrosy* had set up a number of tents using spars and canvas on the beach below. In the boat, Nekrasoff was unmistakable in sky-blue, a dark-uniformed figure that looked like Pechorin beside him, and Starshina Chernyovsky towering head and shoulders above the *matrosy* around him.

'We'd best get back to the others,' Killigrew murmured to Hughes.

The seaman nodded and the two of them were about to turn away when they heard a crackling amongst the foliage as the Russians hauling on the log appeared through the trees behind them. Killigrew and Hughes ducked down amongst the bracken, waiting for the Russians to pass.

Pechorin's *matrosy* beached the gig and the count got out with Nekrasoff and crossed to where Captain Tikhon Maksi-mich Aleksandrei sat at a table in the open air with some of his officers, discussing how the repairs on the *Ivan Strashnyi* were progressing.

Aleksandrei was a heavily-built man with salt-and-pepper hair, the eyes beneath his bristling eyebrows slightly slanted. Of peasant stock, he enjoyed the unheard of distinction of having been promoted from before the mast – back in the days of the war with France – and he wore the Cross of St George on his rumpled uniform. No two officers in the Imperial Navy could have had less in common than Pechorin and Aleksandrei, and yet they were old friends: the captain did not have a chip on his shoulder about his humble origins, and when the count had served on board his first command as a *michmani*, Aleksandrei had learned that if a commoner could be just as good a man as an aristocrat, then so too could an aristocrat be as good as a commoner.

As soon as Pechorin approached, Aleksandrei rose to his feet and, instead of returning Pechorin's salute, seized him in a bear hug.

'Mikhail Yurievich! It is good to see you.' He turned to one of his officers. 'You see, Fedorinchik? Did I not tell you Count Pechorin would not abandon us?'

Pechorin snapped his fingers at two of his gig's crew, who lifted a hamper out of the boat and carried it across to the table. 'I thought this might make your sojourn on this island a little more tolerable,' Pechorin explained. If the *Atalanta* had not had to pursue the *Milenion*, she would have been sailing back to Jurassö this morning anyway. The buckles were unstrapped and the count flicked back the lid with the toe of one boot to reveal the contents: cold meat, white bread, butter, eggs, beluga caviar and other delicacies, along with a couple of bottles of champagne. 'Ekenäs is not St Petersburg, but my valet found an excellent *épicerie fine* down an alley in the town.'

Aleksandrei took out one of the champagne bottles and studied the label. 'The 'forty-six vintage! You never cease to amaze me, Mikhail Yurievich.' He handed both bottles to his steward. 'Put these in the stream to cool.'

'We've also brought the supplies and materials you requested,' Pechorin told him. 'My men are bringing them ashore now.'

'What about Lord Bullivant and his friends?' Chernyovsky growled impatiently.

Pechorin regarded him with amusement. 'What's the matter, *Starshina*? Are you afraid they'll run away?'

Aleksandrei cast a glance at Nekrasoff and Chernyovsky.

'You keep some very dubious company today, Count! A Cossack *starshina*, and a colonel of the Third Section . . . has this bastard come to arrest me for almost losing the *Ivan Strashnyi*, hey?'

Smiling, Pechorin shook his head. 'Captain Aleksandrei, may I be permitted to present Colonel Radimir Fokavich Nekrasoff and Starshina Chernyovsky? Colonel Nekrasoff is the man who permitted Lord Bullivant and his family to escape—'

'I was not the one dallying with a woman on board the *Milenion* when Commander Killigrew recaptured it,' Nekrasoff snorted mildly.

Aleksandrei waved him to silence. 'So my lookouts were right! It *was* the *Milenion* they saw you engage off the west coast of this island.'

Pechorin flushed, still hot with shame at having been defeated by an unarmed yacht, no matter how temporarily. 'You saw that?'

'My men did. They also report seeing some men and women landing from the yacht shortly before you blew it to pieces with your bow chaser. I've already sent some men to hunt them down: it won't take long to find them on an island as small as this.'

'Looks as though the place is deserted.' Thornton was about to step from among the trees when Molineaux stretched out an arm to bar his path.

' "Looks" and "is" ain't the same thing, cully.' The petty officer motioned for him to stay out of sight, and watched the place patiently. He was in no hurry to walk into a potential trap.

The ironworks were not large: a long, windowless wooden building with half a dozen coarse-brick chimneys rising up from the slate-tiled roof at regular intervals; a few outbuildings; a low hut with a shingled roof that probably served as the workers' barracks; and a dilapidated wooden jetty rotting at the water's edge.

'I'll take a closer look,' Molineaux told Thornton when a quarter of an hour had passed without any sign of life. 'You wait here until I signal you.'

'Want me to keep you covered?' Thornton unslung the shotgun he was carrying.

Molineaux shook his head. 'If I get into trouble, you just get back to where the others are waiting and tell them what happened. Mr Killigrew will know what to do.'

Thornton shrugged. Molineaux broke cover, walking across the open space to the workers' barracks. He wiped his neck and the underside of his jaw with his neckerchief. The wind had died and the air was oppressively hot: they would have a storm before the day was out, unless he knew nothing about the weather. Reaching the barracks, he peered through a broken window. Mildewed mattresses lay on the rusting iron bedsteads, and a few shards of broken pottery were scattered across the wooden floorboards. The place was clearly deserted, but Molineaux checked the other buildings anyway before waving Thornton across from the trees. The two of them entered the iron foundry and surveyed the interior with jaded eyes. Someone had taken a sledgehammer to the pyramid-shaped brick furnaces beneath each of the chimneys, and the hot-blast stoves and pig beds had been smashed up. Some storage bins contained a few scraps of iron ore or coke, and here and there a skimming ladle was abandoned on a floor spattered with bird droppings. As soon as Molineaux and Thornton entered, the petty officer heard rats scampering for cover.

'Not exactly ship-shape and Bristol fashion, is it?' he said.

'The Russians must've slighted the place to stop us from using it.'

'They could've saved themselves the bother. I don't reckon an island as small as this has enough iron in it for the navy to bother with the effort of seizing it.'

They were about to emerge into the sunlight from the door at the far end when Molineaux saw a *matros* with a musket slung over one shoulder emerge from the trees less than fifty yards away. Thornton had seen him too, and was about to shoot him when Molineaux knocked the shotgun's barrels up. He pushed the captain out of sight before the Russian saw either of them.

'You want to bring every Russki seaman on this island running?' hissed the petty officer.

'How many Russki seamen can there be on an island as small as this?'

'I dunno, but I'll bet that one ain't alone.'

A matter of seconds proved Molineaux right, when another *matros* emerged from the trees, then another and another, until a dozen of them stood there.

'This island's too small and insignificant to justify a garrison,' said Thornton. 'This must be a shore party from the *Atalanta*.'

'I knew it was too clush when they sailed off without putting a search party ashore,' groaned Molineaux.

The NCO leading the *matrosy* gave orders to his men, pointing around the ironworks. The men split up to search the place, two of them walking straight towards the foundry. Molineaux tapped Thornton on the shoulder and indicated the furnaces. The captain nodded, and the two of them ran across and ducked down beneath the most intact of the furnaces moments before the two Russians entered.

One of the Russians immediately produced a cigarette and lit it with a match, taking a deep drag before passing it to his comrade, who took a thankful puff. Neither of them seemed to be in any hurry to reach the far end of the building, enjoying their crafty smoke while they could, but at the same time they did not seem intent on making a very thorough examination of the place, otherwise they would have glanced behind the furnaces. Nevertheless, it was a tense and uncomfortable couple of minutes for Molineaux and Thornton, who moved round the back of the furnace to stay out of sight of the *matrosy* as they made their way to the door at the far end.

At last, the *matros* whose turn it was to hold the cigarette took a final puff, pinched off the end, and stowed it away inside his forage cap before stepping out through the door, followed by his comrade.

Molineaux and Thornton ran across to the door in time to see the *matrosy* reconvene outside the barracks. Another dozen *matrosy* emerged from the trees, their officer shouting orders.

'Jesus!' breathed Thornton. 'The island's crawling with Russkis!'

The *matrosy* spread out into a skirmishing line and headed into the trees behind the foundry.

'It looks as though they're quartering the island in search of something,' mused Thornton.

'Yur,' Molineaux agreed glumly. 'Us!'

'We must get back to the others and warn them.'

'Plummy notion. Just one problem: they're between us and the others now.'

When Killigrew and Hughes rejoined the others in the forest, the commander had barely had time to tell them about the *Ivan Strashnyi* when Iles, who had been on lookout duty, came running back through the trees from the east.

'Ivans coming this way, sir!' he reported breathlessly. 'Skirmishing line; they'll be here in a couple of minutes.'

'We'd best get moving, then,' said Bullivant.

Killigrew stared at him. 'Where to?'

The viscount rolled his eyes. 'God save us, man! If the Russians are coming from *that* direction—' he pointed to the east – 'might I suggest we head in *that* direction?' He pointed to the west. 'And let's look sharp about it!'

'And get bottled up at the west end of the island?' Killigrew pointed out patiently.

'We could hide in the lighthouse there,' said Charlton.

'Capital thinking, Mr Charlton! The Russians are quartering the island for us; I hardly think they're going to neglect to look in the lighthouse, do you?'

The assistant surgeon hung his head.

'Well, we have to do *something*,' said Lady Bullivant. 'Or are you suggesting we wait here until we're captured?'

Killigrew had to admit she had a point. He looked around for a solution, but saw only trees . . . and then realised he had not seen the trees for the wood. 'Up the trees, quick!'

'I beg your pardon?' Lady Bullivant exclaimed in disbelief.

'It's our only chance! Mr Uren, be so good as to help her ladyship into that tree . . . Fuller, perhaps you could do the same for Miss Maltravers? Attwood, can you make sure Nicholls—'

'I'm perfectly capable of climbing a tree without help!' the maid protested indignantly when the steward tried to take her by the arm. And she quickly proved it too, scrambling up the trunk of one of the pines hardly any less nimbly than Hughes, Iles, O'Leary and Yorath. 'No peeking up my skirt neither!' she added tartly.

'You too, Minty,' Killigrew told Miss Maltravers.

'But . . . we'll be seen!'

'Perhaps,' admitted Killigrew. 'Perhaps not. One thing I do know, we'll be spotted for certain if all of us try to hide here on the ground. Get up as high amongst the boughs as you dare!'

'Eh, begging your pardon, sir, but I don't think I'm in any fettle to go climbing trees,' said Endicott. 'And as for Mr Dahlstedt here . . .' He indicated the pilot's bandaged hands.

Killigrew had not forgotten. 'Charlton, help me drag Endicott over to the hollow between the roots of that tree. We'll cover them over with bracken. You lie next to Endicott, Herre Dahlstedt.'

'You lie still, sir,' Endicott told the Finn as the two of them huddled beneath the tree. 'We'll be all right, you'll see.'

Killigrew and Charlton tore up some ferns and laid them across the two wounded men as quickly as they could, constantly glancing in the direction of the approaching Russians.

After a minute, they stood back to admire their handiwork.

'That'll fool the Russians,' Charlton commented drily, 'if they're blind.'

Killigrew grimaced. The assistant surgeon had a point: the covering of ferns looked about as natural as the Great Wall of China, and almost as obvious. Telling himself it was only obvious because he was looking for it was no consolation, given that the Russians would be looking for it too.

He heard shouting through the trees, the Russians in the skirmishing line calling out to one another as they advanced. Killigrew had run out of time: nothing for it but to scramble up the nearest tree and pray for a miracle. His hopes were not high: they had benefited from more than their fair share of miracles in the twelve hours since they had broken out of Raseborg Castle. He made himself comfortable on a bough on the opposite side of the trunk from where Uren stood on a branch, hugging the bole of the tree with his arms.

He was just in time: the foliage on the trees was thick enough to help hide them from the Russians, but through it he could see the skirmishing line approach, the *matrosy* marching through the undergrowth with their heads bowed. It was a phenomenon he had learned playing hide and seek as a boy in Cornwall: a man searching for another rarely bothered to look up for his quarry, even in woods, and that knowledge had served him well before now.

He caught his breath as one of the Russians passed directly beneath the bough where he perched, and then moved on . . . straight towards Endicott and Dahlstedt.

XX

To the Lighthouse

11.30 a.m.–10.00 p.m., Friday 18 August

Ten yards, nine yards, eight yards . . . surely the Russian must see them; and even if he could not, he was about to trip over them. Killigrew placed one hand on the hilt of his sword, wondering what the hell he was going to do with it if Endicott and Dahlstedt were discovered. His heart thudded in his chest: if they were discovered, all he could do was let the Russians take them – and murder them, in all probability – because to jump down from the trees would only reveal the hiding place of the others.

The Russian below was only five feet from the two wounded sailors now, brushing the bracken with the blade of the bayonet on his musket. Four feet, three . . . he stopped abruptly, and to Killigrew it seemed he was staring right at the bracken that covered the two men.

He's seen them . . . he *must* have seen them . . .

Attwood dropped from a tree some distance away. The Russians did not see him fall, but they heard the thump of his boots hitting the soil, and the rustle of the undergrowth as he set off running through the trees. Killigrew's first thought was that the cook must have panicked: then he realised Attwood was deliberately distracting the Russians, trying to draw their attention away from the others.

It was one of the bravest deeds Killigrew had ever seen: an act of pure self-sacrifice; sacrifice, because it could only have one consequence. Seeing him haring off through the trees, one of the Russians shouted a cry of warning. Another raised his musket to his shoulder and fired. Attwood let out a sob and twisted, sprawling amongst the bracken. The Russian skirmishing line broke as several of the men ran across to where Attwood had fallen. His body was hidden from Killigrew by the ferns, but he saw an NCO standing over the place where the cook had fallen, a pistol in his hand, barking out a terse question in Russian. He took a step forward, and Killigrew heard Attwood scream in agony . . . Jesus, the bastard was torturing him, treading on the wound!

Attwood spat an expletive at the NCO, who fired his pistol, once, before spitting on the corpse at his feet.

Araminta gasped in shock.

The Russian who had been on the verge of discovering Endicott and Dahlstedt had now moved away from where they lay to stand directly beneath her tree. He glanced up, eyes and mouth widening in shock as he saw her and Fuller perched amongst the boughs overhead.

Fuller dropped from the tree, clasp knife in hand, and fell on the Russian, knocking him down amongst the bracken. Landing on top of him, he stabbed frantically at the man's throat. Then he lay still on the Russian's corpse not even daring to look up to see if he had been spotted; if he had, they were all dead.

But the rest of the Russians were all gazing across at the NCO who had murdered Attwood. He ordered two of his men to pick up the cook's body, and looked about, but did not notice that one of his men had disappeared. While the two men carrying Attwood's corpse headed off to their right, in the direction of the lagoon where the *Ivan Strashnyi* lay, the

NCO ordered the rest of the skirmishing line forward, and they continued through the trees.

'Everyone stay where you are,' whispered Killigrew.

They remained in the trees for another couple of minutes, and the commander was about to climb down to make sure the coast was clear when he heard someone moving stealthily through the undergrowth below. He waited, and Molineaux and Thornton stepped into view.

'Where the hell have they got to?' wondered the petty officer.

'They must've been driven off by the skirmishing line,' said Thornton.

Killigrew jumped down to the ground, rolling in the bracken before picking himself up and dusting himself off. 'We're right here.'

'Lumme!' exclaimed Molineaux, starting in fright. He looked up, saw the others perched amongst the boughs, and grinned at Nicholls, who sat immediately above him. 'Now, that's a rare-looking-bird!'

The maid scowled. 'Stop making jokes and help me down!'

'Jump: I'll catch you.'

The maid pushed herself off the bough. Molineaux caught her around the waist to slow her fall. 'You can let go of me now,' she told him.

'Must I?'

She gave him a warning look. He released her at once.

Killigrew gave Araminta the same assistance, without taking the same liberty. 'Thank you,' she said.

Uren helped Lady Bullivant down.

'Are you all right, ma'am?' Killigrew asked her.

She smiled wanly. 'A little shaken, but glad to be still alive.'

'Aye.' Endicott sat up, startling Molineaux and Thornton a second time, and picked the bracken off himself and Dahl-stedt. 'That one were much too bloody close for my liking, and I don't care who knows it!'

'What were those shots?' asked Molineaux.

'They shot Doc Attwood,' O'Leary said grimly. 'Murdered him in cold blood, the bastards!'

'A reminder of the fate in store for all of us, if the Russians capture us,' said Killigrew.

Fuller picked himself up off the Russian he had killed, wiping blood from his right hand with a rag. 'Well, at least I managed to even the score.'

Bullivant rounded on him and slapped him across the face. 'You damned fool! You nearly got us all killed! What the devil d'ye think you were playing at?'

Fuller stared at the viscount with sullen eyes, hurt and angry. Bullivant raised his hand to strike him again, but this time Molineaux caught him by the wrist, staying the blow.

Bullivant glowered at the petty officer. 'Unhand me, you filthy nigger!'

The petty officer's bunched fist came up without warning, clipping Bullivant on the chin. The viscount staggered back, tripped over a tree root and sprawled on his back, staring at Molineaux in disbelief. 'Killigrew! You saw that! Your pet monkey just struck me!'

'Did he?' The commander met Bullivant's gaze with an expression as if butter would have frozen in his mouth. 'Sorry, I was looking the other way. Did any of you other lads see it?'

Iles grinned. 'Not us, sir. Us got summat in us eye.'

The other sailors were grinning too.

'Thornton!' snorted Bullivant. 'You saw it, didn't you?'

'Saw what, sir? I only saw you trip over that root and fall on your face.'

'Damn you, Thornton! You're fired!'

'Good! Because quite frankly, my lord, I've had just about all I can take of working for a miserable, arrogant, mean-spirited bastard like you.'

Bullivant stared at him in astonishment, and rounded on Killigrew. 'This is your doing! You've turned my men against me!'

'You turned them against yourself.'

'You're finished, Killigrew! When I get back to England, I'll see to it you never get another appointment in the navy so long as you live.'

'Quite frankly, I'd rather not have a posting in any navy in which an arrogant, loud-mouthed bully like you has any influence,' Killigrew told him cheerfully, and levelled his shotgun at the viscount's chest. 'Now I'll thank you to be a good fellow and keep your opinions to yourself: one more word out of you, my lord, and instead of trying to save your life I'll take great pleasure in marching you down in person to the beach where Nekrasoff's waiting; do I make myself clear?'

Bullivant sat there, glowering, at a loss for words.

'At the risk of being the sole remaining voice of sanity, might I remind you that we're still stranded on this island?' said Dahlstedt. 'An island that now seems to be crawling with Russian sailors, I might add.'

'Thank you, Herre Dahlstedt,' said Killigrew. 'Right: we need to find a hiding place. Molineaux, what about those ironworks?'

'Uninhabited, sir,' the petty officer assured him. 'And the Ivans have already searched them; reckon we'll be safe there for a while: they won't look for us there again before nightfall.'

'Lay on, Macduff.'

Killigrew and Molineaux led the way through the trees, and the others followed, Araminta helping her father to his feet. O'Leary and Yorath carried Endicott between them, and Iles and Hughes brought up the rear.

When they finally emerged from the trees overlooking the iron foundry, Killigrew noticed there had been a change in the quality of the light. The sky was overcast, a ghastly hue somewhere between off-white and pastel pink, casting a sickly pallor that was at once too bright and too dreary over the scene. He could almost feel the charge of static electricity in the air.

'It ain't a palace,' Molineaux warned the two ladies as they approached the foundry. 'But it's the best we'll find, under the circumstances.'

'Everyone inside,' ordered Killigrew. 'We'll stay out of sight until nightfall.'

'And then what?' asked Thornton. 'Sooner or later the Russians are going to find us. And if we light a fire to attract the attention of any passing ships, it'll only bring the Russians down upon us sooner.'

Killigrew glanced to where the top of the lighthouse, at the far end of the island, showed above the trees behind them. 'We'll just have to find some other way of signalling a ship, won't we?'

As they entered the iron foundry, Araminta wrinkled her nose. 'What's that smell?'

'Guano, ma'am,' said Thornton.

'Really? I thought guanoes grew only in tropical climes.'

Thornton stopped dead in his tracks, leaving Araminta to pass blithely on ahead of him. The captain turned to Killigrew with an expression of disbelief; the commander only shrugged, and turned to his men.

'All right, with any luck we'll be able to stay here for the next few hours, so we'd best get some rest while we can. I want one man on watch at either end of the building at all times. We'll work shipboard watches: Uren and O'Leary take the afternoon watch, Fuller and Hughes the first dog watch and Dahlstedt and Yorath take the last.'

Dahlstedt looked up in surprise, but said nothing.

'The rest of you get your heads down,' Killigrew told them. 'All of you. And no one leaves this building without my say so, is that understood?'

'What if one of us needs to answer the call of nature?' Lady Bullivant demanded.

'You'll have to go behind that furnace,' he said, pointing to Molineaux and Thornton's earlier hiding place.

'That is hardly satisfactory!'

'This whole situation is hardly satisfactory, ma'am; I'm afraid we shall have to grin and bear it.'

'What about food?' growled Lord Bullivant. 'I haven't eaten since breakfast, and all I got then was a few dry biscuits.'

'There isn't any. Unless you'd like to ask the Russians if they'd care to spare us a bite to eat?'

'No food since breakfast!' Endicott muttered while Charlton changed the dressing on his wound. 'When we was in the Arctic, we had to go for days on end without scran! And he's complaining because he's had nowt to eat since breakfast!'

'Take heart, lads,' Killigrew told them. 'If all goes according to plan, we'll be dining on board one of Her Majesty's ships this time tomorrow; and if I get my way you'll all have double helpings, and an extra tot of rum to wash it down with.'

Uren and Iles took up their positions at the doors, and the others settled down to try to sleep. Molineaux sat down next to Nicholls and talked to her while she pretended not to be interested in his attentions. Killigrew found a patch of floor that was clear of bird-droppings and sat down with his back to the wall, tipping his cap forward over his eyes.

Dahlstedt came across and sat down next to him. 'I must confess to a certain degree of curiosity as to how you intend to fulfil that promise, Herre Killigrew.'

'I promised nothing,' the commander told him in a low voice. 'But there *is* a chance.'

'You have a plan?'

'Perhaps. How far would you say it is to Hangö Head from here?'

'About twenty miles. Why?'

'There's usually at least one of our frigates stationed off Hangö Head. I intend to try to signal her.'

'From here?' Dahlstedt thought about it. 'The lighthouse?'

'It's got to be at least a hundred and thirty feet tall. Should be visible from twenty miles off.'

'Barely.'

Killigrew grimaced. ' "Barely" is all we've got.'

'How will you signal? Morse code?'

The commander shook his head. 'I don't know it, and even if I did it would be asking too much to hope that anyone on the frigate would know it as well. But the Russians have stopped operating their lighthouses all along this coast ever since war was declared. I'm hoping that if the frigate sees the one on this island lit up, she'll come to investigate.'

'And if she doesn't?'

'Then we're scuppered.'

'You realise that you won't be able to keep that light on for long. The moment you light it, the Russians from the *Ivan Strashnyi* will come to investigate.'

'I'll have to find some way to black out the light on the east, north and south sides of the tower. Canvas or sacking or something like that.'

'They'll still be able to see the beam.'

'Yes, but it may increase the amount of time that passes before they see it and come to investigate. Especially if I can give them some other problems of their own to worry about. I expect you're wondering why I asked you to stand the last dog watch with Yorath?'

'The thought had crossed my mind. I don't like to stand on ceremony, and I know you're short of men, but I notice that you didn't ask Molineaux or Iles to stand watch. You think they've done enough for one day?'

'Under normal circumstances, perhaps: but present circumstances are far from normal. Molineaux and Iles are going to be busy tonight, which is why I want them to rest now.'

Killigrew tugged the peak of his cap down another inch, folded his arms, and rested his jaw on his chest to signify that the discussion was over.

But if he had hoped to sleep, he had hoped in vain. It was not the discomfort of the floor: in the navy, one learned to sleep whenever and wherever one got the chance. But there were too many imponderables in his plan, too much that could go wrong or simply not happen. He lay awake trying to think of ways to iron out these wrinkles, to come up with contingencies if things did not go as he intended, or an alternative plan to replace altogether the desperate, hare-brained scheme that was all he had come up with so far. On all three counts, he drew a blank. Nothing for it but to press ahead with the plan when the time came, because the alternative was to be captured and executed by the Russians. If nothing else, his lack of choices at least lent him a certain clarity of thought.

After a while, Dahlstedt stood up and picked his way between the men sleeping on the floor to go behind the furnace. Araminta stood up at once and walked across to take his place next to Killigrew.

'You could have handled that better, you know.'

He did not lift his head. 'Handled what better?'

'Your confrontation with papa.'

'There are many things I've done in my life that I could have handled better, with the benefit of hindsight. If there's one thing it's taught me, there's no use crying over spilled milk.'

'No, but only a fool makes no attempt to rectify a mistake. You might at least apologise to him.'

'Go crawling to him begging him not to have me dismissed from the navy?'

'Well, I wouldn't put it quite like that . . .'

Killigrew pushed his cap back on the top of his head. 'But that's what you mean, isn't it?' He shook his head. 'As far as I'm concerned, there's nothing to apologise for. Fuller saved all our lives when he killed that Russian, and we'd never have made it this far if it hadn't been for Molineaux. Damn it, if it hadn't been for Molineaux I'd've died seven years ago on the Guinea Coast.'

'Kit!'

'It's the truth.'

'I don't doubt it; but is it really necessary to curse?'

He stared at her in astonishment, and then shook his head with a wry chuckle. 'Frankly, yes. And I'll tell you something else: if Molineaux hadn't clobbered your papa, I'd've done it myself.'

'Aren't you being a little harsh? I know he can be a crotchety old fellow at times, but he means well; and you've got to admit, he's been under a good deal of strain these past couple of days.'

'I never did tell you about the time he sent a couple of ex-pugs round to my rooms in Paddington to try to convince me of the error of my ways in aspiring to your hand, did I?'

She stared at him. 'They assaulted you?'

'They didn't come for tea.'

She shook her head. 'No. You're lying . . . Papa would never do such a thing.'

'Remember that time we went to the theatre, and I turned up with a black eye? I told you I'd had a fall out riding earlier that day? Take a good, long look at your papa, Minty: he isn't the man you think he is.'

She blanched.

Killigrew shook his head dismissively. This was no time for raking over the coals. 'We've all been under a good deal of strain the past couple of days, in case it had escaped your notice; yourself and your mama included. Your papa is the only one of us who has not conducted himself in a manner that would impress his medieval ancestors.'

'You're just as stubborn as he is!'

'Yes, but not nearly so great a pain in the . . . in the neck. Now if you'll excuse me, Minty, I need my beauty sleep.' Killigrew pulled his cap down over his eyes once more, folded his arms and pretended to doze.

Lieutenant Yurieff checked his fob watch. 'It's getting dark, sir.'

'Still plenty of light to search by,' grunted Pechorin,

slashing at the undergrowth with a standard-issue cutlass: the sabre slung at his hip was a weapon of honour, not a gardening implement.

He had spoken the truth up to a point: even after sunset at eight in the evening, the high latitude meant that twilight would last most of the night at that time of year. But while it was still light out in the open, beneath the pine trees that covered most of the island it was too dark to see one's hand in front of one's face.

'Beregovoi! Go back to the *Atalanta* and fetch some lanterns,' Pechorin ordered his quartermaster. 'We'll meet you at the foot of the lighthouse.'

'Yes, sir!' Beregovoi left the party of ten men, who were searching with Pechorin and Yurieff, and headed back towards the lagoon.

'The men are tired, sir,' Yurieff told the count in a low voice, reluctant to gainsay an officer whom he had always respected until these past few hours. 'Some of them have been on the go since yesterday morning.'

'Killigrew and his men must be just as tired, if not more so,' retorted Pechorin. 'If they can go on, so can we.'

'Captain Aleksandrei's men will have returned to the lagoon by now.'

'Good! Then we will be the ones who find Killigrew and the others.'

'We're on an island, sir. The English cannot go anywhere. They'll still be here in the morning. We can resume our search then.'

'And so will Aleksandrei's men!'

'What's more important, sir? That the English are found? Or that we are the ones to find them?'

'They made fools of us today, Borislav Ivanovich. You saw how Aleksandrei's men sneered at us. The only way we can begin to live it down is if we're the ones who capture them.'

With so many men combing such a small island, he had known it was unlikely that his party would be the first to

408

discover the fugitives' hiding place; but he had neglected to warn Captain Aleksandrei that Killigrew was an extremely dangerous and resourceful individual, and the first men to find him might not necessarily be the one who brought him to heel. He felt a little guilty about that, but told himself that it should have been self-evident that Killigrew was resourceful and dangerous. After all, by now all of Aleksandrei's men must know that the British fugitives had escaped from Raseborg Castle, stolen back the *Milenion*, out-sailed a paddle-steamer and got the better of it armed only with bottles of flaming lamp-oil. If any of Aleksandrei's men put that down to Pechorin's incompetence rather than Killigrew's skill, they would be in for the nasty surprise they deserved when they caught up with the fugitives. Pechorin had learned the hard way not to underestimate his adversary; but he was determined to prove himself the better man in the end.

A yell came from nearby.

'Who's there?' called Pechorin, gripping his cutlass tightly.

'Me, sir. Klossovsky. It's nothing: I tripped.'

Yurieff looked pleadingly at the count. 'Sir . . .?'

Pechorin sighed. 'All right! Let's get back to the lagoon.'

Dark clouds were rolling in from the west by the time they reached the coast. A picquet of *matrosy* at the perimeter of Aleksandrei's camp challenged them on their return. Pechorin identified himself and his men, and as they trudged across the shingle towards the centre of the camp, lightning flickered silently behind the clouds somewhere off to the west. The bright flash picked out a shape hanging from a tree off to their right, black and white with a splash of dark crimson. The flicker of light lasted only a fraction of a second, and it was dark again before Pechorin realised what he had seen.

A man hanging from the boughs of one of the trees overlooking the lagoon, strung up by the ankles.

Thunder rumbled in the distance.

Pechorin crossed to where the man hung and struck a

match to examine his face. A gust of the rising wind blew out his guttering match, but not before he had recognised the face of Lord Bullivant's cook, a third eye gouged in his forehead by a bullet, most of the back of his skull and its contents missing.

'One down, seventeen to go,' a voice said nearby.

Pechorin turned and saw Chernyovsky sitting on a barrel, placidly puffing on a clay pipe.

'You caught him?'

The starshina shook his head. 'Some of Aleksandrei's men. They're in there, celebrating,' he added scathingly, and gestured with his pipe stem to where sounds of drunken revelry issued from a makeshift tent.

'The rest?'

Chernyovsky indicated the trees. 'Still out there, somewhere.'

Pechorin nodded and crossed to the tent. 'The man outside!' he shouted above the hubbub of laughter. 'Who caught him?'

The *matrosy* fell silent at once. One of them stepped forward. 'I did, sir. That is to say, my men and I.'

'What's your name, Corporal?'

'Obukoff, sir.'

'Outside, Obukoff.'

'Yes, sir!' The corporal followed Pechorin out of the tent, and the hubbub of voices was renewed, with an anxious note now. Officers were never good news.

Outside the tent, Pechorin snipped the end off a couple of cigars and handed one to the corporal. 'Do you smoke?'

Obukoff's eyes bugged out of his head at the sight of the fat Havana. 'Yes, sir!' There was a hint of vodka on his breath, but he stood steady enough. 'Er . . . do you mind if I save it for later?'

'By all means, Corporal,' Pechorin told him companionably. 'Where did you find this one?'

'Somewhere towards the middle of the island, sir.'

410

'You didn't see any of the others?'

'No, sir.'

'Tomorrow, do you think you could take me to where you found this one?'

'I'll need permission from Captain Aleksandrei, sir. I'm back on duty at six.'

Pechorin shook his head. 'We're going out at four. More than enough time for you to take us there and get back in time for your watch.'

'Four, sir?'

'The sun will rise at ten to five; but there will be more than enough light for us to see by before then.'

'Yes, sir.'

Pechorin took out a shiny silver rouble and gave it to Obukoff. 'You'll get another one like that when you take us to where you shot the English sailor – provided you say nothing of this to any of your shipmates. Understand?'

The corporal's eyes widened with avarice. 'Yes, sir!'

'Now run along. Get a good night's sleep – I want you refreshed when you come to me at four in the morning.'

'Sir!' Obukoff saluted and hurried away.

Pechorin turned and saw Yurieff looking at him with an expression not unakin to disgust. 'What?'

The lieutenant just shook his head. 'For a moment there I thought you were going to order the dead man cut down, sir. I did not think that bribery was your style.'

'The English have an expression, Borislav Ivanovich: all's fair in love and war.'

Yurieff did not look convinced, but he saluted and marched away.

Pechorin saw Chernyovsky watching him, grinning through his beard. The count walked over to the Cossack. 'Something amuses you, Starshina?'

Chernyovsky shook his head. 'What was all that about? As if I could not guess.'

'If I take you to where the dead man was shot, do you think

411

you could track Killigrew and the others to wherever they're hiding?'

'It'll cost you.'

Pechorin reached into his pocket once more.

Chernyovsky shook his head. 'Keep your silver. All I want is that *negr* petty officer who's with Killigrew.'

'You can have him. All *I* want is Killigrew himself.'

'What do you want us to do, sir?' Molineaux asked on behalf of Iles as well as himself when Killigrew had finished outlining his plan, such as it was.

'Confusion in the Russian camp,' Killigrew told him. 'Chaos. Pandemonium.'

Molineaux grinned. 'Pandemonium is my speciality.'

'No heroics, no unnecessary risks. I'm asking you because there'll be picquets around the Russian camp and you're the only man I know who can sneak past them without getting caught. Iles can cover your back.'

The seaman nodded enthusiastically. ''S'bout time, too, sir, beggin' your pardon. I'se sick to the back teeth with runnin' from these Russkis; it'll be good to 'ave a chance to fight back.'

'That's the spirit, Iles; just don't get carried away.'

'Wouldn't dream of it, sir.'

Killigrew eyed him sceptically.

'Lucifers, sir?' asked Molineaux.

The commander took out the box of matches he had taken from Leong and handed them to the petty officer. 'Good luck.'

'You too, sir.'

Carrying one of the shotguns each, Molineaux and Iles left the iron foundry. Killigrew was about to follow them out, armed only with his dress sword, when Araminta caught him by the arm.

'You're leaving us?'

'Just for a couple of hours. I have to send a message.'

412

'You're coming back?'

'That's the plan.'

She glanced to where her parents sat, and seeing they were not watching, stood on tiptoes to give him a peck on the cheek. 'Be careful.'

He grinned. 'I didn't think you cared.'

'Of course I care!' she retorted, flushing. 'Surely I shouldn't have to explain that . . . oh, you're simply impossible!' She turned on her heel and went back to join her parents.

'Charlton!' called Killigrew. 'You're in charge here until I get back. If I'm not back by dawn, you'd best—' He broke off, realising that if he was not back by dawn, there was no advice he could give the assistant surgeon that would be of the remotest use. If he failed, they would all die, and there was nothing he could do to prevent that. 'Never mind. I'll be back by dawn. Just make sure you keep everyone here until I do.'

'Yes, sir.'

Killigrew slipped out and the smile fell from his face like a mask as he steeled himself for what he knew he must do. He might have made light of the task with Araminta, but he knew that as long as the *Ivan Strashnyi* lay crippled at Jurassö her captain would have lookouts stationed in the lighthouse, keeping a watch for Allied vessels. Since he could not risk the sound of a shot alerting the Russians, there would be no all-too-easy pulling of a trigger to deal with them. There was going to be killing, hand to hand, face to face: harsh, brutal and messy.

The night was turning cold, a bitter wind gusting up the Gulf of Finland, but his brisk pace kept him warm. He followed the south coast of the island, knowing that it was better to stay in the open where the light of the white night guided his steps, grateful that the moon was not yet risen to silhouette him by shining on the sea, making him an easy target. He did not have time to waste blundering through the darkness beneath the trees. Lightning flickered across the sky, and the crack of thunder followed a couple of seconds later. He turned up the collar of the Third Section greatcoat he wore and hurried on to where the lighthouse stood on a rocky promontory at the western end of the island.

The lighthouse was graceful, the sides of the circular tower curving inwards from a broad base, with a chequered red-and-white pattern decorating its middle section to aid identification during daylight hours. In peacetime, its bright beam warned shipping of the dangers of the Jurassö rocks; but the Russians had no wish to help the Allied fleets avoid the rocks, so the lantern room at the top was dark.

He stood in the shadow of the trees, watching the lighthouse from a distance of about two hundred yards. He could just make out a figure walking the open gallery that ran around the lantern room at the top. The man paused occasionally to scan the dark horizon with a telescope, otherwise beating his hands against his sides in an effort to keep warm. The cool breeze blowing at sea level would be much stronger up there.

The only light came from a small window perhaps halfway up the tower. There were no adjoining buildings, so the chances were the lighthouse keepers lived in the tower itself when the lighthouse was in use. Killigrew hoped that, without any duties to perform for the duration of the war, the 'wickies' would have been moved back to the mainland: even if the men were Finns – and Finns who hated the Russians – they would have to be crazy to help a lone British officer when there were over seven hundred *matrosy* in possession of the island. Besides, even the Finns who hated the Russians had no love for the Royal Navy, which had attacked Finnish ports and ruined livelihoods by burning merchant shipping. So if there were lighthouse keepers inside with the lookouts from the *Ivan Strashnyi*, the chances were Killigrew would have to kill them too, or try to. He had no wish to kill civilians, and he cursed the Russians for putting him in this position by trying to murder the Bullivants and their crew; and cursed the Bullivants, whose folly had started this madness in the first place.

He waited for the man on the gallery to disappear round the back of the lantern room, and then ran across the open space between the trees and the lighthouse. Even as he sprinted along the paved track over the rocks, he felt the first few fat drops of rain splash against his face. Reaching the door at the foot of the tower, he put an ear to it and listened until he could hear nothing but the hissing of the rain against the waves. The door was unlocked: he eased it open a crack and peered through, but saw only shadows. Emboldened, he stepped through and closed the door behind him quickly: he did not want any draughts blowing up the stairs to warn the men above that someone had entered below.

He wiped the rain from his face with his hands and ran his fingers through his hair to brush it back out of his eyes, before shaking the drops off his hands and wiping them on the damp breast of his greatcoat. As his eyes adjusted to the gloom, he saw a short passage leading between solid stone walls to a cast-iron spiral staircase leading up. Drawing his sword, he ascended on tiptoe, the staircase leading up about twenty feet through a shaft with solid brickwork on all sides of him. He emerged into a circular room stacked with barrels and boxes. Investigation of their contents would have to wait until he had the lighthouse to himself.

A staircase ran around the inside wall. He followed it up to another storeroom, and another and another, each chamber slightly smaller than the one below. When he guessed he was halfway to the top he paused to catch his breath. The room contained barrels of whale oil to light the lamp above, and there was a hatch in the wall with a joist running out above it, so the barrels could be winched up rather than manhandled up the awkward steps. While he was looking about, he heard someone moving around above him.

Gripping his sword, he ascended the next flight of steps cautiously. Instead of leading straight up into the next room, these stairs ended in a small landing with a door leading off to the right, while the next flight continued up to the floor above. A light showed under the door, and he could hear someone moving about on the other side. He listened: no voices, so either there was only one man on the other side of the door, or there was more than one but they were not talking to each other. He grasped the handle, took a very deep breath, and pulled back on it to free the latch so he could ease it up silently, without the snap of it hitting the restraining bracket.

He eased the door open a crack. A *matros* stood at a wood-burning stove, his back to the door as he stirred something in a saucepan. The *matros* turned to reach for a peppermill, Killigrew pulled the door to again, bracing himself to charge into the room, but the man did not see him. He added pepper to the pan and went on stirring, humming tunelessly to himself.

Killigrew opened the door and stepped silently through. A waft of fish stew slapped him in the face at once. The *matros* stood about twenty feet away: twenty feet of wooden floorboards, each one threatening a treacherous creak. The *matros* had only to shout to warn his shipmate on the gallery above, and Killigrew would find the muzzle of a musket waiting for him somewhere on the way to the top.

Slowly, inch by inch, he tiptoed towards the *matros*. His palm sweated where it gripped the hilt of his sword. If he was going to kill this man he had to do it without giving him a chance to cry out. Get right behind him, close enough to put a hand over his mouth to stifle his screams, and drive the sword's tip into his back, between his ribs and into his heart.

He had halved the distance between them when a floorboard creaked underfoot. He froze, wincing, but the *matros* did not turn, lost in a world of his own. Killigrew hesitated, his heart thudding in his chest, until he realised that the longer he waited, the greater the chance that something would make the sailor turn and see him.

He resumed his advance: ten feet to go, ten more cautious

steps. Nine steps, eight steps, seven, six, five . . . he poised the sword to thrust, reaching out to clamp his left hand over the *matros'* mouth.

A draught caught the door behind him and slammed the latch against the catch with a bang.

The *matros* glanced over his shoulder and saw Killigrew. '*Privet, Czibor!'*

The commander froze.

The *matros* realised that Killigrew was not Czibor, and did a double take. Whirling to face the stranger, he grabbed the saucepan from the stove.

Killigrew was already striding forward. He ducked as the *matros* threw the contents of the saucepan at him, the simmering stew flying across the room to splash over the walls and floor. Killigrew straightened, putting one hand over the *matros'* mouth, pushing him back against the stove and driving the tip of the sword between his ribs. The man's face twisted in shock and agony and he cried out against Killigrew's palm, his death rattle muffled. When the light went out in his eyes and his head lolled, the commander withdrew the blade and the dead man crumpled to the floor.

Killigrew mopped sweat from his brow with his sleeve, and crouched to wipe the blood from his blade on the *matros'* jacket. He straightened and crossed back to the door, glancing up the stairs. Had the man above – assuming there was only one man above – heard the fight? In the panic of the moment, wondering how much noise they had made had been the least of Killigrew's worries; he had not even heard the saucepan hit the floor when it dropped from the *matros'* lifeless hands, but it must have landed with a thump.

Apart from the drumming of the rain on the window panes and the howling of the wind, no sound came from above, which could have meant anything or nothing. Killigrew continued to climb. The door on the next floor led into someone's living quarters: there was a wooden bed there, but no bedding. No ornaments or personal possessions to denote

417

occupation other than a few rough pieces of furniture: a table, an easy chair, some empty shelves, a chest and a wardrobe.

On the floor above, the stairs led straight up into the next room. Killigrew peered cautiously over the top of the steps to see another man's living quarters, likewise deserted. An iron ladder bolted to the far wall led up to a hatch in the ceiling. The hatch cover was off, and he climbed up until he could ease his head through. Twisting his head, he saw the room was in darkness, but another flicker of lightning briefly illuminated it through the large, rain-washed window that the lighthouse keepers would use to check the weather. A large fog-warning bell hung from the ceiling. He was in the watch room, which housed the weights and the clockwork mechanism controlling the rotating light in the lantern room above.

The rumble of thunder followed almost immediately. It occurred to him that a lighthouse was probably not the best place to be in an electrical storm. He hoped this one had a lightning conductor on the roof.

Another ladder led up to another hatchway. He slotted his sword back into its scabbard and closed the hatch below him so he was in complete darkness. Creeping across to the other ladder, he climbed until he was able to press one ear to the underside of the trap door. The hammering rain drowned out any noise the man on duty on the gallery might have been making as he moved about in an effort to keep warm.

Killigrew eased up the trap door at one side, just enough to peer out. A blast of cold air with rain in it smacked him in the face at once. The door to the gallery was open, facing him. No sign of the other *matros*. He lowered the hatch and eased it up at the other side to see the brass 'chariot' on which the lamp rotated when it was in use. Drawing his sword from its scabbard, he slithered up into the lantern room.

The room was circular, surrounded by stout glass panes on every side held in place by the diagonal iron astragals that framed them. Above him, the cupola was topped by a ball vent to allow the smoke from the lamp to escape, so the windows would not become grimy with soot. Through the rain-lashed panes, he could just make out the brass railings surrounding the gallery.

There was no sign of the other *matros* . . . assuming there *had* been another *matros*. Perhaps the man he had killed in the kitchen had been the same man he had seen on the gallery before he had entered the lighthouse. But no, that was ridiculous: the captain of the *Ivan Strashnyi* would not send only one lookout to the lighthouse; and besides, the man in the kitchen had clearly been expecting someone called Czibor. Yet Killigrew had searched every floor of the tower on his way up, and had seen only the one man; the gallery was clearly deserted, which meant there was only one place where the second *matros* could be.

In the lantern room.

And there was only one place he could be hiding.

Killigrew was already throwing himself to one side when Czibor rose up from behind the lantern, musket to his shoulder. The gun barked and the muzzle flash lit up the room as Killigrew landed on the floor and slammed against the wall below the windows. He tried to rise, but he had landed on his right side and it was difficult to push himself up while he clutched the sword in his right hand.

Czibor came around the lantern and kicked him in the wrist. The pain was excruciating. The sword flew from Killigrew's hand and clattered against the wall to fall just within reach. He grasped for it. Czibor kicked him in the side before reversing his grip on the musket. He tried to slam the stock down against Killigrew's head, but the commander rolled in the only direction there was room to go, in towards Czibor's ankles. He punched the man in the crotch, buying himself just enough time to push himself to his feet.

The *matros* grunted and swung the musket like a club, but this time Killigrew managed to catch it in both hands. The two of them grappled chest to chest, Czibor forcing Killigrew back out through the door on to the gallery, where the rain stung his face and his feet slithered on the wet platform. He felt the gallery railing hit the small of his back and instinctively let go of the musket with one hand to brace himself.

Czibor thrust the musket at his throat, forcing him back over the railing. Aware of white breakers crashing against the rocks some 120 feet below him, Killigrew felt himself toppling backwards over the railing.

XXI

Chernyovsky Meets His Match

10.00 p.m.–11.00 p.m., Friday 18 August

Molineaux and Iles paused beneath the trees some forty yards from where they could see one of the picquets at the edge of the Russian camp. Huddled against the rain, their collars turned up, the three sentries silhouetted between the tree trunks looked thoroughly miserable.

Molineaux knew how they felt. Far from providing shelter, the trees above him only channelled the rain so it dripped on him in great, fat drops. But he thanked the rain anyway, because it had driven everyone but the sentries to seek cover in one of the makeshift tents. It had also reduced visibility, and it meant that anyone trying to fire a musket was ten times more likely to get a misfire than a kill.

But it would also make it impossible to set off the gunpowder by laying a powder trail to one of the kegs.

The *Ivan Strashnyi*'s stores were stacked up on the beach about thirty yards beyond the picquet. 'Any ideas?' asked Iles.

'Yur,' said Molineaux. 'You stay here. I don't suppose you've got any string on you?'

'String? No. Us got a reel o' cotton in us 'ussif, if that be any use?'

'Ben, you're a bloody marvel. Give it here.'

Iles rummaged in his pockets and produced his hussif, handing the reel to Molineaux. 'Us ain't gettin' it back, is us?'

'If we get out of this alive, I'll buy you a cotton mill.'

Iles grinned, his teeth showing pale in the gloom. 'Not on a petty officer's pay, you ain't.'

Crawling on his belly, Molineaux slithered off through the undergrowth. His misspent youth had taught him everything there was to know about creeping and crawling silently through the blackest of nights, and he passed between two of the picquets without being spotted. Reaching the stores, he crouched between a stack of crates and some barrels. He could just make out the word 'ВОДА' stencilled on the side, whatever that meant. He was willing to bet it was not gunpowder: the barrels were too large. More likely the powder was stored in the smaller kegs further along the strand.

Using the stacks of material as cover, Molineaux dashed across to the kegs and scrunched down again. He glanced around to make sure no one had seen him: those sentries who bothered to raise their faces into the driving rain all did so towards the trees. Molineaux took a box from the adjoining stack, and crawled behind the kegs. He took down two, setting them next to each other a few inches apart, and placing the box across them to create a small shelter beneath. He reached for the box of matches Killigrew had given him, took one out, cut off the match head with his Bowie knife and discarded it. Next he unwound some of the thread from the reel Iles had given him and tied it to the matchstick.

Molineaux worked quickly, fingers nimble in spite of the numbing rain, eyes constantly glancing up on the lookout for trouble. He took down another keg of gunpowder, prised off the lid with his Bowie knife, and set it down with its open face towards the small shelter he had created. Some of the powder spilled out and immediately became soaked, but that was no matter.

Next he unslung his shotgun, unwrapping the oilcloth rag he had tied about the hammers to keep it dry, and thumbed one back without cocking it. He inserted the matchstick against the hammer to hold it back, and gently eased his hands away. The matchstick held. Hardly daring to breathe, he eased the barrels between the two kegs so that the muzzles lay in the open keg and the hammers were sheltered beneath the box. He put another keg behind the stock to brace it, and wedged the two barrels on either side of the shotgun to hold it firmly in place. Picking up the spool, he backed away, unwinding the cotton thread as he went. His feet scrunched on the shingle. One of the picquets was bound to notice him, but that did not matter: by the time they reacted, he would have reached the trees and would be far enough away from the stack of powder kegs to risk blowing it.

And then his buttocks slammed into something solid. Something that had not been there when he had looked that way to plan his escape route a few moments earlier.

He froze, then straightened slowly and turned to find himself staring up into Chernyovsky's bearded face.

Molineaux forced himself to grin. 'Hullo!' he said brightly, as if encountering an old friend.

'And what you think you do?' demanded the starshina.

Molineaux glanced back towards the stack of kegs. He was only twenty yards away . . . too close, but he would have to chance it. 'I was just wondering what the Russian for "duck" is.'

Chernyovsky knitted his brows. '*Utka?*'

Gripping the reel of cotton tightly, Molineaux threw himself flat and braced himself for the explosion.

Nothing happened.

He glanced towards the stack of kegs, and swore.

Chernyovsky reached down, grabbed him by the collar and hoisted him to his feet.

Molineaux held up his hands. 'Something was supposed to happen there.'

The Cossack smashed a fist into his face.

Killigrew found himself on the wrong side of the gallery railing, dangling by one hand, his right shoulder screaming with agony. He had dislocated it six years earlier, and now it felt as if he had almost wrenched from its socket a second time. He tried to grab hold of the rail with his other hand, but Czibor leaned over him and tried to smash the stock of his musket into his face.

Struggling to grip the slippery railing, Killigrew swung himself away from the blow, painfully conscious of the long drop to where the breakers smashed themselves furiously against the rocks below. He managed to catch hold of the railing with his other hand and hoisted himself up so he could get his feet on the platform. Czibor drew back the musket to smash the stock into his head. Killigrew swung his feet under the railing, his head dropping below the blow, the sole of his boots smashing into Czibor's kneecap. The *matros* collapsed with a scream. Killigrew swung himself back on to the platform, sobbing with relief at having something solid beneath his feet, and the railing between himself and that long, awful drop.

Czibor writhed on the platform, clutching his shattered kneecap. Killigrew grabbed him by the front of his jacket and tried to hoist him up so he could topple him over the railing, but the *matros* drew his bayonet from the frog on his belt and tried to thrust it into his side. Killigrew dropped him and twisted away, the bayonet's blade slicing through the fabric of his coat. He turned and stumbled back into the lantern room, scrabbling on the floor in the darkness for the fallen sword.

Czibor managed to haul himself to his feet, struggling to stay upright as he sought to keep the weight off his left leg, and hobbled towards the door. Killigrew forgot about the sword and turned to face him. Jumping up, he caught hold of the lintel and pulled himself up, kicking out with both legs as he did so. His boots slammed against the *matros'* chest, driving him back against the railing. Czibor toppled over and plummeted from the gallery with a scream that was whipped away by the wind.

Killigrew slammed the door against the wind and the rain and leaned against it, gasping for breath. 'Alone at last,' he muttered.

It was only a matter of time before more men came to relieve the two lookouts. Glancing through the window in the direction of the lagoon, he saw no sign of the diversion Molineaux had promised him. He tried not to worry about it: he knew the petty officer would not let him down.

He descended to the ground floor and barred the door. On his way back up to the lantern room, he paused to search the storerooms on the lower levels until he found what he was looking for: red lead paint. Tucking two of the largest brushes he could find in one pocket, he picked up two cans and carried them back up to the lantern room, where he threw the contents of one against the windows on the north, east and south sides. Then he began to spread it about, holding one brush in each hand, before daubing more paint from the second pot to cover the gaps. After his life and death struggles with the two Russians, the act of painting was oddly soothing. Soon his hands stopped shaking and he found himself whistling 'The Girl I Left Behind Me'.

When he had blacked out the windows as best he could, he collected a hurricane lamp from the living quarters. He patted himself down for his matches, and belatedly remembered he had given them to Molineaux. Well, this was a lighthouse, wasn't it? The wickies could not light the lantern with prayer. He searched about, but it was almost impossible in the darkness. Then he remembered what the first *matros* had been

425

doing when he arrived, and made his way down to the kitchen where he lit the lamp's wick with a glowing ember lifted out of the stove with a set of tongs.

He carried the lamp back up to the lantern room and examined the lantern itself. It was of the Argand type, with two tubes to blow oxygen on to the oil-fuelled wick to give a bright, clear flame with a minimum of soot. There was a parabolic mirror behind the wick, two prisms on either side, and a Fresnel lens in front to concentrate the beam. He checked the oil reservoir: empty.

He made his way down to the oil room to fetch a can, and trudged wearily back up the three flights of stairs and two ladders that led up to the lantern room. He filled the reservoir and replaced the cap.

With the windows blacked out, he had to step out into the wind and rain on the gallery to see if Molineaux had blown up the gunpowder on the beach, but all was dark in that direction. Had the petty officer let him down? Well, he was only human. But he was not the sort of man to quit: if he were still alive, he would be trying to fire those kegs.

Killigrew could no longer wait for the diversion, however. Dawn was only a few hours off, and when it came, the crews of the *Ivan Strashnyi* and the *Atalanta* would resume their search, leaving no stone unturned this time. The sooner Killigrew sent his signal, the sooner the frigate stationed off Hangö Head would come to investigate . . . assuming they could see the light on a foul night like this, and assuming their curiosity was piqued by it. Too many imponderables, too few alternatives. He took the glass flue off the hurricane lamp and used it to light the wick. The flame burned clear and bright, and the apparatus intensified it so much that Killigrew was dazzled even without his face in front of the lens.

The light was already shining in the right direction, but a winking light was more likely to catch the eye than a steady one. He descended to the watch room below and studied the mechanism. As far as he could tell, it operated on much the

426

same principle as the grandfather clock in the hallway of the family home in Falmouth. There had to be a key somewhere. He fumbled about and found it hanging from a nail on one wall. He wound the two weights up as far as they would go, then set the pendulum swinging. The apparatus whirred and grated, and he did not need to stick his head up through the hatch above to know the lantern was rotating on its chariot.

He made his way down to the living quarters and slumped into a chair. He had done all that could be done: all that was left to do was hold the lighthouse against anyone who came to investigate the beam. Even with the windows blacked out around three-quarters of the lantern room, the beam would pick out the slashing rain and be visible from the lagoon . . . or perhaps visibility was so poor, the men at the lagoon would not notice. Still, the lookouts' relief was bound to turn up sooner or later. In a while, he would make his way downstairs and plan his defence, but for now he just needed a moment to catch his breath . . .

And then the mechanism that rotated the lantern also struck the fog bell that hung in the watch room, deafening him.

Startled, he leaped clean out of the chair. It was so loud, they must have heard it on the mainland, never mind down at the lagoon.

Captain Miles Standish was dreaming of his favourite Haymarket whore when a knock on the door ripped him cruelly from her arms. He sat up in his bunk and found himself back in his cabin on board the second-class paddle-frigate HMS *Buzzard*.

'Who is it?' he yawned.

The door opened and Lieutenant Slater was silhouetted on the threshold. 'Sorry to disturb you, sir, but the lookouts have spotted a light off the port bow.'

'What sort of a light, Mr Slater?'

'A flashing light, sir.'

Standish blinked at him.

'You know, sir . . . like a lighthouse?' Slater prompted him.

'Is there a lighthouse in that direction, Mr Slater?'

'Yes, sir. I've checked the charts and there's one on the island of Jurassö, twenty-two miles west by north of our current position.'

'Mystery solved, then.' Standish turned over to go back to sleep. 'In future please be so good as to refrain from disturbing my sleep with trivialities, Mr Slater.'

The lieutenant hesitated on the threshold. 'It's just that . . . sir, none of the lighthouses on the Russian coast have been in operation since the war broke out.'

'So?'

'So why is this one on now?'

'I really couldn't say.'

'It occurred to me it might be a signal of some kind.'

Standish rolled back and blinked at him. 'What sort of a signal?'

'I don't know, sir. And – with all due respect, sir – we're not likely to find out if we don't go to investigate.'

'Admiral Napier's orders are quite specific, Mr Slater. We're to maintain position off Hangö Head, observing any shipping movements, until he sends us further orders. I have no intention of abandoning my post to go and investigate some mysterious light. Now kindly be so good as to resume your duties on deck and let me get back to sleep.'

'Aye, aye, sir.'

Chernyovsky growled something at the sentries who left their posts at the picquets to crowd round where the Cossack stood over Molineaux: the petty officer was willing to bet it was something along the lines of 'Leave him! This one's mine!'

The *matrosy* backed off. Chernyovsky drew his Cossack knife from his belt, twisting it so that the wicked blade glinted in the lights from the surrounding tents. 'I cut you up like slaughtered pig, *negr*!'

428

Still seated on his backside – where the starshina's punch had landed him – Molineaux waved him away irritably. 'Why is it you coves always have to show off?' he demanded wearily. 'For all you know, there could be a dozen of my mates watching you from the woods, getting up to all sorts of mischief that will allow us to escape, but do you think to go and take a look-see? No, you've got to start showing off your muscles, playing with your cutlery!' The petty officer put one hand down on the shingle beside him as if to push himself to his feet, then closed his fingers around a fistful of pebbles and flung them into Chernyovsky's face.

The Cossack reeled. Molineaux jumped to his feet, drawing his Bowie knife from the sheath at the small of his back. 'Oh-kay, Don Cossack: you want to play with knives? Let's play!' He lunged at Chernyovsky's face with his blade. The Cossack jerked his head aside, but the lunge had been a feint; Molineaux changed the direction of his attack at the last moment, slashing at the Cossack's wrist. But Chernyovsky parried it with his own blade.

The two of them backed off, circling. 'You've done this kind of thing before, ain't you?' Molineaux said accusingly.

Chernyovsky grinned. 'Once or twice.'

Molineaux lunged again, but this time he did not bother with a feint, slashing through one of the cartridge pouches stitched to the breast of the Cossack's tunic. He darted back quickly, but not quickly enough: Chernyovsky's riposte slashed through the fabric of his sleeve – and the shirt beneath that – to draw blood from his forearm. The petty officer gasped in shock.

The Cossack grinned. 'Or three times, even.'

The wind drove the rain into Molineaux's eyes, making him blink constantly. He could hardly see Chernyovsky, let alone strike at him. He tried to circle round so he was the one with his back to the wind instead of the Cossack. But Chernyovsky was aware of the advantage their relative positions gave them, and refused to let him pass.

In spite of the rain, more and more *matrosy* emerged from their tents to watch the fight. They cheered when Chernyovsky's blade darted forward to draw another line of blood from Molineaux's cheek. The petty officer clapped his right hand to the stinging pain.

'Why do I always end up playing against the home crowd?' he wondered out loud in an aggrieved tone. 'Some of you Ivans might cheer me, you know, just to even things up. Ain't you never heard of supporting the underdog?'

'Foolish English sentiment,' jeered Chernyovsky. 'Save your breath, *negr*: you need it to fight.'

'Save your own breath,' Molineaux retorted. He stepped in close, stabbing with the Bowie knife, but Chernyovsky's left hand clamped over his wrist, staying the blow. In the same instant, the Cossack tried to stab him in the heart, but Molineaux caught his wrist with his own left hand. The two of them struggled chest to chest. Chernyovsky had the advantage of both height and strength, and he drove Molineaux back into a marquee that had been set up as a sort of mess for the *matrosy* from the *Ivan Strashnyi*. The petty officer tripped over a chest, crashed into a table, and the two of them rolled over it. They broke apart, and when they stood up both had lost their knives.

Chernyovsky at once seized Molineaux's neck in his massive hands, and slowly began to squeeze. The petty officer drove a fist into the Cossack's stomach, without any apparent effect. He gripped Chernyovsky's wrists and tried to prise his hands away from his throat, in vain. All he could see through his swimming vision was the Cossack's leering face. He felt himself blacking out.

And at that moment the fog bell in the lighthouse tolled sonorously.

The sound made Chernyovsky glance over his shoulder, without loosening his grip on the petty officer's throat. He said something in Russian to the *matrosy* crowding behind him.

Molineaux gave up trying to prise the Cossack's hands from his throat. Feeling his legs turn to water, he fumbled for the box of matches Killigrew had given him. He managed to extract one, and struck it against the side of the box.

At the rasping of the match head, Chernyovsky turned to look at him, and glanced down in bewilderment at the match flaring between them.

Molineaux touched the flame to the gunpowder spilling from the cut cartridge pouch on Chernyovsky's breast.

The Cossack's eyes grew wide as realisation finally dawned. '*Nyet!*'

The powder flared. Molineaux flung up an arm to protect his eyes. The adjoining cartridge burst, and the one after that. Screaming in agony, Chernyovsky let go of the petty officer to beat at the cartridges that exploded across his chest like a strip of Chinese firecrackers.

Molineaux threw a fist at his jaw, spinning Chernyovsky around. He braced himself against the table behind him and kicked the Cossack firmly in the seat of his trousers, sending him staggering towards the entrance of the tent. The *matrosy* who crowded there scattered to avoid the flaming Cossack. Chernyovsky staggered across the shingle outside, tripping over to fall across one of the kegs of gunpowder, splintering it.

'Oh, *hell*!' As the first explosion shredded Chernyovsky's torso, Molineaux pushed over a table and threw himself down behind it.

The rest of the kegs exploded, filling the night with light, heat and noise. The tent was blown away from above him and a wall of hot air slammed the table against him as a roaring sound filled his ears.

As the noise faded and pieces of burning debris fell down all around him, Molineaux looked up to feel the rain against his face, reassuring him he was still alive. There were *matrosy* everywhere, some of them lying unmoving on the shingle, others staggering around with dazed expressions and

431

smouldering clothes. One of them was shouting, but no sound that Molineaux could hear came from his mouth.

Time to leave.

He picked himself up and sprinted for the trees. None of the Russians followed him: they had enough problems of their own. He thought he had made it when he slammed into a body in the shadows of the woods. He saw a burly figure standing over him, levelling a shotgun at his head.

'Ben!' he shouted. At least, he thought he shouted, but the words sounded oddly muffled inside his head.

He saw Iles' teeth flash whitely in the gloom as he answered, but could not hear him. He realised the explosion must have deafened him.

The seaman repeated the question. Molineaux shook his head and indicated his ears. 'Can't hear you! Gone deaf!'

Iles shook his head in exasperation and hauled Molineaux to his feet. The two of them fled into the night.

Colonel Nekrasoff was fast asleep in one of the cabins on board the *Atalanta* when the explosion ripped through his dream. He got up, dressed hurriedly, and made his way on deck to see the chaos and confusion ashore where burning debris littered the beach. Pechorin's gig had been lowered from its davits, and Nekrasoff could see the count being rowed ashore through the driving rain.

He grabbed Yurieff. 'What's going on?'

The lieutenant shrugged. 'There was some kind of commotion on the beach, and then there was a big explosion . . .'

Nekrasoff's hand tightened on the fabric of Yurieff's sleeve. 'Killigrew! Where's Pechorin going?'

'To investigate, I expect.'

'Get me ashore.'

Yurieff looked dubious. 'He did not say anything about letting anyone else go ashore—'

'I don't give a damn what he said or didn't say. It isn't up to him. Now get me ashore, damn you!'

One look at Nekrasoff's face convinced the lieutenant it would not be a good idea to argue further. 'Vasyutkin! The dinghy!'

Nekrasoff stood drumming his fingers on the bulwark while the sloop's dinghy was lowered from its davits. The crew rowed it round to the foot of the accommodation ladder, and Nekrasoff climbed down to take his place in the stern sheets.

On the beach, Captain Aleksandrei was trying to draw order from the chaos, commanding some of his men to re-establish the picquets and others to tidy up the mess. There was little point trying to put out the fires: the rain had all but done that already.

The two Cossacks who had rejoined the *Atalanta* with Chernyovsky at Odensö Island now stood looking forlornly at the crater where the gunpowder kegs had been stacked. 'Where's your *starshina*?' Nekrasoff demanded.

'Gone,' one of the Cossacks said mournfully.

'Gone? Gone where?'

Both raised their eyes towards the heavens, the rain hammering against their beards.

'What does that mean?' demanded Nekrasoff.

'He's dead,' said one.

'Blown up,' said the other.

'Idiot!' Nekrasoff made no attempt to make it plain whether he was talking about Chernyovsky or the Cossack who had just spoken. He whirled on his heel and looked about for Pechorin, but the count had vanished into the rain.

He approached Aleksandrei. 'Where's Pechorin?'

The captain frowned and looked about. 'I don't know. He was here a moment ago.'

'He said he would not be long,' one of the *matrosy* added.

Nekrasoff grabbed him. 'Did he say where he was going?'

'No, sir. But I think he was going to the lighthouse.'

'What makes you say that?'

'Well, he glanced towards it, said "wait here", and ran off

in that direction.' The *matros* pointed. 'He must have seen the light.'

Nekrasoff thought the *matros* was speaking metaphorically. 'Light? What light?' Then he glanced up, and through the rain he saw a faint beam emanating from where the lighthouse was, although the tower itself was invisible in the dark. Then the beam was gone, only to briefly reappear a few seconds later. Had Pechorin turned on the light? No, he had not had time. Why would he turn on the light, anyway? Why would anyone want to turn on the light, for that matter?

'You and you!' he called across to the two Cossacks. 'Come with me!'

Aleksandrei had seen the light too now. 'Perhaps I should send some more men with you?'

Nekrasoff shook his head. 'Keep your men here in case it's a diversion. Three of us should be enough to deal with whoever lit that light.'

Molineaux had recovered his hearing by the time he and Iles reached the iron foundry, and the pair of them were laughing.

'When you create a diversion, Wes, you don't muck about!' said the seaman. 'What 'appened to that macky bastard Cossack?'

Molineaux grinned. 'He finally met his match.' The petty officer glanced to where the top of the lighthouse was just visible above the trees to their right. He could see the beam of the lantern slicing through the rain each time the lens pointed to the west. 'Looks like Mr Killigrew managed to get that light on.'

'Did you ever doubt 'ee would? 'E's got us this far, din't 'ee? You know summat, Wes? For the first time since the Russkis fired on us boat at Vitsand Sound, I'se startin' to think we might just live through this business.'

They stepped through the door of the foundry, grateful to be out of the rain. The interior was as black as pitch. 'Seth?

Red?' Molineaux called into the darkness. 'You there? It's us: Wes and Ben.'

Someone struck a match and applied it to the wick of a hurricane lamp. As the yellow glow filled the large room, Molineaux saw the others huddled on the floor . . . and a dozen *matrosy* standing around them, keeping them covered with muskets.

'Think again, Ben,' he told Iles wearily.

A man in the uniform of a Russian naval lieutenant replaced the glass flue over the wick and shook out his match.

Four more *matrosy* stepped up behind Molineaux and Iles, depriving the seaman of his shotgun and tying both men's hands behind their backs.

The lieutenant stepped up to face Iles and drew a pistol from the holster on his belt, thumbing back the hammer and pressing the muzzle to the seaman's nose. 'Where is your Commander Killigrew?'

Iles made a suggestion that would not only have required unusual nimbleness and acrobatic agility on the lieutenant's part but also a complete lack of shame and self-respect. The lieutenant slashed him across the face with the pistol, the sight scoring a line of blood across the seaman's cheek. As Iles sank to his knees with his face screwed up in pain – without giving the Russians the satisfaction of hearing him cry out – the lieutenant turned to his men.

'It is no matter,' he said, in English for the benefit of the prisoners. 'There are not many places he can hide: it will be dawn in a few hours, and we will find him soon enough.' He concluded with a curt order in Russian. 'Now, get moving, all of you!' he added.

The Russians herded their prisoners to the door.

XXII

Mano a Mano

11.00 p.m.–Midnight, Friday 18 August

Killigrew was sitting on the bottom steps of the spiral staircase on the ground floor of the lighthouse when he heard footsteps approaching the door.

As soon as he had recovered from the shock of the fog bell tolling, he had scrambled up the ladder into the watch room to stop it from ringing by taking off one of his kid gloves and pulling it over the clapper; but by then the damage had been done.

He had found the musket in the kitchen and loaded it from the dead *matros'* cartouche box. Now he picked it up and levelled it down the passage at the door, waiting, ready to sell his life dearly. The longer the light stayed on, the greater the chance that someone on board the frigate stationed off Hangö Head would notice it. Even if his own life was forfeit, at least he could do everything in his power to make sure the others had a chance to escape; not that that was much.

The footsteps stopped right outside the lighthouse door, and he heard someone try the doorknob. He slipped a finger through the trigger guard of the musket and braced the stock against his shoulder. Why the hell had he decided to come here alone? He should have brought Hughes, Fuller, O'Leary and Yorath with him: then the two *matrosy* would not have given him nearly as much trouble, and the five of them would have been able to defend the lighthouse much longer than he could hope to alone.

The footsteps retreated, then returned at a run. The door shuddered as someone threw his shoulder against it.

Killigrew remembered what Strachan had told him in the Arctic, what seemed like a lifetime ago: 'Always got to be the hero, haven't you?' And it was true, he had to admit to himself. He could tell himself that it was all part of being a naval officer; but it had been his choice to join the navy, and anything he might say about being from a long line of naval officers was all a load of gammon. He loved his job: the paperwork was a bore, and asinine superiors could be a headache, but it was worth putting up with those minor irritations for the excitement, the danger . . .

The man outside threw his shoulder against the door a second time, and again it held.

. . . for moments like this.

Killigrew smiled in the darkness. This was what being a hero was all about: even if he lived to tell the tale, the events of the past few days were unlikely to merit more than a couple of lines at the bottom of the 'Naval Intelligence' column in *The Times*, but he was not in it for the glory. The moment . . . that was the thing. Live for the moment. After all, it might well be his last.

But not if he could help it.

The door burst open on the third attempt. Killigrew sighted carefully at the figure silhouetted on the threshold, but even as he squeezed the trigger the man threw himself flat on the floor.

Killigrew caught his breath. Was the man dead? He took a cartridge from the cartouche box, but before he could tear it open and empty it into the musket, the man on the floor called out to him.

'Is that you, Killigrew?'

'Pechorin?'

'I had hoped it would end this way: just you and I, *mano a mano*. By the way, you can stop reloading that musket. You are reloading, aren't you? I'm afraid I can't see too well in this light, but there are six rounds in my revolver, and if I empty them all in your direction I think I can be reasonably confident that at least one bullet will hit you.'

'What makes you think I'm not armed with a revolver?'

'Give me some credit! I know the difference between a musket and a revolver when I hear one.'

'Really? I'm always impressed when someone can hear a shot and tell me exactly what make of gun it was. Speaking for myself, I can't tell a shotgun from a pocket pistol. What makes you think I haven't got a second musket primed and loaded?'

'If you had, you'd have fired it already. Even a runner-up in the East Falmouth Junior Pistol Shooting Championship of 1835 couldn't miss at this range.' Pechorin stood up. Killigrew could see he was not lying about having a revolver.

'So, where does that leave us?'

'At the bottom of a lighthouse that's light is on when it should be off. I'd be grateful if you'd help me alter that situation.'

'And supposing I say no?'

'Then I'll have to shoot you. Not very sporting, I know, but there is rather more at stake here than our rivalry.'

'What rivalry? We have no rivalry, Pechorin.'

'I beg to differ. Now, up the stairs you go like a good boy. And please remember that my revolver is lined up on your back.'

Killigrew turned wearily and ascended the steps once again. Both of them were out of breath by the time they reached the living quarters. Killigrew was about to climb the ladder to the watch room when Pechorin stopped him.

'Ah, no, I think this is far enough.'

'The mechanism that controls the light is on the next floor up.'

'Yes, and you go up first and slam that trap door on my head as I try to follow. I think not.'

'You can't blame a chap for trying. Now what? Do you want to go up first?'

Pechorin smiled, and shook his head. 'An interesting situation, is it not?' he said, crossing to the small window without taking the revolver off Killigrew. 'For obvious reasons, you want the light to stay on; I want it off. We both have a good deal at stake. I think this gives you sufficient incentive.' He opened the window with his free hand. A blast of cold air and rain howled through. Pechorin tossed the revolver out.

'Intriguing!' said Killigrew.

'I see you have your own sword.'

'Something I picked up along the way.'

'You know how to use it?'

'You're the one who's the fencing champion of all the Russias.'

'Afraid?'

'A tad apprehensive, yes.'

'Come now, Mr Killigrew. You may act all modest, but I've a sneaking suspicion you're a little more skilled at fencing than you're prepared to admit. This is good: where would be the challenge, if you were not?'

'I'm not getting out of this, am I?'

Smiling, Pechorin shook his head.

'Very well,' sighed Killigrew. 'Just give me a chance to catch my breath. I've been up and down those stairs a dozen times tonight—'

Abruptly, he lunged across the room and caught Pechorin in a rugby tackle without giving him the chance to draw the sabre. The two of them slammed back against the wall and fell to the floor, grappling as they rolled across the boards. Pechorin rolled on top. Killigrew managed to draw his legs up between them and, placing them squarely against the

Russian's chest, he catapulted him back across the room. Pechorin turned to brace himself against the wall and stood there, gasping, while Killigrew picked himself up.

'You fight dirty, Mr Killigrew.' Pechorin put one hand on the hilt of his sabre. 'But you will die like a gentleman, even if you cannot fight like one.'

Drawing the sabre, he whirled.

In time to see Killigrew's feet disappear through the hatch into the watch room above.

Pechorin swore and scrambled up after him, pausing at the top of the ladder to thrust his sabre up through the hatchway in case Killigrew was waiting to slam the hatch down on him. But Killigrew had already clambered up the next ladder in the lantern room.

' "You will die like a gentleman, even if you cannot fight like one".' Somewhere above Pechorin, Killigrew mocked the Russian's accent. 'This is the nineteenth century, Count: no one talks like that any more. Frankly, I don't believe they ever did, outside of romance novels, and I suspect you're guilty of reading one too many.'

Snarling with rage, Pechorin flung himself up the second ladder. As his head emerged through the hatch, Killigrew slammed the cover down on him. Pechorin dropped his sabre and fell to the floor below, clutching his head.

'Seems you were right about me slamming the trap door on you,' said Killigrew. 'Sorry about that.'

Pechorin ascended the ladder again, this time thrusting his sabre through the hatch and throwing the cover clear before climbing up into the lantern room. He gazed about, averting his gaze as the lantern's beam swept over him. There was no sign of Killigrew in the room, which meant he had to be outside on the gallery; the light reflecting off the glass on all sides made it impossible to see out even where the panes had not been painted over. Pechorin reached for the door handle.

Killigrew dropped down from where he had been clinging to the iron stanchions that supported the cupola. Pechorin staggered under his weight, and the commander hooked an arm around his neck.

'Drop the cutlery, Count, or I'll break your neck.'

With a roar, Pechorin launched himself backwards. Killigrew was smashed against the glass behind him, once, twice, three times . . . the panes of glass shattered, but the astragals held firm, preventing the two men from toppling out on to the gallery. The wind and rain howled through. Pechorin broke free of Killigrew's grip, slashing at him with the sabre. The commander dived to the floor, performing a forward roll around the side of the rotating lantern. He rose to his feet so the lantern was between him and Pechorin. The beam hit the count full in the face, forcing him to avert his gaze. Killigrew drew his sword and lunged, but Pechorin recovered quickly and parried with ease. As the beam swung round towards the commander, he dived for the door and tugged it open.

The shrieking wind hit him like a solid wall, and he would have staggered back on to the point of Pechorin's sabre if the shock of the icy blast had not stunned the count as well. Killigrew forced himself out on to the gallery, whirling sword in hand to face the door. The rain still slashed down, slicing through his greatcoat, and lightning rent the sky, each flicker accompanied by a crash of thunder.

The beam dazzled him again, and Pechorin chose that moment to lunge through the door. Killigrew barely managed to sidestep in time. The count slipped on the rain-washed platform and skidded against the railings, almost losing his grip on his sabre as he reached out to brace himself against the handrail. Killigrew slashed at his neck, but Pechorin got his own blade up in time to parry, driving the commander back with a counter-thrust.

Spreading their feet, leaning into the wind that whipped their hair about their heads, Killigrew and Pechorin faced one another, sword-point to sword-point. Pechorin performed a *balestra*, lunging forward to thrust at Killigrew's chest. The commander parried, but the thrust was a feint, and Pechorin followed through with a *remise*. Killigrew parried awkwardly, and the count's blade slashed through the fabric of his greatcoat, drawing blood from his side. He tried to riposte while Pechorin was still close, but the count responded with a counter-riposte that forced the commander to twist away. Pechorin sprang back, grinning.

He's actually enjoying this, the bastard! thought Killigrew.

The commander did not wait to let Pechorin get his breath back, using a nimble *flèche* to bring himself close in to the count, thrusting at his face. Pechorin parried, but when Killigrew's thrust proved to be another feint, the count was waiting for it and parried the *redoublément* effortlessly before following up with his riposte. Killigrew counter-riposted, and sprang back.

The two of them fenced back and forth around the outside of the lantern room, feeling one another out, looking for the patterns in each other's style, the set-pieces that could be anticipated and turned against their opponents. Killigrew much preferred fencing to shooting – any fool could point a gun and pull the trigger – but fencing was about brains as much as skill, trying to anticipate one's opponent, thinking three of four moves ahead. He had a slight advantage here, for he had already watched Pechorin fence in the duel with Lord Dallaway. Perhaps he had suspected it might come to this sooner or later, which was why he had been so keen for the match to take place, never dreaming that it would end with Dallaway's death.

But fencing was not much fun against an opponent who was clearly more skilled than he was, and if their sparring now taught him one thing, it was that he was clearly outclassed by the Russian.

'You *are* good,' Pechorin acknowledged with a grin, shouting to make himself heard above the wind and the thunder. The two of them closed, swords crossed between them, faces inches apart. 'I'm glad to find your skill with the blade exceeds your skill with the pistol. You should not hide your qualifications under a bushel.'

'In that case, perhaps I should warn you about my other sporting accolade,' Killigrew shouted back, the rail behind him hard against his spine.

'Oh?' Pechorin forced him steadily backwards until his feet barely touched the platform. 'And what is that?'

Killigrew brought his forehead down sharply against the bridge of Pechorin's nose. As the Russian staggered back, the commander kicked him squarely in the crotch.

'Dirtiest fighter in the Royal Navy, eighteen fifty-four.'

Pechorin doubled up in agony, but still had presence of mind enough to slash at Killigrew with his blade. The commander evaded the wild cut with ease, but had to grab the rail with his left hand as his feet slipped on the platform.

'Have you no honour?' Pechorin hacked at his head, and Killigrew barely brought his sword up in time to parry. The force of the blow was enough to jar his right arm.

'You make a lot of noise about honour and being a gentleman, for a man who was trying to blow an unarmed ship carrying two women out of the water earlier today.'

'Nekrasoff's orders, not mine.' Pechorin swung again, and again Killigrew barely managed to parry it. 'Make it easy on yourself, Commander. I promise you a swift death.'

'And what about the Bullivants? Will you give them a swift death, too?'

Pechorin slashed again. 'I do not make war on women.'

Killigrew parried. 'Nekrasoff does. What do you think he's going to do with them, if you kill me?'

'I shall deal with Nekrasoff after I have dealt with you.' Pechorin launched into a series of brilliantly executed thrusts and cuts, driving Killigrew back around the gallery. 'Where are you going, Commander? You cannot run for ever!'

'I don't intend to! I've got bad news for you, Pechorin: don't you know the villain always loses?'

Pechorin smiled, and forced Killigrew to duck with a swing aimed at his neck. 'That's only in those romance novels you were talking about earlier. Anyhow, what makes you think *I'm* the villain? Yours is the country supporting a backward, heathen state that butchers innocent Christians by the thousand.'

Killigrew parried Pechorin's next cut and tried to follow up by slipping under his guard, but the count twisted aside. 'Turkey may not have the most enlightened regime in the world, but that doesn't give Russia the right to invade the Ottoman Empire! International disputes need a congress of nations to decide things peacefully, not unilateral action by an Empire scarcely less backward and autocratic than the Turks'!'

Pechorin slashed a rent across the breast of Killigrew's greatcoat. 'Cowards talk while heroes act!'

'No, Count: heroes think before they act; only cowards bully smaller nations!' Sick of being on the defensive, Killigrew launched into a set piece of his own, driving an astonished Pechorin back the other way around the gallery. 'Besides, do you really think the Tsar plans to replace the Sultan with a more enlightened regime? Or will he set up a puppet state to expand the Russian Empire even further, and take control of the Bosphorus?'

'History will judge us.' Pechorin finally managed to stand his ground, and no matter how many feints and thrusts Killigrew tried, he could not penetrate the web of steel the Russian wove between them.

Killigrew was gasping for breath. His arms ached with the exertion of this prolonged bout, and the weariness accumulated over the past couple of days was catching up with him with a vengeance. He remembered his old fencing instructor's advice on what to do when faced by a clearly superior opponent: the straight thrust. No feint: any skilled fencer always made his initial thrust a feint, before launching into the reprise, *remise* or *redoublément*; and any skilled opponent was ready for the feint.

'God will judge you, Pechorin! And I intend to see to it he gets a chance to do so at the earliest opportunity!'

He thrust. No feint: a straight thrust to the heart, unwavering, unstoppable.

Pechorin brushed the thrust aside with a bored expression, and then lunged, pinking Killigrew in one shoulder.

The commander staggered back with a gasp of shock. He sank to his knees, one hand on the handle of the open door to the lantern room for support, the blade of his sword touching the platform as if he was too weak even to lift it any more. He felt another wave of dizziness sweep over him. *Oh Christ, not now,* he thought desperately. *Dear God, let me stay conscious just a few moments longer . . .*

The count smiled triumphantly. 'You're finished. Credit where credit is due: you were a worthy opponent. But the game is ended. Goodbye, Mr Killigrew.'

Pechorin lunged, thrusting the blade at the commander's throat.

Killigrew pulled the door away from the side of the lantern room, using it to shield him from the thrust. The tip of the sabre scraped against the glass. Killigrew slammed the door, trapping the blade. Pechorin tugged at the hilt, but his sabre was firmly caught between door and jamb. Realising he had been outmanoeuvred, he stared at Killigrew in horror.

'You know what they say, Count,' the commander told him. 'As one door closes . . .' He thrust the point of his sword deep into Pechorin's stomach. '. . . another one opens.'

The count stared down at the wound in shock and disbelief, and then raised his eyes to meet Killigrew's. The commander twisted the blade and withdrew it.

Pechorin crumpled. Letting go of his trapped sabre, he slumped against the railing. He tried to push himself up, but his legs gave way and he fell, slipping under the railing to plunge into the night.

Killigrew leaned on the rail and gazed down to where he saw the count's broken body sprawled on the spume-washed rocks below. He opened the door once more – Pechorin's sabre clattered on the platform – and staggered into the lantern room. He found an oily rag and used it to wipe the blood from his own blade before he slotted it back into its scabbard. Then he clambered gingerly down the ladder to the watch room below. As his feet touched the floor, someone touched him on the back of the neck with something cold and metallic. He turned and found himself staring down the barrel of Nekrasoff's revolver. The colonel was flanked by two of Chernyovsky's Cossacks, who levelled their carbines at the commander.

Nekrasoff smiled broadly, and hit him on the temple with the pistol's grip. Killigrew saw the colonel's face waver, and then the floor was rushing up to meet him, and the light finally went out.

XXIII

No Witnesses

Saturday 19 August

The following morning dawned bright and clear, the sun shining once more, the previous night's storm little more than a half-remembered dream. After a brief conference with Aleksandrei involving much angry gesticulation but which nevertheless ended with the captain turning away in disgust to wash his hands of the business, Nekrasoff marched the fifteen prisoners away from the lagoon, with an escort of two dozen of the *Atalanta*'s *matrosy* armed with muskets, under the command of one of the lieutenants from the *Ivan Strashnyi*. Iles and Hughes carried Endicott between them on the litter.

The Russians herded the prisoners through the woods at the centre of the island to the south coast, not far from where the fugitives had landed the previous morning. They were made to stand in a row, spaced a few feet apart, and three of the *matrosy* passed along the line with bundles of spades, handing them one each. Not a good sign, Killigrew could not help thinking.

'Dig,' ordered Nekrasoff.

'I beg your pardon?' spluttered Lord Bullivant.

'You heard me: dig!'

'I'm the thirteenth Viscount Bullivant! I do not dig!'

The lieutenant stepped up to the aristocrat and pistol-whipped him. Bullivant sank to his knees with blood running between his fingers.

'Dig!'

'Why should I?' sobbed the viscount. 'You're going to murder us anyway.'

'Better later than sooner,' Lady Bullivant said pragmatically, and started to dig with little ability and less enthusiasm.

'What are we supposed to be digging?' asked Araminta. 'Some kind of ditch?'

Killigrew gave her a look.

'Oh!' She blanched when realisation finally dawned.

Killigrew attacked the soil with the spade as viciously as he would have liked to attack Nekrasoff. The anguish of having come so far only to fall at the final hurdle was like a knife in his guts.

'Twenty-six of them, fifteen of us,' observed Molineaux, digging next to Killigrew. 'Reckon we could take a few of the bastards with us, sir.'

'Not yet, Molineaux: something may yet turn up.'

'Gotta be a way we can get them in closer,' the petty officer muttered out of the corner of his mouth. 'Maybe if I pretend we've dug up some buried pirate treasure . . .'

'No tricks!' barked Nekrasoff.

As they dug, Hughes began to sing 'Rule, Britannia'. His voice sounded cracked and hoarse, and yet soon all the other prisoners joined in: apart from 'Rule, Britannia! Britannia rule the waves; Britons never, never, never will be slaves,' none of them knew the words, so they sang that couplet over and over again, drawing strength from one another in what none of them doubted was their final hour.

Nekrasoff marched up and down the line, inspecting their handiwork. 'Enough!' he told Molineaux, who in spite of his efforts to delay had dug a pit deep enough to contain a body.

'Help her.' He indicated Araminta, who was making heavy weather of the task. Presently Killigrew was ordered to help Dahlstedt, who was struggling even to hold the spade with his bandaged hands, and Hughes was ordered to help Lord Bullivant.

Within an hour, the graves were dug, each of them standing on the lip of one with their backs to the sea, while the *matrosy* moved behind them, aiming their muskets at the back of the prisoners' heads.

Killigrew turned to face his own would-be executioner. 'If you're going to kill me, at least have the sand to look me in the face when you pull the trigger.'

The *matros* did not look happy about that, so Nekrasoff pushed him aside and drew his revolver from inside his coat, levelling it at the commander's forehead. 'With pleasure. I'm going to enjoy killing you, Killigrew.' He lowered the revolver's muzzle, aiming at the commander's throat, his chest, his stomach. 'You're going to spend a long time dying, Commander. Any last words?'

'Yes: "Look behind you".'

Nekrasoff threw back his head and laughed. 'Now really, Commander! Is that the best you can do? After the resourcefulness you've shown thus far, I'd expected better of you.'

The Russian lieutenant had turned ashen. 'I think you should do as he says, sir.'

Nekrasoff frowned, and backed away from Killigrew before glancing over his shoulder.

A frigate was sailing around the next headland, less than a cable's length from the shore, the French *tricolore* flying from her mainmast.

Killigrew smiled. 'No witnesses, you said?'

Seeing the French ship, one of the *matrosy* broke. Slinging his musket from his shoulder, he ran past the prisoners towards the trees.

'Come back here, you coward!' The lieutenant levelled his pistol and fired, but the shot went wide. The running man just

449

redoubled his efforts. The lieutenant snatched a musket from one of the other men. Molineaux launched himself at the Russian before he could fire and threw him down on the ground. While the two of them grappled, rolling over and over, the rest of the *matrosy* panicked and began to run to the trees. Four of them covered less than a few yards before they were brought down by Hughes, Fuller, Iles and O'Leary, who snatched up their spades to go on the attack.

Killigrew was still staring down the barrel of Nekrasoff's revolver. 'It's over, Colonel,' he said softly.

'For you, it is,' agreed Nekrasoff, and began to squeeze the trigger.

Araminta caught him around the waist in a flying tackle that would not have disgraced William Webb Ellis. As Nekrasoff squeezed the trigger, Killigrew felt the bullet sough past his ear. Araminta sank her teeth into the colonel's wrist. He screamed and dropped the revolver, then punched her on the jaw and broke free, rising to his feet to run after the others.

Killigrew dropped to his knees and took her in his arms. 'Minty! Are you all right?'

'Do I look as if I'm all right?' she snapped back. 'That brute punched me!'

He could have laughed with relief. 'You stupid ninny! You almost got yourself killed!'

'Well, I like that!' she protested indignantly. 'I just saved your life!'

'So you did.' He took her head in his hands and planted a big kiss on her astonished lips, before grabbing Nekrasoff's revolver and rising to his feet. The colonel was already out of range, disappearing into the trees. Molineaux sat astride the Russian lieutenant and was slowly but surely throttling him with the musket the lieutenant had taken from one of his men. Lord Bullivant had waded knee-deep into the surf and was waving frantically at the French frigate. He need not have bothered: a swift glance assured Killigrew that the ship had already dropped anchor and was lowering boats into the

450

water. Matelots and marines armed to the teeth were shinning down the lifelines.

Killigrew grabbed Dahlstedt. 'When they get here, tell them to circle around the island and head off the *Atalanta*, before she escapes!'

'A sailing frigate against a paddle-sloop? They'll be lucky: the *Atalanta* already had steam up when they marched us away from the lagoon. The French ship will never catch her.'

'It's got to be worth a try. At least they'll get the *Ivan Strashnyi*.'

'Where are you going?'

'After Nekrasoff.' Killigrew sprinted across to the trees. He heard Dahlstedt crying out after him, but turned a deaf ear.

He ran through the trees, his exhaustion forgotten. There was no room in his heart for elation at knowing that, whatever else might happen, the Bullivants and what was left of their crew were safe now: all that mattered was catching the man who had tried so hard and so ruthlessly to eliminate them all. No one knew better than Killigrew that violence was not always the answer, but there were some men who were beyond redemption, beyond any kind of rehabilitation; men so steeped in villainy it was impossible to punish them proportionately for their crimes. There was only one thing for such men: if nothing else, a bullet in the brain would at least prove their executioners had enough mercy left in them to provide a cleaner and quicker death than they deserved. Nekrasoff was just such a man, and Killigrew was in no doubt that he could perform mankind no greater service than to exterminate the Third Section colonel once and for all.

He was halfway through the woods when a fusillade rang out ahead of him. Bullets whipped through the undergrowth as a great cloud of smoke billowed from the *matrosy*'s muskets. He threw himself flat amongst the bracken, cursing his folly for failing to anticipate that Nekrasoff would leave a rearguard to hold off any pursuit. As the Russians reloaded, Killigrew crawled through the undergrowth on his belly, trying to outflank his ambushers. It seemed to take forever to get into an advantageous position, and all the while Nekrasoff was getting further and further away.

Just when he thought he had covered enough ground to slip past the Russians and make his way down to the lagoon, he heard a twig snap behind him. He rolled on his back to see one of the *matrosy* standing a few feet away, his musket already levelled. Killigrew brought up the revolver, but too slow. A musket barked, and the sunlight dappling the forest floor sliced the gun smoke that bloomed between the trees into golden shafts. The commander and the Russian stared at one another, and then the blood ran down the hole in the *matros'* forehead and he keeled over to reveal that the back of his head had been blown off.

Killigrew twisted and saw two men standing off to his left, both levelling rifled muskets: one with smoke curling from the muzzle, the other pointed at the commander. Recognising the hooped guernseys and bonnets of matelots of *la Royale*, he dropped the revolver and threw up his hand. '*Ami, ami! Je suis un officier de la marine britannique!*'

'*C'est un anglais!*' one of the matelots exclaimed in surprise, and as the other hauled Killigrew to his feet he saw two dozen more matelots advancing through the trees to engage the Russians. The woods became noisy with the rattle of musketry, and soon the air was thick with the sulphurous reek of gun smoke. The skirmish was short and one-sided: realising they were massively outnumbered and their smooth-bore muskets were no match for the French rifles, the Russians turned and fled back to the lagoon.

Some of the matelots made to go after them, but their officer called them back and ordered his men to reform. More matelots were tramping through the trees from the beach on the south side of the island, and those men who had fired their muskets reloaded.

The French officer took advantage of the lull in the battle to interrogate Killigrew. 'Who are you?'

'Commander Christopher Killigrew, HMS *Ramillies*, at your service.'

'It's oh-kay, monsewer!' called Molineaux, running up with the matelots, musket in hand. 'He's with us.'

The French officer nodded and proffered a hand. 'Lieutenant Henri Halévy of the *Scaramouche*.' He indicated Molineaux. 'This man tells me there is a Russian two-decker in the lagoon. This is true?'

Killigrew nodded. 'The *Ivan Strashnyi*, but she's going nowhere. It's the paddle-sloop *Atalanta* I'm worried about: she'll get away, if we don't hurry.'

'*Alors!*' Halévy waved his men forward with his revolver, and Killigrew took a musket from a dead Russian as the matelots advanced through the trees once more.

News of the *Scaramouche*'s arrival off the south coast had reached the Russian camp, so that by the time Killigrew and Molineaux charged out of the trees with the matelots, only a handful of the *Ivan Strashnyi*'s crew were prepared to put up a token resistance. Of the remainder, half were wading or swimming in a vain attempt to catch the *Atalanta* as she gathered way, steaming out of the lagoon, while the rest sat disconsolately on the shingle, waiting to be taken prisoner. From the look of it, some of the *Ivan Strashnyi*'s officers had boarded the *Atalanta* to escape, but Captain Aleksandrei had refused to abandon his crippled command. As the matelots surrounded the men on the beach, covering them with their rifles, Aleksandrei came forward to proffer his sword hilt-first to Lieutenant Halévy.

Seeing the French had everything well in hand as far as the crew of the *Ivan Strashnyi* was concerned, Killigrew sprinted along the rocky shore until he was able to bound up on to a large boulder overlooking the mouth of the lagoon. The *Atalanta* was already moving out to sea, but she was still less than a hundred yards away, close enough for Killigrew to make out Nekrasoff standing with his back to him on the quarterdeck.

He brought the musket up to his shoulder, took careful aim – remembering to make allowance for the crosswind – and pulled the trigger.

The hammer fell with a dull snap.

Killigrew was mortified. He thumbed back the hammer and fired again, but again the percussion cap failed to ignite the powder charge. Seeing his quarry escape him, he threw the musket down in rage and frustration. When he looked up at the paddle-sloop, he saw that Nekrasoff had seen him – and recognised him – and was waving a mocking farewell from the taffrail.

Killigrew heard heavy breathing behind him. He twisted to see Molineaux climbing up the boulder to join him, carrying a rifled musket. 'Is that thing loaded?'

Gasping for breath, Molineaux shook his head.

The commander clenched his fists at the sides and glowered after the *Atalanta* as she steamed away from the island, heading back towards the Finnish coast. There was still no sign of the *Scaramouche*.

'The bastard's getting away!'

Molineaux put a hand on his shoulder. 'Never mind, sir. You can't win 'em all.'

Killigrew shrugged his hand off irritably.

'Anyhow, reckon we did beat him,' said the petty officer.

'And just how do you work that out?'

'We got the *Ivan Strashnyi* . . . or the Frogs did, at any rate, thanks to us. And we're still alive, ain't we? And the Bullivants too.'

'And what about the ones who didn't make it, Molineaux? Todd, Mackenzie, Attwood, Burgess, Ogilby and Searle? All dead, because of Nekrasoff. Beating him isn't enough: I want to know this world has been cleansed by his death.'

'Maybe the Tsar will do the job for you. His superiors will be none too pleased about the way he let us escape. Even if they don't scrag him, all he's got to look forward to is a prolonged holiday in the Siberian salt mines.'

'Not that swine. His kind always finds a way to wriggle out of trouble.'

The petty officer nodded soberly. 'Reckon we ain't heard the last of him, then?'

Killigrew shook his head.

'Good.' Molineaux shouldered his musket. 'That means we'll get another shot at the bastard.'

There was not room on board the *Scaramouche* for all the Russian prisoners, so Capitaine Meilhac settled for taking Captain Aleksandrei and his remaining officers on board, and a token three dozen of his *matrosy*.

'We cannot afford to have the prisoners on board outnumbering the crew!' Lieutenant Halévy explained to Killigrew as they prepared to climb into the last two boats to row out to the frigate. Dahlstedt and Endicott had already been sent on board the *Scaramouche* with Hughes, Iles, Thornton, Uren, Fuller, O'Leary and Yorath, and were having their wounds tended by the frigate's surgeon.

'This island is as effective a prison as any we can provide,' Halévy continued. 'I doubt the Russians will risk sending any more ships this way before we can return with a couple of transports to pick them all up. As for you and your companions, we should be joining the rest of the fleet before nightfall; you'll be back on board your ship in time for supper.'

'You couldn't make it a little later, could you?' asked Killigrew. 'Even in the wardroom, the food on board the *Ramillies* leaves a lot to be desired, and I've always had a fondness for French cuisine.'

Halévy grinned. 'I'll have a word with *mon capitaine.*'

'We owe you our lives,' said Lady Bullivant. 'It is most fortunate you saw Mr Killigrew's signal.'

The Frenchman frowned. 'Signal? What signal?'

Killigrew's jaw dropped. 'You mean . . . you didn't see the light in the lighthouse?'

Halévy shook his head. 'We just happened to be passing,

that is all. We chanced to spy some figures on the coast of an island supposed to be uninhabited, and came to investigate . . . what is so funny?'

Killigrew had thrown back his head and was laughing heartily.

'I'm glad you find it so amusing,' Lord Bullivant said sourly. 'You'll be laughing on the other side of your face when Lord Aberdeen hears of the disgraceful way you and your men conducted yourselves. And someone's going to pay for the destruction of the *Milenion*—'

'Rodney?' interrupted Lady Bullivant.

'Yes, m'dear?'

'Do put a sock in it, there's a good fellow.' She steered her husband towards one of the boats.

As the matelots pushed it out through the surf, Killigrew realised that Araminta was still on the shore. 'Aren't you going with your parents?'

She shook her head. 'I'd rather go with you.'

Killigrew grinned, and crooked his elbow so she could slip an arm through it. Along with Halévy, Molineaux and Nicholls, they made their way down to the remaining boat.

In the stern sheets, Molineaux sat next to the maid on the thwart in front of Killigrew and Araminta.

'Makes a nice change, to have someone else rowing *me* for a change!' the petty officer remarked. 'Now, what would you do in this situation, sir?' He pretended to notice Nicholls sitting next to him for the first time. 'Ah, that's it!' He slipped an arm around the maid's waist and drew her to him, kissing her passionately. She tried to push him away, then abandoned the pretence and let herself enjoy it. The matelots pulling at the oars cheered them.

'Nicholls!' hissed Araminta. 'There are people watching!'

Molineaux broke off the kiss with a scowl, and turned to address Killigrew. 'Begging your pardon, sir, but you couldn't follow my lead, could you? Reckon it's the only way to choke her luff . . . sir? Sir!'

456

The commander had keeled over backwards and sprawled on the bottom boards, unconscious.

Halévy felt for a pulse in his neck, and then prised up one of the commander's eyelids. 'Out like the light,' he said. 'But he lives: he has merely passed out. Exhaustion, I expect, poor devil.'

Nicholls fumbled in her pockets. 'I've got some hartshorn, if you want to try to revive him.'

Molineaux placed a hand firmly on her arm. 'Let 'im sleep. He's earned it.'

Afterword

The war that subsequently became known as the 'Crimean' War was anything but. At the time – and for a few years afterwards – it was known simply as 'The Russian War'. It is remembered as the 'Crimean' War because that is where the British and French armies focused their activities after they landed there in the autumn of 1854 (having already fought a desultory campaign of sorts in the Balkans) and it was in the Crimea that the best remembered episodes of the war – Inkerman, the Alma, the Charge of the Light Brigade at Balaklava, and the siege of Sebastopol – took place.

But if the British army focused its attention on the Crimea, the Royal Navy attacked the Russian coasts wherever it could reach them. The navy's fleets were active not only in the Black Sea and the Baltic but also in the White Sea, as well as the Pacific, where an attack on Petropavlovsky was thrown into confusion when the rear admiral commanding the Pacific squadron, David Price, committed suicide in his cabin moments before the attack was due to take place.

It was in the Baltic, however, that Britain's hopes for a swift conclusion to the war were focused. The Russian capital, St Petersburg, was the prize, lying at the eastern end of the Gulf of Finland. It was never taken: the maritime fortress of Kronstadt barred the way. The Baltic Campaign proved to be the climax – or rather, the anti-climax – of Vice-Admiral Sir Charles Napier's long and adventurous, if not always distinguished, career. His orders were simple: to prevent the Russian fleet from escaping into the North Sea, and to 'look into the possibility of doing something in the Åland Islands'. He followed these instructions to the letter, the 'something' he did in the Åland Islands being to mastermind their capture, with the invaluable assistance of the French.

But so much more was expected of a man with Napier's reputation for exceeding his orders. When he did not attempt to reduce Kronstadt and capture St Petersburg, the British public soon became disillusioned with its hero, and turned on him at the prompting of the Admiralty, which needed a scapegoat and found one in Dirty Charlie. It is true that Napier enjoyed poor relations with his subordinates – never a useful quality in a military commander – and that by 1854 he was well into his sixties and had lost his former verve. But one cannot help but be disappointed by Keppel and other senior captains of the fleet who wrote letters home to the press, criticising Napier behind his back for his lack of boldness. To some extent Napier made a rod for his own back before the war started by boasting of how much he hoped to achieve, although as war drew closer he began to warn people not to expect too much. Did Keppel – an otherwise brave, able, intelligent and humane man – really think that an attack on Kronstadt was feasible with the vessels at Napier's disposal, or was he merely motivated by long-standing dislike of his former captain?

Indeed, *was* an attack on Kronstadt feasible in 1854? Nelson would have been horrified by the suggestion that wooden ships be pitted against granite-faced shore batteries, but Nelson never had the benefit of steam-driven ships. Napier was not to know that the Russian guns at Kronstadt were hopelessly outdated, or that Russian gunnery was so poor – nor was Keppel, for that matter – but in spite of these, Kronstadt was a strong fortress; stronger than Sveaborg, which was bombarded the following summer, and certainly stronger than incomplete Bomarsund. Even with their poor gunnery and obsolete cannon, the Russian batteries at Kronstadt might have wrought terrible damage amongst deep-draughted Allied ships struggling to manoeuvre without accurate charts in the shoals surrounding the fortress.

As 1854 wore on, Napier wrote to the Admiralty explaining that it might be possible to attack Sveaborg, but not without gunboats and mortar vessels. The First Lord of the Admiralty, Sir James Graham, wrote back instructing him to make the attack, but refusing to commission the gunboats and mortar-vessels he needed. Graham was looking ahead, convinced that after Russia was beaten Britain would find itself at war with its then ally, France, and he did not want to waste money on gunboats and mortar-vessels when the navy should be building ships of the line to meet the French threat. Both Graham and Napier were caught between the rock of British public opinion and the hard place of the Russian batteries: an attack on Kronstadt or Sveaborg might well have resulted in the destruction of a great part of the British fleet, but a failure to attack would lead to outrage at home. Instead of supporting his former friend, Graham passed the buck to Napier, leaving the decision in his hands. There was really only one choice Napier could make: not to attack. On his return to Britain in December 1854, he was effectively dismissed, with the implication that he was a coward, and thus he ended his career with his reputation in undeserved tatters. Only lately have naval historians begun to reassess his abilities: Napier was no Nelson, but he was perhaps one of the best admirals Britain had in the Crimean War, and certainly better than the man who replaced him, Richard Saunders Dundas.

Pioneered by Samuel Hahnemann in the first half of the nineteenth century, homeopathic medicine is much older than most people realise. Pyroglycerin – which has a number of different chemical names, but is today best known as nitro-glycerine – was invented by the Italian chemist Ascanio Sobrero in 1846. Tested by Drs Hering, Davies and Jeanes at the Hahnemann Medical School in Philadelphia, it was recommended for treating a number of diseases, and used by homeopathic practitioners to cure headaches, toothache and neuralgia.

Perhaps the most intriguing phenomenon of the Crimean War – and indeed of warfare of the mid-nineteenth century as a whole – was that of the 'war tourists'. Aficionados of the memoirs of Sir Harry Flashman will know that Fanny Duber-ley thought nothing of travelling with the army to the Crimea, but then her husband was the paymaster of the 8th Hussars, so this was perhaps excusable. Indeed, it was nothing unusual for soldiers' wives – from the colonel's lady to Judy O'Grady – to travel with the regiment. Less easy for modern minds to comprehend was the behaviour of those gentlemen of leisure who took their yachts to the Baltic to watch the British fleet in action: Lord Lichfield and his friend Lord Euston, later the sixth Duke of Grafton, with the *Gondola* of the Royal Yacht Squadron; Lord Newborough with his iron steam yacht *Vesta*, who took his female cook and housemaid with him; a Mr Campbell on board the *Esmerelda* of the Royal Western Yacht Club; the owners of the schooner *Mavis* and the yawl *Foam*; and last but by no means least – in ghoulishness, at any rate – the Reverend Robert Hughes, Fellow of Magdalene College, Cambridge, and his brother, aboard the *Wee Pet* of the Royal Thames Yacht Club.

After the capture of Bomarsund, Hughes and his brother went ashore to have a good gawp at the corpses of some Russian soldiers killed in the bombardment. 'Those are the first Russians I have seen clean and sober yet,' was his brother's light-hearted remark. The Hughes brothers later made a nuisance of themselves by sailing too close to the Russian batteries during the bombardment of Sveaborg, and had to be towed clear by a British warship, but none of these tourists was, to my knowledge, ever captured by the Russians; it would have served them right if they had been. Perhaps their ghoulish curiosity is not so difficult to explain: they did not have the benefit of satellite television to beam pictures of the slaughter into their homes even as it happened.

The Reverend Robert Hughes is also one of our informants on the activities on the less-well-recorded civilian ships that accompanied the fleet. Some, like the cutter *Sparrowhawk*, sold French brandy and Dublin porter to sailors with the fleets; others provided services only hinted at in the journals and diaries of the officers accompanying the fleet. 'Three times service, one of these "no go – too much of anything is very bad",' Lieutenant Emil Theorell, an officer of the Swedish navy who served with the British as an interpreter, wrote in his diary for 30 July 1854; while Dr Edward H. Cree, ship's surgeon on board the steam frigate *Odin*, cryptically remarked: 'Some of our lieutenants went boarding strange ships' in his journal for 20 April. Of course, it may well be these 'strange ships' were the venue for tea parties and games of whist; I leave it to the reader to make up his or her own mind.

Killigrew and the North-West Passage

Jonathan Lunn

1852: The most famous rescue mission ever attempted.

Joining the search for Sir John Franklin's ill-fated voyage has long been a dream for Lieutenant Kit Killigrew, R.N. However, a captain more interested in personal glory than the safety of his own crew soon turns the voyage into a reality more akin with Kit's wildest nightmares. And just when he thinks it can't get any worse, a creature of almost mythical proportions starts to pick the crew off one by one . . .

Killigrew and the North-West Passage evokes in terrifying detail the true horror of an Arctic winter – the mind-numbing cold and desolate landscapes – and a darkness which seems almost to permeate men's minds. It's Jonathan Lunn's most chilling and exciting novel yet.

Praise for the Killigrew series

'A hero to rival any Horatio Hornblower. Swashbuckling? You bet' *Belfast Telegraph*

'If you revel in the Hornblower and the Sharpe books, grab a copy of Jonathan Lunn's action-packed saga' *Bolton Evening News*

'On a par with Douglas Reeman or Bernard Cornwell' *South Wales Argus*

'A rollicking tale with plenty of punches' *Lancashire Evening Post*

0 7472 6525 9

headline

Now you can buy any of these other bestselling Headline books from your bookshop or *direct from the publisher.*

FREE P&P AND UK DELIVERY
(Overseas and Ireland £3.50 per book)

An Evil Spirit Out of the West	Paul Doherty	£6.99
The Outlaws of Ennor	Paul Doherty	£6.99
The Templar's Penance	Michael Jecks	£6.99
Seven Dials	Anne Perry	£6.99
Death of a Stranger	Anne Perry	£6.99
The Legatus Mystery	Rosemary Rowe	£6.99
The Chariots of Calyx	Rosemary Rowe	£6.99
Badger's Moon	Peter Tremayne	£5.99
The Haunted Moon	Peter Tremayne	£6.99

TO ORDER SIMPLY CALL THIS NUMBER

01235 400 414

or visit our website: www.madaboutbooks.com

Prices and availability subject to change without notice.